C000261065

New Origin Stories

Edited by Ra Page

First published in Great Britain in 2022 by Comma Press.
www.commapress.co.uk

A CIP catalogue record of this book is available from the British Library.

ISBN: 1912697408
ISBN-13: 978-1-91269-740-3

The publisher gratefully acknowledges assistance from Arts Council England.

Printed and bound in England by Clays Ltd, Elcograf S.p.A

Contents

CONTENTS

Introduction

The Moral Economy of the Proto-Hero

'... there are others which as marked with Becca, but they shall not be named now...'
– Rebecca letter, 16 December 1842

On the evening of 13 May 1839, in an outbuilding of Glynsaithmaen Farm, in the Welsh hills of Preseli, a crowd of local men gathered, dressed in bonnets and petticoats – some perhaps with masks or blackened faces – to set out under cover of darkness to destroy a nearby tollgate. Tollgates were a new way of taxing rural communities – hitting tenant farmers, labourers and lime-sellers the hardest. The men would be led by an appointed 'Rebecca' (on this occasion one Twm Carnabwth), with the others calling themselves her 'daughters', after the Biblical figure blessed to have a thousand million children who would one day 'possess the gate of those who hate them'. Although conceived as a one-off act of defiance, this event set a precedent for widespread civil disobedience three years later, when gangs of *Merched Beca* ('Rebecca's Daughters') gathered at tollgates across the region to perform a short scripted dialogue before smashing them to the ground. 'Wait! It feels like a big gate put across the road to stop your old mother,' the appointed Rebecca would recite, feigning bad eyesight. 'We will break it down, Mother!' the 'daughters' would reply. 'Nothing stands in your way!'[1] So widespread were these protests that by early 1843, according to historian G. A. Williams, 'south-west Wales had become ungovernable; there seemed to be no law west of Swansea.'[2]

The use of umbrella-identities by protesters fighting for a shared cause is a tactic that runs through early nineteenth-century British protest. A decade before the so-called 'Rebecca Riots', agricultural workers in southern and eastern England were fighting the mechanisation of farm work under the pseudonym 'Swing'. In Nottinghamshire, less than two decades before that, textile workers smashed stocking frames under the name 'Ludd'. Indeed, collective pseudonyms can be traced several centuries further back, at least as far as the poacher riot at Penshurst, Kent in 1450, where those arrested gave the name 'Servant of the Queen of the Fairies' to the local magistrates. Sometimes the identities began as real people, but grew larger-than-life in the collective imagination in the aftermath.[3] Some acquired worldly affections in the form of military pretensions: *General* Ludd, *Captain* Pouch (Midlands Rising, 1607), *Captain* Ann (Maldon Food Riots, 1629), etc. But more important were their subversive flourishes, the ways they broke with everyday social norms and even claimed supernatural affiliations. Pouch went round with a leather bag tied to his waist that he claimed had magical contents. Ludd dressed in a blue and white spotted cotton dress, according to police reports, despite being of huge build. Always, at the heart of these actions, was an essentially performative identity, drawn from the ancient rural tradition of 'rough music' or charivari.[4] To quote Rhian E. Jones: 'Staging an elaborate performance or ritual before a protest would have made the event feel both familiar and justified. Meanwhile, dressing up in masks and costumes – particularly costumes which blurred the boundaries of identity – was a way of creating a liminal space and enhanced persona in which protesters could take extraordinary actions which overstepped the bounds of what was possible in their everyday life.'[5] It was a tradition, therefore, of contained chaos, designed to rectify a social wrong; a moment of agreed disorder within a context of wider, durable order. To put it another way: cosplay in the name of doing good.[6]

The book in your hands proposes a hypothesis: that the modern, American superhero – as we've come to know them through films and comic books – has some origin in these dressed-up resistance figures; that there is some DNA in the American superhero that can be traced back to these protest heroes, or dare I say, 'proto-heroes'.

It's a bold claim, perhaps. The worlds in which the two sets of characters operate couldn't be more different: the British proto-heroes concerned themselves with local grievances; the American superheroes with saving the world (or at least the whole of Metropolis/Gotham/New York City). Similarly, the moral codes by which they lived couldn't have less in common. At best, the American superhero is a 'morally neutral' enforcer of the status quo, that is to say, a souped-up policeman fighting scaled-up petty crime; at worst, he is a self-appointed vigilante delivering vengeance without the cumbersome red tape of a judicial system. Being 'morally neutral' means being complicit, of course, and fetishising vigilantism borders on libertarianism (in the American sense), especially when the vigilante in question is a billionaire son of Gotham. To put it bluntly, the American superhero props up a reactionary, pro-capitalist view of the world.

By contrast, the British proto-hero fought to protect a pre-industrial, pre-capitalist way of life, where market forces and the profit motive were not the be-all and end-all of existence, and when the basic cost of living was still largely affordable because it was protected. In studying the food 'riots' of the eighteenth century, E. P. Thompson claimed that in almost all cases, there was some 'legitimising notion' at play – a belief by the people of the crowd that they 'were defending traditional rights or customs; and, in general, that they were supported by the wider consensus of the community' – what Thompson famously called 'the moral economy of the poor'.[7] The ambition of the proto-heroes that came on the heels of these riots was – unlike their world-saving descendents – simply to put food on the table.

But we often become the opposite of our forebears, so perhaps we shouldn't be surprised that the proto-hero apple has fallen so far from the tree.

To test this theory, twelve authors have been tasked with updating these protest personae and re-costuming them, not just in modern dress, but in superhero outfits, complete with superpowers and localised missions to 'do good' (in a social justice sense, rather than a merely crime-fighting one). Authors have set their stories in near-future Britain, and have trained their heroes' superpowers on causes that bear some correlation with those of their historical namesakes. Thus, The General (a modern-day Ludd) rails against automation and employee monitoring in the distribution and service industries; The Captain (a modern-day Ann) plunders billionaires' bank accounts and donates the spoils to charities fighting poverty; and a gang of single mums calling themselves 'Servants of the Queen of the Fairies' raid chain stores for basic provisions for local foodbanks – nappies, baby formula, loaves of bread.

Each story is accompanied by a short 'origin story' – an afterword by an historian who consulted on it, introducing us to the original historical figure, their cause and their context. It is interesting to note how many of the original protest figures shared a common concern around what we might call a pre-modern sense of public access – be that access to common land (before enclosures), to roads (without paying tolls), or to basic provisions like grain (before a free market allowed middlemen and export trade to drive prices sky-high). This issue is equally reflected in the contemporary stories: Pouch battles to win back and protect personal data; Lady Skimmington fights to stop her council from selling off part of a local park; and Jack-a-Lent uses her superpowers to free her own local public spaces from the emblems of past oppression (slaver statues).

The short story might not be the most obvious literary form in which to resurrect these proto-heroes. But in an experiment like this, it has two things going for it as a form: it lends itself, structurally, to the underdog's point of view (there is no space for the back-story of privilege, only the front-story of having to start from scratch all the time); and it sets a precedent for fast and accessible serialisation, by subsequent writers and fans – the kinds of remixes, reboots, team-ups, and spin-offs that the superhero meta-narrative – or rather 'expanded universe' – is built on. Having said that, this is a launch party, so for now, all bar one of these characters exist in isolation, in a world where, as far as they know, their superpowers make them unique.

One or two characters have been included that perhaps bend the rules slightly – Cassivellaunus, didn't become a collective identity but was rather an anti-colonialist resistance leader, not unlike Queen Boudicca, who fought Roman occupation and wasn't averse to bit of dressing up himself, frequently donning a cloak of invisibility, according to Welsh mythology; and Hermione wasn't originally an individual, but a ship, famous for its mutiny, on which countless sailors in later years claimed to have served, often just to frighten others into showing them some respect.

Perhaps the oldest genuine performance piece in this long history is the story of the Cuckoo (dating back to King John's reign), which sits at the end of this book, and brings us neatly back to Gotham – not the city of Batman, mind, but a small village, pronounced 'goat-ham', in Nottinghamshire, with its bizarre tales of elaborate hoaxes once performed by villagers to prevent a toll being set on the road passing through it. It's an apt setting to close on – to counterpose the dark, fearful backstreets of DC territory, or the glittering skyscrapers of Marvel country – quiet but defiant, with its twelfth-century church, its long-since filled-in pond, and, in the corner of a nearby wood, its mysterious burial ground. A peculiar place, much like Britain itself.

Ra Page
January, 2022

Notes

1. The full script went as follows:

   Rebecca: 'What is this my children? There is something in my way. I cannot go on....'
   Rioters: 'What is it, mother Rebecca? Nothing should stand in your way.'
   Rebecca: 'I do not know my children. I am old and cannot see well.'
   Rioters: 'Shall we come and move it out of your way mother Rebecca?'
   Rebecca: 'Wait! It feels like a big gate put across the road to stop your old mother.'
   Rioters: 'We will break it down, mother. Nothing stands in your way.'
   Rebecca: 'Perhaps it will open...Oh my dear children, it is locked and bolted. What can be done?'
   Rioters: 'It must be taken down, mother. You and your children must be able to pass.'
   Rebecca: 'Off with it then, my children.'

2. Gwyn A. Williams, *When was Wales? A history of the Welsh*, Black Raven Press, 1985, p193.
3. In the case of Rebecca, the opposite might be true. Though the character was fictional, organisers - specifically Twm Carnabwth - tried to reverse-engineer a 'real world' origin story, claiming the clothes the first Rebecca rioters wore were borrowed from an old maid called Rebecca who lived in the foothills of Preseli, being the only woman tall enough and large enough in the village. Local records fail to bear out the existence of any Rebecca in the area.
4. Also known as 'skimmington' in southern and western England, as 'Ceffyl Pren' (wooden horse) in Wales, and 'riding the stang' in Scotland and Northern England, with each version having regional variations.
5. Rhian E. Jones, 'Rebeccaism', from *Resist: Stories of Uprising*, edited by Ra Page (Comma, 2019), p155.
6. It's important to make a distinction here between the fictional collective personae of this protest tradition and mere acts of

anonymity (with or without the cover of a pseudonym). 'Rebeccaism' (as Rhian E. Jones calls it) is about owning the fiction and prioritising the collective within that fiction. By contrast, purely anonymous actions claim to cover the identity of a real, non-fictional individual whose authority would only grow if their true identity were ever revealed. This is what happens when a potentially progressive movement like Anonymous has its tactics stolen by fake-whistleblowers like QAnon, so named after their original perpetrator's claim to have high-level 'Q Clearance' in real life. Anonymous protests claim everything about them is real.

7. E.P. Thompson, 'The Moral Economy of the English Crowd in the Eighteenth Century' from *Past & Present* No. 50 (Feb., OUP 1971), pp78-79.

Pause

Luan Goldie

IZZY AND I WALK the perimeter of where the park café used to be. It's still there of course, hidden behind the wooden hoardings the council put up last month after the old building was broken into. It was the third time it had been vandalised, the windows smashed, the walls sprayed with crude depictions of Mayor Thomas stuffing the pockets of his tacky purple suit with handfuls of cash.

As a kid, I used to hate that the café had so many windows. The whole front of it was glass and Dad used to inspect each pane for fingerprints, evidence that I hadn't cleaned it as well as he'd like. 'If we can't keep our windows clean, people will think our kitchen's not clean either,' he'd say. Though Dad's kitchen at the café was always spotless. Everything around Dad was spotless, cleanliness being one of the few things he had control over in his life.

Izzy climbs on a bench and tries to see over the hoardings. 'It's a mess in there,' she says.

'Get down,' I tell her.

Her black pleated school skirt flies up as she jumps back, igniting a cheer from the drug dealers who occupy the opposite park bench.

'Iz,' I say, 'was that really necessary?'

She shrugs and plucks at the long grass. The council used to keep it cut. Even after they stopped opening the public toilets and fixing equipment in the swing park, the grass was at least kept below knee length. I guess they no longer need to pretend to care; it's not a park any more, just some sketchy bit of land, a neglected eyesore. Nothing worth fighting for.

'I hope people turn up tomorrow,' Izzy says as she steps towards the hoardings and taps at one of the remaining posters. It had been a challenge keeping the posters up, the council being so quick to tear them down, as if peaceful protest was no longer allowed. I even had a call from one of Mayor Thomas's aides, asking me to 'reconsider' my plan. 'You won't be making a scene will you, Ms Allen?' she asked. To which I replied, 'Yes, that's my entire objective.'

'It'll be so embarrassing if no one comes,' Izzy says. 'Especially with all this effort you've gone to. You know it's meant to be baking hot as well? I'm looking to get a tan,' she says, checking the colour of her arms, which are two shades lighter than the dark orange of her face.

I make a conscious effort to stop grinding my teeth, to stop taking her disinterest so personally. She checks her reflection in the screen of her phone. 'I get why you're doing the whole cross-dressing thing,' she says, 'but you're going to sweat buckets in that ugly suit. Why don't you wear a dress instead? Sex it up a little.'

But tomorrow's not about being sexy; it's about humiliating Mayor Thomas. People used to be dazzled by his expensive suits and talk loaded with promises, but things are changing. People around here are ready for a more honest leader, someone in tune with the community. Too bad they didn't want all this when the perfect candidate was right here, before their eyes. Back when Dad was still around.

'Did you tell your friends from school to come along?' I ask, thinking of the slightly rowdy, yet large group of girls Izzy spends most of her time with.

'Yeah, kind of. Well, they're busy, you know.'

'They're fifteen. What could they possibly be busy doing?'

'Going Westfield,' she says.

And I see that longing in her eyes, the one that threatens to pull her away from me and what she increasingly sees as 'my causes'. Of course she doesn't want to 'waste' her Saturdays being politically engaged. She'd much rather spend hours trying on clothes she'll never buy and eating McDonalds. But we were never brought up to be 'those kinds of girls'. We spent our childhoods giving out leaflets on the high street, wearing CND badges and marching as soon as we could walk. Though looking at my sister now, you wouldn't think it.

'Izzy, there's a woman over there.'

'So?' she says, not even looking up from her phone.

'So, go and give her a leaflet. Please.'

She rolls her eyes and takes one of the leaflets from my bag. The woman moves closer, pushing an empty buggy while a toddler in a letterbox-red hat dawdles behind. 'Excuse me,' Izzy says, employing her sickly-sweet voice. 'Can I give you a leaflet about tomorrow's event in the park?'

The woman doesn't break her stride so I cut in. 'Tomorrow Mayor Thomas and P&B Housing are having some tacky photo opportunity to promote the housing development they're planning on building over this land.' I swear Izzy yawns but I carry on. 'We, the people, want to show the mayor and his fat cat friends that we'll not –'

'You're protesting against the development?' the woman asks.

'Yes,' I say. 'We've already lost our community café this year, let's not lose our beloved park –'

'Beloved park? Really?'

I follow her eyes and notice that even though it's 4pm on a warm Friday afternoon the park *is* pretty empty.

'And that café,' the woman says nodding behind us, 'I never knew when it was meant to be open. No one used it.'

'Actually, it was used all the time. It was a real space for the community.' At least it was when Dad was well enough. Of course I tried to keep it going, though the rumours about his illness put people off, as if his madness contaminated the place. It was also hard to run a business on my own, while studying and keeping Izzy from spinning out of control.

'Anyway, I prefer Costa on the high street.'

'Me too,' Izzy mumbles. 'What I'd give for a latte right now.'

'Companies like Costa don't care about the community. They're not going to offer toddler groups or discounts for pensioners or yoga for young people.'

'Yoga?' The woman laughs. 'You do realise this isn't Hackney? This is all stuff the area could do without.'

'Okay, so the café wasn't for everyone, but surely you care about the potential loss of another green space.'

'Mum-may, look!' the little boy calls, delighted with the insect crawling up his arm.

Perfect timing. 'See,' I say, 'this is why parks are important.'

'Hardly a park is it?' the woman says with a slight scoff. 'It's a scrappy piece of land no one really uses or takes care of.'

'But *you're* here. *We're* here. And,' I look around for others but there are only the drug dealers, though thankfully one of them has a football and is performing knee ups. 'Look, those teenagers are here too. Everyone is enjoying the park.'

'There are plenty of parks around here,' the woman says, 'nicer ones.'

'People need outdoor space. Over a third of residents in this area don't have gardens.'

'We need homes.'

'We need clean air. The air around here is practically poison.'

'I know that actually,' the woman snaps, her patience wearing thin, 'because my son has asthma. And you know what doesn't help? Being in cramped, damp, temporary accommodation. So, no,' she says handing the leaflet back to Izzy, 'I won't be coming to your protest.' She calls her child over and starts making her way up the path.

Izzy knocks her shoulder against mine. 'Can we go home now? I'm starving.'

'You really couldn't care less about this, could you?'

'Well, maybe that woman's right.'

'She's not. And it's not okay for our council to keep selling off our green spaces for profit, treating clean air like a commodity we could save on.'

Izzy starts scrolling. *'Why stop progress,'* she reads. *'The park is full of drug dealers, safer to stay indoors. Good on the mayor.* These are all comments under your post about the protest.'

'Okay, enough.'

'Don't you ever worry that you've read the community wrong? That perhaps people do want more homes.'

'People don't know what they want. They're not thinking about what it will mean to lose this space. It breaks my heart.' A crisp packet gets caught in the breeze and skips along the tops of the hedges. 'I hate the idea that he could come home and none of this would be here any more.'

Izzy tuts. 'I knew this was about him.'

'Dad put years into this park, running community projects, after school football, litter picking. He dedicated his whole life to helping the people around here.'

Again, she rolls her eyes, she does this on purpose, and to show me she's over it, that she couldn't care less.

'If only he'd got to finish his campaign, to fully run for mayor, he would have won. I know it. I just know it.'

'Well, he didn't. Because he was too busy disappearing off to God knows where.'

'The disappearing, it wasn't his fault. He had other things going on, things I… things I can't explain. But he cared. And when he comes back –'

'Look,' she shouts, 'it's been three years. He's not coming back.'

As her words hit, the hot sensation I've come to dread begins to spread from my feet and up my shins. I once asked Dad to describe how it felt when it happened to him. 'Like a storm rolling in,' he'd said. It's not the same for me, but then, I can't do what he can.

The boys on the bench laugh at something and Izzy is back on her phone.

'Stop looking at that,' I say, slapping it from her hand.

'What's wrong with you?' she shouts, grappling in the grass for it. 'Are you mad?'

'I need your support on this.'

The heat now fills my stomach, tingles my fingers and I can feel it rising up my throat. The woman with the pushchair is parked up, as the child twirls, disappearing into the long folds of grass, only his red hat visible.

'None of your campaigning is really about *saving our green spaces*,' Izzy says, and I recognise the mimic. How boring she must find me. 'It's all about Dad. About you wanting to prove something.'

'It's not –'

'You don't listen. In fact you're not listening to anyone, not me, not the community. You're just crazy about this place. You're crazy, just like him.'

'Stop it,' I scream as the heat floods my head.

Then. Everything. Stops.

Pause.

The grass no longer sways, the red hat is stationary. The laughter from the dealers can no longer be heard, only seen as their eyes are squeezed shut, their mouths opened wide. One of them stands with his leg frozen at an angle, the ball airborne above his knee.

Then, cutting through the silence is a gasp. It's Izzy. How?

'Why is it so quiet?' She looks around, her face etched with fear.

The pause, as I've come to know it over the years, has always been capable of stopping everything except me. So why is Izzy still moving and talking? Why is she witnessing this?

She rubs her head, 'I feel sick.'

'It's okay, Izzy. It's okay.'

Her eyes dart around, between the static child, the motionless football, the unmoving red buses which can be seen above the treetops. 'Everything's stopped. Nothing's moving.'

'I know. But it's okay.'

'Okay? Are you crazy?'

'It'll start again, usually in a few minutes,' I take her hand.

Though minutes is a best-case scenario. What if everything stays paused for hours, like it did once when I was a child? I sat there on the kitchen floor between my parents, looking up at their faces contorted in anger. I didn't know what was worse, the fear of hearing them scream at each other, or the fear of the world not restarting.

I feel the fire inside my body recede, a flash passes my eyes and everything slips back to normal.

★

Back home I sit on the kitchen counter, nursing a whisky from a mug. Izzy has said little but keeps glancing over at me, as if trying to work out what I have failed to all these years.

On the door rail hangs the big boxy purple suit for tomorrow's protest. Everything about it has been picked to communicate how wrong the mayor's plans are, how awful it would be in the long term to have a tower of so-called luxury flats rather than our park. I've pinned Monopoly money to the lapels and an oxygen mask hangs from the back pocket. How can I stage my protest after this? How will life go back to normal when another person has seen what I can do? Even if it is my own sister.

'So?' Izzy says. 'Are you going to tell me?'

I put my head in my hands and part of me wishes it would happen again, not a long pause, just one which would give me enough time to gather my words and form an explanation. But they never come that close together. There used to be months between them, though now, as I get older, they're more likely to happen every few weeks.

'Talk to me,' she pleads. 'Was it you?'

I laugh dryly, that nervous habit I picked up from Dad.

'Please. Tell me the truth. Did you do that?' There's a wobble in her voice, a rare display of weakness, enough to make me feel ashamed, not that I've kept this secret, more that I wasn't able to protect *her* from knowing it.

'Yes,' I say.

'How?'

'I don't know. It happens sometimes.'

'This has happened before?'

'Yes. A few times.'

'What is it?'

I shrug.

'It's like you stopped the earth turning or something.'

'Of course not. Not the earth. Just what's in front of me. For a few minutes.'

'How do you know the whole world didn't stop?'

It's too big to think about, too scary to comprehend.

Izzy gets off the sofa and goes to the balcony, stepping outside into the warm evening. She looks at the traffic below then turns to me. 'Do it again,' she demands.

'I can't.'

'Why not?'

'It doesn't work that way and also, why would I? It's not like I enjoy it. It's wrong. And I – I'm scared of it.'

'What else can you do?'

'Nothing.'

'And who else can do stuff like this? You can't be the only one.'

The next part is so obvious I wish she'd put the pieces together herself and spare me having to drag it all out.

'Dad?' she says. 'Dad could do this too?'

More, I think, *he could do so much more.* 'Dad was a complicated man. He had lots of –'

'Why didn't he teach me?'

Is this really her issue? 'Are you serious?'

'He always favoured you. I was always just the baby.' It's Izzy's most common complaint in life, how she came of age too late for Dad to ever get to know her as anything other than a fussy little schoolgirl.

'Well, you have to teach me?'

'No,' I snap. 'I can't.'

'Show me how.' She leans over the balcony again and looks down, focused on the movement of people below. 'What did you do? You got angry? You screamed? How does it work?' she squeezes her eyes shut and I grab her by the arm and pull her back inside.

'Do you have any idea how lonely it feels when everyone and everything around you stops? When you're the only one able to move and talk? When your own family stare right through you?'

Izzy shrugs her arm from my grasp. 'But you're not alone in it any more. Are you?'

I lay awake most of the night, as I have many nights before, thinking about this ability I have, this thing of no use. I don't even understand it. I take out my notepad to record today's pause. I had first started logging them around three years ago, right around the time the pauses seemed to change, going from less of a suspension of time and more to a skipping of it. It was only ever few seconds, a minute at most, like the forwarding of a film. And I only noticed because when things moved again I would find that people were a few steps in front of where they'd originally been, or the sandwich they'd been eating had more bites than before.

Though today's pause was, thankfully, just that, a pause. A short snapping of time brought on by stress and worry.

I don't get out of bed until way past nine the next day. I potter about, read the news and tidy the flat. I make pancakes which Izzy refuses to eat when she finally crawls out of bed, instead making herself toast and eyeing me suspiciously.

At midday I dress for the protest, carefully dabbing on the wolf-grey beard which Mayor Thomas sports. The beard still splits people, some thinking it unseemly for a person of such importance to have facial hair, while others see it as a marker of him being a man of the people, rugged and ready to muck in. As if he would ever do anything to dirty one his infamous £600 suits.

'Are you ready?' I ask Izzy.

'For what?'

'I'm not in full cross-dress for no reason, am I?'

Despite herself she laughs. 'The beard, it strangely suits you.'

'Come with me. Please?'

She sighs and looks back at the TV which she's been blankly staring at.

'We've worked on this protest for weeks now. You can't miss it to sit home watching crap on Netflix.'

She nods. 'Okay, I'm coming.'

We gather looks as we walk up the high street towards the park, handing out leaflets about the true cost of P&B's development on our environment. We talk people into following us, to disrupt the photo opportunity Mayor Thomas has been bragging about on social media all week.

'It's overwhelming to think you can control all this,' Izzy says, indicating the crowds and buses around us.

I ignore her, focused instead on how many people are tagging behind us as we walk.

'So it *just* happens and you can't stop it?'

'Can we save this conversation for when we're somewhere less public?' I whisper.

'Do you get a warning when it's about to happen? Like a message from beyond?'

'Stop,' I say as we enter the park where a crowd, larger than I expected, gathers. It reminds me of the old days, back when Dad used to arrange Family Fun Days at the café. It's what I thought I could recreate when I took over running the place, but instead I ran it into the ground.

P&B Housing have gone all out. There's an ice cream van, a free BBQ and young pretty women giving out balloons and branded tote bags. There's also a small marquee labelled 'Marketing Suite', surrounded by glossy impressions of how the area will look after its 'regeneration'. Sparkling tower blocks filled with happy, skinny residents holding coffee cups and laughing over the balconies of their rabbit hutches.

'*Skim Park, a dynamic new neighbourhood for our shared future*,' Izzy reads. 'Whoa.'

'What absolute bullshit.' A few people gather closer to take photos of me. 'I need to start.' It's time.

I walk over to where the cameras are set up in front of a little stage. Mayor Thomas stands beside it being briefed by one of his aides.

'Mayor?' I call to which he turns.

'Ms Allen. How nice to see you again.' His composure slips momentarily as he notices my outfit.

'I have some words to share with the community,' I say. 'I hope you don't mind if I use your stage for five minutes?'

'Ms Allen, this is simply not how things work,' one of the aides call after me. 'Surely *your father* explained this to you?' she says with a smirk.

I push my reaction away as I step onto the stage and raise my megaphone, 'Ladies and Gentlemen,' I call. A few turn to look, but it'll take more than my suit to distract them from free burgers. 'I'm here to tell you, that these flats, they won't be for you. These flats,' I say, pointing to the adverts, 'will be to make money. Money which will be pumped into P&B Housing. They're not really building them for us. So why should we give up our parks and trees for *them*.'

Mayor Thomas moves closer and laughs a little, as if trying to lighten the mood. 'As I've explained to Ms Allen, on *countless* occasions, this development will be incredibly eco-friendly. It will feature a rooftop garden and rainwater harvest systems. Let's also not lose sight of the fact that it will be a huge boost in our effort to combat the *criminal* shortage of housing.'

'Affordable housing is it? At £450k for a one bedroom?'

The crowd hushes, I have their attention now. As I look out I'm surprised by how many have joined and how many more are now streaming through the gate. Maybe the posters worked after all. Perhaps all those leaflets did the job.

'What about a shortage of green spaces? What about the increase in childhood obesity? The lack of clean, safe spaces for people to enjoy in this borough?'

'And what about the rent cuts for businesses?' someone in the crowd shouts. There's jeering which Mayor Thomas frowns at before plastering back on his listening face.

'Yeah, let's talk about those business rates? You were meant to bring them down.'

Then, more voices. 'And they've got money for fancy flats, yet can't fix the potholes on my road.'

'The school needs more money, for books and teachers. Thirty-one to a class.'

'The fly tipping too, it's appalling.'

Mayor Thomas turns to his aide and whispers are passed.

I look down at Izzy, who mouths at me, 'Say something.'

'People, please,' I call, and while my voice through the megaphone is loud, my audience's interest is elsewhere. The crowd begins to thicken around Mayor Thomas as more and more people step forward to question him, holding him to account for every one of society's ills.

'Our borough has many issues,' I try, 'but the most urgent threat is the closure of our park and of this development.'

It's like no one is listening. I notice Izzy's friends, they wave and move closer to the stage, one reaches out and grabs my legs, unsteadying me. Is she drunk?

'Oh come on. We were promised a bit of anarchy today,' she laughs.

The boys she's with start laughing too. Then they reach for me, attempting to drag me from the stage. 'Stop,' I shout. But they take one leg each and raise me above their shoulders. The pack cheers as I'm hoisted up, and surrounded by so many faces and lenses I can't help but raise my megaphone and call into it, 'Save our park. Save our park.'

Even Izzy looks enthusiastic.

Some join in with the chant and there are shouts about other things, which get lost in the growing din.

'Save our park. Save our park.'

I'm pulled from the boys' shoulders and passed over to the crowd, my megaphone falls away and I'm faced to the sky. It's quite unsettling being fully reliant on a bunch of strangers to keep me from falling to the ground. 'You can put me down now,' I call but no one listens.

Where are they taking me?

'Put me down,' I squirm.

Across the sea of heads I see Mayor Thomas, red-faced and flustered, his suit jacket flapping as he too is lifted into the air. From the back, a small scuffle breaks out and I feel that switch in the atmosphere as my peaceful protest gets pumped with too much negative energy, as it becomes something else, something unplanned and nasty. At the side of the stage a shovel, adorned with a red ribbon, and a bottle of champagne sit untouched. While my objective was always to disrupt the ceremony, to humiliate Mayor Thomas at his own 'party', I never pictured it like this.

I'm passed towards Mayor Thomas, like some weird parade.

'Calm down,' I call, but my voice is swept up and lost within the clamour. 'This isn't why we're here.'

They struggle to hold me and I begin to slip, my legs hanging down.

'Money-grabbing pig,' someone shouts and a bottle flies overhead.

Then. Everything. Stops.

Paused, without warning.

How? I didn't even feel it coming.

I slide from the loose grip of the person holding me.

'Izzy? Izzy?' Where has she gone? I've never seen the park so busy before. I'm not going to find her in all this.

Mayor Thomas is suspended mid-air, as if thrown. He looks stressed, no terrified, and besides him his aide reaches up with one hand, her other holding the phone, probably calling the police.

I hear laughing and then the sound of a single pair of hands clapping. Izzy stands at the side of the stage, bright-eyed. 'I did it,' she shouts. 'I can't believe I did it. Look at this one,' she points to a man up the side of the café, taking a piss by the hoardings. 'So, how do I restart them?' she asks. 'Not that I want to. I think we should walk around. Explore. God, we can do anything.'

'No.'

'Come on, this is great.' She starts pushing the people, 'Urgh, so weird.'

'Izzy, stop. Stop touching them.'

'Why? It's not like they can feel it.'

'It's disrespectful.'

She laughs and even I recognise that it sounds a little stupid. But for me dealing with this, alone, all these years, I had to develop a set of rules to feel at least some control over it.

'Look at him,' she points to Mayor Thomas, his face contorted in terror. 'He's such a joke. But people love you, this has been amazing. You need to run for mayor. It's so obvious.'

I follow her around the outskirts of the crowd as she prods and pokes people, inspecting the beads of sweat stilled on foreheads, the many faces caught in anger. 'It's unbelievable,' she mumbles.

'Stop,' I say, 'will you please stop.'

'So, will you do it?'

'Do what?'

'Run for mayor.'

'Izzy, this isn't the time to have a chat about my career.'

'It's the perfect time,' she laughs. 'Look around, we have nothing but time.'

'I don't want to go into politics. Dad tried it and it almost broke him.'

'Good job you're not Dad then. Look what you've done today. You've got all these people to give up a sunny Saturday to come and watch you parade about in a crappy suit. Look up,' she says.

There's a flock of birds still in the sky.

'The clouds aren't moving, we've literally stopped the world turning. We can do anything, Izzy. Don't you see?'

'No. You're getting carried away.' I step towards her, my baby sister, the one who missed so much, who always felt like she arrived after the party finished. I take her hands in mine and immediately there's a tingling, then the heat. It's almost unbearable but for some reason I can't let go. It's as if we're fused together, charging one another up. The heat travels up my arms, burning all the way across my chest and head until a light flashes.

★

Dad looks well. His face shines with health and the lines, which were once deep across his face, have smoothed out.

I'm sitting on the kitchen floor, the kitchen floor of my childhood.

He comes towards me, his face pulling up into one of his wide smiles. 'Girls,' he says, 'you did it.'

Girls?

Izzy sits behind me, rolling a red bus backwards and forwards. She's about three or four years old. I remember her like this, chubby and cheeky.

'Girls?' Dad says again, scooping Izzy from the floor and pulling me to standing. 'I'm so glad you found a way to rewind. Now this time when we go forward, we'll do things properly.'

Origin Story: Rough Music

Rhian E. Jones

YOU DON'T NEED TO be a historian to recognise that the past is always with us. It can take the form of personal memory, or collective memories held within families and communities, as well as more officially recorded histories. The continuity of past and present, even in contexts that seem very far apart, is demonstrated by the many unresolved political, social and economic issues that affect our daily lives. Luan Goldie's story, inspired by the seventeenth-century Western Rising and the long history of protest by ordinary people over land use and ownership, proves that past and present are more closely intertwined than we might think.

The sixteenth and seventeenth centuries in Britain saw significant changes in use, access and ownership of land. Previously, even though ordinary people may not have owned much or any land themselves, they were able to make use of public land, rivers and forests – 'the commons' – to farm, hunt and fish, grow crops, carry out small-scale mining, gather fruit, grains or wood for fuel (known as gleaning), and to graze their livestock. This changed dramatically after 1625 when Charles I, having run up deep financial debt for the Crown, which owned the majority of the country's land, began to sell off much of this land to the local gentry for personal, leisure or business use. Across the country, formerly public land was closed off with fences, hedges or other field boundaries, communally-farmed land converted to private pasture, and land depopulated of those who lived and worked on it, in a process known as enclosure.

For ordinary people, enclosure meant the loss of access to resources that were vital for supporting and sustaining themselves, and which they had been able to use for generations. In addition to poorer peasants who relied on common land for food and fuel, and those who made a living through agricultural smallholdings and mining, artisans and self-employed labourers such as weavers, tailors and carpenters, whose products depended on forest produce, were also affected by this loss, as were those who lived on the land itself. As shown in Luan's choice of a public park as a modern equivalent to the enclosures protests, there were also deeper issues around who has the right to use and enjoy public space.

In the Forest of Dean, Gloucestershire, local 'free miners', a group who had been granted customary, but not legal, rights to mine for ore in the area, found that enclosure threatened this traditional lifestyle. Led by John Williams, their protests against enclosure formed part of the Western Rising, a series of riots which took place during 1626–1632 in the Forest of Dean, Gillingham Forest on the Wiltshire-Dorset border, and Braydon Forest in Wiltshire. Events like the Western Rising show that ordinary people didn't passively accept their expulsion from the land, but opposed it in acts of public protest in order to continue using or occupying the land. Opposition could entail simply ignoring the new division of land, turning livestock onto enclosed fields and pastures, holding protests outside the homes of the gentry, or more violent direct action like destroying the new fences and hedges which blocked established rights of way or setting fire to property. These protests could involve large groups of people, like the Western Rising, or they could involve single or a few individuals trespassing or poaching to gather food or fuel as they had previously done. Occasionally groups established camps or built rough dwellings to physically occupy land.

Anti-enclosure protests were massive, widespread and long-lasting, continuing for decades in some cases, and made it obvious that these changes were negatively affecting the everyday lives and livelihoods of ordinary people. However, in a pre-democratic era, these people lacked the kind of political influence that could lead to the process being halted or reversed. Those affected by these changes had no opportunity to vote on them or to voice their concerns to an elected representative, particularly as enclosure worked to the benefit of those in power. (Even today, as Luan's story shows, elected officials who work against the community and for the benefit of private developers can, in fact, be part of the problem.) Landowners could treat these protests as dangerous riots and call on their employees and local military resources to break them up. Participants in the Western Rising, like those in other areas, faced arrests, huge fines, and imprisonment or public punishment in stocks and pillories. In the end, the riots were put down, often violently, and the lands sold off for private use, with some residents compensated for their loss but many not. Despite their short-term disruption of the imposition of enclosure, protesters ultimately could not win against the political and legislative turns towards private ownership and use of land. Enclosure and privatisation accelerated in the early nineteenth century with the development of industrial capitalism, and these changes went on to shape the world we live in.

Although there is little evidence that these different local communities communicated or coordinated their actions against enclosure, they used similar tactics such as public parades and traditional costume, including male rioters dressing in women's clothing. John Williams was a notable example of this, leading his protests under the name 'Lady Skimmington', an alias used by a number of men involved in the Western Rising. This use of a mythical leadership figure, and the particular costume involved, highlights how pre-industrial protests often drew on the folk custom and traditions of their local communities. Many anti-enclosure protests could seem more like a carnival, including the use of costumes, symbols and 'rough music' produced from everyday or household objects by blowing horns, drumming, ringing bells and banging pots and pans. These elements were taken from community rituals known as charivari – 'skimmington' was a local variant on this name, used across the West and South of England.

At its heart, charivari was a public shaming ritual oriented around a kind of street theatre. It was used by communities to uphold local traditions and to express moral outrage at breaches in social norms and conventions, which could include domestic violence or adultery. It both made visible a conflict within a community and attempted to address it. The usual form taken by charivari was a mass procession through the local area, soundtracked by 'rough music' from the crowd and sometimes including dancing, singing or chanting, and an effigy or an individual dressed up to personify the object of the protest. While it's important to note that charivari in its original context was often used to uphold norms and relations that were socially conservative, patriarchal, and heteronormative, its evolving use in economic and political protest could see it used for more progressive ends.

Pre-industrial communities also had traditional festivals and carnivals where parading and dressing in colourful costumes and masks formed part of the occasion. This could include cross-dressing or wearing animal masks or skins. These costumes symbolised the freedom of the occasion and expressed that, during this period, those who took part were free from everyday rules and laws. Many costumes were meant to symbolise 'the world turned upside-down', suspending normality – including aspects of social and political relations – for a temporary period of anarchic enjoyment. This exposure of power structures through inverting them was understood to be only time-limited, with things returning to their 'proper' order after the carnival or festival's end. Luan's protagonist, by dressing as the local mayor to identify the protest's target, both draws on this tradition and inverts it, becoming a kind of 'Lord Skimmington'.

Historians have analysed the use of elements of carnival and charivari for political protest – both anti-enclosure and later industrial and social conflict, including Luddism and the Rebecca riots – as attempts by ordinary people to repurpose these familiar things in order to respond to a new situation. Using carnival costumes and symbols that traditionally expressed freedom from law and order enabled them to defy the new laws put in place by landowners, and through costumes like cross-dressing they were demonstrating their view that the changes being imposed meant, to them, a world turned upside-down. Like charivari, anti-enclosure protests were intended to uphold local customary rights, to draw public attention to a breach in the moral, social or political code that a community was used to, and to resolve it. Using elements familiar from traditional local rituals lent political protests a familiar frame of reference that their participants – and their audience – could easily understand. Finally, the collective nature of the protest provided a visible contrast with the individualist mentality behind enclosure, which gave a single individual ownership of what had previously been a collectively used and maintained resource.

From the nineteenth century, as Britain developed a recognisably modern democratic system, spontaneous and chaotic protests by local communities gave way to more organised movements which focused on national politics. These had the goal of improving living and working conditions by gaining democratic representation for ordinary people through trade unions, the Chartist movement and the birth of the Labour Party. Despite the growth of more constitutional protest centred on parliamentary reform, more carnivalesque protest of the older kind persisted throughout the nineteenth and twentieth centuries, particularly on issues of importance to local communities. In recent decades, we have seen protest on issues of broader and international scope also continue to use costume and symbolism, often in creative and spectacular ways, such as the stylised Guy Fawkes masks used in many Occupy protests or the *gilets jaunes* movement.

Luan's story attests to the fundamental importance of public space and the value of land to ordinary people. Even though the use of land for farming and food-gathering is much more limited in the Britain of today than it was at the time of the Western Rising, ownership and access to land is still a vital concern. Issues of gentrification, housing quality, and high rents continue to affect communities and to reflect racial and class divides. The Covid-19 pandemic and resulting lockdown has highlighted the stark inequalities between households with access to gardens or local parks, and those confined to overcrowded HMOs or bringing up families in small flats and tower blocks without space for exercise or leisure.

Today, local communities continue to voice concern at plans, frequently led by multinational property developers, to 'regenerate' an area in ways that end up pricing out local residents through lack of affordable housing, or excluding them from newly-built shopping centres, parks and leisure complexes. This trend has been referred to as the 'social cleansing' of many of the country's major cities, with rentier capital replacing industrial capital as the basis of neoliberalism. Protest over rents, housing and public space, defending customary rights against landowners, employers and multinational corporations, has been a permanent feature of the past few centuries. Echoes of anti-enclosure protest and opposition to unequal property relations informed movements from the Levellers and Diggers in the English Civil War to the 'mass trespasses' on gentry-owned land carried out by ramblers and left-wing activists in the early twentieth century.

Awareness of this continuum of protest, and of the long-standing nature of many of the problems we face today, can inspire, facilitate and strengthen contemporary activism. References to the history of particular protests, and their continuity with current struggles, can sometimes form a deliberate part of contemporary political movements, such as the banners carried at trade union marches – often themselves of historical significance and usually displaying significant moments or figures in the movement's history. However, there are many less concrete and tangible elements to protest history and tradition, particularly carnivalesque protests, in which participants used everyday objects in creative ways for costume or symbolism or took physical direct action to demonstrate their views. As illustrated in Luan's story, the strategy and tactics of protest can recur across history as the problems that ordinary people face – and the ways in which they attempt to redress them – crop up time and again.

After That, Is This

Courttia Newland

Mum used to say, 'Always look at the hands,' and I'd laugh like it was foolishness, or pretend she hadn't spoken, but you know what? She was right. Hands tell a story, that's facts, even if certain people don't speak their language. You know the signs, it's obvious.

And I'm perched on the footbridge rail arching the river, cold metal forcing an ache in my sit bones, trying not to be seduced by the fact it's lit up and glowing, those twin counterweights on either side reminding me of oversized rabbits' ears, or miniature tornados frozen mid-whirl, depending which way my head tilts. Failing to ignore the starlight glint of lovers' padlocks, hundreds clasped firm all over the bridge. And the evenly spaced lamps every metre or so hurt my eyes, especially the one right beneath me, and truth be told probably reflect the glare of my pale face, although no one's there to notice this time of morning. Drunks, ravers, women on the game and men who follow like kids entranced by the piper, all somewhere else, for unknown reasons. Paving stones empty, grey brickwork clear as the blank canvas of overcast sky.

And I'm thinking: this is stupid. And I think, Pero and Frome, Pero and Frome over and over, it's fucking annoying.

Both at the same time, my eyes stinging from tiredness and lights. Still I perch, and don't move.

I could, easily. Get up, go home. Take a sip from my bottle of white rum, undress. Sleep. Or try.

But I don't.

So what *do* I do? Look at my flipping hands. Turn them over, palms up, exchanging dark for light. Pero and Frome.

Mine are kinda odd. Slim as the rest of me, tiny boned, the fingers somehow elongated, like I have more joints than humanly possible. The fist I make surprisingly large, the splay when I let go further than I imagine a split second before it happens. It reflects the lights too, only the palms mind. The other side, the darker skin is greedier, sucking glow into cracks and bumps, gleaming with defiance, pleased with herself. Figures. There, right side up, I see the dotted patch of scar tissue where spattered oil got me years ago, the shell of knuckles darkened by parkour, crisscross scars and yet-to-heel lightning strike cuts desecrated terrain. Blunt, cracked nails, bitten and gnawed.

And I don't want to know, looking towards the trees and buildings. The slosh of water beneath me a reminder. I put both hands on the railing, filling my lungs until my chest swells, tasting the bitter grit of exhaust fumes. Air cracks and swirls before me like one hundred mile an hour winds, the space before me wrenches apart. Darkness forms within that tear of known reality, like a mother's call to come home. I kick off from the railing, step inside.

Hers were paler, slim like mine and rough with use. Tiny as the dolls I cherished, sometimes I compared theirs with Mum's, amazed how similar they looked. Small and dainty, super pretty, shining with cocoa butter that gave them an almost plastic sheen. Pinprick freckles, faint, hardly there. When I was real young, they were soft and plump at the heels. I'd trace the thin brown lines of her palms with a finger, sitting on her lap while she watched *Casualty*. Heart line, life-line. Two kids, apparently.

We'd laugh at that, although it almost turned out true. As I got older, Mum's hands lost their weight and shine, to become skinny and grey, roughened by bleach. No amount of Palmer's able to stop the coarse scratch when I rubbed my soft flesh against them, until she pulled away.

When I step out on the other side, it's cold. Air crackles like surging power lines, static raising hairs at the base of my skull, although I won't turn back. I need to concentrate on what's in front me. The paving slabs are dark with the aftermath of rain. A waxing gibbous moon's overhead, frosting the area, and when I snatch a look at the sky, I can't find it, the clouds are too thick. I'm stepping forwards, cautious. Two years ago I adopted a calico rescue cat named Blake to keep me company in my flat. He won't be held by anyone, even me, is very prone to scuttling half-freaked when I stomp though the place, and runs from anyone who comes to the house (a rarity) like he's struck by lightning. It's easy to imagine the way I walk, hands poised at my sides, trying to keep my head straight and rely on peripheral vision, makes me look like my poor, traumatised cat.

The square's dark and still, an upward thrust of turrets, narrowed windows and yellow brickwork like smoker's teeth. Though I can leave any time, I feel hemmed in. I'm not used to it, not since I grew into my skill. Before, in life, I always felt trapped by the circumstance of simply being, until I learned that giving in to the pressure squeezing my skull and temples is silly. It's been a long time since then.

And I'm here. Beneath the shadow of lead casting, the static curling hair of his wig falling limp against round shoulders, the fleshy jowls and protruding nose, ankle-length jacket falling open, betraying the portly figure of a man to whom good dining was consistent, less luxury than unacknowledged necessity. While thousands of miles from where he'd lived and this likeness stood, people ate tossed scraps, their bellies crawling with hunger. And I stare into the face of a man who can't see mine, tension migraine sharp, pressing against my temples and forehead. An ache in the muscles where my neck meets spine, musing at the myriad ways it hurts to look.

A clanking, creaking noise. I react like Blake, whipping around and inevitably they've appeared, the source of my enclosed anxieties, those who wish to imprison me, physically, mentally, spiritually, take your fucking pick. As it was.

Tonight, I assume they believe they've done their homework. The bulk of my forthcoming assault is formed by a group of six men, women, I can't actually tell who's who, dolly-step advancing, a net held taut at four corners, two more lifting up the front and back. They're shuffling because the net must be weighty, I mean, there are globed weights at the corners, true, but it's mostly because the actual material itself is dark with paint, probably quite heavy. If I had to make a guess, I'd say it was some kinda lead coated rope. Ironic if you think too hard. I don't have the time.

Positioned on either side of the Net Bearers, another two dark-clothed figures move slowly towards me, double-pronged objects with orange handles raised. These lot are half-crouched, difficult to see in dim light. They point the objects at me from an angle just above their hips, so they must be weapons. The Object Handlers fan out, blocking my pathway, or that's what they think. No one speaks, the clanking continues, everyone moves in utter silence.

To a person, The Group wear face masks, metal kneepads, helmets and other forms of protection, another reason they walk like the living dead. Any visible skin is blackfaced, and I'd be offended but I can't talk. The net looks cumbersome, unwieldy, and makes a fair bit of noise. I reckon they've been told about me.

I sweep my head left to right. Start to laugh.

That seems to annoy them, which is great, it's what I need. I'm hoping it makes them clumsy. A Handler on my right makes the first move, kneeling forwards and thrusting with the object like they're fencing. It touches my leg. There's a sound like a fly caught in an electric trap, and I pull away, too late. I scream, unable to stop myself. My thigh's been stabbed with a thousand tiny needles, it's agony.

A cattle prod. They've fucking stung me with a cattle prod.

The Group close in, knowing they can hurt me. I've gotta move quick. Lifting my hands, fingers splayed, I push air at them, hearing my teeth grind.

Nothing. Fucks sake.

The Net Bearers are up in my face, I recognise their plan. My mind shrieks panic, my stare's wide-eyed. I'm scared.

I've got three seconds, max. So I drop to the floor, ignoring the sear of pain in my right leg, use that arm to keep me balanced, sweeping with my left foot. That brings down the one who shocked me. I push off straight after, gasping with effort, and kneel over their body to throw a punch into their solar plexus with all my strength. Connection jars my knuckles and forearm. That does the trick. Breath erupts, I smell dank cigarette along with lager, the bitterness of oily food. They're wheezing, out for the count, can't breathe.

I keep my motion fluid, grabbing their fallen prod, and dive into a roll just like practice, coming back on the other side before the second handler, short and stout, already puffing. Some idiot told them it would be easy; put me down, quick call to feds, a couple of tins back at the ranch, job done. They're flailing, who's scared now? A weak thrust of a shaking prod goes over my head, uncommitted, it's perfect. I'm kneeling on my weak leg, my yell of pain a war cry as I jab hard, teeth gritted, connect. Hold it there, I won't let go like they did.

Second handler screams like they're being beat by their mum. I try not to relish that. They fall.

Oh, shit. Net Bearers.

The first thing I note when I swing around is they're struggling. The wretched net would've only got heavier the longer they hold on, their muscles weaker, and the other thing is, I've moved innit? That wasn't meant to happen, I was supposed to be on the floor convulsing from prod shock. It means they have to shuffle round in unison to find a better position, and even if they've practiced like I have, none have the agility of a real me. I roll away once more to put some space between us. My leg still tingles, but I've got some feeling back as long as I don't favour it too much.

It's almost over, even if they don't know it. I hear my mother's voice, see the Net Bearer's black-gloved hands. Thin material, better for grip.

As a test I push downwards, towards the floor. The paving slab beneath me crackles blue energy, almost splitting to reveal the darkness. I pull back and it closes up, speckled, grey.

I'm grinning, looking up.

'Don't fuck with Jack-a-Lent, yeah?' I tell them, deep and masculine. Splayed hands chest high, I push.

My intention's to maim, not kill, so when straw needles materialise below my poised wrists like strands of hair from electric-blue pores, they're warning shots, not for real. If I wanted to put them down permanently, I would've used stones, not dried grass, and aimed for their heads. God knows where the materials come from, I've never tried to find out, although I can bring anything through the portal, bullets or water, bricks or sand. I only have to imagine, so it's lucky for these lot people like me want equality, not revenge.

Still, the needles travel at high velocity, it's gotta hurt. I make them strike the tips of their fingers, smiling a little as they scream, drop the lead net meant to dampen my powers, watching them fall to the ground rolling and kicking like upturned insects. Who's cockroaches now? A few end up on their sides, and I can't resist pushing strands into the flesh of their arses for good measure. There aren't many laughs in this line of work. I grab fun where I can.

The Group are a bundle of shadows making odd shapes, groaning. They're no threat. Even so, our beef was pretty noisy. I need to speed things up.

And I'm walking across the square past a curled-up body, still writhing like a worm in hot sun. They say something in a voice raw with alcohol that almost makes me jump.

'Why don't you go and clean up your own mess, you prick?'

'Get fucked,' I whisper, before I clock it's the accent, they hear the South West no matter how I disguise my voice. The best thing I can do is shut up, walk away.

Beneath the statue, we lock eyes. John Cass, designed by Louis-François Roubiliac, an English merchant and major developer of the Transatlantic Slave Trade with direct links to slave agents in the Caribbean, as well as African forts. Originally cast in lead circa 1751, this particular work was moved to its current location, the Guildhall, back in 1980, years before I was born. Several fibreglass copies exist, including one at the John Cass Institute, its original location, and another in the entrance lobby of the London Metropolitan University Archive. I'll get to those another night.

One final look upward, a matter of pride. Now I'm here, face to leaden face, it feels better, a civic duty. I open a portal behind John Cass the length and width of the statue, the unstable hole a gaping wound glistening at the centre, torn and ragged at its edges. Fissured air crackles. I relish darkness, push him inside, and close the portal for good.

Recently, I've been occupied by the role of masks in our cultural traditions. How they tally with what I'm doing, my task. For us, masks are a way of putting on another face, usually of someone who has passed. Engaged as a physical mechanism, they allow the wearer to transform into another entity, influencing the spirit, or spirits they appeal to. There's power inherent in that which either draws people in or forces them away, alongside a performance element that can't be ignored, whether it occurs on the African continent or the wider diaspora. We can be chosen or volunteer our services due to specialised characteristics symbolised by the mask, qualities attained or initiated into. I wear mine, of sorts, in honour of these traditional ancestral values, though of course they're echoed in European cultures throughout the ages. I'm not sure why the West is so confused by the practice of mask wearing, when they've performed similar rites for hundreds of years.

I use white paste made from chalk powder instead of something heavy and restrictive, painting my entire face. Occasionally, if I think I'll be amongst company, I might wear a home-sewn face mask, though they're difficult to fight and travel in, and I prefer the freedom of paint. While I researched the historical significance of African masks, I found a number of books on the folkloric traditions of Bristol. The muse was unexpected, matching almost everything I'd experienced since I came into the skill. Etched in thin textbook pages, I read all I could about the legend of Jack-a-Lent.

A portal closes behind me, as I step into my bedroom to see darting orange fur, the curled question mark of Blake's tail whisk away. Poor thing. I doubt he'll ever get used to it. I would lock him in his cage when I go out on tasks, but that's just cruelty to animals. I wait a minute, fingers rested on my heart, getting my breath back. It takes a fair bit of energy to travel by portal, not just physically, in my head. Often it's tougher than engaging with Group members. The further away from Bristol I go, the worse it feels.

My leg smarts, the sting of grazed hands, elbows and knees sparking lightning-flash pain. I've banged my hip and spine rolling on concrete, even though I tucked in my head like I was taught. A throbbing ache I didn't notice until now makes my lower jaw fall in agony, hands clenched in fists. I swear, bent over. Blake arrives as if he never left in righteous panic, surefooted, leaping random piles of clothing, rumbling thunderous content and winding around my sore ankles. I ease myself onto the bed, grunting, and he jumps onto my lap. We fall into our routine, me stroking from head to tail, him pawing my lap in left to right rhythm, purring. It's almost as if the Guildhall fight never happened.

I sit a minute, trying to breathe normally. The street outside's filled with pre-emptive silence that's unusual. Most nights, I hear the continual whirr of passing bikes and young conversations, the heartbeat of bounced footballs, drunken, shouting voices telling everyone their business like anyone cares, mostly people I know, even if I don't understand the language, I recognise voices. Music's constant round here, leaking from windows or neighbour's houses, tinny phones as kids sing the latest 1 Extra track in loud, cracked tones. I'm on the ground floor and sometimes it feels as if they're in here with me, ready to go in my fridge for milk, ask if I want tea. Not everyone loves Ends, but that's their business. They don't know it, if you're not Easton you can't. It's the feeling of being a part of something you can't force, or create, it either happens or it don't. Like family, pretty much. I grew up a way from Landsdowne Court, where I am now, on Gordon Ave with Mum and Dad before it all went to shit. So I know.

I give myself a quick check over. The knee of my trackie bottom's frayed, not all the way, the black material semi-translucent as sheer tights. The elbows of my matching hoodie are similar, and the white JL letters I stitched above my left breast are dark with muck. I roll the bottoms down from my waist to just above the knee. The skin there's clouded red, flushed with anger. I press with a forefinger, gasp and swear again. That's not gonna heal for a while.

It's my first big proper fight, the first where stakes were raised because they'd planned how to deal with me. They're getting smarter, less a smatter of random people vex 'cause Colston drunk Bristol harbour juice. They're getting to know me, and what I'm doing. That makes them dangerous.

The flat's small, only a few limped steps from one room to another. In the bathroom, I search a mirrored cabinet, pushing aside bottled perfumes and nail polish, dental picks and hairbands, trying not to look at my face. When I can't find tape and dressing, I slam the cabinet door, forced to see what I avoid. My white painted face, a pale moon floating above the midnight dark of clothing. Uniform. I refuse to say costume, that's just stupid. I've never been into superheroes, never read comics or watched anime. I haven't seen that programme everyone raves about on HBO, despite my cat's name. It's coincidence, promise. Whenever Comicon made its mythical way to us each year, me and my mates would sit on a bench outside Bristol Temple Meads station, passing Scrumpy cans with our hoods up, talking shit about the cosplay fools dressed in wispy lime dresses, wearing plastic Elven ears (always pink), or dolled up as Potter wizards. Fucking idiots.

Now look. Not much difference between us, ancient traditions converging with modern myths, both simple means of human beings communing with Gods, angels, deities, ancestral spirits, whatever the fuck you call it. Thinking back on those piss-taking days and the way those cozzers ignored us, I'm struck with a tingle of guilt because I always remember Mum insisting I was different, even back then. I just didn't want to know.

It stings, my limp hurts, I've got no choice. I'm going into work.

Those early days were fearful beyond understanding. My first time, terror worse than I'd known. Mum sat me down, I couldn't have been older than eleven or twelve, wanting to explain something I remember she said. Dad was at work, his presence ghostly in the house, the odour of aftershave roaming corridors and rooms, desperate to remind us what had been. A hint too faint to catch, or inhale. A moment, before it was gone.

I'd long been sneaking looks at any textbooks I could find, mainly Dad's academic stuff, so I thought I knew what she was gonna say. Something about monthly blood cycles and my first steps into womanhood, not being scared or freaked out by pain, what it felt like her first time. I'd read enough novels, including Mum's battered old copy of *Are You There God? It's Me Margaret* and a few chapters we hadn't covered in biology classes, to feel as though I knew what was coming. Only there was no way. When she started on about hands in what seemed like her usual ritual, I sighed frustration, my chin resting against one palm. I thought I'd piss her off. Instead, she smiled, just watching me.

I asked what was up. To this day, I'll never forget a single word she said. Mum sighed, shifting until her knees were pointing at me. Cocoa butter gleaming, the way I always wished mine could. 'I suppose practical's better than theory,' she said at her trainers, before she lifted her hands like she was trying to stop something, and the portal appeared in the air before us, a broad oval the size of a hallway mirror, hovering a metre or so from where we sat.

Years later, I'd remember when I saw a boy being pushed into the swimming pool by his dad. The snapshot fear that lit his face. His screams, silenced by water. The surprise tightening my eyes and mouth, my vivid certainty he would drown. His anger as he resurfaced, beating the pool with a fist, only splashing himself as his dad laughed, and laughed.

Growing up, tough love was all we knew. It made me what I am today, so I don't blame Mum for pushing me. Back then, every single one of us was pushed. It was supposed to toughen us up.

Going through a portal these days is like dipping my head beneath water. The noises of the world are inconsequential, mute disturbances with no bearing on the underworld. Constant humming fills my ears. I can't see much. Everything is blurred and out of context. It's calm, peaceful. It wasn't always that way.

Back then, that first time, I screamed, fought, thrashed. If Mum hadn't pulled me out, I would've drowned. Even though I know how messed up it was, to be initiated so brutally, I can't help feeling grateful she rescued me.

I'm in Bell Hill Tesco's stockroom, and yes, full disclosure before anyone says a word, this *is* where I work. Alright? I know I'm slightly taking the mick, but I don't see why I should faff around with all night pharmacies when I can get what I need here. And it's not stealing technically, because as soon as I'm on shift and the tills open, I'll slip in the money and it's done, like I paid for real, and it's not as if I can wait, can I? I've got proper work to do.

Like so many of these Express places, way back when this was a pub. The Bell. Not too imaginative, but it was St George. Mum tells stories about it being her local, growing up. It's where she hung out with her parents and their mates, and their kids when she was young, even though she weren't supposed to, where she had a first pint as soon as she was legal, probably even her first snog (or one of many I'm guessing). I know for sure it's where she met my dad. Yes indeed, Mum and Dad could've swapped flirty glances and bants right on the spot I'm walking this minute, hunting for clean up tape. What a ride, eh? Life.

It's dark, and I don't switch on the light because, you know, just in case. We close at eleven and open again at six, and quite often the night shift stays pretty much overnight, loading deliveries, stocktaking or cleaning, and I would hate for screw-faced Yogita, my manager, or the perpetual strop that's my good mate Owen to find me here with no reasonable explanation. Sure, I could portal somewhere else and cause even more trouble when they saw it, but why would I want to do that? If I'm caught, I'm done for either way.

I conjure up a small portal, not even open, just a crackling electric-blue sphere of energy below my wrist, so I don't fall over or anything. I point and search, bending down before a low shelf, muttering and counting myself lucky that what I'm looking for isn't locked up with all the serious medicinal supplies, the Calpol and Panadol, Imodium and Anadin. My next shift's not until the weekend this rotation, all the more time to gear up for customers queued without face masks, arguing whether the rule's two metres or one, Owen scanning items beside me with a face like a cadaver, more life in the statues I portal than him. He's not a bad one or nothing, just nineteen and bearing the scars of a past drug habit, quite serious I guess. Faded marks the colour of distant galaxies on his arms he normally keeps covered up, shirtsleeves buttoned at the cuff, unless we're in the stockroom, alone. Smaller ones on the back of both hands, which he tries to push into his pockets, and make another ritual. We know a few of the same people, so I reckon he thinks I'm cool. Most of the time Owen looks like he's had a surprise hit of Spice, and he's stuck at the till trying to claw back consciousness by portalling himself down to the banal reality of shop floor.

A row of microporous tape, another of wound pads beside it. I take a couple of each, listening for the stockroom door; no doubt they'll come in handy if The Group keep turning up at statues, trying to stick me like a stubborn cow that needs herding. The leaf green boxes tumble into my free hand. They're light and fit in my hoodie without any trouble.

Outside, I hear it. The unwieldy industrial vacuum cleaner firing up, baritone conversation on shop floor. Time to go.

On Pero's bridge I rest against emaciated metal, knees up, sitting on the cool slabs of concrete, trackie leg pulled up from the ankle this time. It's not comfortable, I don't even care. I suppose I could've done this at home, it's probably easier, yet something about the feel of night, water lapping beneath me and the atmosphere does something. It's calming, helps me see, more or less feels like home anyway. The skies are clear, the moon easier to catch than it was in London, straining with the brilliance of its mirror gleam. I sever flimsy microporous tape with my teeth, attach it to the wound pad and apply both to my reddened leg, absorbing the stagnant quiet of the city in wait, listening for disruption.

Nothing comes.

And I don't know what it is, maybe the stillness, maybe my thoughts. Maybe the void I'd come from moments ago. It all rushes me, as I push the dressing tight against my thigh, alive to spiked pain, release and let my head fall back until I'm looking up at clouds racing like expelled smoke. I think about the moon and sun and relationships of symbiosis, how one thing doesn't quite work without the other, connection and disconnection, what either achieves. How we reflect what's in our proximity, or refuse the source. Whether it's choice at all, perhaps mundane coincidence. And I'm being vague, I'm sorry, I know it's not helpful, but the truth is, neither are the thoughts swimming through me, because I'm imagining Mum and Dad, commerce and profit, cold lands and dark continents, and whether the thing I give a shit about is even worthy of being my focus. I'm seeing the idiot on the floor, face painted black, curled up against the hard, gritty concrete, giving a whispered order through clenched teeth. And it's not like I haven't thought about it before. Look at the hands. So true. Right here on this bridge, before Guildhall, even before The Group tried it the first time, after Colston came down amongst a ripple of anger and protest, I'd been thinking the exact same thing.

It's nothing I suppose. A space between this world and beyond. A dead zone, void. Liminal, intellects might say. Not people like Mum.

Maybe it's the place she floats in now, languishing, alone and waiting for us, or where my sister came into being all those years ago. A space of *before*, of things without form. The ancient world, older than our Blackness. At uni, caught up in those things, I practiced double study, spending half my time on a useless history degree, the other searching for texts that might apply to the darker world I knew existed. I was my dad's child after all.

That first time, when Mum pushed me in, the roaring was loud as waterfall. I tumbled and rolled like a kid who'd taken a trip running, until a firm grip clasped my wrist. A tug. Solid ground beneath my feet, a hurried intake of air filling my chest. The bruised sky, everything real.

I stood on the edge of a damp, wooden jetty. A wide expanse of river spread before me, glistening buildings making a wall of the opposite side. Dark windows of moored boats lay at rest, bobbing and sleepy. Something caught my eye. When I turned my head in that direction, I saw an obscure half sphere of radiance some miles away, almost a fallen sun half buried in land, an arc of concave illumination that seemed holy, unimaginable. My surroundings, real as they felt, might have not been reality at all. When I looked at the nearest statue it was unlike those I usually avoided, head ducked to the floor so their cold gaze wouldn't pierce me. A proud African woman, hands lifted, rainfall locks draped behind her, chin tilted towards the moon.

Mum stepped in close beside me.

'This is why we use our portals with intent,' she muttered, looking around. 'Without that, you get yourself lost.'

I opened my mouth to argue, but she'd already taken my hand. There was nothing, immersion, and we were home.

I spend the remainder of my night, or morning, whichever way you chose to see it, performing my task. The locations I travel to span the length and width of the country; once, I even crossed the channel to portal a John Nicholson likeness, on behalf of my Indian brothers and sisters in Armagh. In Grosvenor Road, Chester, the equestrian statue of Viscount Comberbare, owner of 420 enslaved Africans. In City Hall, Cardiff, and St Pauls Cathedral, London, Thomas Picton, renowned torturer, slave owner and Governor of Trinidad. The bust sized monument of Sir Edward Wynter, owner of several eighteenth-century Jamaican plantations, adorning Battersea Church, south London. And then the infamous; Rhodes at Oriel College, Oxford, several of Robert Peel, whose family wealth derived from slavery and made him the man he became, much like my mother's toughness made me, in Leeds, Bradford, Tamworth, Manchester. Statues of Lord Nelson, protester against the abolishment of slavery and close friend of Simon Taylor, owner of more than 2,000 enslaved Africans, in Great Yarmouth, Norwich, the Isle of Anglesey and Deptford Town Hall. Duplicate Colstons at the Girls' school and Society of Merchant Venturers in Clifton, Bristol. Francis Drake, Robert Blake, Clive of India, H.M. Stanley. Prime Minister William Gladstone, whose father John received the largest compensation pay out for lost slaves in the UK. So many names, so many men. Such a task.

I've heard people say it's up to local communities to debate what statues should come down, and which should remain. I'm not really one for long talk, so I make portals expand, push statues in and collapse them again until my eyes are dazzled, my chest seizes, and I find it difficult to breathe.

Beneath the imposing height of Beckford Tower, Bath, I lean against chilled stone. My chest wheezes. Leaves whisper around me. The quiet of the cemetery behind is mute fog. It's too much. No way I can portal them all. The task would take years, and possibly harm me. My head lifts, it aches. At the tower base, there's a sign. It says William Beckford and his family inherited wealth from Jamaican plantations, and yet the tower, raised by Beckford himself, has been turned into a museum with the intention that its connections to slavery might be fully explored.

I stand, my breath returns. The tower will stay. I open a portal and enter.

Sometimes I know people watch me. Hidden in shadows made by alcoves or edges of buildings, gravestone still, or so they believe. Somehow, I sense their presence. It's connection, like a television on in another room. Tingling, underlying sensation. I can't see them, and still, I know them well.

They're not enemies, uh uh. Not like The Group. And I'm not sure how they follow me, only it's something symbiotic like moon and earth, another occurrence I haven't worked out yet.

Here's the other thing. They never *do* anything. Like, they stand or crouch or whatever, and just watch what I do. Portalling, I mean. I felt them initially after the protests, when I'd been portalling statues a few weeks. My research wasn't as good as it is, and one of my friends swore down there was a slaver's statue outside Wills Hall, where I'd lived as a fresher. I'd never seen anything, but they insisted. Even though Google backed me, I learnt that Wills' extensive family wealth derived from slave-grown tobacco, and thought I'd better check it out, just in case. That was a down day for me, I was thinking of Mum a lot, so I waited until one in the morning, reheated my earlier dinner from the chippie, wolfed it down in a blind attack on my Ikea plate, and went.

Only, I wasn't at Wills Hall. On the far side of the main road, opposite St Michael's, I stared into lights. Feathery rain came down, slanted by wind, making pavements and the dark road glisten, and it was quiet, unusual for such a busy street. Considering how I'd got there, I crossed metres from the traffic lights, trainers slopping against tarmac. I'd been thinking of her, hadn't I? I'd portalled by intent, unconscious or otherwise.

The A & E façade resembled a hotel. Odd brickwork the colour of scrubs and hospital face masks, a sliding door entrance complete with transparent awning, shielding smokers from rain. No one there at this time. I sleepwalked closer, past the NHS infirmary sign, and when sensors picked up my presence and the glass slid in an awkward, jerking movement, I started, awakened. The whine of electrics was loud in the night. Interior lights were bright, painful, bringing to mind the steady pulse at my temples. Mum was wheeled through here, the ambulance parked sideways on the pavement, doors gaping, yards away. Complications, they told us. She'd asked for a homebirth, disappointed with herself when the midwife went into another room talking quiet, phone pressed against cheek, a hand against her free ear. Sitting on hard plastic chairs with Dad, his fingers sweaty and tight around mine, we waited to be called.

I knelt on the pavement, knee rested on the shallow edge of a puddle, disregarding sodden chill seeping through cotton into my flesh, the first instinctive tingle of being watched by a stranger huddled beneath an oak tree, my self-flagellating urge to visit the worst place on earth, everything.

And just like it happened months ago, I'm not where I should be. I look around, shoulders slumped, even though I can't be annoyed with myself. It's the lake at St George's Park where me and Dad used to come, where we'd kick a ball around in wind and rain, before he'd go off to teach at the Workers' Education Association. A wide-open, grassy space, people jogging and walking dogs, the prime spot to bun weed in a huddled teenage group when I got older, listening to music on our phones, hoping we didn't see anyone we knew. All those warm summer nights laid on the grass with a hoodie beneath my neck, watching clouds roam like idle nomads. I've done it again. Portalled somewhere without meaning to.

I sit on damp grass, thinking back, uncaring about the spreading patch of cold on my rear. One time, we were sitting on the benches when some guy started an argument with a group of four men. Big blokes, Muslim, the guy on his own, and white, and I dunno what happened but when we looked up the white guy had two big fuck off machetes in each hand, pointed at the grey path, walking slowly towards them. He was shouting 'Come on then! Come on!' None of the Muslim guys backed down though. They just stepped to him like it was nothing, and I thought it was instant bloodshed, until a police car went by, and they all left separate ways like a drop of rain making contact with earth. It was broad daylight as well, about half three that afternoon.

I think of powerlessness, incredulity. The whispering person, writhing on Guildhall concrete. And that's enough.

Whenever I go there, I'm surprised. The apartment's low ceilinged, like the product of an earthquake, and I always think it's good he's not that tall. The rooms are pretty big, even if functional. One bedroom, a living room, the kitchenette and pit of a bathroom with a window opening onto the stone stairway, the blank faces of apartment doors. That's it. Only the necessary. It's almost as if more would be too unwieldy, overwhelming or confusing, so the bare minimum will do. A sagging futon/sofa with some weird hippy blanket draped on top faces a dusty 20" telly from the 90s. There are pictures of me graduating, me and Mum wearing kid's birthday hats, me, Mum and him taken in an obvious selfie, the background minimal and long forgotten, kinda like the place he lives.

I try not to turn up too often. I don't want him to know I've been there, restless and lonely, pacing the Moroccan rug bought from some imitation French souk, listening for steps on the stairway, a key in the door. It's not a good habit to develop, creeping about personal spaces where I shouldn't be, and as soon I do, the guilt's like dank rainwater on my flesh, cold and uncomfortable. I find myself doing random shit like picking up menus I can't read, sushi bars and Indian restaurants, all the prices in euros, mouth watering and teeth grinding from withheld tears.

I don't know why he never came back, much less why Dad would live somewhere more student flat than anything I ever had. It's just enough to understand I can visit, and smell the growing summer miles from where it all went wrong, secure in the fact he might be better there.

I've heard about this place, although I've never come inside. When my mates wanted anything, back when I was a teenager hanging with the mandem, before I went uni, I'd hand over my money and wait on the corner of Warwick Road, pacing. Dunno why. I looked up at the streetlights, studying cobwebs and the way colours split into tiny, insect-sized rainbows. A lot of the time it was spitting, or very cold. It always seemed to take ages before they came back, trading stories about the Snyders', talking about the potency of their dro, or molly, whatever I chipped in on. It always happened the same way.

And I'm standing in their living room, still as a stranger. Snoring rumbles around me, more than one person I reckon. I'm wary of moving because all the lights are switched off, and if this place is anything like certain other houses I've been to, I know there's shit all over the place. Especially the floors. I push my right foot forwards, sliding across carpet and straight away I hear a rattle as I make contact. Sounds like a tin can. I'm not sure about what I'm doing here, I could get myself in a lot of trouble, but it's been niggling me, and if I want to be the change and all that crap it means I've got to do more than push a few statues into the void. I've got to try harder, do better.

So I make a small portal beneath my wrist, like in the stockroom. Just enough to see by. And it's exactly what I expect, the image I pictured walking to and fro across the street years ago, a completely different me.

Ricky Snyder, lanky and gaunt, sprawls on a sofa. Head back, mouth open. Legs spread open so far I can see the hairy bulge of thighs, into the darkness of baggy shorts. Hannah, his long-time girl, sleeps beside him, curled up foetal, a sofa cushion squeezed under her chin. I swing the portal light around, using tiny steps, trying to keep quiet. There's Nick and Raff Watson, Ricky's cousins, one in an armchair, the other prone on the floor. Both good-looking, rough as hell, everyone knows who they are. I turn back around.

When I lower my outstretched hand to the coffee table, it's all there. Empty tins, Rizla packets, a ton of self-sealed bags. Crumbs and dustings of white, brown, green, even tiny crystals of purple that reflect the light of my portal. Everything, like everyone said, and I don't know why I'm surprised. The Synder's always served up the whole estate.

The writhing person whispers, close in my ear; 'Go and clean up your own mess.' I'm nodding, biting my inner cheek, it's true.

I open the portal wider, just a touch. It's crackling, obviously I don't want Ricky, or any of them up. I push in the lot, all the tins, drugs, electric scales, even rolling papers. A part of me screams inside at what I'm doing. What'll happen if they find out it's me. I creep around the room best as I can, avoiding debris, and find a couple of plastic shopping bags hidden beside the sofa where Ricky sleeps. When I look inside, one's pungent, the other sterile, and there are larger blocks in each, no doubt what they've chopped off and weighed. No sense being all timid about it. I push those inside too.

When I think of Mum, and Owen, and all my mates that struggled with the yoke, it makes my jaw clench, and my face screw up. All the difference that absence might have made. The time wasted. The ruin of lives.

And the portal gets wider. I'm not controlling anything, it's the urge. It grows behind Ricky, so wide I see the askew slant of his upper teeth, their size reminding me of rabbits for some reason, and I'm repulsed by the thought, and I feel the push coming from my gut, building intensity like the need to burp or fart, growing and rising from my body, coming out.

A cry. Brief, simple. Momentary, gone. Upstairs, from a room unseen, and I know what it is. The kid. Of course, Ricky's kid.

I've seen them in the Tesco's. A boy trotting behind him, mostly Hannah, every now and then the big man Rick Snyder himself, can't be older than 5, podgy arms and legs, green eyes and freckles, cuter than anything. Always baffles me how out of all the shit and pain caused by us, we still possess the ability to create beauty, almost despite ourselves. How we don't even have to try, we just float along led by our whims and out it comes, something so perfect and real. Yeah, we fuck up eventually for the majority of our time, but that first manifestation, our truest expression, can't help but arrive moulded in the image of what we're supposed to be. Our apposite form.

And that's it. No matter what was said, or how I feel. I can't. In my right mind, thinking properly, there's no way.

The sun will come up soon. I'm tired, but actually okay. One last look at my hands, and I'm gone.

Origin Story: From Jack-a-Lent to the Fall of Colston

Dr Richard Sheldon

University of Bristol

SHORTLY AFTER 19 JULY 1749 when tolls began to be levied on travellers and goods making their way towards Bristol from the South and the East, a group of men, some of them in disguise, some with blackened faces, assembled and processed together towards toll gates on the Long Ashton Road. On the night of Monday 24 July, 'a great body of the country people of Somerset […] making prodigious shouts […] fell to work with hatchets, axes, etc.,' destroying toll gates at Bedminster just to the south of the city. The next night came attacks on toll gates and houses on the Eastern Toghill Road. These protesters were described as 'naked with only trousers on, some in their shirts,' others had blackened faces in clear defiance of the notorious 'Black Act',[1] a statute which prescribed the death penalty for going about in such a disguise following the activities of a band of protesters against the loss of common rights in the Royal forests who became known as 'the Waltham Blacks'.[2] These initial protests led to a summer of confrontation between the rioters and the Turnpike commissioners backed up by the city authorities. Toll gates and houses were rebuilt and guards appointed to protect them and oversee the collection of tolls, a reward for information of £100 (a small fortune in today's money) was offered for information on the protesters.

The wider background to these protests lay in the sweeping agrarian and commercial changes that preceded and paved the way for the industrial revolution in Britain. Innovations including the expropriation of common lands and resources through enclosure, the imposition of work discipline and surveillance in industry and agriculture, the removal of consumer protection legislation that sought to ensure a fair provision and, above all, the privatisation of common resources in the name of the few rather than the many all marked this period. Wild animals, forest fruits, roots and herbs, and fallen timber now became exclusively owned commodities protected by the full weight of the law and the awful spectacle of the gallows. As well as the commodities of agrarian capitalism and consumer goods the roads would also have become conduits for the newly wealthy on their way to the social scenes of Bristol, Bath and London. The emerging free market was not free for all. Previously the highways of England had been considered ancient 'rights of passage', communal shared resources for all, now increasingly they became thoroughfares for the better off.[3]

As an integrated national market for both essential food and luxury items developed, the transport network required improvement. Such improvements were backed by investors who sought a return on their capital. A local group of investors with interests in improving the speed and ease of road transit had clubbed together to form a trust investing in improvements to the road surface. In return, they erected toll gates on the road charging a fee or toll to travellers in order to pass. In the absence of effective political representation for the poor (only property-owning males possessed the right to vote) there was instead the tradition of collective bargaining by riot. Paradoxically, 'traditional' culture became a strategy and a flexible set of tactics for rebellion and a repertoire for resistance. Bristol itself was still the nation's second city at this time and at the heart of an expanding network of trade and commerce with the South

West, the Midlands, Bath and London. Manufactured goods, fuel, farm produce and a growing list of groceries from near and far were being transported. The roads were also frequented by those who had made their fortunes from slavery and its associated products. The Bristol turnpike roads were at the start of a boom in the construction of turnpikes that lasted until the 1770s. There had previously been a rash of protests at the construction of tollgates in the Bristol region between 1727 and 1735 when protesting mine workers had destroyed tolls, processed through the city, and even levied their own tolls on goods and travellers.[4] For a time, the authorities and the investors behind the tolls were forced to retreat and exempt the miners from charges. Later, in 1793, a notoriously bloody riot exploded when tolls were levied to cross Bristol Bridge.

Strange as it seems to us, resistance was staged in the name of tradition. A customary culture in part real, in part a nostalgic reinvention of tradition, was a resource for resistance. Jack-a-Lent drew upon what the historian E.P. Thompson called the moral economy of the poor. Rather than the chocolate box retreat of today, the English countryside in the eighteenth century was both the home turf and the battleground of nascent capitalism.

The colliers of Kingswood Forest, a notoriously riotous and forthright community, 'a set of ungovernable people',[5] had protested in the past. At one stage of the protests, holes were bored into the gates in order to pack them with explosives and blow them up, suggesting a clear link to mining communities who would have had the hardware and expertise to perform such an action. On 26 July, the 'country people [...] in a prodigious body, with drums beating, and loud shouting, armed with cutting instruments fixed in long staffs,' returned. Some of the protesters were disguised as women. Gates were destroyed as well as the tollhouse which was in the process of being rebuilt after the previous attack two nights before. A gate on the Dundry Road was also destroyed by a crowd led by 'two chiefs on horseback; one with his face black'd, and the other a young Gentleman Farmer of Nailsey [Nailsea], well known, carried the Standard, being a Silk Handkerchief on a long staff…' The rest, led by three drummers, were armed 'with some weapon or others promiscuously, as rusty swords, pitchfork, broad axes, guns, pistols, clubs.' On their hats and caps they had the initials JL to signify they were the 'Jack-a-Lents' and all were to be addressed as 'Jack'. Outside the George Inn, they ranged themselves 'by beat of drum, huzzas, and a hunting horn'.

Jack-a-Lent was a figure appropriated from carnival folklore as carnival itself was largely a lapsed custom in protestant England. The precise mechanism of transmission is lost to us along with much else, yet he allows us a kind of lens through which we may momentarily recapture popular theories of justice and retribution. In the sixteenth century Jack-a-Lent had been a straw effigy pelted by boys, perhaps as a relief for tensions generated by the privations the six weeks of Lent. Jack was occasionally recorded in the English West between the seventeenth and the nineteenth centuries but in truth we know little about his meaning or why he was chosen as the eponymous leader of the protests of 1749.[6] In 1766, the tale of Robin Hood was published in chapbook form championing him as 'the terror of forestallers and engrossers' (capitalist speculators in the grain trade neglecting the needs of the poor, respectively: those who bought before the market, and those who bought in order to withhold corn from the market and cause prices to rise).[7]

When the Jack-a-Lents reached Redcliff Hill on the Southern edge of the city the rioters would have been in sight of Queen's Square, an exclusive housing development financed by and in many cases inhabited by merchants who had grown rich on the slave trade. Today, just off Queen's Square lies Perro's Bridge, erected in 1999 and named after the black servant of Bristol's slave trading Pinney family, for a long time the only physical acknowledgement of the city's long connection to enslavement. A month after the riots, in August 1749, an anonymous letter was sent to the Mayor of Bristol threatening to burn down the merchants' Exchange building beyond Queen's Square on Corn Street if the new tolls weren't removed and the men taken prisoners by the city authorities released. This grand building had been completed and opened in 1743, based on classical and Venetian architectural models it also trumpeted the position of Bristol at the cutting edge of the world economy. Above the doors of the Exchange on its front façade was, and are, carvings of an African woman and an Indian man. Inside the exchange are plasterwork heads representing Asia, America and Africa symbolising Bristol's wider colonial and commercial entanglements in the business of enslavement as well as the luxury trades associated with the expansion of Britain's growing role in the world economy. Hundreds of merchants met here and in the adjoining coffee houses and taverns. East Indian traders would deal in Indian textiles, profits from which were reinvested in the triangle trade of the Atlantic: metals manufactured in the Bristol region were sent to the West coast of Africa where they were exchanged for enslaved humans, who were then shipped to the Caribbean and America to labour on sugar and tobacco plantations.

North of Totterdown – where the protesters destroyed tolls on the Wells Road after being thwarted in their attempts to march on the Old City – lay Easton, an area known for its large-scale extraction of coal, clay and sand, developed for housing in the nineteenth century and partially demolished and rezoned again for new roads and housing estates in the 60s and 70s, where 2021's Jack lives. The running down and closure of Bristol's manufacturing industries in the 1990s cast many of the city's residents into unemployment, social exclusion and the problems that come with them. Striking levels of deprivation and exclusion – quite at odds with the city's more recent assiduously cultivated image as a hipster Elysium – resulted and to a large extent remain. Bristolians participated in the riots of 1980 sparked off by brutally insensitive policing and the 'Suss Laws' (though largely unnoticed in comparison to the inner-city disturbances of St Pauls in the same year) as well as in the urban riots of 2011, often disparagingly, and tellingly, known as 'the Chav Spring'.[8]

Perhaps the sense of release experienced by the community

during the 2020 Black Lives Matter protests, which famously culminated in the toppling and dunking of slaver Edmund Colston's statue, felt something like the post-Lent release of the first Jack-a-Lent processions, coming as they did after months of enforced lockdown due to the COVID-19 pandemic.

On 7 June 2020, thousands of Bristolians and others of all races gathered to demonstrate their solidarity with the global struggle of Black people against racism made manifest in the killing of George Floyd in Minneapolis thirteen days before. The statue of Edward Colston, a notorious slave trader, was toppled by a group who came equipped with tackle for the job. Joyous crowds then rolled and dragged the statue past Perro's bridge where it was thrown into the River Frome.

A long stone's throw away from Colston's now empty plinth stands the figure of Edmund Burke, erected in 1894 and paid for by the Wills family of Bristol tobacco product manufacturers (as in the Wills Hall mentioned in Courttia's story), commemorating his tenure as the city's MP between 1774 and '80. Burke is generally celebrated as a hero and remembered as an opponent of the slave trade. Though undoubtedly on the right side of history when it came to his public statements on the issue, when push came to shove in 1792, his actions behind closed doors did not match his public stance. Following the revolts of enslaved peoples in the French Caribbean of 1791 he began to oppose emancipation believing it to be an uncontrollable movement. As the economic and strategic interests of the West Indies were too important to the British state and economy to lose along with their revenue, he shifted positions and did not support Wilberforce's Abolition Bill placed before parliament in 1792.[9] Just as we should remember and celebrate the actions of protesters we still need to attend to the figures who continue to ornament our public spaces. It was good that both aspects of Bristol's past were remembered in 2020. It is better still that we can understand the 2020 protests within the wider, natural tradition of redressing wrongs on the lanes, streets and squares of our cities when democratic means have been exhausted.

Notes

1. In the economic downturn that followed the collapse of the South Sea Bubble of 1720, the 'Black Act' was passed in 1723 in response to a series of raids by two groups of poachers, known as the Blacks from their habit of blacking their faces when undertaking poaching raids. The Act and its various extensions over the years was notoriously harsh, specifying over 200 capital crimes (including, for example, not just the burning of haystacks, but also the merely threatening of doing so). Under this Act, the legal rights of defendants were strictly limited. For example, suspects who refused to surrender within 40 days could be summarily judged guilty and sentenced to execution if they were apprehended. See E.P. Thompson's classic study *Whigs and Hunters: The Origins of the Black Act* (Harmondsworth: Penguin, 1975)
2. For a detailed account of the Jack-a-Lent protests of 1749 see Andrew Charlesworth, Richard Sheldon, Adrian Randall and David Walsh, 'The Jack-a-Lent Riots and Opposition to Turnpikes in the Bristol Region in 1749' in *Markets, Market Culture and Popular Protest in Eighteenth-Century Britain and Ireland* (Liverpool: Liverpool University Press, 1996). Unless otherwise indicated all historical evidence relating to Jack-a-Lent is drawn from this source.
3. See E.P. Thompson, *Customs in Common* (London: Merlin, 1991) for a collection of essays on the eighteenth century as seen from below and from the inside out. For the wider world currents of history in this period see Peter Linebaugh and Marcus Rediker, *The Many-Headed Hydra: The Hidden History of the Revolutionary Atlantic* (London: Verso, 2000) and David Armitage and Sanjay Subrahmanyam (eds.) *The Age of Revolutions in Global Context* (Basingstoke: Palgrave, 2010)
4. On these earlier protests see Andrew Charlesworth (Ed.) *An Atlas of Rural Protest in Britain 1548–1900* (London: Croon Helm, 1983) pp. 119–121.
5. See R.W. Malcolmson, 'A Set of Ungovernable People' in J. Brewer and J. Styles (Eds.) *An Ungovernable People* (London: 1980) for a study of the Kingswood miners

6. See Ronald Hutton's *The Station of the Sun: A History of the Ritual Year in Britain* (Oxford: Oxford University Press, 1997) pp. 172–173.
7. *The Exploits of the Renowned Robin Hood, the Terror of Forestallers & Engrossers and the Protector of the Poor & Helpless* (London, 1769)
8. See Owen Jones, 'Why 'chavs' were the riots' scapegoats', *The Independent* 1 May 2012
9. See the account in P. J. Marshall, *Edmund Burke and the British Empire in the West Indies: Wealth, Power and Slavery* (Cambridge: Cambridge University Press, 2019). On memory, commemoration and slavery in contemporary politics see Jessica Moody, *The Persistence of Memory: Remembering Slavery in Liverpool, 'Slaving Capital of the World'* (Liverpool: Liverpool University Press, 2020) and for Bristol Madge Dresser, *Slavery Obscured: The Social History of the Slave Trade in an English Port* (London: Bloomsbury, 2016).

Absence

M. Y. Alam

IN THE MIDDLE OF it is this little girl. She's not the tidiest or most fashionable kid you'll ever see: tatty pair of jeans that might have been the in thing a couple of decades ago, third generation hand-me-down trainers and a T-shirt so worn the cartoon figure and speech bubble are just about visible. I didn't think there were still kids dressed like her: you know, poor looking. But she's got an ice cream, and she's licking at it, watching him, not alarmed by what must seem a crazy man. If anything, she seems entertained.

'Little girl,' says Cass, quietly. 'Go away.'

She keeps licking her ice cream and slowly moves her head from side to side.

'She can't see me, man,' I say. 'She can't see me or hear me. And neither can anyone else.'

'Is that a fact?' asks Cass, sighing. 'Then why are we talking?'

Sure, I got to think about that one. I mean, maybe he's immune or something.

'Could be you're imagining –'

'Imagining? Did you just say *imagining*?'

Cass stops, shakes his head, then, crouching a little, looks at her. She's still enjoying the milk, vanilla, sugar and whatever else they put in ice cream.

'Little girl, tell me what you see.'

For the first time, the girl looks down, gathering her thoughts, and then clears her throat. It's an odd thing, her *ahem*-ing as if she's just about to make some big speech to an audience. This one, she's an odd little girl, I decide.

'You,' she says, looking at Cass directly. 'You're funny.'

Which makes me wonder: if looking at Cass is so funny, then how come she's not laughing?

'Funny?'

The little girl nods, goes back to her ice cream, and I'm sure she sneaks out a burp – quiet, and short. The mound of ice cream on top of the cone has shrunk. I wonder how she's going to deal with the rest of it. Maybe she'll start by nibbling at the edges along the top of the cone and tackle the rest after. I bet she's one of those who bites off the bottom, and then sucks, filling the tube, the bit you hold, the handle. I favoured the biting the tip of the handle and sucking method, myself, back when I was a kid. Most times, I didn't even think about it. It was ice cream, not rocket science.

'Funny how?'

She is now working her way along the top edge of the ice cream cone. She's enjoying this part especially. Not my ideal method, but not bad, either. You see, you get wafer and ice cream in every bite. And that's good – nothing worse than just dry wafer, right? I mean, who likes that?

'Do you always do this?' she asks, not looking at him, still fixed on the ice cream.

'Do what, little girl?' says Cass, then throws a glance my way. 'What do you mean?'

The little girl pauses eating and looks at what she has left. The outer edge of the cone top is gone. Just the wafer tube, half loaded with melting ice cream.

'Talk to yourself,' she says, all matter of fact, as if it's a normal thing to do.

Cass blinks a couple of times, shakes his head and sighs again.

'Fuck me,' he whispers.

'You should not do that,' she says, then bites off the top of the cone, in one go, adding as she chews, 'You swore. That's not a nice thing. It means you have a small vocabulary.'

Sounds like something her grandparents would say, but I'm really enjoying this. I would love an ice cream right now, I tell myself. As you get older, you forget about eating van-bought ice cream, and instead you might go for the ones you get in the shops. Nothing like the stuff you get from a van, though.

'Yeah,' I add, teasing Cass. 'Swearing's not cool, man.'

'You shut up. Just shut up.'

I smile it off. This is typical Cass, getting all excited and making it a big deal. It's not that he's always angry; he's not a crazy like that. Most times, he's gentle, I suppose: *a gentle giant*, people have called him, at least until he loses his shit. No. Most of the time, he speaks in a quiet way, and he's usually careful with his choice of words. But he's a big man – no overweight slob or nothing – but, you know, there's some meat on him; a solid fourteen stones if I had to guess.

'Is that a wig?' she says.

'What? Wig? No: my own hair, little girl.'

'Dead locks,' she nods, like she knows all about it. 'That's what you call your kind of hair.'

'Yeah, something like that,' says Cass.

The thing that nearly always annoys him is social media, with all its idiots posting videos and messages about anything and everything. Cass being Cass, with his history and all, has interests of his own, and so, he reckons himself an 'influencer' – which I think means he tells the world he knows something no one else does. Wasn't always the type to move like that, but as he's grown in age and size, so has his mind. Well, that's what he says at any rate.

'Tell her they're not dead locks,' I say, for some reason hoping he'll correct her.

Annoyed, Cass tells me to shut my mouth. Again, he lets loose a curse. Not a big one, but PG, probably: *Fucking*, but not in the sexual way. Just fucking as in *just shut your fucking mouth.*

'Why do you keep doing that?' she asks.

Cass replies, as calmly as he can:

'I'm sorry. You're right: I shouldn't swear, but he's making me cross right now.'

The little girl nods, like she gets it: really gets it.

'My friends make me cross sometimes. But we never swear.'

'Yeah,' says Cass, throwing me a glare, 'Friends can be a pain.'

Neither of us has any real friends, except for each other, I mean. Neither of us have any siblings but Cass didn't even have a dad. By default, this made us each other's best friend. As kids, we didn't take school too seriously, either; not when there were shops to lift from, car stereos to thieve, vehicles to TWOC and robs to go on. Still in our teens, we moved into more regular, but more risky ventures. And that's where things went wrong for Cass, more than me. Thanks to being fed to the coppers by our supplier, he did a three-year stint at Her Majesty's pleasure. I'd visit as often as I could. I think that meant a lot to him and truth is, it meant as much to me. Inside, he got into books, then education – it was either that or pumping iron. Cass, he could always handle himself if he had to, so maybe he figured schooling and books would help him pass his time. When he got out, he went to university and started some airy-fairy degree. He wanted me to go with him, but that stuff, it's for the birds.

'Why aren't you inside?' asks Cass, flicking his head at the school behind us.

She shrugs and tells him:

'I never liked school.'

For the first year of his studies, that's all he'd ever talk about – his stupid degree which, apparently, helped him make sense of the world. Only now, he was using words he never used before – not necessarily big words, but new words. He started to sound different. He sounded, well, like he was educated. He loved all that; the lectures, books, the essays to write. It allowed him to think, to focus and the idiot even thought he could make a difference. Sure. Like I said, it's for the birds, all that.

'You shouldn't miss school. School's important, little girl.'

She burps another little girl burp. I don't think she meant it as a response, but it seemed like that's exactly what it was:

'Ha! She burped you, Cass.'

Cass shakes his head, mutters something to himself and straightens up. I'm still laughing when I tell him:

'She owned you with that burp, bro.'

'Shut up, please: just shut up.'

'Sorry,' I say, adding. 'She did burp, though. Does that qualify as a diss, you think?'

So, while at university – *uni*, he'd call it, like it was his friend or something – he gets interested in the kind of things people like us don't usually bother with. Sure, those things hit and hurt us, but we don't talk about them. For Cass, that was the problem. According to him, politics, race, poverty, crime, equality and every other damned thing that's left to experts who don't know shit about it, was actually our problem to sort. One time he came out with something weird: 'People like us,' he said, 'we're talked about as if we can't speak for ourselves.' Bollocks: it's not that we can't speak for ourselves. We choose not to. What's the point speaking when you know you'll be ignored?

Long and short of all that was *uni* changed him, changed his outlook. For the first time in his life, he found a greater purpose. Personally, I couldn't see the point. It's just talk, right?

'Cass, you need to believe me.'

'Just stop. Stop this, man. It's not funny any more.'

During the second year of his degree, he got tight with a student on his course. He'd had girlfriends before, but not like her. He told me one time, a month or so into the relationship, that it wasn't just her looks he'd fallen for, it was her mind, as well. Not a good sign. The man, he melted when he was with her, or even when he talked about her. Just mushy bullshit that I knew would come back and bite him in the arse. I wish I'd been wrong. A few months later, she hits him with it, and hits him hard. She'd outgrown poor Cass. Told him the relationship had been fun while it lasted but had run its course. Wasn't going anywhere and they weren't growing, she said. She didn't mention that she was growing into one of her lecturers – some creepy, upper-class poser in tweed, more than twice her age, no doubt cash-healthy but weak in the ticker department. He was a historian, but his views weren't appreciated by a lot of people, at least, not openly; you know: Britain's lost its way, the Empire had been great and good, and now immigrants ought to be thankful for being here. That's right: he was a Tory, but not one of the newer, friendly kinds who used all the right words and made out that they gave a shit about ordinary people. Cass described him as an 'an unapologetic, old-fashioned, elitist, one nation Conservative', whatever the hell that means. Maybe it just means he was a twat.

'Okay, little girl. If you don't go to school, you'll regret it later, when you're older.'

Funniest thing about this twat was his name: Caesar. Rex Caesar. Why bless your child with one dog's name when you can use two, right? His parents, they must have hated the sight or sound of baby Rex to do him that way. Cass, meanwhile, his name is awesome. His mother, she chose it even though she knew it was unusual, and with kids being kids, that he'd be teased to hell and back: Cassidy Vellaunus. According to his mum, Cass was named after an ancient Welsh freedom fighter or some such. At least Cass's name, it had a decent back-story.

Cass's mum fell in love with a Black man called Edwards. Cass was born the same year as me and even then, not so long ago, she got the looks and remarks from decent, self-righteous, and law-abiding sorts every time she was out and about with baby son, husband, or both. As good as outcasts, they moved from Wales to here where things weren't that much better. His old man, originally from Barbados – *though actually as a matter of fact, originally from Africa, actually, if you think about it*, according to Cass – he never got to see Cass grow up. Cass's mum tried to get some measure of justice, but she had no chance. She told us once that Cass's dad was killed at a time when police brutality, stop-and-search and even deaths in custody were almost expected if you weren't white. Cass and his desires to make the world better come from the same place; it just took a bit of education to get him all radicalised and uppity. A lot of what his mum said also found its way into Cass and lucky him, he could actually go out into the world and experience it for himself. Don't get me wrong: I got the same kind of shit growing up, but until you actually lose someone to it, it's always going to be theoretical, and not existential. Those are more of Cass's words, by the way.

After being heartbroken, and betrayed by the woman he thought he loved, Cass left his precious *uni* but his passion – if you can call it that – for all that political stuff, has grown and become deeper. At times, he sounds like Malcolm X with a Yorkshire accent. He's become something of an activist: you name it, he's on it like a flash – hugging trees, saving whales, boycotting corporations, being anti about capitalism, sexism, racism and anything else that pops up. He goes on the marches, joins these groups that are full of maniacs and idealists in equal measure, and of course, has to drop his science on whatever social media is running hot. He has followers, apparently, but that's something everyone else has as well. To me, it sounds like one giant circle jerk where everyone in the world is invited to work themselves into a frenzy, puke out some bollocks in 140 characters or less, and then repeat the whole process ten seconds later.

Cass still has an unhealthy interest in his ex-woman and her newfound love, Rex. I'm forever telling him he needs to let that poison out of his system, to put it in the rearview, but he's still a bit obsessed with her, always asking himself what he did wrong, wondering how things could have been different. It's not like he stalks them, but he 'follows' them online, which is not a good idea, either. Over the years, Rex has become a real mover and groover among other idiots who see the world like he does: God bless the Queen, honour the British Empire, resent Europe, loathe immigrants, put Britain first and all that shit. To Cass's horror, his ex seems to have morphed into the same thing. He couldn't believe it; that someone could switch so easily. Maybe Cass and her breaking up was a good thing, after all. Since then, that's been him: social justice warrior/ wanker at large, putting the world to rights, one tweet at a time. As much use as farting in a gale.

★

Cass's phone makes a few noises; social media giving him more cause for concern. I tell him to delete that shit off his phone because all it does is make him angry. Instead, he usually responds with some holier than thou shit like: *People should be angry*. Anger? What does that solve? Anger won't stop any of it.

'What's your friend called? The one you're swearing at?'

'What? Oh, him?'

Cass looks my way but bobs down again, getting eye level with her.

'Ignore him,' he tells her.

'Don't ignore me, little girl,' I say, knowing it makes no odds. 'My name's Faisal. What's your name, then?'

I realise that this could look very, very dodgy: a fully-grown man talking to a little girl – who seems to be on her own, by the way – does have more than a creepy vibe to it. Ordinarily, with all the shit about grooming kids, I run a mile from white girls, even if they're in their twenties. But this is not an ordinary moment in my life, so it doesn't matter where I go, what I do or say – no one can do a thing about it. Well, except maybe Cass.

'Yeah, what's his name?'

'He just told you,' smiles Cass.

'Who?' she asks.

'Him. He just told you his name. He asked you your name as well.'

'No, he didn't.'

Still, I have to wonder, where are this kid's parents? Does she have any? Is she some ice cream-eating orphan Annie, who waits outside her school watching people argue, judging their performances? What's this kid's deal? Now that I think about it, she's the creepy one.

'You want me to tell her again?'

'You: shut the hell up. She heard you,' says Cass. 'You heard him, right?'

She shakes her head.

'No. He must be invisible,' she offers.

'Maybe she's deaf, as well,' I offer. 'Or is it not called being deaf any more?'

'Shut up,' says Cass, gritting his teeth, then turns back to the girl: 'He's not invisible. No such thing as invisible, right? He's just here, standing right next to me.'

She shrugs and denies, but helpfully adds: 'Ghosts can be invisible.'

I wasn't wrong: this is one creepy little girl.

'He's right here,' insists Cass.

'Well, I can't see him,' she says. 'You're funny.'

And that goes on for a few more rounds, with Cass getting more frustrated with each rebuttal and her finding it funnier, like Cass is the one messing with her. I have to confess, it does start to annoy me a little, as well. She could be making it easier. It's like this is some game for her.

'Cass.'

He ignores me.

'Cass, you prick. Listen to me.'

He looks at me, takes in a deep breath and says:

'What?'

'Watch this. Seriously, you're gonna love this.'

I walk over to her, crouch down so my head is close to her head, my mouth a couple of inches from her ear.

'What do you think you're doing? What the–'

I let rip an almighty yell. Loud and long. I don't think I've ever made a noise quite like it – I could have been in a heavy metal band had I known such levels of loudness were in me.

'What are you doing? Stop it, you're making a scene.'

Obviously, Cass is missing the point I am making here; and it's an obvious point at that. That's typical of him. He's so intelligent and so well read, informed and engaged with all this stuff going on in the world, but he misses things in plain sight. Wood for trees and all that.

'You see?'

'What are you doing?'

What I am doing is screaming into a little girl's ear and she is reacting, how? She isn't. Therefore she is either deaf, or whatever it's supposed to be called now – which she isn't because otherwise how would she have heard Cass's ramblings and ravings for the last ten minutes? Alternatively, she simply cannot hear me. Or see me. There's that, too.

'Are you talking to him, again? Your friend?'

Cass stands but doesn't speak, which is my cue. Just to prove the point, I move around to the little girl's other side, and blast more noise into her head. Again, nothing. She does not hear me. I stand upright, brush non-existent dust off my shoulder and, facing Cass, say:

'The defence rests. Or prosecution. Whichever. I rest my case is the point I'm making.'

This does not seem to give Cass any reassurance. He turns away from us both and starts walking, muttering to himself. Before trotting off to join him, I tell the little girl, who's now licking her fingers clean of runny ice cream:

'See ya later, little girl. You've been very helpful. And go home: you should not be out alone like this. Lots of strange people around. Go home, little girl.'

*

Cass just won't accept it. He tells me he's thinking of getting some help – medical kind of help.

'This isn't normal.'

'I know. Don't you think I know that? But it's real, man. It is real.'

I suppose it might be a process, him coming to terms with this. Cass told me about how his mum dealt with things after his dad died. There are supposed to be different stages to loss and grief and this thing might be the same. Denial: he reckons I paid off the little girl to play along with this sick little joke, which I'm pulling on him for the purpose of shits and giggles. Sure, I like a prank and joke as much as the next man, but this would have taken some precision planning not to mention serious acting from the little girl. Anger: well, for him, anger was a good and regular thing so nothing unusual in that. Bargaining: didn't seem to be the case, either – it's not the kind of thing you can bargain with. Depression: well, he's too caught up in his changing the world bullshit to get depressed. Acceptance: we had some way to get to that part of the process. Actually, it's probably nothing like grief. More like madness.

*

We continue arguing as we walk – well, mostly it's him telling me to leave him alone and to stop messing with him. No matter what I say, he's standing his ground: he can see me, and so can everyone else. He doesn't notice, or perhaps chooses to ignore all those passers-by staring at him as he talks to himself. Like I said, wood for trees. Around the corner from his place, there's our regular convenience store. I tell him to hold on as we approach the shopfront:

'Hear me out. Just do this and you'll see.'

With a bit of reluctance, he walks into the shop, with me next to him. I tell him to ask the man behind the counter for playing cards, and the man gives him a deck with red backs.

'Two fifty,' says the shop man. He's maybe 40, and suspicious of everyone, not just people like Cass or me.

'Ask him now.'

'Would you like to see a trick?' asks Cass, with not a hint of enthusiasm in his voice.

The shop man shrugs, returns the change and says: 'Go on then.'

We do the trick. The shop man is impressed and seems glad to have experienced this. He asks for an encore. So we do it again, this time with fifteen cards.

'How the bloody hell are you doing that? Some kind of bloody black magic voodoo?'

Cass is about to bite, discipline the man, but he lets it slide. I think maybe Cass enjoyed doing this.

'I'm psychic,' smiles Cass.

Even the customers, initially queuing up behind Cass are now feeling the awe. They ask him for more. Cass does more. The customers give him rave reviews, and each one wants him to do a trick for them. One or two pull out their phones and film the antics and upload them somewhere, keen to bask in someone else's glory.

As we leave, the shop man tells him he should be on the stage. I agree. That could be one hell of an act. Cass doesn't seem too taken by the idea but is instead racking his mind for the how and the why, both of which remain a mystery to me.

Nothing happened, not that I can recall. Cass insists it must have been something, even if it was nothing out of the ordinary. By the time we get back to the place I call home, Cass is asking me to retrace my footsteps from the moment I noticed my own lack of presence, which happens to be this morning, soon after I woke up.

At first, I thought I was dead; you know, walking around, people not seeing or hearing me – I was pretty spooked about that. I mean, who wouldn't be? But I could touch people – you know, push them, move them – except they didn't know what was going on and that freaked the hell out of them too. So I ran over to Cass's joint. Which leads us to where we are now: Cass playing at detective, trying to work out what made me this way.

*

So I'm sat here while he's throwing out theories, asking questions and repeating my responses. So far, we've established that it's not because of radiation, an insect bite, a meteorite, some weird fog, a military or medical experiment, or aliens sticking things up my arse. Nothing weird has happened. Cass cracks his knuckles, which is what he does when he's in serious thinking mode.

'Right,' he says. 'We'll work through this. Don't worry.'

'Worried? Why would I be worried?'

'You're not worried?'

Truth is, I am. A bit. I mean, who knows what else will happen to me because of this. And what about when this gets boring, or interferes with being whatever the hell normal means these days? What if I can't have a relationship, or have kids, raise a family? Not like I really want that right now in my life, but still, you know, it could happen.

Cass asks me about everything that happened yesterday, which seems pointless because he was with me for most of the day and we've been through that once already. What's the point?

'Because: could have missed something. We need to be detailed, precise. We'll keep doing it until we get somewhere.'

'Right, so like being interviewed by the coppers, then?'

'That's right. Except we're not looking to catch you in a lie. We're looking for a moment, and a possibility that explains this.'

I woke up, checked my phone, saw his message about going into town to get a new phone. I was in the mood to buy some new kicks, so I figured why not. I grabbed a shower, had a mug of sickly-sweet and black tea because the fridge is knackered and the milk had turned.

'Tea: I had tea without milk.'

'What? You think you drinking black tea made this happen?'

'Ah, no. That'd be stupid, right?'

Got changed, moped around in the flat for a bit, then headed out to his place.

'Anything unusual happen on the way over?'

'Come on, man: like what? I saw two dogs fucking in a field: does that count?'

I resume the telling of the day as it unfolded: we legged it into town, walked past people and shops; I bought a bag of crisps and Cass ate most of them – so it's not magic crisps, either. After that, Cass went into every damned phone shop around, but in the end decided not to upgrade. I thought about hunting around for a new pair of Sambas, but the ones on my feet might have a few more months left in them. So we walked back home. And that was it.

'Oh,' says Cass, deep in thought, obviously remembering something. 'Oh shit.'

'What? What is it, man?'

'What about when we walked past that homeless woman?'

I don't know what he's talking about.

'You know,' says Cass. 'The one who was begging.'

I think back: still nothing.

'How can you forget? She was old, scrawny and she looked like she was crying, man.'

She was. Cass, soft arse that he is, handed her a few coins with a smile. He doesn't like doing that usually, not because he believes beggars are part of some larger criminal enterprise, but because his 'argument' is that it doesn't solve the problem longer term and that it should be addressed 'structurally'. By that, I thought he meant building more houses but he didn't. It means something else, apparently. Some of this stuff he comes out with when he's in that zone, it's like another language, I swear.

'Well, what about her?'

Cass swallows and looks at me like I'm about to die, or I'm dead already.

'She cursed you.'

Ridiculous.

'I remember exactly what happened. She asked you for money.'

'She did?'

'And you: you told her *piss off*. Called her an old bag or something. You idiot.'

'What? No, I didn't.'

Actually, I probably did. Not that I tell beggars to piss off by habit, but I was in a bad mood, having wasted three hours moping around various phone shops for no reason, other than Cass's smartphone being the centre of his universe.

'Yes,' says Cass, nodding gently. 'And she said something to you: she pointed at you and she said something.'

Shit.

'She cursed you.'

She did.

'That's got to be it.'

I remember her gnarly, crooked forefinger jabbing at me, stabbing at me, her one cloudy, weeping, grey-blue eye searing something into my soul, while she mumbled through lips hiding a mouth containing what was left of her teeth.

'What she say, Cass? What she say?'

Cass shrugs:

'I don't know. Sounded foreign. It wasn't English.'

Cass laughs, not because it's funny but because he might be convinced of his own explanation. Seriously? I mean, *seriously*.

'You didn't see her; she was as good as invisible to your eyes. You were deaf to her voice.'

'What?'

'Yeah: she cursed you, with the same curse that's on her. That's got to be it.'

'That's what you're going with? An old gypsy woman's curse.'

'Don't say it like that.'

'What?'

'Gypsy curse.'

Truth is, sometimes even Cass gets a bit mixed up with what you're supposed to and not supposed to say.

'It's not like I was being rude or racist about it, Cass. I'm just saying: maybe she was a gypsy, maybe she wasn't.'

'Still, not cool.'

Like an idiot, I say:

'What? What's not cool?'

At which point, Cass takes it upon himself to give me a damned lecture:

'What we have to bear in mind,' he starts, 'is that these words you use, they're loaded, and they're rehearsed without any attention to the hurt they can inflict.'

'What?'

'Words have power, man. Think about the negative connotations of words like "gypsy" or "curse", or even "witch".'

Damn. Now he was doing the air quotes thing. I knew I should have kept my mouth shut.

'First of all, you're the one who said she cursed me, Cass. And second of all, curses and witches are not good. I mean, witches can mess you up with curses, right? That's how they roll.'

'Well, that's what we're led to believe through the embedded nature of "conventional wisdom", sure. But the occult is not neutral. It's not waiting to be interpreted and rehearsed. It's been fashioned through centuries of demonisation and othering, of making normative and real those we are told to fear, hate and see as the enemy within.'

'What?'

'What I'm saying is these words and ideas don't exist out there in a natural state, devoid of any context, history or politics.'

So now it was just noise coming out of his mouth.

'No, witchcraft, the occult and even race has been imagined and made real through centuries of very specific types of use, use that's framed already marginalised and oppressed groups – like women, Catholics, Jews – into our social "others", outcasts and scapegoats. By the time you and I come to reference them, even in ordinary conversation, we already know they are something to fear, to become anxious about and find suspicious.'

I'd heard that before, or variations of it; immigrants, asylum seekers, the unemployed, the gays and let's not forget, people like us; not white, born here, but not from here, not really. Cass knew and felt this more than me, with everything his parents went through. I mean, hell, his old man, he died because of that shit.

'So,' I start, not really sure how to get things back on track. 'But it was a curse, or whatever you wanna call it. That's what you're saying.'

'Yeah,' says Cass, not looking very confident about it all of a sudden. 'It does sound ridiculous when you say it out loud, like that.'

We went through the rest of the day, and nothing else stood out as unusual or freakish enough to explain my cloaking. But things were different, now. I realised everything would change. Cass's acceptance had the effect of dropping a weight on my head. How the hell was I supposed to get on with life like this? I mean, sure, being invisible and unhearable sounds like a blast, but it means you're not there. Like that old homeless, poor and maybe gypsy woman, you might as well not exist. For Cass, meanwhile, this situation posed interesting opportunities, and he wasn't talking about magic tricks.

'This could be good,' he says.

'Right. Good,' I say, not convinced at all.

'No, listen. We can do stuff. We can change things.'

So, surprise: he started droning on about how the world was messed up and how us being like this could change things.

'Us? I'm the only one like this, man.'

'I'm the only who can see you, though, right?'

'So far.'

'Think about it. It doesn't have to be a curse. It could be a gift. With this, we could challenge, disrupt and subvert.'

Another one of his mantras. And saying the word 'mantra' is another thing he's always saying as well. He's full of all these little pearls. Sometimes, like now, it can get real tiring.

'What are you talking about? You're the only who can see me, Cass. How am I supposed to do anything now?'

'I got your back, my brother,' says Cass. 'I got you. It's going to be alright.'

★

For a while, he went on about 'projects'; mostly small, but ambitious plans that he thought would make the world a safer, more just, tolerant and better place. We could target banks, multinational corporations, the petrochemical industry, big pharma, news organisations, political lobbyists, coffee shop chains and also those other evil bastards who exploited the workers, the minorities, and of course, poor old mother earth. I had to nip that shit in the bud, which I did by floating something else, something much more personal to him. I was tempted to bring his dead dad into it. When you think about it, that's the only reason he's become what he is: for him, despite sounding like a social justice wanker, it's always been real and so damned raw. But it has to come from him – he's the one who has to instigate, own and deliver that precious, but pointless, revenge, or whatever the hell it is. So instead, I went for the more obvious 'project'. When I laid it out, he made like he wasn't so sure, but I had him. In any case, my project was way better than any of his wild, unrealistic and spectacular ambitions. Of course, we had to make sure it was kept low profile:

'Real cloak-and-dagger stuff,' smiled Cass.

'And I'll be your cloak.'

★

Thing of it is, it wasn't even hard. They make it easy for you. With all the stuff these people say and do behind closed doors, it's like shooting fish in a barrel. All you have to do is light the fuse and step back. Didn't take long for the news channels to get hold of it, and then the tweeting millions got annoyed and did what they do best; circulate it amongst themselves, shame the sinner into submitting apologies, demand his head on a platter and the next thing you know, he's decided to withdraw and focus on his garden, writing, family, whatever.

After Rex, we broadened our scope. We hit an actor next.

Then there was a politician who was into some real weird shit. We kept going after that. Cass even drew up an ever-growing shit list populated with newspaper columnists, talk radio presenters, a load of politicians, some big-wig CEO corporate types – not a day went by without another name being added. Thing of it is, each one of these projects had its costs. Not like we're a pair of billionaires who can afford to spend their way into delivering their version of justice. So, sure, I've taken a liberty or two – I'm not mugging old ladies or anything. We all got to live so I've done a few things that could be considered illegal but tomayto, tomahto, eggs, omelettes, heat, kitchens and other cooking-related idioms. And yes, idiom is another gift that Cass felt the urge to explain without me asking.

*

We're both still keeping an eye out for the gypsy/non-gypsy woman – sorry, perhaps that should be Roma, or maybe 'traveller'/'non-traveller' – in the hope that we can convince her to take back her curse, if she did curse me in the first place. So far, no dice. Meanwhile, I'm doing my best to carry this without losing my mind – questions are always popping into my head: what if I become present again? What if I suddenly reappear in public, or in the middle of one of Cass's projects? More worrying: what if I don't? I do occasionally have to run a test. Once a month or so, Cass and me hang around that school, and we check in with the creepy little girl to see if she's still unaware of me. She's always wearing the same outdated, grubby clothes and she's always eating an ice cream with no variation to her method. You got to respect the discipline she's got. I enjoy the conversations Cass has with her. Cass doesn't seem to mind, either and he's told her he has dreadlocks, not dead locks. She says he's funny and she even talks to him about her own imaginary friends; one of them's a dead child from what sounds like the Victorian period, another has a chicken's head for a head and she has one that's a social worker. Like I said all along, she's one creepy little kid, that one.

Origin Story: Freedom Fighter vs Rex

Professor Richard Hingley
University of Durham

M. Y. ALAM'S SHORT STORY is not a retelling of the tale of the ancient British leader but does draw part of its context from Britain's pre-Roman past. The name of the main character, Cass, is derived as we are told from the ancient British warrior leader Cassivellaunus; the university history lecturer who steals Cass' girlfriend is named Rex Caesar, presumably a reference to Julius Caesar. These classical references are evidently not intended to be taken too literally in Alam's piece of creative writing. Cass was named by his mother with reference to an ancient Welsh freedom fighter, while Rex Caesar is 'an unapologetic, old-fashioned, elitist, one nation conservative' who views the British Empire as great and good and thinks that immigrants should be happy to be here.

Alam is reflecting critically upon Britain's historical past as an imperial power by drawing upon imperial Rome. 'Rex' is the Latin word for 'king', while Caesar is the title adopted by Roman emperors from the time of Augustus (ruled 27 BC to AD 14) to reflect upon the military and political achievements of Julius Caesar. Julius Caesar has a direct connection with our tale since he invaded south-eastern Britain in 55 and 54 BC and fought against Cassivellaunus – the leader of the British peoples (or 'tribes') who chose to resist Rome. The name Cassivellaunus is thought to have meant 'handsome and good'.

That much is recorded history, since Caesar wrote his own account of his invasions of Britain in his work, *The Gallic War*, which provides much of what we know about Cassivellaunus. Caesar was busy conquering Gaul (France) for the Roman Empire but could not resist also travelling to Britain, which was comparatively unknown to the Romans. Caesar tells us that the anti-Roman Britons united to fight Caesar under Cassivellaunus, and, although he had long been famous in war, it was only the arrival of Caesar in Britain that led to this Briton's military prominence. The Iron Age (pre-Roman) peoples of Britain were divided into numerous local groups and generally only united to fight outsiders who threatened their security. The resistance to Caesar was divided as some leaders sought Caesar's friendship, while those that wanted to fight the Romans followed Cassivellaunus.

In Caesar's account the British resistance was overwhelmed and Cassivellaunus' stronghold, his *oppidum*, was overwhelmed. This *oppidum*, which was probably sited somewhere to the north of the Thames, was the main target of Caesar's campaign during 54 BC. Caesar tells us that the *oppidum* was in a dense woodland and surrounded by a bank and ditch. It was overwhelmed and Cassivellaunus, according to Caesar, surrendered: he will have been one of the British leaders who supplied hostages and tribute to Caesar before the great commander returned to Gaul and then to Rome. All this, of course, was recorded by Caesar himself, although it is generally believed that he had won a significant victory in Britain before he withdrew. The Romans were not to return to Britain for another century, when the emperor Claudius led an invasion in person which gradually led to the conquest of much of mainland Britain by the later first century AD.

So the Cassivellaunus that M. Y. Alam draws upon is evidently a freedom fighter, but why should he have been Welsh? Caesar suggests that Cassivellaunus ruled to the north of the Thames and the Roman military under Caesar never reached the far west of Britain. The area of modern Wales was not conquered for over 150 years after Caesar withdrew. We have a second account of the actions of Cassivellaunus in the writings of the twelfth-century monk, Geoffrey of Monmouth (*The History of the Kings of Britain*). Geoffrey had clearly read Caesar's account but his Cassivellaunus was a much more powerful figure who decisively defeated a rather pathetic Julius Caesar, sending him back over the Channel in disgrace. And Geoffrey's Cassivellaunus is very much a Briton since medieval accounts suggested that the peoples of Wales were the direct descendants of the ancient inhabitants of Britain.

A powerful usurper called Caswallon, presumably also Cassivellaunus, appears in the fourteenth-century Welsh medieval masterpiece called the *Mabinogion*. This has directly inspired M.Y. Alam's tale, since Caswallon puts on a magic cloak of invisibility so no one would see him kill six men when he seized the throne of Britain from the rightful king. So Cassivellaunus in these two medieval accounts is a Welsh warrior leader who overwhelms a powerful leader. Archaeologists and historians tend not to believe simple origin myths that connect modern peoples directly to ancient ancestors today, since the country that we call Wales was a medieval creation and the population of the whole of the British Isles has long been highly mixed.

But how about Rex Caesar? There is a long tradition in England of using the Roman Empire as a model, or an ancient parallel and precursor, for the British Empire. People who adhere to this interpretation usually hold a very positive view of both imperial institutions as upholders of civilisation and order. For them, resistance leaders such as Cassivellaunus were seeking to hold back the tide of history. The Latin language has long been the key tenet of elite education in the most prestigious (expensive) of our public schools. At the launch of the exhibition about the emperor Hadrian at the British Museum in 2008, Boris Johnson introduced the event by speaking in Latin to an international audience for over five minutes, causing some consternation. Roman archaeologists have reacted critically to such elitist perspectives that link imperial Rome to civilisation. The 1990s in the UK witnessed the development a 'post-colonial' Roman archaeology that aimed to heavily critique the elitist perspectives that had been inherited from the Victorians and Edwardians. Roman archaeology today focuses much of its attention on the discrepant identities of the people living in the Roman province of Britannia, including the large-scale migration of people from other areas of the Roman Empire. The old focus on Roman towns and villas has been replaced by an interest in all groups within society, including slaves and women in addition to elite men.

Rex Caesar in this short story stands for a tradition of elite education that, in archaeology at least, is well past its sell-by date. The attitudes of certain of our politicians, of course, is a very different matter.

Hermione

Pete Kalu

– NO! NO! NO! She's going into the water again!

The child turned. Her legs thrashed the blanket that held her down, bursting the safety pins that had attached it to the mattress. She sat up in her hot wetness and screamed, her body stiff, salt eyes frozen wide. When her lungs were exhausted of air, she gulped, and her face turned towards the curtained window where there was only darkness. The uneven patter of her grandmother's feet on the staircase didn't abate the child's heaving. Then her grandmother was above her, bending, Nana's sour, mouldy smell enveloping her, easing her back down into the sheets, smothering her in pickle and oats and old sweat and then the blanket over her again. – But she's in the water, Nana!

– Hush child. Your mother's on a boat at sea. Goodness sake, she's a fisherwoman, that's what she does.

– No, Nana, she's sinking. She's going down and down and down into the blackness.

The child was pointing. The grandmother tracked her finger. The window. Beyond that, the sea. – Yes, she has gone far out to sea. But her boat is strong, and she will come back in time.

– In time? You don't understand. Time is overrated.

– And you're not making sense, Safiya. Have you had a bad dream? Let me twirl your dreamcatcher for you.

– Hush, grandma, leave it, you're too late, she's on the water's bottom now.

Ignoring the child's sleep-addled mutterings, her grandmother tucked her in, kissed her brow. – She told you that she's carrying another child, didn't she? A brother or sister for you. Soon you won't be so lonely. Do you know babies love water, and before they are born, all babies live in water, did your mother tell you that?

– Talking is overrated, Nana. Please be quiet.

– You make me laugh. Shall I sing you a song? People used to come from miles to hear me sing. *The girl with the sea-green eyes and a voice that can calm an ocean* was my billing. Let me sing for you.

– You're going to anyway, Nana.

Her grandmother chuckled. – Yes, I'm going to sing anyway.

And she sang. And the dreamcatcher turned. And the child subsided into sleep.

Her grandmother stayed on the bed a few minutes watching this strange child's lips shape noiseless words until her breathing steadied. Then she went over to the window, drew back the short, threadbare curtain and stared into the brewing black-grey.

*

It was no easy place to do it, but, from Folkestone, if you knew the waters – the banks, the submerged cliff lines, the tidal patterns, the troughs and middle currents – it was possible to go out there and catch fish. Hermione had advised the skipper a little further East into the deep, but the skipper worshipped his sonar, and she knew not to press him. There was a streak of the irrational to him and when it flared, things got messy. Now she worked with the others to run the nets out. No easy task. Gill net fishing required a long, lead-weighted net that could fall 90 fathoms to the bottom of the channel; and also patience, as with all fishing.

She saw them as glints first. Shards of light in the blackness. The midshipwoman swept a searchlight across and picked it out, an assemblage of planks and floats – a raft more than a boat. It was flimsy; the glints, she figured, were mobile phones, being waved. It was not yet past the lurid orange marker ship that split French from English waters. Were they trying to reach their fishing boat? The *Helena*'s gill net was dropped: they couldn't move towards them. Nor could they move away.

The skipper was frustrated about something and came to Hermione aft, by the shelter deck. The net had snagged in the deep. She swallowed an *I told you so* and her eyes flicked to the bobbing craft.

– I saw it, the skipper said in response, – On the sonar. And I've called it in. There's a glut of these things. The coastguard'll make it over when they can.

– Border Force?

– Yes.

– Why don't we do something? The swell is rising. They could founder any moment?

– And lose the net, cut it away so we can reach them?

– Yes.

– The cost would finish us. All of us, with how it is at the moment.

She looked into the murk again. Those lights. When she turned back, he was still there, silently pleading with her. She stayed quiet, forcing him to speak. He shouted through the spray:

– Will you go down, to free the net?

His voice was gruff, hating to ask, to acknowledge this thing she and only she could do.

– If I go, then afterwards, will we assist the craft?

– Of course.

He stepped away as he said it, ostensibly to check the dhan flags being picked out by the searchlight now, but for sure too, to avoid acknowledging the concession. Hermione read him and considered. While they were here, at least they were not moving away from the flimsy raft and the people clinging to it. She would go down.

Apart from the skipper and two of his family, the crew of the *Helena* were all women. It had not been easy. Some in Folkstone – husbands, boyfriends, civic leaders – would be quick to gloat if their business failed; behind doors they would wave aprons at them in derision: *Women cannot fish.* Three of the female crew were around her now, asking, and she told them yes, she was going down. The regular questions came upon their faces: – *How do you do it? How do you stay underwater so long, and without equipment? How do you even see down there? It's like you have a superpower.* Admiration edged with bewilderment. Hermione shrugged all this off. They gathered tight around her as she shed her clothes, then she slipped overboard.

Descending the murk, she cleaved the water. Her eyes made their adjustments automatically. She found the snagged net and cut the heavy-weighted leadline. It had caught on cliff rock. she freed it and spliced it in a temporary repair. Then thrust back up. They were waiting at the starboard edge. The few men turned away as she raised her arms and the women hauled her out and clothed her. Dressed, still dripping, she crossed the top deck to the wheelhouse, and ducked her head in.

– It's free now, she told the skipper.

The skipper turned. – We can haul up?

She nodded. – Yes.

As the net came sprawling over the sides at the stern, hands watched the fish sluice and spool into the steel catch trough. Its drains flooded and gulped. Hermione looked out across starboard into the gloam. The lights from the raft were still there, but five or six where before there had been nine or ten, and those handful dimmed. The raft was close enough now that she could see things: that some were bailing water with buckets, that a series of polystyrene cube floats had been lost from its undercarriage, that the raft was listing, that they had no life jackets. They were tall, obsidian figures, folded into the raft's crevices, many arms and legs linked and braced as if by fixing their limbs together they could keep the raft itself from breaking up.

On board the *Helena*, the net was full in. Hermione heard the skipper fire up the engines and watched the churn of dark new waves. But the *Helena* didn't pull in the direction she'd expected. Instead it began putting distance between itself and the raft.

But he'd given his word.

She crossed the deck to the wheelhouse again, flung open the door. – You promised?

The skipper half-turned. Stress blotches patched his face. The eyes that rose to meet hers were a trough of trickery and evasion. – The owners, he said, – they picked up my message and their lawyer sent a direct order to clear out, not to get involved because it's the Border Force's work and we could be liable if anything went wrong.

– But you promised.

– I'm sorry.

– Come on, Harry. Look! She was pointing. Through the wheelhouse rear window, they both could see – she made him see – that the raft's planks had worked apart, the now four-metre swell had wrenched the stays holding the contraption together. Now its starboard was fully in the water, the remaining floats askew, its deck slowly submerging. An arm disappeared. The figures now all gone into the water's maw.

The skipper pushed the engines, making away.

Cursing him, Hermione fled the wheelhouse. – If you won't..!

– No, Hermione, no!

The skipper cursed, threw the engines into idle.

Hermione ran to stern. The women saw her, called out – the danger of the engine blades turning – but she was overboard in a moment, gone into the waters.

The skipper stood on deck and yelled Hermione's name amid a stream of curses.

– She's gone deep? he asked them. It was an attempt at innocence as much as enquiry.

The women were not fooled. They looked to one another. They'd been gutting. They had fishhooks.

– Don't be stupid, he said to them as they advanced.

– Use the radio then, one of them said to him, – at least radio.

They went with him into the wheelhouse, knocked off the autopilot.

The *Helena* circled and its searchlight swept the waters. Yet nothing human heaved up from the dark weight of water, only planks and a twist of rope caught in a vortex and pulled swiftly back down. After 30 minutes, with the tidal waters surging ever stronger and the Border Force boat cutting across and flashing them a *desist*, reluctantly, the women agreed. The skipper set course back to port.

⋆

Immersed in the deep, Hermione cleaved water, touched the pink sand of the seabed. She found five there, limbs loose, clothing sucked off by the waves, their lungs taking in water; they were still present, if barely: resigned to death. She took one into her arms and pressed him close until she could feel the crusted sores of her shoulders and inner arms splintering, the crusts splitting off and attaching to the one she hugged. She found his lips. He kicked as she pressed the insides of her lips right into his, felt her crusts there breaking again, knew they were attaching to him; she let go. He had enough of her now to breathe water, and she saw the welts spread into his arms, his shoulders, become sores, become mini-gills. He could extract oxygen now from the water, at least for a while until the crusts fell away. She saw his eyes focus, his mind absorb the marvel, then he looked back at her in wonder, how he was not dead, how he was somehow breathing. She pulled two others to her and did the same, the wincing hug, the kiss, the break of her scars and their adhesion to them. Three was all she had managed when rip currents took the others. But three was three. And one was a child whose hand she now holds.

One of the two men goes to talk, gesturing with a hand.

She stays him: Talking is overrated. It's okay. You're okay. You don't need your mouth to talk any longer.

How? they both ask.

There is oxygen in water, she explains, think how fish survive. I have this too. In my arms, the inside of my lips. I broke some of myself off, pressed the crusts into you both. Now you can too. Breathe. At least while the crusts stick to you. Which is long enough to reach the ship.

Our boat up there?

No, one down here. Link hands. We'll walk the seabed together and reach it. We have time. We're in another time.

They don't understand, but they walk. Others pass them by. Sunken African figures, tall and dark-skinned like them. More questions spill.

She smiles. Africans. From slavery times. From *The Henry Lascelles*. They call themselves the Blue Devils. They are on their own journey.

But?

Yes, it's confusing. Down here, we are in sea time. There is no past here, everything is now, for as long as you can breathe. For as long as the cells on your arms and mouth keep working. Then you must emerge into air. Let's keep on. We have time.

They walk on, and the two men turn to each other and talk, and one bends down and picks up the girl, though there is no need because she walks more than fine, she is the strongest of the three. The girl kisses the man who bent to pick her up and calls him Daddy.

Hermione feels the switch of the currents. She leads them round an unstable sandbar, circles the seabed's cliff then descends the sloping bed where the press of water is greatest.

The ship is there and they all four see it. The battle on board is still raging as memory, as past, submerged in the waters of oblivion yet right there, right before them. The rafters point, query.

They are Hermiones. They are from the ship, the *Hermione*. They're here for you.

But those clothes. What happened to time? This is two hundred years before now, isn't it?

Then. Now. Watch. You see the woman there? This is Hermione. This is who I was. Who I am.

*

Hermione had sneaked onboard and had passed muster, Captain Pigot never noticed. She was the lightest, most agile of three sail mates, and at trials after three other topmast sailors had jumped ship, had been assigned with two others working out on the topsail yardarm, scurrying in the winds to battle sailcloth. They were young for topmasters and the captain declared them Boys, and henceforth to be referred to as such and paid as such. She was Boy 3 of Boys 1, 2 and 3, and she was fine up there, strong and skilled enough after two years on ships, well able to tough the slap of canvas, the rope's slip and burn, the howl and tug of blistering wind with Boys 1 and 2. David and Edwin. The skipper's caprice was their death certificate: You're all too slack! Too fucking slow! This is no floating Republic! This ship shall be run by my authority and my authority only! Who hauls down last to deck tonight will be flogged! Fear spread among the three topmasters. They huddled and conspired. For Hermione, it was not only the prospect of ripped flesh, but also the danger of her secret revealed. The two others knew this and had sworn to secrecy. Being lightest she was always assigned furthest out the topmast and so would be slowest down. It looked grim for Hermione, but the Boys made a pact. To leap as one. And trust in God.

At the captain's shout, they leapt. It was down to God now and the winds to decide who landed last, who would be flogged. God Himself was capricious that day. Their desperate leap and fall onto deck from the topsail yard arm amused the captain. That the sailors reported all three dead from the fall was proclaimed the just punishment of slackers. The captain had them thrown overboard.

Down Boy 3 went, into the black and airless. There is a point, at the cusp of death, where the body surrenders, and all creatures who have seen this, recognise it. Boy Hermione was at this door, limbs askew, lungs no longer burning but filling, when she felt her envelopment. Some creature come to feed on her. She didn't resist. The octopus's tentacles wrapped around her swiftly. Suckers attached and she felt herself being crushed, waited for the life spirit to ebb away. The octopus had its mating arm in her face now, thrusting into the cavern of her mouth, attaching to the lip membranes there. She sensed some fillip spread from her lips and mouth outwards across her shoulders, into her arms, saw welts rise, become small suckers, crusted gills. And realised, somehow, she was breathing. Now the octopus was gone, shooting away, trailing iridescent purple-pink tentacles. She watched it, a species she'd never seen before, and saw it stop, slowly sink, fall inertly to the ocean bed, stirring ripples of sand there: its gift of life to her had been its death spasm.

In a heave of lung, Boy Hermione broke surface. The battle on the *Hermione* was still raging. She heard the cries, saw gun-flash, heard the slash and thuck of sabres. She swam to stern and crew saw her, threw ropes, hauled her over the gunwale. She learned from them the captain was dead, hacked, slashed and finished, and the ship now a republic under crew's orders. That night on the *Hermione* they celebrated. Cheers rang out. We are all Hermiones! All hail the mutiny!

Only in the dead of night, when the grog and revels were being slept off by the others, did Boy Hermione allow herself tears. For Boy One and Two. For all the world's fallen Boys.

When Boy Hermione woke and turned to look across the sea at port, she saw obsidian bodies swimming towards the ship. She hailed them, ran out ropes.

*

Come with us.

They have broken the surface of the waters now, and see ropes being thrown for them from the ship.

I can't. I have a child.

I can be your child!

Hermione cups the child's ebony face. I wish, I wish, she says to her, and gives her a kiss. Now go. Swim across, and they'll take you on board, you'll sail with them. Where you land, I don't know but it will be somewhere. And at some time. Now. Beyond now. Before now. I can't say. But you will have your allocated time here on earth. So, go. Sail with them. I will be with you. I will never leave you, and if you want to see me, you will see me.

We'll remember you.

Go. I must leave now.

She kisses the girl a final time, then dips underwater.

*

The child was inconsolable and the social worker, trained as he was in assuaging the irrational, however deeply felt, fears of small children forcibly separated from their loved ones, was sympathetic, but firm:

–Your mother is with the nurses now. She is in the best of care. She will be ready to see you soon. Not now, but soon.

– No no no, said the child. – She is with ShipHisHead. She is with the ghost ships and the slave ships. She's down there and the octopus has bit her, and the octopus has died. And now she will die too if I don't find her!

– Safiya, stop this nonsense. This kind man is trying to help you, he's trying to tell you something. Will you listen? Take your hands from over your ears.

– Hush, Nana.

The grandmother turned to the social worker. – I'm sorry, she has a vivid imagination and, combined with the stress and her sleepless nights, it makes her sometimes uncontrollable.

– It is well, the social worker said. – Inshallah, she will heal, as will her mother. You are the legal next of kin? She is your daughter or daughter-in-law?

– Yes.

The social worker made a note on his pad, then stroked a stray tuft of hair from Safiya's forehead. She was sprawled in one of the counselling room's orange, upholstered chairs.

– Your mother's fine. Sleep, child, sleep deep.

Safiya continued muttering, even as her eyes closed.

The grandmother leant forwards and whispered to the social worker: – What I don't understand is, how did she know her mother was in trouble? She can't view the sea from her bedroom window, not at night. And her mother doesn't take a phone.

– It's not unusual, the social worker replied softly. – She will be reading signs in how her mother holds herself. The onset of the malady, the illness, there will be small tells that the child picks up without even knowing, and then her nightmare comes.

– They said she was dragged out of the sea?

– Yes, your daughter was pulled from the sea. The coastal ambulance team know her. She's done this before. There is no suicide ideation, they say, only delusion. She will be in the Unit for another few days, for her own safety. They are running a few blood tests now. As a precaution. The social worker took the grandmother's hands. – Don't worry, it will all work out.

The grandmother nodded. The social worker went to say something, hesitated, stopped his tongue.

– It's okay, said the grandmother, – you can tell me. My heart is leather. Remove the stones from your mouth.

– I shouldn't say this, I could be sacked, but I overheard the doctors talking about your daughter. I taped it; it was so strange. They were not the usual doctors. They were from one of the

Prime Ministers' Initiatives to distract from his terrible policies. They belonged to D.I.R.T., the Deviants Investigation & Research Taskforce.

The grandmother grimaced. – What were they saying?

– I'm not sure. It didn't sound well. But here. Listen. I don't understand it fully myself.

The social worker pulled out his phone, selected the file and pressed *Play*. Two voices could be heard amid a scatter of bleeps and the clack of a keyboard. The first voice was even, conscientious, the second a blither spirit:

– Her mitochondrial DNA. It came back saying she is one percent Cephalopod. Octopus. Should we dial that in?

– No. Just note it on the file. Probably a lab error.

– And her mouth cavity contained what looked like tiny gills on the buccal mucosa. A similar feature on the inner arms and shoulders. Do we phone those through?

– We are all descended from fish, right? Let's just do this job and no more. File photos if you have to, but then be done with it. Let's not create more work for ourselves than we need to. Don't feed the monster. Coffee?

– Yes. No sugar... okay. The file's sent.

– God, I hate this job.

Origin Story: Striking Back Hard

Niklas Frykman

IN THE LATE SPRING of 1797, Britain was hit by the largest, best organised, most sustained working-class offensive of the century. For the imperial elite, it could not have come at a worse time. After seeing each of their continental allies cowed into submission by the force and fury of the French Republic's revolutionary armies, Britain now stood alone, face-to-face with a vast European coalition bent on invasion and regime change. All that stood between them and success was the might of the Royal Navy's home command, the largest concentration of seaborne violence ever assembled. At its core was the gigantic fleet that lay at the Spithead anchorage just off Portsmouth, and it was here, on Easter Sunday 1797, that the 'great mutiny' began.

When the first phase of the mutiny drew to a close in early June, it had spread from its initial appearance at Spithead to the Cork and Plymouth naval stations in the west, all the way to the Nore anchorage at the mouth of the Thames and the North Sea fleet in the east. Altogether, some 40,000 men onboard more than 100 vessels rose up, overthrew their officers, and for two whole months refused to do the work of war. Initially, the navy's high command and the government were conciliatory, prepared to offer the men their first pay raise in a century and a half, but when the mutiny took a more revolutionary turn in late May, and the most radical of the mutineers declared the fleet to be a floating republic, the British state unleashed its full repressive force, crushing the mutiny, imprisoning hundreds of insurgents, publicly torturing and executing dozens.

The government's terror-tactics did not contain the spirit of mutiny. As ships left home waters for British colonial possessions overseas that summer, news of the great mutiny spread around the world. Shipboard rebellions broke out in the Mediterranean fleet, at the Cape of Good Hope, even in the navy's tiny Indian Ocean squadron. But nowhere did the conflict between officers and crews erupt with the same ferocity as it did in the Caribbean, where the British frigate *Hermione* had been stationed since the outbreak of the war with revolutionary France in 1793. After four years of service in the toughest theatre of that war, and just a few weeks after receiving news of the collapse of the great mutiny in England and the vicious repression that followed, the crew of the *Hermione* rose up, slaughtered ten of their sixteen officers, and then set sail for South America. Arriving at the port of La Guaira (in today's Venezuela) a week after the revolt, the Hermiones surrendered the ship to the Spanish authorities – thus adding treason to the crimes of mutiny and piracy (because they had unlawfully seized the ship) already on their heads – and then dispersed.

Even by the grim standards of the eighteenth-century navy, Captain Huge Pigot's rule onboard the *Hermione* had been extraordinarily cruel. In the best of times, he flogged frequently and completely without mercy, and when drunk, he lost all restraint. In the week before the mutiny, he conjured up a spurious reason and then demoted, flogged, and humiliated a junior officer, mostly, it seems, for being popular with the crew. Three days later, Pigot exploded again. This time, some of the topmen moved too slowly for his liking, and so he cursed and threatened them, promising the last man down a severe flogging – three panic-stricken men slipped and fell, crashed onto the deck, all three instantly dead. Pigot refused to honour them with a proper sea-burial and ordered the bodies to be dumped overboard instead. The next morning, he flogged over a dozen men for having appeared unhappy about the events that took place the day before. Two days later, yet another three men were flogged. After that, however, no one was ever to suffer Pigot's wrath again. The Hermiones had had enough. That same night, they rose in violent revolt.

Once they had laid hands on their officers, the mutineers knew there was no turning back. Normally, the Admiralty dealt with the unsettled aftermath of a mutiny by singling out and punishing a small group of ringleaders, while allowing the majority of insurgents to fall back into line without too many questions asked. But not this time. The Hermiones' decision to meet the officer corps' terror-tactics with even greater counter-terror-tactics could not be allowed to succeed, or else the navy's established hierarchies would be continuously subject to forceful challenges from the lower deck. And so, as soon as news of the mutiny had made its way from La Guaira to the British naval station in Jamaica, and from there on to London, a transatlantic manhunt got underway that sought to track down, try, and execute the fugitive Hermiones. It was mostly a failure. Out of an estimated crew of approximately 160 men at the time of the mutiny, only 35 were ever captured. The rest got away.

Their success in alluding capture also meant they would leave little trace in the historical record, and we can therefore only guess where they might have ended up. It seems likely, and contemporary rumours confirm, that while some settled down in Spanish America, the majority drifted back to a life at sea. Much like impoverished migrant workers in the twenty-first century, eighteenth-century sailors were extraordinarily cosmopolitan in their outlook and experience, used to being tossed this way and that by the centrifugal forces of a world at war. They frequently jumped ship, crisscrossed imperial boundaries, and obscured their origins and identities as a matter of course. For the Hermiones, disappearing back into the fluid, multinational world of deep-sea shipping was a simple matter, and the few who were discovered and handed over to British naval authorities had mostly themselves to blame: they simply could not stop bragging about the mutiny, and eventually someone snitched.

Historians have often portrayed the *Hermione* as an extreme outlier, explained solely by Captain Pigot's grotesquely violent regime, and universally regarded, at the time and afterwards, as nothing but a sad tragedy. But this was not so. As long as the cycle of revolutionary wars continued, and crews continued to be routinely beaten and tortured to within an inch of their life in the name of naval discipline, the *Hermione* continued to sail throughout the Atlantic world as a kind of ghost ship, firing the imagination of disgruntled sailors and simultaneously stalking their officers' worst nightmares. Whenever there was trouble below deck – and not just in the British navy – captains were quick to suspect that a fugitive from the *Hermione* had somehow snuck onboard and was now infecting the rest of the crew with his mutinous spirit. Sailors used that fear as a weapon, muttering the word *Hermione* under their breath within earshot of their officers, toasting its memory from within the safety of a disorderly crowd below deck. Some even went so far as to wrongfully claim to have been onboard the *Hermione* at the time of the mutiny, a dangerous but exhilarating game of stolen valour. Convicted mutineers were almost certain to hang by the neck, but the lower deck celebrated them as heroes for having struck back hard. For one spectacular, but fleeting moment they had turned the tables on their oppressors, and, for that, they were honoured and immortalised by their fellow tars.

Further Reading

Ann Veronica Coats and Philip MacDougall, eds, *The Naval Mutinies of 1797: Unity and Perseverance* (Woodbridge: Bordell, 2011).
A. Roger Ekirch, *American Sanctuary: Mutiny, Martyrdom, and National Identity in the Age of Revolution* (New York: Pantheon, 2017).
Niklas Frykman, *The Bloody Flag: Mutiny in the Age of Atlantic Revolution* (Oakland, CA: UC Press, 2020).
Jonathan Neale, *Mutineers* (London: Bookmarks, 1998).

Lady Swing

Bidisha

ELLE WAS CLOSING THE shutters of the library when she saw the group, dressed in dark workwear, by the gates of Halfway House. They beckoned to her and she went out to talk to them.

'Pellman,' she greeted the skinny man at the front. Pellman laboured on the farmlands around the estate. Elle had worked with him for years.

'It's time,' he said. The others nodded agreement.

Elle glanced back towards the great house. Her boss, Tom Foote, was pottering about in there somewhere. He was the owner of Halfway House and the last son of the family that had once owned the surrounding village of Mayvel.

'You sure?' Elle asked.

'Time for change,' said the woman behind Pellman. Elle recognised her as Caroline – she worked at the food bank down in Blandford Forum. 'We've had word from the others – the whole West Country from the chalklands to the coast. They're on board.'

'The great reset. It's coming,' said Pellman.

'Won't you attract notice, going to all the estates like this, all in black?' said Elle.

'We *want* to attract notice,' said Pellman, gripping the gates. 'We're a warning and they'll get plenty more if they ignore us.'

'Just be careful,' said Elle.

'We've *been* careful,' said Caroline. 'We thought you were with us on this?'

'I am,' said Elle. 'It's just... I've been managing this place for nearly two decades.'

'And in all the time you've been here, have *your* conditions improved?' asked Caroline.

Elle looked sheepish. She had signed all the petitions and attended some meetings in town. The other workers on the estate often talked to her about their troubles and she listened. But she herself preferred the shadows.

'That's the problem,' said Pellman. 'We've been down in the ditch so long, we've grown loyal to our masters. You're really a girl from the terraces, down Brewhouse way, like me. Have you seen that part of town recently? Most of those terraces are condemned.'

'I haven't,' admitted Elle.

'They're your roots. Our families are centuries old, just like Foote's. We're just as valuable.'

Tom Foote was waiting for Elle when she re-entered the house. In muddy yellow trousers and a red jumper speckled with hay, he stood munching an apple.

'I was out with the horsies,' he said. 'Rosie's off her feed – I nicked this from her.'

Elle found it hard to believe that as well as being the Marquess of Halfway House, Tom was an actual MP with a cushy job in Westminster – not that he was ever at Parliament.

'What was Pellman on about?' he asked.

'Oh, just... the midsummer fair. They're helping out.'

'They're getting a bit comfortable, don't you think? Coming up to the gate like that?' said Tom, picking hay off himself and dropping it onto the floor.

'Pellman's been with us forever,' she said. This was the most she dared to answer back.

'You know, there were riots here 40 years ago. I remember it, I was kicking about after coming down from Cambridge. It started the same way: weird groups of ragtags and malcontents gathering at night. Pellman's parents among them, no doubt.'

'What did they have grievances about?' Elle asked carefully.

'Same reasons as ever. They call it 'food poverty' these days. Hasn't it ever been thus? Too much work, not enough pay, not enough food. They don't understand the economics. *Our* fridges are empty! The estate hardly turns a profit! We can barely heat the house!' Tom stomped out past her, still harrumphing as he slammed the door.

After clearing up Tom's dropped hay and muddy footprints, Elle went back to the library and logged onto the estate's accounting system. She always felt tiny in the grand room, but it had the best Wi-Fi signal. She pulled out her phone. A sequence of messages scrolled along: 'Shipwrights + carpenters union ok', then 'Stonemasons joining Weds.' Finally, 'Big guns: West Country Industrial Alliance up 4 it. Everyone's on board. Paper mill, textiles, factory unions. Tonight.' Elle texted back a thumbs up emoji.

The kitchen staff had clocked off by the time Elle's day finished. She made herself a sandwich in the staff kitchen, washed up and took some hot chocolate up to her room on the second floor. It was the old nursery and a bookcase in the corner still held a small collection of fairytales, picture books and adventure stories. Tom's own quarters were at the other end of the house. All the other staff lived out, in cottages on the estate. The seasonal workers and casual, short-term staff lived in trailers and Portakabins on the periphery. Elle got into bed and lay awake, counting down the minutes.

At four, her phone lit up right next to her face on the pillow. One word, repeated: 'Go go go go.' She got up, grabbed the black tracksuit, black wool cap and gloves off her chair and put them on. The summer heat was stifling and Elle felt like she was burning up. The grounds were vast and still. She let herself out through the small security door in the gatehouse and felt rather than saw her way towards the trees on the left. She wasn't afraid; she found the forest familiar and protective.

Elle heard a low whistle through the darkness. A few steps on, she heard it again. She pursed her lips and whistled back. The woodland ended on a long peak above Blandford Forum. Climbing up on the rickety wooden fence, she looked down over the local area: the knot of A-roads and roundabouts, the centre of town, the retail park, the housing estates and the grid of narrow, terraced streets where she had grown up. In the distance was a line of impoverished villages known casually as the Black Chain – Black Hill, Black Dyke, Black Haw and Black Moss – through which, 500 years ago, witch-finders had marched, hanging and drowning women as they went.

The industrial sweep lay to the northeast. The factories were hulking, crumbling black shapes. Elle focused her gaze on one in particular, a clothing manufacturer whose boss, a millionaire who looked like an ageing footballer, kept his workers on four quid an hour and refused to update their equipment or give them sick pay. She narrowed her eyes onto one window pane in the near corner. She felt a warm, pleasant rush, a surge of good energy spreading from her core out to the surface of her skin, and her ears began ringing finely, a thin zing like a struck tuning fork. The glass of the factory window gleamed. Then it flashed and shattered. She saw a flame dancing through the jagged opening. Elle held her breath. More of the windows on the top floor of the factory broke open and fire began to gut the building from within. A strong smell of acrid, molten plastic reached her, as black smoke collected around the factory. The air grew hotter and a fire engine could be seen racing along the A350.

Elle backed away and cut along the edge of the wood. She kept stopping to look back at the burning factory and the increasingly ferocious flames.

She stumbled through the dark, clinging to the fence and pulling herself along. The land curved upwards, overlooking the part of the West Country the tourist books called 'God's garden'.

It swept from the soft, surfable coast up through green arable land, past the bogs and marshland towards the ghostly chalklands. Overlooking everything were estates like Halfway House and villages like Mayvel, where Tom Foote's family had lorded it for centuries.

Just as the ground levelled off, Elle thought she saw a shadow moving between the trees. She ducked behind a trunk and whistled but got no reply. She whistled again, and clapped once, sharply – but to no response. After a few more moments, during which her instincts were certain there was something out there, though she could neither see it nor hear it, she continued on, her skin prickling uncomfortably.

The grounds rose steadily. Elle thought she might be at the Buckley Estate by now, or perhaps she'd arrived at their neighbours, Wicklow House. Soon she would see the white light at the top of Halfway House gate twinkling through the trees. Up there somewhere, on the brow of the hill, the old gallows used to stand. There were plenty of entries from the old court accounts and execution broadsides referring to the wooden frame and its dangling rope.

The sun was fully up now. Back at the house, Elle changed and immediately drove out in the old, creaking Jeep, to pick up supplies for the midsummer fair. A group of factory workers was spaced out along the side of the road that led to the industrial estates, holding handmade signs saying SAVE OUR JOBS and LIVING WAGES and STRIKE TO FIGHT. Some had their kids with them, who were shouting and clapping.

'Stand up for your rights!' the kids shouted. 'Fight for a future!'

Elle beeped in support. She went to the booze wholesalers, where she was a familiar face; some of the younger workers would be bartending at the fair, cash in hand. Back on the estate, Elle unloaded the supplies into a barn, parking the Jeep alongside the other, everyday vehicles – Tom kept his beloved powder-blue Aston Martin and black monster truck lovingly stabled in a different garage altogether.

Pellman and his crew arrived later that day and reported to Elle. Together, they set up marquees and benches on the long stretch between the boathouse and the rose garden.

'How did it go last night?' Pellman asked her as they were positioning a trestle table.

'Good.'

'Did anyone see you?'

'I was careful.'

'The factory owner's gone spare,' Pellman grinned. 'He was sitting with his head in his hands this morning in the pub. And the letters?'

'They've gone out.'

'They'll have an effect,' said Pellman.

Elle shivered as she remembered the messages she'd written, the only lights in the library her laptop screen and phone. It was sneaky, but even disturbing other people was a way of connecting with them. To not feel like a total invisible nobody. Each one signed 'Lady Swing', after the old high gallows ground.

'To compel people, to get them to do what you want, you have to make them afraid,' Pellman said, not for the first time. 'Talk to someone in the only language they understand.'

'I know, I know,' Elle sighed.

'Letters aren't violent. Words aren't violent,' said Pellman. 'Fires in empty factories don't hurt anyone.'

Guests began arriving after lunch. A section of the estate's grounds was being used as a car park, with young cadets from the local army barracks acting as stewards. There were five-a-side football games, tug of war matches and a boat race starting from the boathouse on the river. Every win and loss was toasted at the stands the local brewers had set up. Tom Foote was striding about like a true country squire, his loudhailer gripped in his hand: 'Who's it to be this time? Last year it was Higher Whatcombe – can Lower Whatcombe reclaim the cup? And we've got the Pimperne Rowers versus Shroton departing in five.'

There was an atmosphere of innocent release, of pure relaxation, and Elle felt proud of everything she'd done – as she did every year. By twilight, a local band was playing, some people were dancing and others were pushing each other about beerily. Elle was stone-cold sober.

She'd come to Halfway House as a history graduate fresh out of Exeter Uni, to help Tom edit his book about Mayvel village, then been taken on as his PA. At first, she felt like a custodian of a place she had admired since childhood – Halfway House was one of the reasons she studied history in the first place. But after twenty years, she realised, she was just a serf, her wages unchanged, working for room and board and little more than pocket money on top. She should count herself lucky. Her parents and other relatives had all worked in the factories and warehouses.

At the bar, a guy in a rugby shirt and his red-faced friends got up, linked arms and jumped in unison, shouting a local folk song: 'Ohhhh, *who's* a dirty girl from Dewlish and *who's* a Holwell whore? *Who's* a Bloxworth bugger and *who's* a filthy jackdaw? *Who's* a fool that walks the Cove and gets bummed on Harland Moor? *Who's* a Durdle donkey and who's a Portland bore?'

'And now we play… Blast the Priest!' bellowed Foote's voice over the megaphone. A roar went up across the site. 'All we need is a volunteer!'

'I'll do it!' shouted a man whom Elle recognised from the Blandford Forum actuary's office. He clambered onto the stage, snatched the black priest costume from Foote's hands, put it on and began delightedly sliding about, dodging handfuls of kitchen sludge and mouldy fruit, which Pellman's crew offered to the crowd in buckets.

'Down with priests! Down with the church! Damn your god and up the devil!' yelled the crowd as they re-enacted the old village ritual.

Elle went down to the boathouse, where she found a group of very young teenage girls sitting close together, hunched over a Ouija board.

'Where did you get that?' Elle asked, keeping her distance.

'In the games room,' they said. Elle had opened up the back parlour in case anyone wanted to play pool or drink a quiet sherry, and the cabinets were indeed full of old board games and battered decks of cards, although she'd had no idea about the Ouija board.

'It keeps trying to spell out Fuck,' one of the girls laughed.

They all watched as the planchette spelled F, then U, then X, then whizzed back to the centre. Next time round it spelled F – A – U – X. Elle stared, but she said nothing.

'Faux? It's calling us a bunch of fakes in French?' asked a girl, her voice drawling and posh.

'It's not working,' said another, who was lounging back. 'Forget it. I'm not going to be insulted by a dead Frog.'

'I know you're not kids, but please be careful,' Elle said. 'These are ancient grounds – people lived and died here long before Halfway House was built. You don't know what you're letting in.'

She took the board from them and the girls let her do it – they were bored and done with the game.

'Why would a spirit visit *here*?' said one of the girls. 'The tourists say how beautiful it is. But so what? There's nothing. Farm. Factory. Hospitality – food and bevs. Retail. We'll be getting up at 4am pulling calves out of cows' arses for the rest of our lives.' She looked at Elle. 'You've been here forever, haven't you?'

'Ages,' Elle agreed, feeling ancient.

'Don't you get scared?' asked another girl. 'Halfway House. It's creepy.'

"Halfway' is just an Anglicisation,' said Elle. 'One of the men in the Foote family married a woman whose surname was Halfte and he named it for her. The house itself isn't that old. It's Victorian. Certainly not haunted.'

Elle took the Ouija board back to the parlour, passing a troupe of historical re-enactors dressed as the Yeomanry Cavalry, in replica uniforms from the early 1800s. They looked happy after their afternoon of fake skirmishes with fake opponents. Without changing out of their clothes, they climbed into their Hondas and Toyotas and drove away.

Elle hung about the exit of the car park, saying goodbye to the last guests. She got chatting to one of the car park workers, a young army cadet called Jez – 'Short for Jezebel,' she said, rolling her eyes. Her mother, Marine, had lived and worked on the estate for a couple of years now.

'I might crash at the cottage tonight. We're on leave from the barracks. If that's okay with you?'

'Of course,' Elle reassured Jez.

'I'll probably get in and have an instant argument when she sees this.' Jez plucked at her army uniform. 'She thinks people should work on the land and reclaim our pagan freedoms. She's probably why I turned out so straight-edge.'

'Who's "she" – the cat's mother?' said a voice.

'Mu-um,' said Jez, turning red. Marine had been helping Pellman clear the site. They now stood waiting for a sign-off from Elle.

'We'll come back tomorrow,' Pellman said as he got in his van. 'We've picked up anything that could be blown away. I'll go to the dump first thing.'

Elle waved Pellman off. Marine put her arm around Jez.

'What were you two talking about?' Marine asked.

'Law and order,' said Elle, grinning. 'How we should rise up.'

Marine looked at her closely.

'Oh really? And where do you stand on that, Elle?'

'I have sympathy. I see where the protesters are coming from.'

'I admire these young activists,' said Marine. 'I like their zip and fearlessness. Sometimes you need to clear the air. I'm always surprised that *you*, Elle, can bear to work here. Your surname's Faux, isn't it? You're a historian, you must know the story.' She turned to Jez: 'Generations ago, one of the Foote sons fell in love with a Faux woman – and his brothers dragged her out and hanged her on a gibbet! Right there on the gallows on the hill.'

Elle frowned.

'It's just a story. I never found evidence to back it up. We all have the same surnames repeating for centuries and being copied and miswritten and misremembered. It doesn't mean we're all descendants.'

'Of course they're not going to write it down,' said Marine. 'How the young men of the richest family in the area murdered their sister-in-law. If it's true, it's the Footes' fault that the women of the Faux family grew up poor in the years that followed.'

'They were poor to begin with. Marrying into a rich family once doesn't guarantee wealth,' said Elle.

'Not for that poor woman it didn't. I'll tell you something, Elle, the whole place reeks of resentment. That's why there are uprisings every few years. It's land memory. Like muscle memory –'

'Oh, Mum. Stop,' said Jez.

'You couldn't possibly believe all that!' laughed Elle.

'Oh, she does,' said Jez stonily.

Elle stayed until every last person on the site had clocked off, every power source shut off and every door fastened shut. The furniture hire people would come to collect tomorrow, as would the suppliers who'd left things overnight. Along one edge of the estate, close by the rose garden, was a wall of boundary stones, dating from a time when there was no town and no Halfway House, just the small stone church, cemetery and lanes of Mayvel market.

She was woken up by a white van at the front gate, beeping to be let in. She'd let the gatehouse staff off for the day after the fair and even if Tom were up and about, it wasn't his job to let the staff in.

She unlocked the chain of the gate, opened the gates and waved the van in. The driver, a stocky blonde fellow, rolled down his window as he passed.

'Boss-man not around?'

'I haven't seen him,' she said.

The man brought the van in a little way and cut the engine.

'I'm Schaffer,' he said. 'Friend of Pellman.' Elle nodded. 'You coming to town today?'

'I can't. I have to clean up,' Elle said.

'And at night?'

Elle backed away from the van, looking towards Halfway House. She knew their movements, if not their conversation, were being captured on the CCTV cameras which Tom rewatched during his occasional bout of aristocratic paranoia.

'Pellman said you were game,' he pressed.

'I really just need you to do your work today, Schaffer. Your actual work.'

'Right,' he snickered. 'Gotta earn a wage while we can.'

He started up the engine again, crunched across the gravel and turned right, rolling onto the grass down towards the boathouse.

Elle went back inside to find Tom Foote in the library holding an enormous mug of tea in one hand and a piece of paper in the other.

'I've just received the most dreadful email,' he said, pushing the paper towards her.

She took it, but she already knew what it said.

'Foote, be careful in the night. Blood for dinner. Love and devotion my "Marquess", Lady Swing,' she read out.

'What do you think?' said Tom, gulping his tea and staring anxiously at her.

'It's ridiculous.'

'It *is* ridiculous,' he agreed with relief. 'As MPs we get all sorts of crazies writing to us at Westminster, or the Blandford Forum office. Bribes, death threats, complaints about the neighbours, you name it. But nothing comes to the house. It's not Hugh Swing's wife, surely? I know him from the Commons, they're lovely people. And there's something else, Elle,' said Tom, looking even more distressed. 'It's about the animals.'

Elle frowned as she gave the letter back to him.

'The animals?'

'It's horrible.' Tom sank down on an over-stuffed green velvet sofa. 'Someone's interfered with the animals. We don't know when. The cameras didn't catch them. Whoever did it, they knew where the blind spots were. Flossie down at the stables called me and I came here to look for you. It's all just happening at once.'

He looked up at her helplessly. Without another word, Elle strode out, crossed the long balcony and walked to the working area of the farm. At the stables, their main stablehand, Flossie, waited pale and tight-lipped.

'I called the others and told them not to come in,' Flossie said, opening the doors to the stables.

They went into the dark interior. Instead of poking their long noses forward over the half-doors, the horses shied far back in their stalls, pawing the ground.

'What's that smell?' Elle asked.

'Fear. And blood.'

In the last stall lay a foal. Its eyes had been gouged out and there were long knife slices along its belly and its side, from which its innards spilled in a mess of dark, slimy flesh.

'Oh my god,' said Elle, retching.

'They killed the mother too. In the same way. She's in the other stall.'

Elle pulled herself up and looked over the wooden rim of the stall. The beautiful mare was in there, collapsed on the ground, violently maimed and already covered in flies. For some reason, Elle's immediate thought was that Schaffer had done it – he had a smirking menace about him. But she had no proof of that.

Flossie was pacing the narrow space between the rows of stalls.

'Don't tell anyone about this. Fear spreads panic,' said Elle, thinking *that's exactly what Pellman wants.*

'I've already called the police,' said Flossie.

Elle gulped, then said, 'Of course. This is a crime. They'll want to talk to… everyone.'

Elle and Flossie checked on the sheep, the cows, the henhouse and the few goats they kept. A hefty, frowning man in his fifties approached them at the sheep pen, his tread heavy. This was Timbold. He'd worked at the estate even longer than Elle.

'Has she seen?' he demanded. Flossie nodded. 'We've penned up the others. They won't get to them,' he said to Elle.

'That's very good of you, Tim.'

'And it's the same with the pigs. They've gone for a sow.' He clenched and unclenched his fist around the metal gate of the sheep pen. 'They didn't do it for stealing. They did it for pleasure. They took nothing.'

Just like Flossie, Timbold paced, only the way he walked had a rough, bull-like quality. He swung round and stopped short.

'I'll tell you what it is. It's the devil,' he spat. The word 'devil' rang out and echoed lightly off the nearby outbuildings. 'Only the devil comes in the night like a bloody coward,' Timbold ranted.

'We need to talk to our casual staff, the summer hands. We can't rely on superstition,' said Flossie.

'Once upon a time we knew what to do with the devil – and his servants. They used to drown witches in the river – same one we have our races on. But the devil's very clever you see. There's plenty of talk about people walking a-night between Chettle and Tarant Monkton and seeing all sorts of demons. And who's to say they didn't?' he asked, raising his chin before trudging off.

'The long-timers here get madder by the season,' tutted Flossie, watching him go. 'If you indulge him he'll tell you about how his great-grandad was an executioner who was haunted by all the people he hanged. His family go back to the Domesday Book.'

News about the animal attacks spread within a couple of hours. Elle saw Tom Foote pacing the balcony and talking urgently into his phone, and the next morning there was a rugged, unmarked black vehicle parked by the side of the drive. A muscular man with a stern face watched from the driver's seat, unsmiling and unblinking, as Elle, Pellman and Marine checked him out.

'What's with the militarisation?' asked Marine. 'Elle, did you organise this?'

'Nope. It must be Tom's doing. Some kind of private security. He wouldn't do it unless he was really scared.'

'Scared of us!' Pellman grinned. 'Scared of his own staff, rising up.'

'He's scared of the Mayvel Beast that haunts the grounds,' said Marine. 'The beast with a grudge! There are plenty of stories.'

'That's us,' said Pellman. 'They think we're animals. Only good for being worked to death.'

They had met early that morning because Pellman and Schaffer were leading a demonstration in the New Town, which had sprung up literally in the shadow of the retail park. Elle drove them down there. Everything was made of the same stained grey concrete slabs. Charity shops and workers' cafés alternated with hair and nail salons, betting shops and chicken takeaways.

The march was peaceful at first. They were surrounded by tradespeople of all kinds, from farm workers and casual labourers to groups of factory machinists and shop workers from Blandford Forum. Pellman went up to the front while Elle and Marine fell behind.

'What's the plan?' Elle asked.

'We walk to Mayor Clarke's office, get him to come out – we know he has a planning committee now, thanks to a friend on the inside – then we get him to listen to us, and we go away quietly,' said Marine. 'And get this – they've got my dear daughter and her chums to keep us in order. So it's middle-aged radicals versus young squares in uniform.'

They marched slowly down the middle of the road towards Mayor Clarke's office in the centre of the New Town. Everyone jeered as they passed the small police station which, as always, had its shutters pulled down tight over its front desk. Elle couldn't remember a time when she'd ever seen it open to the public. At the corner, they were joined by a new group of rather solid, intimidating-looking protesters.

'They work at the prison,' Marine told Elle. 'HMP Guys Marsh. I was their landscaper when they first opened up. They got me to lay down lawn around the fences. No flowers, no shrubs, no bushes. Horrible place.'

'What are they marching for?'

'Same as everyone else,' shrugged Marine. 'They're all on zero-hours contracts.'

Schaffer and Pellman passed a megaphone between them, shouting, 'We want simple things. Better conditions. A living wage.' Then everyone joined in, shouting, 'Reform the system or burn it down!'

'Can I join you?' said a voice on Elle's other side.

It was Caroline, the woman from the Blandford Forum food bank. She introduced herself to Marine.

'I only volunteer at the food bank after hours. I'm an English teacher at the Sixth Form Academy,' said Caroline as she fell into step with them. 'I do the breakfast club for the kids, and then I man the food bank for their parents after school. You know what some of the grown-ups tell me? That they're being offered food and allowances instead of wages.' She nodded over towards the industrial district whose factory tops and warehouses could just about be seen through the smog over the nearby buildings. 'The factory workers have it worst. They're running them into the ground.'

'It's bad karma,' said Marine.

'Oh, I don't believe that stuff,' said Caroline. 'I moved here from Plymouth when I got married. The people round here indulge in far too much hocus-pocus.'

They came to Mayor Clarke's office, but he had clearly been forewarned and they found the building's reception empty, its doors closed. A couple of baby-faced army cadets stood outside, politely guiding the protesters to 'Continue on, keep walking.'

'You know what this is about, don't you?' said Marine, pointing at the guarded doors of the mayoral office.

Elle shook her head.

'The local elections,' Marine explained. 'None of the officials want to get mixed up in activist business, not even the reformers. They don't like to get their hands dirty.'

At the crossing, some bouquets of flowers wilted, commemorating a road accident. They skirted the hikers' path that set ramblers towards the chalklands and took the turning for the industrial panorama. Everyone was holding their phones and filming themselves and each other, tweeting about where they were.

Elle heard shouts from further up the line.

'Watch it burn! Watch it burn!'

Elle could feel the air getting hot. They were getting close to the old wool factory, where the machines were decrepit and the wages and conditions hadn't changed in decades.

'The workers there, they're all girls I went to school with, and their sisters and mums,' said Marine.

'Mine too,' said Elle.

'And you're about fifteen years younger than me,' Marine said. 'So nothing changes.'

The air grew dark and acrid and all around them people were beginning to choke and cover their mouths. Elle saw Caroline several steps ahead, rubbing her eyes, which streamed with tears. About a hundred yards in front of them, everything was obscured by thick grey smoke: the wool factory, engulfed in flames. Through the choppy darkness, Elle saw Pellman and Schaffer. They were yelling and waving their arms to keep people back, but the fire was too loud. The air was too bitter to inhale and waves of heat rolled through them from the blaze.

'All the stuff in the factory's burning,' Elle managed to say, her eyes screwed tight, 'the plastics in the machinery, all the equipment. It's toxic.'

'This is what we came to do,' said Caroline.

'Die of poisoning? It's not safe,' said Elle, her throat tight.

They backed away and fanned out around the front of the factory entrance. The flames centred deep within the building and burned through the middle of the roof. Every so often there was a crash from inside the factory as something broke. There were shards of glass shattering, metallic crunches and the heavier, blunter noises of walls and ceilings falling through. The women workers from the factory cheered as the factory was destroyed, their faces shining with sweat and soot. But then they were confronted by another group, who'd been standing silently further back with their arms crossed and now approached them, almost squaring up to the women.

'How is this helping? We're just hurting ourselves,' shouted one of the challengers.

'We tried reasoning with them. They didn't listen. Now they have to,' a woman shouted back to her.

'They won't. They'll punish us. We'll end up inside for criminal damage. Let me guess: you don't have kids. We don't want a revolution, we want to put food on the table.'

'None of *us* set the fire,' the woman from the cheering group shot back.

'Neither did we,' said the woman who'd confronted her.

Elle watched the exchange, her eyes stinging from the fire. *This has all happened before,* she thought. *Workers attacked clothiers who used spring looms here – maybe even on the same ground.* The women in front of her continued to argue, until the urgent pulsing of sirens silenced them. The marchers were pushed to the side by advancing police cars, followed by two riot squad vans full of uniformed officers. People scrambled out of the way.

'Elle, watch out!' shouted Caroline, but it was too late. Elle spun around and found herself in front of a police car, which bore down until she felt its bonnet pressing into her legs. She stared into the eyes of the police officer driving the car. He revved the engine. She could see him smirking. The air around them was dark and blistering, even though it was the middle of the day. Everyone else had backed off, many filming while others hammered on the roof and boot of the car.

The car inched towards her, exerting its pressure. Elle could feel the sheer horsepower of the engine and, for one second, was taken with the delusion that she could actually withstand it pushing her. The thought vanished as the car forced her up onto the pavement and backed her against the brick wall. Elle heard other police officers shouting out of their vehicles, yelling a warning to the driver, but he ignored them – and so did she.

The car pressed against Elle and then, just as she had done when looking at the abandoned factory, she felt a rush that was far more powerful than her fear. Her heart beat hard, the surface of her skin grew warm and once again her ears began ringing. She closed her fists, not tightly, took a deep breath, and looked straight into the driver's eyes. The police officer's expression changed, his eyes growing wide and alarmed. He looked down, and then jerked back and began thrashing as flames rose up from the inside of the car, in front of him, licking up the dashboard to the inside of the windscreen and windows, turning them black. The police car rocked, and through the scorched windscreen Elle saw occasional flashes of the police officer's grasping hands. *If he rolls the windows down,* she thought, *it'll make the fire worse*. So there he was, trapped and alone.

The protesters stood and watched, not lifting a hand, as the police car filled with smoke and hoarse cries of panic rose up from the policeman trapped inside. Elle didn't move a muscle. The police car bucked again and stalled, lost power and slid backwards. There was a second of silence – and then a man ran towards the hot car. He covered his fist with his coat and yanked the driver's side open. A huge ball of stinking black smoke billowed out. Coughing, his eyes tightly shut, the man reached inside and dragged out the police officer, who lay on the ground, motionless. A crowd surrounded him and a woman dropped to her knees, saying 'Give him space.' The policeman stirred and coughed and the people around him drew back as he sat up shakily, clutching his chest and gasping for breath.

Elle ran, with Marine following close behind. Soon they were lost in the crowd, which surged around them. Once the crowd had rounded a corner, the pair of them ducked behind a building and sank to the ground.

'Are you okay?' asked Marine, staring at her.

'Fine, fine.' Now it was over, Elle felt weak and out of breath.

'Thank god he reversed. I thought he was going to crush you.'

'I thought so too,' said Elle. She rubbed her legs where the car had pressed into her.

'What did you say to him?'

'Nothing.'

'What did you do?'

'Nothing,' said Elle, but Marine wore an odd smile.

'What did you say your surname was again?'

'Don't you start,' said Elle.

'Nothing to be ashamed of. Witches are folk heroes.'

'And they burned for it,' said Elle. 'Or they swung. Once upon a time they thought *all* spinsters were witches.'

'You can say what you like. Don't worry, I'll keep your secret.'

'Don't be ridiculous. You realise that's what everyone says when they hear my surname? Timbold calls them the devil's servants.'

'Timbold's crackers,' said Marine.

Elle stood up.

'Come on. Let's find Caroline.'

'Great, another sceptic,' grumbled Marine, but she got up all the same and followed her.

Elle didn't tell her friend that, in fact, she'd actually first become interested in history when saw her own surname in a pamphlet in the local museum. Back in the Middle Ages, some of her namesakes had been tried as sorceresses. A young woman and her three sisters who lived with their widowed mother; the entire family had been hanged. The thing was, the girls had plenty of uncles and male cousins, all of whom married and had children, and none of their descendants got hanged for witchcraft. The name meant nothing. Of course, in her teenage years she'd fantasised that she was a descendant of these famed, doomed witches, smitten by the idea of being somebody, not a nobody.

Elle and Marine rounded another corner. The crowd was now rough and mixed; people had lost the friends they had come with and mingled together, moving restlessly around the perimeter of the wool factory that continued to burn, pumping out dirty smoke.

There was a shout from a muddy area beside the factory – 'Disperse! Disperse!' – as yet more police cars drove up to block them in.

Elle spotted Caroline sheltering inside the entrance of the abandoned paper mill further down the street. She and Marine joined her – Elle wanted to get as far away as she could from the burning police car, and from the staring eyes of the protesters back at the factory wall.

The paper mill had never been restored. Young people in the locality held raves and dance parties there across the summer; first the police broke them up, now they ignored them. The place was an eyesore, and a perilous one at that, with crumbling walls, sagging ceilings and pitted floors. Inside was a mess of rubble, graffiti, flammable rubbish and the original equipment, now rusted and even more dirty and dangerous than before. The huge metal doors stood rusted open and all the rubbish from the street blew in and rotted.

The further away they got from that burned-out police car, the more the heat and buzz bled out of Elle's body. A cold self-disgust and regret filled her instead.

'There's something happening up there – I heard arguing – someone might be in trouble,' said Caroline, before leading them up a metal staircase onto a rickety platform.

Next to the platform was the cavernous metal belly of an empty paper vat.

In the corner of the metal landing, they saw Schaffer, his stocky frame bristling as he grabbed an older man by the collar. The older man was purple in the face and gurgling incoherently as he gripped Schaffer's wrists. Schaffer had lifted him off his feet and pressed the man against the railing above the rusty vat.

'Schaffer – stop!' shouted Elle.

'Stay out of it, Faux, you want this as much as any of us,' he growled. He was staring deep into the eyes of the man he had by the neck.

'No I don't!' she shouted.

'Then what?' snarled Schaffer.

'Let go of him,' said Marine, her voice echoing off the walls of the vat.

Grimacing, Schaffer threw the man into the vat. He landed with the sickening crunch of bones breaking.

'Oh, god!' shouted Caroline, backing away.

Schaffer was breathing hard. For a second he stared at Elle with a gloating look, as if they were kin. She looked away, horrified.

'That's the foreman from the textile company,' said Marine. 'Caroline – *Caroline* – call an ambulance. Tell them what happened.'

Caroline snapped to it and reached into her pocket for her phone.

Schaffer heaved himself away from the railings, stalked past them and thudded down the metal stairs as if he had no care in the world, before breaking into a run towards the exit. None of the women stopped him.

'I can't get reception,' said Caroline. 'Let's go down.

The three of them clattered back down, Schaffer nowhere to be seen.

'We need to call the police as well as an ambulance,' said Elle as they approached the exit of the decrepit mill. 'Don't go far. They'll want to talk to us.'

Marine looked at Elle quizzically while Caroline talked to the ambulance dispatchers, pacing and biting the edge of her thumbnail.

'Schaffer's a thug,' said Marine. 'Half the pubs in Blandford have barred him.'

'He lost it back there,' muttered Elle. *And what did I just do?* she asked herself, before pushing the thought away.

'Are you sure you want to stick around?' asked Marine.

'I don't know... I don't know, I'm spent,' said Elle. Her head was full and she needed to think.

Up the street, at the wool factory, the crowd of protesters had begun to disperse. They were heavily outnumbered by the police. An ambulance with its lights flashing but its sirens off nosed through the crowd towards the mill. Two paramedics got out. Caroline came forward and led them towards the metal steps and the vat. People who were on their way home from the protest stared as the paramedics were joined by two more colleagues from a second ambulance stuck behind the crowd. All ran into the mill. More police vehicles parked up and surrounded the paper mill.

'Stay where you are,' shouted the officer closest to them, getting out of the car.

'Don't say anything,' said Marine to Elle under her breath. 'We got to the top of the stairs, we saw some guys arguing, and we froze. Then we legged it.'

Elle nodded. The women separated and waited for the police to approach them. Elle looked down at herself – her dark cotton top, jeans and hiking boots were similar to what many women in the crowd were wearing, and she knew her face was nondescript.

Elle, Marine and Caroline were spoken to by three separate police officers. Elle told the WPC the story she'd agreed with Marine. The WPC took Elle's contact details and raised an eyebrow when she gave her address at Halfway House.

'Does your boss know you're here?' she asked Elle.

'Tom? He doesn't mind, as long as I do my work and...'

'Don't bring trouble up the hill,' the police officer finished for her.

'Something like that,' Elle muttered.

'Know anything about these messages that've been going round?' asked the WPC.

'Messages?' said Elle, unable to stop a tremor in her voice.

'Poison pen letters. Malicious communications. There've been online threats going round all the country houses. Signed Lady Swing. Any idea who that might be?'

Elle gulped and shook her head.

'You stick to signing petitions, if you want things to change,' the officer told Elle. 'Don't get mixed up in these protests, they attract all sorts.' She pointed up to the vat. 'This assault. Recognise the man who did it?'

Elle shook her head.

'I fled – I didn't want to be next.'

At the end of the road, two burly officers could be seen dragging Schaeffer back to where the police cars were parked. Schaeffer was scowling, his face red and caked with sweat, but he didn't put up a fight. As he was ushered past and shoved into the back of a car, a strong animal stink seemed to follow him – and as if she'd read her thoughts, the police officer said to Elle, 'Heard you've had trouble with the animals, up your end. Any idea who that might be?'

Elle shook her head. The other police officer, a young man, was still talking to Marine, only they seemed to be having a friendly conversation, chatting and laughing. Marine was deliberately not catching Elle's eye.

'I hear all sorts about the estates,' said the WPC. She pointed her pen at herself. 'Blandform Forum constabulary. I'm the youngest on my team, but my bosses, they're men in their sixties. And they say every generation, it comes in waves. Sightings of an animal in the woods and whatnot. And every time, there's animal maimings. Always at a solstice. Winter or summer. Then it goes quiet for twenty years. It coincides with civil unrest. Unrest among the people.'

'What… kind of animal?'

'One that likes to keep itself private,' said the police officer. She put away her notebook, returned to her car and sat down in the driver's seat, leaving the door open. 'I grew up on a farm – my parents own Winterbourne Poultry. One thing I know: animals don't turn against each other for no reason. The only one that does that is the human animal. A species predator: that's what we call one that harms its own kind.'

The WPC shut her car door with a slam, waited for her colleague to get in beside her and reversed sharply away from the paper mill.

Marine was waiting for her a few steps away.

'What were you joking with that policeman about, Marine?'

'He's a friend of Jez's, been to our house loads of times. Meanwhile it looked like *you* were getting a proper telling-off.'

Elle shook her head.

'I don't know how much she believed me.'

'The way to lie effectively is to tell half the truth. I saw the guy, but not clearly. I was there, but I came late. I know him, but not well. You don't fib outright, you don't invent anything. Just hide half the truth. Split it off.'

Just then two fire engines finally came tearing down the street, more than an hour late, to tend to the fire at the wool factory. Elle declined Marine's offer of a calm-down drink in a cosy nook at the Chalk Way pub and headed back home in the Jeep. As she joined the long line of vehicles heading back to the roundabout, she thought about the liar who hides half of themselves. Was that what she was? A split, hidden creature? A species predator. She turned up the old dial radio to drown out her thoughts, but all she heard were voices fighting through the eerie, crackling static.

For the next few weeks, everyone lay low. Elle started work at eight every morning instead of nine, read all the messages that came to her but didn't write any, or respond to anything.

One Saturday morning she accompanied Tom to a local

election hustings at Blandford Forum, where Tom and his opponent, Horley, presented their arguments to an audience of well-heeled local people.

On the face of it, Horley wasn't that different from Tom Foote. They were both well-bred men of a certain age. But Horley emitted a strange, nervy energy and there was often a frantic grin on his face. His eyes never settled on anything for long. He was an outlier; the Foote family had been in power here for generations.

Things went fine until the end, when a woman put up her hand and asked, 'And what'll you be doing about law and order? It doesn't feel safe any more.' She glanced around as she spoke, as if danger lurked in that very room.

'No it doesn't,' Horley jumped in, 'and in fact, Madam, I can share with you that down at Sherston a respectable man called Cresswell was ambushed by a gang of young men *not* from the area demanding better work conditions in the paint factory and I have it on very good authority that these young men are affiliated with illegal foreign gangs and if that's the truth we shouldn't be afraid to say it. We don't know what they want and our English prisons are filling up with them. I mean animal maiming for heaven's sake! Who in a civilised country does that? It's tribal. And I'm a local boy myself, not a city lad. I remember the disagreements we had with the lads from neighbouring towns – but that was harmless. Anyone know the lingo? If you were from Sturbridge you were a 'Vinney', if you came from Shapwick you were a 'Crab-Fighter'. Anyone know the name of someone from Wyke Regis?'

'A "Mer-Chicken"!' shouted a man in the audience, grinning. Everyone laughed.

At the end of the hustings Tom Foote was ushered away by his team to a room at the Old Courts pub for some cold sandwiches and a debriefing session. Elle walked out of the hall and noticed the food bank opposite, in the empty shell of the old library. The food bank was a makeshift affair with rickety plastic shelves holding dozens of packets of pasta and jars of sauce and a small selection of fresh fruit and vegetables.

Caroline was behind the table – Elle hadn't seen her since the protest at the wool factory and the paper mill. They greeted each other, making no reference to that day.

'How did the hustings go?' asked Caroline.

'Badly,' said Elle, adding 'I mean for Tom. Horley's gaining support. Can I help?'

'You can stack these, if you would.'

There was a box of chickpea cans on the floor. Elle went behind the table and began putting them on the bottom shelf. Caroline collected all the vouchers that local people had given her in exchange for food and clipped them together. There were dozens of them from that week.

'Horley talks a big game about "the people" but I've never once seen him down here,' she said. 'I had a meeting with him a few months ago about some things he could put on his manifesto. I mentioned higher wages, better conditions for factory staff, a bit of money for operations like this and when I mentioned local casual workers unionising he basically ended the meeting. At least Tom has manners.'

'Tom has sympathy –' Elle began, then stopped short. 'Sorry. I have to keep reminding myself I'm not his campaign manager. He already has one, and I'm pretty sure he's being paid a heck of a lot more than me.'

Caroline joined her, putting the last of the tins on the shelf.

'Have you heard from Pellman at all?' she asked Elle.

'He still works occasionally on the estate. But we're coming up to the August holidays now and everyone gets their time off,' said Elle neutrally. She lined up the cans of supermarket own-brand chickpeas. 'Why do people donate this stuff? Do they believe the poor deserve only the most boring, worthy, own-brand food? What about chocolates and caviar? This is a wealthy area, but they're so stingy.'

'Elle, they've arrested Schaffer,' Caroline said quietly. 'Grievous bodily harm. He pled guilty. The police are taking that day very seriously. They're looking to trace all the protesters.

They're sentencing Schaffer tomorrow. I think you should show your face. It looks suspect, otherwise.'

Elle gulped, then nodded. A queue had formed in front of the table. Caroline went back to her work, Elle returned to the Jeep.

The next day she, Marine, Flossie, Pellman and Timbold – his hair plastered down with some kind of pomade – sat next to each other at the magistrates' court. On the other side of the room was the injured foreman's extended family – a woman in her fifties with two sets of parents, a couple of peaky looking teenagers and about half a dozen surly men. The man himself was sitting right at the end of the row, his face closed and impassive, his leg out, a set of crutches leaning next to him.

'I don't believe in courts. There's different kinds of justice,' Timbold was muttering loudly, 'some by law, some by the hand –'

'Oh will you stop *chuntering on,*' hissed Marine.

Elle looked out of the window at The Old Courts pub, where they'd all agreed to go for a drink afterwards. She'd never noticed the design painted on the wooden sign before. A pyre, a gallows and a ducking-stool. Were *they* old symbols of justice? No, she realised, they were the three things they used to kill witches.

A door slammed and Schaffer was led in, tightly flanked by two court officers. His face was raw and nicked, with bruises around the jaw and a cut eyebrow. He looked sulky and resentful, as always. The families on the benches next to Elle stirred unhappily when they saw him.

'We'll get you back, you Halfway lot,' one of the men on the victims' side sneered, but was shushed sharply by the court bailiff.

'All of this pain and trouble' said Elle to Marine. 'And all because Schaffer couldn't hide his feelings. He couldn't control himself. He hurt another person.'

'He controlled himself just fine. We tried talking to them nicely – it didn't work. Now it's time for us to show our feelings. If they can't act out of common decency they can act out of fear instead. A "little warning" isn't misplaced,' Marine whispered back. 'Blood gets spilled. These things happen. You're lucky you can defend yourself.'

'Please don't joke about that.'

'The police officer driving that car could have ended up with a lot more than smoke damage.'

'Stop, Marine,' said Elle, squirming. 'I was frightened. I panicked. He was threatening me.'

A woman in a tailored jacket, sitting high up and square centre in the room, was talking down at them. Elle tried to listen, but being in the court made her feel exposed and guilty. The lady said, 'Mr Schaffer has admitted his crimes, sparing his victim and his friends and family the pain of a trial. However, taking into consideration his long record of disturbances and altercations, I have no choice but to recommend that he be taken into custody on the charge of grievous bodily harm for a minimum of four years –'

There was a roar of triumph from the benches, which was immediately superseded by the loud wail of the fire alarm. Two hassled-looking clerks burst in, saying, 'Evacuate! This is not a drill!' Everybody looked around in confusion, even Schaffer and the officials on either side of him. He was hustled out of a side door. Elle and her friends stood up and the clerks ushered them towards the fire exits. Behind them, in the foyer, were a couple of large metal street bins piled with burnt rubbish, emitting sour smoke and covered in fire extinguisher foam.

'Hardly an arson attack,' said Flossie. 'It's probably just kids messing about.'

The foreman's family went out first, walking close together and hugging each other. Elle and her friends followed at a respectful distance. Elle found herself in step with Pellman as they shuffled through the bottleneck at the exit and came out into the staff car park at the back of the court.

'What're you so smug about, Pellman?' said Elle.

'They knew this was coming. We warned them. But they

went ahead anyway. You know who they're trying in the other rooms? They call them 'ringleaders' – ordinary lads from Chettle and Chippenham who're just as angry as we are, with good cause. Two lads from the distribution centre in Shaftsbury.'

'They'll still be sentenced. Maybe even more harshly for all your mischief.'

'All *my* mischief? We're in this together, Faux fire-witch.'

'*What* did you call me?'

'Just joking,' he said. He clapped her on the shoulder. 'Still, a bit of myth-making's no bad thing. All the great rebels had a legend around them – Robin Hood, Guy Fawkes, Dick Turpin the highwayman.'

'I'm not any of those guys,' said Elle, turning away.

'How do we know you didn't start the foyer fires?'

'Because I didn't.'

Pellman's eyes sparkled.

'That's what I like: you suspect me, I suspect you. Chaos is the tool of the masses,' he crowed. Then his expression changed and his face grew hard.

A police car pulled into the car park, very slow and deliberate. Elle's heart began to pound as she instantly recognised the driver: it was the officer who'd questioned her in the paper mill. The officer was unaccompanied. As soon as she got out of the car, she shouted over to her, 'Elle Faux? I need you to come with me.'

Elle froze as the officer advanced slowly, her hand to her hip. What did she have there? Not a gun, surely. A Taser perhaps.

'What do you want to talk to me about?' said Elle.

'I think you know. What you've done. What you are.'

'I'm not anything,' said Elle. She was backing into the corner almost without realising it.

'We know what you tried to do.'

'And what is that?' said Elle.

'Murder. Attempted murder.'

There was a gasp from the others, and jeers of satisfaction

from Schaffer's supporters. The police officer, Elle noticed, was quite breathless. Elle wondered if this was one of her first serious arrests, wondered how nervous she might be.

'What're you talking about?' she said, to buy time.

'We don't take kindly to people who try to hurt our colleagues.' The police officer was loosening a clasp on the side of her belt.

'I never put my hands on anyone,' said Elle.

'You don't need to. I'm talking about arson. Death by fire.'

'I don't know what you're talking about.'

'You did something. I know it. You've been getting better at it. Practising, I'll warrant.'

The police officer seemed to be about to say something else – something about the abandoned factory Elle had torched, no doubt – but instead she closed her mouth with a decided smirk.

'But that's for us to investigate,' she said, grinning.

Elle was almost backed into the corner between the court wall and the car park fence. She felt that warm, pleasant surge again. That wonderful rise of strength. *An animal with nothing to lose will fight to the death – fight for territory, fight for survival*, she thought. *Fight to protect their own.* She had seen that among beasts both tame and wild in all her years at Halfway House. She rubbed her hands together; her palms were warm. The police officer had almost closed the distance between them. They locked eyes – then they were both distracted by the officer's walkie-talkie squalling into life.

'We've had another report of animal maimings up in Black Haw. Can we get someone up there, please?' said the crackling voice urgently. 'Animal maiming in Black Haw, specialist units.'

'Elle, run!' shouted Pellman, and Elle ran straight towards the police officer, meaning to knock her off her feet, but the officer's instincts were sharp. She grabbed Elle and slammed her to the ground. Elle crashed down, winded. The officer knelt on Elle's neck, pulled out the yellow plastic discharger of a Taser, put it to her stomach and shot her with it.

When Elle came round, she was lying on the ground twenty feet away from where an ambulance stood, square in the middle of the court car park. Dozens of onlookers were staring down at her, as police officers bustled to hold them back. She felt her entire body throbbing with light and heat. As she attempted to get up, the ring of officers around her locked arms, and she realised they were all wearing bullet-proof vests and helmets. As she reached out to them, they shrank back.

'Careful,' said one to his colleagues.

Behind the police cordon and immediate crowd, Flossie clung to Timbold. Marine stood a few yards further back, talking to some police officers, huddling with them just as if... just as if, Elle realised, she was one herself.

'Marine,' she tried to shout, but she could barely raise her voice. 'Marine, tell them.'

Marine stopped talking to the police officers and turned to Elle with a frown. Her face, usually so animated, was cold and uninterested as she glanced down at Elle.

'Marine,' said Elle again.

Marine curled her lip.

'Who're you calling Marine? It's Agent Haines to you.' Her voice was unmistakably jeering, her tone completely different from the one Elle was used to. As she walked towards her a lanyard she was wearing seemed to flash the word 'DIRT' at her.

Elle laughed emptily, her throat dry. So that was how they knew. She had been played. The officers watched her, grinning, as she absorbed it all.

'I... thought we were friends,' said Elle. How small and humiliating that sounded, she thought.

'Nah. I'm not friends with people like you. Deviants. Why would someone like me want to hang round with someone like you? We uphold the law. Look what you do.'

Several feet away, half-covered on an ambulance gurney, was the charred body of the police officer who'd tasered Elle. Her uniform had melted onto her skin and all her hair had burnt off. Elle remembered now. The voltage had hit her, like waves of sharp white flame, then reversed, shooting back along the thin, buzzing wires. Elle's eyes slid from the horrible sight and met Pellman's gaze. He stood, loose and exhilerated, watching her. His face wore a sloppy grin.

'What do I do?' she asked, trying to sit up. The police officers tensed up.

'You mean *did*, Firestarter. You're a cop killer,' said Pellman.

Elle held up her hands and felt the heat build in them. She could feel her strength coming back. After all, as the legends said, it was difficult to kill a witch. The police officers and even Elle's friends braced. Her last thought, before she got up and ran, was: *That's a hanging offence.*

Origin Story: The Spectre of Swing

Rose Wallis

In the autumn and winter of 1830, unrest spread rapidly across rural England. Crowds of agricultural labourers forcibly demanded charitable relief and better wages, tearing down threshing machines that deprived them of work. Collective action was accompanied by more spectral manifestations of the labourers' grievances, incendiary fires and threatening letters signed by the ominous hand of 'Swing'.

Once considered the 'last labourers' revolt',[1] the Swing disturbances are now understood as more than a last-ditch attempt to stop the onslaught of agrarian capitalism. This was a complex response to the experience of enduring economic depression and the breakdown of social relations – not an organised movement as we might understand it, but a coherent expression of shared grievances. The forms that protest took were reasoned if not peaceful, drawing on a long-standing repertoire of action that enabled the otherwise disenfranchised to exert pressure on their employers and the authorities to uphold their 'right to subsistence'.[2]

Bidisha's story, set in the contemporary South West, captures the breadth and depth of Swing as a response to persistent hardship shared by more than the agricultural community. The resonances with current experiences of austerity and all that has entailed – cuts to social welfare, a greater reliance on charity, job insecurity – are all too palpable. So too are the social divisions that underscore acts of protest and how they are perceived. Permeating this re-imagining of Swing are contested notions of what constitutes a legitimate protest, debates that again resonate in the present.

At the end of the French Wars in 1815, England fell into a deep decline. As international markets opened, the price of domestic produce fell, and farmers found themselves unable to afford to pay adequate wages to workers or employ them at all. Where labourers were hired, it was often on a daily basis, offering them little security; and with the demobilisation of 250,000 British soldiers, competition for work only increased. To mitigate these circumstances, impoverished workers applied in growing numbers for relief from the parish. From at least the 1790s, local authorities had drawn on the parish rates to supplement poor wages – something akin to our system of income support. As the war continued and times were made harder with persistent harvest failures, this system became more regularised; but increasing demand pushed local taxation up adding to the financial burden on rate payers.

The worsening economic crisis fuelled the breakdown of social relationships. Not only did the labourers resent their employers but tenants turned on landlords, and landlords on their tenantry. Farmers called on the landed gentry and the church to reduce their rents and tithes to allow them to pay better wages and their own rates. They in turn were criticised for allowing wages to be supplemented from the public purse. The labourers' sense of entitlement to parish relief was cast as the chief cause of 'idleness, vice and profligacy';[3] but for under- or unemployed workers, attempts to cut relief constituted an attack on what had become a customary safeguard against destitution.

Popular reaction to these conditions, manifest from at least 1816, if not 1795 – although not continuously – was not confined to 1830. In East Anglia and parts of the South West, riots had broken out in 1816. In 1822, crowds destroyed threshing machines across Norfolk and Suffolk. Indeed, in some parts of the country, Swing was the latest battle in an ongoing 'rural war'. But just as the conditions that prompted Swing were not limited to 1830, they were likewise not specific to the rural community. Certainly in the South West, textile industries had been in decline for some years with competition from Northern factories and foreign markets. Disputes amongst the weavers had broken out in 1822 and 1823; and strikes and disturbances had also taken place amongst Somerset papermakers, and Dorset flax-workers. The Radical journalist, William Cobbett, blamed the dejected state of the weavers at Frome on the 'bluff manufacturers' who called upon the local volunteer forces and magistrates to keep the poor in check, threatening them 'when they dare to ask for the means of preventing starvation for their families.'[4] It is perhaps unsurprising therefore, to find threatening letters penned to urban manufacturers across the South West in 1830 attacking the use of industrial as well as farm machinery, and declaring that 'Swing must of necessity soon be here.'[5]

Swing protesters' demands were varied, including minimum wage rates, more poor relief, and on occasion more affordable food prices; but Swing is perhaps most often associated with the destruction of threshing machines. Their introduction had replaced hand-threshing, and pushed wages down as their operation required no specialist skill. Forcibly removing them created opportunities to work, and higher rates of pay. Much like the Luddites of the industrial Midlands and North, the destruction of farm or manufacturing machinery was not an attack on technical innovation, but a means of exerting pressure on employers to improve workers' conditions; part of a tradition of 'collective bargaining by riot' that extended back into the eighteenth-century.[6]

These collective actions were ordered and relatively restrained, not marked by a tendency to initiate interpersonal violence at least. They were underpinned by a sense of legitimacy that was demonstrated through their openness and community participation, often taking place in broad daylight with great clamour. An almost holiday atmosphere was evident at one meeting of labourers at Winfrith in Dorset. The men, attended by their wives and children, were described as 'particularly well-dressed, as if they had put on their best clothes for the occasion.' They had 'advanced rather respectfully, and with their hats in their hands, to demand an increase in wages.'[7] The local authorities rejected their request and forcibly dispersed the crowd. Indeed, it was aggressive intervention on the part of the authorities that was more often the source of any violent altercation.

Threatening letters and fires were perhaps as characteristic of Swing as machine-breaking, but they appear as more covert forms of dissent. These were acts committed in secrecy with stealth to evade detection, which threatened or enacted violence and destruction. They were not public manifestations of righteous indignation in the same way that crowd actions were. However, such covert methods should not necessarily be understood as less legitimate forms of popular protest. They were part of the repertoire of actions employed by rural communities, not unique to Swing, which might be used in combination with collective action. These were psychological weapons.

Threatening letters served as both expressions of the labourers' grievances and warnings prior to collective action or arson. Farmers were told to put down their threshing machines or risk their removal by force or fire. Western clothiers were likewise advised to 'do away altogether with damned Power looms... you had better alter the suffering or youl loose [sic] More than you have gained these 7 years.' In case the recipients of this letter were in any doubt of what was at stake, it concluded 'burning and cutting.'[8] More explicitly violent statements were also made: two Wiltshire farmers were warned that if they didn't pay their workers a fair wage 'destruction will come like a thife [sic] in the night when every thing is still and Calm and quiet... Blood for Blood. All Pay.'[9] As well employers, magistrates, clergymen, and those responsible for the administration of poor relief, were similarly reminded of their obligations to the labouring poor or face retribution. One clerical justice was labelled 'the Blackguard Enemies of the People on all occasions, Ye have not yet done as Ye Ought.'[10]

Many (although not all) threatening letters were signed by 'Swing'. The lone word invoked a double meaning: the act of field workers swinging a flail in unison, and simultaneously the threat of judicial punishment and a body swinging from the hangman's rope. On occasion the letters' authors amplified the sense of impending danger, by hinting at a more pervasive and organised movement, signing off 'Captain Swing' or professing to be one of his 'agents' working amongst the recipient's community. Certainly more than one south-western magistrate was convinced that there was a 'system of threatening letters' distributed by agitators from outside the region. Even in areas where there had been little or no open protest, the spectre of Swing, manifest in threatening letters and fires, was enough to stimulate action, to remove machinery or to grant concessions.

Arson was viewed with particular abhorrence by the authorities, as nothing more than vengeful and wanton destruction that warranted the ultimate sanction at law; it was, as our superhero Elle reminds us, a hanging offence. The language used to describe incendiaries – fire-starters – invoked an unholy 'other'. As one panicked magistrate described them in 1830, 'a set of Hell Hounds who are carrying devastation through every part.'[11] It was even decried as un-English:

'It is for the honour of our country, it is for our credit as men, that we must find out and punish these cowardly miscreants. Englishmen were never assassins! Englishmen were never incendiaries.'[12]

Animal maiming, while not especially prevalent during Swing, was, like arson, an established tactic and one that elicited similar disgust. The perpetrators were also considered 'fiendish', 'inhuman monsters if not the devil himself.'[13] It might be hard for us to consider the slaughter of animals with any less repulsion, but in the context of agrarian society, we must recognise the status of livestock as property of considerable value. Incendiaries and animal maimers no doubt intended to terrify and injure their victims, but not in any bodily way. The destruction of property created financial hardship for the owner, and while this might have limited further their capacity to provide employment, it was a potent symbolic act: attacking the basis of the victim's wealth and power, gained at the expense of the impoverished labourer.

Despite their clandestine perpetration, fires were also public statements. In the context of Swing, we might consider arson in a similar way to the tradition of 'rough music': action intended to shame and expose the victim. A burning hay rick, barn, or manufactory, could be visible over great distances, lighting up the night sky and drawing a crowd who might celebrate, or just watch the conflagration, rather than help to put it out. Much like the anonymous letters, they could, and did, serve as a warning, provoking the propertied classes to address the needs of the poor.

Deals were brokered to address the labourers' grievances either in response to, or to prevent unrest. Without any sort of approval for the protests, many among the propertied and local government acknowledged that agricultural labourers had legitimate cause for complaint. These local concessions were countered with extensive and rigorous prosecutions, making examples of the most 'serious offenders'. Unsurprisingly, arsonists and those considered responsible for the most extensive and violent attacks on property faced the harshest penalties. Likewise, non-agricultural workers were singled out for not sharing – it was claimed – in the genuine distress of farm labourers. The same language used to describe incendiaries was adopted to distinguish between legitimate and illegitimate protest, attributing unrest to 'foreign' agitators, elements outside the rural community. In Dorset, at the opening of the court of Special Commission convened to try Swing offenders, Judge Alderson attributed the disturbances to the designs of 'interested and wicked men', those who 'endeavoured to dissever the bonds which hold society together.'[14] By blaming 'outsiders', the authorities downplayed the extent of social divisions and divested Swing of its scope as a movement that united labourers across occupational communities.

While some of the wage increases secured by the protesters were sustained into the 1830s, social divisions became more sharply defined. The New Poor Law passed in 1834, put an end to wage supplements from the parish; and the levels of unrest experienced in 1830, as well as the Reform riots of 1831, were used to drive the extension of professional policing into smaller urban and rural communities from the middle of the decade. In their report, the Poor Law commissioners attributed Swing to the maladministration of the relief system: disorder and conflagration were the product of 'minds already depraved by the baleful effects of compulsory relief.'[15] The social contract that underpinned the labourers' customary expectation of support was broken.

The apparent 'failure' of Swing, and its more destructive and threatening elements have perhaps contributed to its characterisation as a reactionary rising, one that sits at odds with the more peaceful or 'progressive' tactics and formal organisation of later labour movements. More recently, however, historians have drawn out the formative role Swing played in the articulation, and struggle for employment rights and standards of social welfare that continued to inform workers' protests throughout the nineteenth century.

Nevertheless, the central tension developed in Bidisha's story concerning legitimate and illegitimate protest persists. In August 2011, the then Prime Minister described the summer riots of that year as 'criminality, pure and simple.'[16] More recently, in 2020, those responsible for toppling the statue of the slaver Edward Colston amidst the Black Lives Matter protests, were described by the Home Secretary as a 'criminal minority who have subverted this cause'.[17] Environmental protesters have similarly been branded as 'eco-crusaders turned criminals.'[18] However, as other contemporary commentators have highlighted, there is a danger in confining social unrest to 'random acts of anarchy' perpetrated by a deviant minority.[19] Rather like the 'othering' of Swing and the official narrative of unrest promoted by the authorities in its aftermath, representing these contemporary protests in this narrow way does little to consider the economic and social contexts that underpin them: austerity, the climate crisis, now Covid-19, and the more entrenched social divisions and inequities that these circumstances have brought to the fore.

Notes

1. J. L. and B. Hammond, *The Village Labourer 1760-1832* (Longmans, Green and Co. 1912) chapters 11 and 12.
2. P. Jones, 'Swing, Speenhamland and rural social relations: the 'moral economy' of the English Crowd in the nineteenth century,' *Social History* 32:3 (2007), 274.
3. Evidence of Justice Stone of Somerset, Board of Agriculture, *Agricultural State of the Kingdom,* Part II (London, 1816) 13-14.
4. W. Cobbett, *Rural Rides* (first published 1830, this edition, Penguin, 1967) 339.
5. The National Archives (TNA): HO 52/9 f. 633, enclosure of an anonymous letter signed 'Swing' received by silk manufacturers Nalder and Hardisty at Shepton Mallet, Somerset, November 1830.
6. E. J. Hobsbawm, 'The Machine Breakers', *Past and Present* No. 1 (Feb. 1952), 59.
7. H. G. Mundy (ed.) *The Journal of Mary Frampton, from the year 1779, until the year 1846* (London, 1885) 361-2.
8. TNA: HO 52/9 f. 633 enclosure of an anonymous letter signed 'Swing' received by silk manufacturers at Darshill near Shepton Mallet, Somerset, November 1830.
9. TNA: HO 52/11/5 f. 11 Copy of a letter received at Codford St. Peter, Wiltshire, November 1830.
10. TNA: HO 52/7/102 f. 231-2, letter to Rev. Huntley at Kimbolton, Huntingdonshire, November 1830.
11. TNA: HO 52/9 f.90 Justice Berney to Home Secretary Lord Melbourne, December 1830.
12. Public address from the High Sheriff of Norwich and Justices, *Bury and Norwich Post*, 24 November 1830; also printed in the *English Chronicle and Whitehall Evening Post* 25 November 1830.
13. J. E. Archer, '*By a Flash and a Scare'. Arson, animal maiming, and poaching in East Anglia 1815-1870* (Breviary Stuff Publications, 2010) 131.
14. Dorset History Centre: D-SEY/JP/019 *The charge of the Hon. Mr Justice Alderson to the grand jury of Dorset at the opening of the special commission at Dorchester, 11 January 1831.*
15. UK Parliamentary Papers: 1834 (44) Report from His

Majesty's commissioners for inquiring into the administration and practical operation of the Poor Laws. Report of Henry Stuart Esq. appendix A, p. 361.

16. David Cameron, address to the House of Commons, 11 August 2011. Hansard. https://publications.parliament.uk/pa/cm201011/cmhansrd/cm110811/debtext/110811-0001.htm

17. Priti Patel, address to the House of Commons, 8 June 2020, Hansard. https://hansard.parliament.uk/commons/2020-06-08/debates/212DD2A6-B810-4FDE-B3BD-1642F5BA1E86/PublicOrder

18. Priti Patel, address to the annual conference of the Police Superintendents' Association, *The Guardian,* 8 Sep 2020.

19. See for example comments made by Vanessa Kisuule, Twitter 7 June 2020, and Kerry McCarthy question to the Home Secretary, House of Commons, 8 June 2020, Hansard. https://hansard.parliament.uk/commons/2020-06-08/debates/212DD2A6-B810-4FDE-B3BD-1642F5BA1E86/PublicOrder

Unloved Flowers

Gaia Holmes

HE HATES THE MORNING train stuffed full of commuters setting off for work as he comes home after a long night shift. Even through his cotton face mask he can smell the cacophony of odours: toothpaste, aftershave and brash colognes still wet on jaws and necks, the particular odour of upholstered seats warmed by bodies, leather, polish, rubbery trainers and the sickly-sweet notes of Starbucks spiced chai. Within five minutes of the journey, the quiet green perfumes of the garden centre – compost, pond weed and the fat, almost sexual, tang of tomato plants – are quickly subsumed and he becomes one of them, almost, except for the soil beneath his fingernails and the dead fish in a Tupperware in his work bag. Just about everyone is stroking or tapping the screens of their phone. The sun's just coming up, wheat fields a dull gold in the light, eagle on a telegraph pole, swallows swooping, deer. The woman sitting beside him is researching off-grid techno-detox holidays. She scrolls through Instagram photos of barefoot people and yurts and campfires... package holidays, 'be free with the trees', 'Wild women'. The man across the aisle is in some angular virtual world shooting killer robot rabbits and outside there are trees, the smell of rain and foxes, a kestrel, a field humming with the blue of cornflowers, a heron, a huge lolloping hare. Look up! Look out, he wants to shout into the crowded carriage but he doesn't. Instead, in his head he says hello to the oak, the ash, the elder as the train slows at the junction. Spring. Things growing and singing. The dull winter world renewed, refreshed with green, beaded with bud. Look up. Look out. There's a cow. A still thing. People ping and bleep and slurp and rustle. People are squashed together. Thighs touching thighs. Shoulders touching shoulders. They have learned to tango with their elbows as they stroke or tap their screens and fold themselves in. A baby strokes her mother's face waiting for something to flash, ping or light up. Meanwhile he takes a flat browned old oak leaf out of his pocket, balances it on his knee, taps it gently so it makes a papery sound, runs his fingertip down its midrib so it whispers. No one hears. No one looks. No one notices it turning green.

Scrawny, scratchy hair like gorse. At school, they bullied him, shoved grass down the back of his shirt, put dead mice and dog shit in his school bag, called him Swampy because, when he sweated, he smelled like the stagnant pond by the allotments behind the playing field and, as he got older and his bones started to fit, and things started sprouting, his sweat got more and more loamy, mulchy. He suffered bullying throughout his first year then, in his second, a gang of them slathered a whole tube of Veet over his head and his eyebrows and held him down until it burnt most of his hair off. After that he stopped talking, so his parents took him out of school. At school he stood out because he was 'different'. Now he's the sort of person you don't notice, the sort of person who holds open a door for someone and ends up standing there holding it for ten minutes as countless other people take the opportunity to mill through without thanking him, without even acknowledging him, as if his role in life is to hold doors open for ungrateful people.

Wasps and bees love him. Maybe it's the sugar in his sweat. Maybe they can smell the flowers he dreams of – all those wild meadows between stations full of borage, vetch and clover. In the past he has led swarms away from frightened picnickers like the Pied Piper, he's lifted nests from neighbours' rafters with his bare hands. He's never been stung. Cats are wary of him, but dogs love him too and it's for that reason he got the job at the garden centre straight away without even presenting his CV. At the job centre they'd done a 'job match' for him and the search came up with 'security guard' and, as it happened, 'George's Garden Centre' on the outskirts of Brighouse was looking for a night guard so his job adviser booked him an interview there and then and even though he knew he wasn't exactly 'security guard material' and he'd never forcibly removed anyone from any premises and he had weak knees and was no good at running, he had to attend the interview or he'd be sanctioned. When he got there, he was hired within five minutes simply because Beverly the toothless Akita liked him.

'You're the first one she hasn't tried to savage during the interview. Can you start next week?' George asked and shook his hand.

It isn't a fancy Yankee Candle sort of garden centre. It sells flora, fauna, muck and goldfish. He works the night shift from Monday to Sunday, one week on, one week off. He patrols the perimeter every hour with Beverly and a torch. Though she has no teeth, Beverly makes a good guard dog. When she hears an unfamiliar noise, she turns into a vicious hell hound, snarling and growling, straining on her lead and puffing up to twice her size. If you're her friend, as Connor is, she's as soft and loving as a docile Labrador. At midnight they have a snack; weak tea and Bourbon Creams for him, and a Garibaldi biscuit soaked in a saucer of milk for her. He loves the aquatic section the most. Each morning around 4am he spends a little time there absorbing the calm hum of the water filters, the darting glitter of the Comets and the Fantails and the slow, bumbling drifting of the bulbous guppies. Like bees, wasps and dogs, they seemed to like him and always come to peer through the glass, head-butt his fingertip when he dips it into the water. The weekly death toll is high. He gets used to the sight of fish floating belly up on the surface of the water. He gets used to fishing them out with a slotted aquarium spoon, putting them in a Tupperware box and dropping them into the river on his way from the station, giving them a proper send-off. Sometimes, before they die, he sees them fading, wishes he could give them the kiss of life, breathe them back into being. But the ones that live seem to triple in size within weeks. They outgrow their aquariums and George has to put them in the pond with Lola the huge, ghostly twenty-year-old koi. 'Are you feeding things special stuff?' George asked him one morning. 'Because everything's growing like mad and I'm sure Lola's been getting her gold back since you started here?'

After the Veet incident at school his hair had grown back quickly, much stronger and thicker and it wouldn't seem to stop growing. His mum had to trim it regularly because it grew an inch a week. He also started experiencing a strange, dull ache which the doctor diagnosed as 'growing pains'. He grew so much that they constantly had to buy him new clothes and shoes. When he reached the age of nineteen, he finally stopped growing. And, at the age of 21, after ten years of silence, he started talking again. He still doesn't talk much though, only if he has to or if there's something he wants to say. He doesn't do small talk but he's rarely in a situation where small talk's required because he doesn't go to pubs, bars or clubs and since he's moved into the flat above the newsagent's he hasn't got to know anyone, but he doesn't really mind. He's happy in his own company or with toothless Akitas or cold-water fish and he rarely feels lonely. So the job at the garden centre is perfect for him.

There are several living landmarks he likes to take note of as he walks back from the station after his night shift. After work he's always knackered and the landmarks spur him on up the hill. There's the sleeping cat and the chilli plant in the window on

Hopwood Lane and the rooks' nests in the tree at the edge of the park and the ducks gorging on the daily offerings of rice and stale chapattis by the pond, and there's the lawn of the Hazelwood Care Home which gets yellower and yellower every day as the spring dandelions take over. He likes dandelions. He thinks they're much more alive and exciting than bedding plants. Much more gutsy than a primrose or a cultivated begonia. Dandelions remind him of his Granny Amy.

After his parents had taken him out of school, they didn't know what to do with him, so they sent him to stay with his granny during the week. He liked it there because everything was a little wild and there was always something happening in the kitchen: dark wine bubbling in demijohns, bottles of Ginger beer exploding, things pickling and steeping in jars. The house seemed to breathe like a living thing. It was never completely still or quiet. It was his granny who had kindled his interest in plants and his fondness for dandelions. Dandelions were her favourite flower. She'd rather a bouquet of dandelion than a bouquet of roses. She said if she had a garden, she'd fill it with them. She explained to him that though roses were beautiful, fragrant, well-loved flowers, dandelions had so many more tricks, like soft little medicine cabinets. In spring, she drank dandelion tea for her blood and her 'waterworks'. In winter, she drank dandelion wine for her spirit. In Dandelion season, she took him out to gather what she called the 'food of the gods' and as they picked, she'd tell him the story of Theseus the Greek hero who defeated the Minotaur. Before the defeat, in order to build up his strength, the Goddess Hecate fed Theseus Dandelion salads for 30 days. Connor used to nibble on the bitter leaves as a teenager hoping they'd make him stronger and braver, bring his voice back.

Today as he passes the care home, he sees a young woman down on the lawn on her hands and knees cutting off dandelion heads with a tiny pair of nail scissors.

'You have to dig them out at the root,' he tells her, 'because if you just chop them off at the stalk, they come back thicker and stronger.'

'I know. I tell them that every time they ask me to go and neaten up the garden but they don't listen. I like them. I think they're cheery and Elsie, one of our ladies, loves them – she can't see properly, thinks they're daffodils. If it was up to me, I'd just let them do their stuff, but they say it makes the place look tatty. It's funny isn't it… how someone decides a weed's a weed?'

'Yeah,' he says. 'My grandma used to say they're just unloved flowers.'

'I like that. That's a good way of putting it.'

There's a precious pocket of wilderness on the outskirts of the bald grey town by the old coal yard near the railway. Before he got the garden centre job, he spent a lot of time there listening and watching. Despite the roar of rail, road and siren, at dusk on a summer's day, the blackbirds out-sung the noise of traffic. There were owls too. Sometimes he saw the urban foxes dragging polystyrene takeaway trays through the gap in the fence to eat their scavenged dinners in the sanctuary of the undergrowth. He was amazed how nature fluttered and flourished in the heart of such a pruned back town. Sometimes he took a can of beer and a bag of chips, made a night of it, lay on his back watching the bats skim gnats from the dark then lit a fire. A few weeks ago, he decided to take a detour on his way home from the station to see what had grown. He was ten yards away from the gap when he saw someone going in. It looked like a woman and he didn't want to scare her, so he held back, waited a few minutes then peered in. Things *had* grown. Tents. There were lots of them, some were small and domed, some were crude ridge tents made of thick green tarpaulin and rope, one or two of them were those flimsy pop-up 'festival tents' patterned with rainbows. The place looked okay there despite the odd bit of rubbish. The rosebay willowherb was towering around the edges and the saplings had grown a good foot. He decided he'd have to find another spot for his lager, chips and bat nights and walked on.

The next time he passes the waste ground, it's early. He smells wood smoke and bacon drifting from behind the fence and he sees her again, this time coming out of the gap, the woman he'd seen the other night. She's dressed in a pale green uniform. He vaguely recognises her and wonders if it's from his morning commute and then he remembers where he's seen her before. It was outside the care home cutting back the dandelions with a pair of nail scissors.

She jumps a little when she sees him, looks as if she's been caught out, as if she's going to snap at him but then she seems to recognise him and smiles.

'Ah, it's the dandelion man! Good morning, Mr Dandelion Man… we were right about the dandelions. They've gone bonkers. Elsie's well chuffed. Have a nice day, Mr Dandelion Man,' she says, waving as she hurries off towards town.

A few days later he sees her again on his way home from work. She's out in the garden of the care home with the nail scissors.

'I know,' she says when she notices him. 'It's a waste of time… they're getting the proper gardener in next week and it'll be death by herbicide for this lovely lot. I needed some air so I'm just *pretending* to garden. It gives me a break from the PPE… have you just moved into a place near the railway station? I'm only asking because I never used to see you there and now I see you all the time?'

And he tells her how he used to go there most weekends. How he loves the fact that you can still find a little bit of wilderness if you look hard enough. He tells her about his 'nights out' there with chips, beer and bats. He tells her about the owls and the hedgehogs and the foxes and the sweet smell of melilot in the early evening after a sunny day.

'Yeah, it's amazing isn't it? All that stuff practically in the middle of town. Thank god for that little wilderness… I'm living there. In a tent, just temporarily, until I can sort things out...I get the impression that you don't poke your nose in, ask questions, so I thought I'd tell you because you're probably wondering why you keep seeing me there... They're still there... the bats. Tally put up some bat boxes for them to roost in winter. They're going mental at the moment. There's loads of them. You should come back and see them. No one will mind. Come on a Friday night and I might join you. I don't do much at the weekend. I usually just go to bed early with a book and a torch. It'll be good to have something to look forward to.'

He goes there at dusk on his next Friday off bearing four cans of lager and two hot parcels of chips. She's waiting for him by the gap when he arrives.

'Welcome back to your little wilderness, Mr Dandelion Man,' she says, ushering him through.

There's no one else about when they get inside though there are a few lights glowing through some of the tents and the murmur of voices.

'It's usually quite quiet at this time of night. Some of the tenters go to sleep early because there's nothing else to do. Some of them go out begging or busking. You'll probably meet Matty soon. He usually brings me cakes from the discount section on Friday nights.'

The bats start coming. Lots of them. They lie on their backs looking up at the fleeting black frenzy of wing and dip.

'It's amazing, isn't it? It's like they're scribbling on the night. God, there's loads of them!' she says.

'It's the best time of the year for them... a dry night as well. There'll be tons of insects in the bushes, midges and moths. It'll be like a banquet.'

Once the sky grows still again, they light a fire and open another can and she tells him about the other people that live in the tents.

'I don't think you make assumptions, do you? Most people do. They assume that if you're homeless you're a junkie... Three months ago, I could never have imagined that I'd be living down here in a tent, but bad things happen, don't they? Sometimes you lose control. See the army tent over there?' She points across the waste ground, 'That's Matty's. He was a nurse… had a nervous breakdown during the pandemic. He's still not right but he's a sound bloke… sometimes he goes off on one… it's frightening but it's more of an inward thing than an outward thing. He wouldn't hurt anyone, and he's kind… and that one there, the blue one… Florin, Maria and little Sofia live there… awful what happened to them. People started getting funny with them when all the Brexit palaver happened. They got threatened. People kept chucking bricks through their window… pushing lit fireworks through their letter box so they got themselves on a waiting list, but it got so bad they had to leave… the red one there, that's Barefoot Sam. He's got problems… mental health problems… he's always talking about the garden of Gethsemane and saying he'll meet me in Jerusalem and coming out with these weird conspiracy theories… and the big, green square one… that's Tally's. He was the first one here… just wanted to drop out… get away from it all… .and then we all turned up and ruined it for him! He makes stuff with scrap wood… garden ornaments, hutches, bird tables, bat boxes, benches, bug hotels, that sort of thing. He does alright with it… people are into 'rustic' at the moment… He knows a lot about nature, well, about everything really… makes tea with weeds… cooks funny stews with flowers and mushrooms and roadkill. We call him Lord Tally because he's sort of the boss here. Get's wound up if we don't respect the place. He went mental when he saw Sam snapping bits off the trees to burn… told him to stick to burning dead things…'

The next time Connor meets Jess at the coal yard, Tally introduces himself and lays down on the grass to join them for the dusk spectacular of bats.

'It's good to see someone appreciating the creatures,' he says 'They're in the world's bad books at the moment… people blaming them for the plague. They've been culling them in some countries. They say, the scientists say, that the virus came from horseshoe bats and they're probably right, but it's not their fault. It's not the bats' fault. We're so arrogant us humans, and we're never to blame, are we?!'

He sits up, sighs, raises his mug to the sky.

'…And the meek shall inherit the earth… Here's to the meek!'

The bat nights with Jess and Tally become a regular thing. He goes to the coal yard on his weekends off until the end of October when Jess finds a bedsit on Balmoral Place. It's tatty and damp and only slightly warmer than living in a tent would be, but there's a 'proper' bed and actual taps with running hot water – one of the many things she missed whilst she was living on the site. They still see each other every other weekend but the bats have gone into hibernation so, instead of going to the old coal yard, they take their chips and lager up to Albert Rocks and watch the beams of car headlights zig-zagging up and down the skinny roads of Norland Steeps and discuss who might live in the tiny cottage right up on the tops above The Hobbit Inn.

It's almost spring when he goes back to the old coal yard to see how everyone's getting on and when he does, he sees a development notice wrapped in plastic and zip-tied to the fence above the gap. The notice states that whole site will be cleared and replaced with a car park. A few years ago, the town suddenly seemed to start breeding new car parks. Every week some new shrubbery, garden square or old shop would be plucked, demolished or filled with concrete and slowly all the town's green bits were buried beneath asphalt and tarmac. It all happened after they flattened the indoor market. He remembered going there to buy odd bits with his granny; loose-leaf tea, plungers, fuse wire and big 50p bags of bruised bananas from the greengrocers. Now there's nowhere in town where you can buy a single loose potato or a cheap bag of random fruit. When the market went, the cherry trees in George's Square went. The buddleia at the top of the Woolshops went. The grass and the picnic benches in The Piece Hall went. They carpeted Westgate Arcade with Astro Turf and installed spikes high up on the stonework where the pigeons used to roost.

When he gets in, he sees about fifteen new tents and polythene structures filling the space. Tally's outside, sawing away at a wooden pallet.

'You've missed a lot. It's all been happening down here... police, drug squad, ambulances, fire engines. You name it, they've been here,' he says 'Loads of new people moved onto the site just after Jess left... a real mixed bag of characters... it's not like it was when Jess was here... lots of people really struggling, scared, running away from someone. One of the police was telling me that cases of domestic violence doubled during the last lockdown. We've got lots of young ones now...things going missing... lots of trouble... but it's hard for them to find anywhere, especially now, at the tail end of "the plague". The hostels are all full. Look,' Tally points at a lidded yellow plastic bucket, 'The council even gave us our own needle disposal unit.'

'Have you thought of moving, pitching up somewhere else?' Connor asks.

'Well, you know as much as I do, it's a pretty bald town... not many green spaces left... and I sort of feel responsible now, for this place and these people, so I've decided to stick it out to the end, which won't be long now. Have you seen the sign?'

Connor nods.

'I've told them I'm not shifting. Matty says he'll do the superglue trick if he has to, and the young lads are getting excited... talking about tying themselves to the trees. I don't think we stand much chance because what the world needs now is more car parks, isn't it? More bloody car parks.'

'Where will everyone go? And what about all the wildlife? What about the bats... they're an endangered species... isn't it against the law to uproot an endangered species?'

'Yeah, I tried that one with them, but the law seems to be particularly bendy these days, especially when it comes to the *developers*… and as I said, our beloved bats aren't exactly the flavour of the decade. Stay for a brew and I'll tell you more about the newcomers.'

Connor agrees and, whilst Tally's making tea, he has a good look at all the trees and shrubs that frame the bright man-made tents and the polystyrene benders. As he's looking at a fluffy catkin bud forming on a branch, a young lad comes limping across the yard towards him.

'Alright mate? You thinking of moving onto the site?' he asks.

'No, I'm just here to see Tally.'

'You couldn't spare a fiver so I can get a taxi to the hospital could you… it's my leg. It's killing me…'

And he rolls up his trouser leg to show him an angry, scabby puce and red patch on his calf.

'Bloody hell. That looks bad.'

Connor gives the lad a fiver, he thanks him and hobbles off towards the gap.

Tally comes out of his tent with two mugs of tea. He nods at the lad.

'So you met Scott then? Did he show you his leg and ask for some money for a taxi?'

'Yes. It looks really bad his leg does.'

'It's an ulceration from injecting. Matty's had a look at it. He told him he'll lose the whole thing if he doesn't get it seen… that money you gave him… well, he won't be spending it on a taxi.'

'As I said. There's a lot of people with serious problems down here. We lost a girl last month… hypothermia. Her name was Hayley. Scott saw her begging outside Tesco just after Christmas. She was all scared and bashed up, so he brought her down here and we sorted out a tent and some bedding for her. Matty used to make her a brew every morning and one day she didn't answer when he called into her tent. He opened it up and found her just lying there. It was awful. It's been such a bad winter. After Hayley died a few of us started skipping, looking for palettes and bits of wood to put on the tent floors so the cold's not coming in through your back. We try to light a big fire every night and the church has started bringing the soup wagon down at the weekend. It's cold and desperate. You know it was my own choice to live here, but for most of the others it's not a choice. It's their only option. It's become a dysfunctional sort of sanctuary and the developers are going to flatten it. They're going to uproot these vulnerable people and this wildlife and those wintering bats.'

As he walks home from the coal yard, he thinks of the way Tally described it as a 'sanctuary' and remembers what Matty had said about the place one of the times he'd joined them for a bat night. He'd told them that when he'd first pitched up there, he was in a mess. He'd never *wanted* to be there, but after a while when summer arrived and the flowers were in bloom and the birds were singing, he started thinking it was where he *needed* to be, somewhere wild and alive after weeks of working on the hospital ward amongst all that dying. He said it had helped him to 'reset' himself. It had become his salvation, his haven. Connor thinks about the way it has become so important, so necessary, for so many people, tries to imagine it gone, flattened, buried alive, tarmacked over, covered with cars, and he begins to ache. The ache runs through the whole of his body. It's the sort of pain he imagines he might feel if he was bound to one of those medieval torture racks. It's as if he's constantly being pulled and stretched and he's sure he can hear his bones cracking. He tries painkillers but they barely take the edge off. His clothes and his shoes nip. Everything seems too tight. When he has a shower, he's shocked to see how long his toenails have become, curling inwards where they've pressed up against the toe caps of his shoes and as the week progresses the pain moves to his skull, hums through his jawbone, pounds behind his eyeballs and he experiences an awful sensation as if his scalp's splitting. He phones in sick. Takes more painkillers washed down with whisky. Knocks himself out.

He sleeps for days dreaming of things being uprooted, people being dug out of the earth, bleeding roots instead of legs... Rentokil men with tanks of weedkiller strapped to their backs hosing the tents and the tenters... everyone raw and red, the smell of burning hair and scorched skin. Jess's hands turn into pairs of nail scissors and she hacks away at the bulldozers, tries to cut them up. He awakes and his body is gummed to the sheets by the thick, resinous sweat of his fever. The flat smells like a ploughed field after rain. His feet itch and when he looks, he sees there are tiny mushrooms growing between his toes and clods of moss beneath his nails. The pain in his skull has dulled a little but his head is heavy and when he touches it he feels that his hair has grown whilst he's been asleep, twisted itself into worry knots, dreadlocks and it hangs in thick ropes down his back.

The phone rings. It's Jess telling him it's all started to kick off at the coal yard. When he puts the phone down, he hears a flapping noise coming from the kitchen. The dead guppy he brought back from work to put in the river a week ago has come back to life.

Since the Veet attack at school all those years back he's managed to get through life with little conflict. He's been verbally abused but never punched, kicked or pushed, so when he gets to the coal yard and sees the bailiffs in their high-vis jackets trashing the tents, he feels both angry and frightened.

Fear triggers the memory of Veet, its awful stench – synthetic roses, bleach and burning hair. The men are merciless, working their way around the yard leaving a trail of tents behind them like burst balloons.

Lots of the tenters are there, some shouting, some crying. Tally's waving a bundle of papers in the air. Matty's pacing up and down with his head in his hands. Barefoot Sam is sitting cross-legged strumming the remaining two strings of his guitar and singing 'All things bright and beautiful, all people great and small.' Jess is trying to reason with the men.

'They've nowhere else to go!' she says. 'You can't move them until you've found somewhere else to put them... some of them are just kids...'

'They're all just junkies, love, they'll find another hole to crawl into.'

'They're all just people! They're *people*.'

Scott's standing outside his tent, pleading with one of the bailiffs.

'Don't wreck my tent, mate, please. Just give me five minutes to get my gear out before you trash it.'

'You've had five weeks pal. Now move!' and he pushes him out of the way. Scott falls, lands on his bad leg and begins to groan.

Connor stands for a few more seconds surveying the sad, raggle-taggle tenters as the burly bailiffs scatter their lives and trample over their homes. Then he starts walking towards them.

'Look lads! It's a Swampy!' a bailiff says 'Come to protect your junkie friends have you? Gonna tie yourself to a tree?' and he's laughing. All the bailiffs are laughing, but there's fear in their eyes and there's fear in their laughter.

For the first time in his life Connor is ready to hurt someone. He's ready to break the bailiffs' noses, punch them to the ground and bully them back but something has happened to him and he can't move his legs. His toes have taken root. He's bound to the earth and things are growing up around him, spreading out from him, snaking, sprouting and whispering – dandelions, rosebay willowherb, foxgloves. A beautiful tide of weeds is flowing from him, flowering, shooting up between the bailiffs and the machines and the tents. Suddenly, down in the old coal yard, it's summer in the middle of spring and the air is alive, crackling with the soft shrapnel of seeds and buds, teeming with moths, butterflies and the mass of bats that have been nudged out of their winter torpor by the tension.

Connor's fingers have become bindweed, inching greenly, trailing way down below his knees. There are big white flowers breaking into bloom from his knuckles. He remembers what his granny had taught him about bindweed – thunder flower, young man's death, choke weed, throttle vine. She called it 'the biggest bully of the weed world'. One of the most invasive, the strongest, so strong it could choke a man if it had the will.

Connor gives it the will.

Origin Story: Ad Hominem

Dr Chris Cocking

GAIA'S CHARACTER, DANDELION MAN, is inspired in part by a real-life environmental activist who was also known as 'Swampy' (real name: Daniel Hooper). Swampy was a reluctant hero of the UK's direct-action environmental protest movement in the 1990s, who first came to prominence at the direct-action protests against the construction of the A30 bypass, in Devon, from Honiton to Exeter during 1996–97.[1] As part of these protests, he occupied tunnels dug under the proposed construction site, at Fairmile and elsewhere, and became known as the 'human mole'. He later gravitated towards similar protests against the second runway at Manchester Airport,[2] and became something of a national media celebrity (especially in the tabloid press).

However, and (perhaps similarly to Gaia's Dandelion Man), Swampy was somewhat of an accidental hero in that, when the eviction started, he had been among a smaller group of people than originally planned down in the tunnels at Fairmile. The local Under Sherriff for Devon (who was responsible for overseeing the eviction of the camps) decided to start the eviction late on a Thursday evening (they usually started by securing a perimeter around the protest camps just before dawn), as he had rightly assumed that most activists would be in the pub at that time, as that was the day that their Giros[3] arrived!

So, by a quirk of fate, Daniel Hooper and a very small number of other, suitably nicknamed activists (such as 'Muppet Dave' and 'Animal') were the only ones down the tunnels during the eviction, and as such were propelled into media fame when they finally emerged above ground after being coaxed (or dragged) out by bailiffs.

While Daniel Hooper may have been the most famous activist to be called Swampy, it is worth highlighting that he wasn't the only (or even the first) environmental activist to be given this nickname. There were others who adopted the name before he became associated with it. When I was at the protests against the A34 Newbury bypass in 1996–7[4] there was another 'Swampy' on the camps, who was mainly known for his raging alcoholism. I remember him sitting round the campfire with a tin of super-strength malt barley beer, vomiting in it, and then trying to pass it round to share with others (we all politely declined!). I also remember people adopting the name spontaneously during protests since Swampy came to fame. So, for instance, during a protest by Brighton & Hove Albion football fans at the final game at the historic Goldstone football ground in Hove in 1997,[5] a dreadlocked protester who scaled the outside gates was cheered on with chants of 'Swampy' by the crowd. Therefore, it seems that the name 'Swampy' became a more generic name to describe people who looked (or smelt) like they had been in a swamp; indeed Gaia's character, who appears to graduate to the new name of Dandelion Man seems to have developed this earlier nickname for similar reasons.

I didn't know Daniel Hooper personally when I was involved in the anti-roads protest movement, and other than once sitting with him in a pub in Bristol with a group of mutual friends, I don't think that I ever met him. However, it seemed to me that when he became well known, he was a rather reluctant spokesperson for the environmental movement, and hardly appeared to enjoy his newfound fame. Like Gaia's character, Daniel seemed to have also been a little uncomfortable with being called Swampy. He was quite shy and perhaps even a little awkward in his media appearances, and was never the most vocal or outspoken of his generation of protesters – some of whom stood out much more at the protests than he did. This was most apparent when he made what was seen by many as quite an embarrassing appearance on the satirical BBC news quiz *Have I Got News for You*[6] in April 1997 at the height of the media hype around him. At one point, he was shown a picture of Neil Hamilton (who at the time was the local Tory MP for Tatton, the constituency that included the Manchester Airport protest camp where Swampy had been based) and he asked who he was – to roars of laughter from the panel and audience. The media spectacle around Swampy reached levels of near self-parody when he posed in a posh Armani suit in a fashion piece for the *Daily Express* (although in fairness to him, this was no doubt done very much tongue in cheek, and I understand that the money he received for doing the photo shoot went towards paying his court fines). This lampooning of direct-action protests continued apace, and in 2000, the comedian Sacha Baron Cohen sent his character Ali G to do a spoof mini-documentary of the eviction of tree protesters in Crystal Palace, London[7]. For someone who could have been up those trees just a few years previously, I found it rather excruciating to watch (at one point, protesters turn on Ali G and berate him for not taking it seriously), even if, privately, I could see the humour in it

Following this wave of Swampy hype, there was something of a backlash from the grassroots environmental movement against the media sensationalisation of protest lifestyles. While some individuals may have privately wished for the kind of media coverage Swampy enjoyed, there was a deeper ideological concern that by focusing on individuals, the media was trivialising the broader environmental issues that Daniel and others were protesting about. This relates to the concept of recuperation that is popular in situationist anarchist theoretical perspectives,[8] which suggests that mainstream culture often successfully co-opts radical movements in a process that diminishes their radical edge, makes mainstream culture itself appear more inclusive and flexible and, of course, monetises the images, iconography and styles of that 'radical' lifestyle. Examples of this range from rumours that Swampy's name had been copyrighted by someone who wanted to write children's stories based on a character that was a human mole, to the appearance at the Victoria and Albert Museum of a display of the clothes worn by 'Fraggle'[9] a member of the Dongas Tribe that protested against the construction of the M3 motorway through Twyford Down in 1992–94.

It could be argued that the media creation of the 'Swampy' character was a result of the anti-roads protests openly professing to having a leaderless structure. With any political movement, the media always needs to 'personalise' it, that is to reduce it to a few personalities (or just one) so that it can both categorise it and undermine it with a*d hominem* attacks. Something similar happened in April 2019 when Extinction Rebellion protests shut down parts of central London. Despite continually asserting its leaderless structure, the media attempted to a impose a 'figurehead' on the protests in the form of actress Emma Thompson, who appeared at one of the sites. By focusing on her, the media could get its definitive sound-bite (an interview with her mid-protest), and then attack and mock her for flying transatlantic specially to attend the event.

Following all the unwanted attention Daniel Hooper received, it is perhaps noteworthy that for a long time afterwards, he personally spurned the limelight and refused to speak to the media.[10] However, over time Hooper has become more confident as a public speaker and in recent years his media appearances have been much more polished, such as when he and his sixteen-year-old son were recently reported to have dug new tunnels against the construction of HS2 in Euston Square, February 2021.[11]

A final point to emphasise is that Swampy and the wider environmental protest movements were not entirely passive targets for the media. Indeed, they were able to exercise some agency in how they were represented in popular discourse, and even make the mainstream media look foolish sometimes. So, for instance, in April 1997 when he was at the Manchester Airport protests, Swampy announced to great media fanfare (and front-page headlines) that he was standing for Parliament in the forthcoming general election, under the slogan 'Dig for Victory' (a propaganda phrase from WW2), only to later announce that it had all been an April Fool's joke, no doubt resulting in the tabloid editors who ran with the story, feeling rather gullible![12] On a broader level, although 1990s environmental protests predated smartphones and live streaming, they pioneered the use of handheld video cameras and proved themselves media savvy in the way they used them. It was common for activists to create their own media outputs instead of just trying to negotiate positive coverage from the mainstream media. For instance, the 'No M11 Link Road' campaign that predated the A30 protests that brought us Swampy produced the critically-acclaimed, low-budget feature documentary, *Life in the Fast Lane.*[13] Such grassroots films often caused more of a stir than their humble budgets might suggest, sometimes even having their screenings banned.This happened, for example, with *On the Verge*,[14] a film about a campaign against a Brighton-based arms factory, EDO MBM Technology Ltd, which saw its premiere at the Duke of York Cinema cancelled when the police put pressure on the council, which in turn stopped the cinema showing it, banning it on a film certification issue (even though the police are not meant to intervene on film certification issues).

This latter documentary was made by the Brighton activist newsletter SchNEWS, which also happened to publish a spoof diary (loosely based on *The Secret Diary of Adrian Mole*), written by yours truly, about an accidental, hedonistic, fictional protester called 'Dumpy' who also falls prey to trivialising media coverage,[15] and who isn't a million miles away from how the Swampy persona was misrepresented in the mainstream media. In short, these movements weren't without their own media awareness.

In small, grassroots ways (such as the comedy event 'Have I Got SchNEWS for You'),[16] Swampy's generation of activists were able to reclaim some of the narratives about their work that had been dictated by the mainstream media. Furthermore, while they may never have developed the superpowers that Gaia's character acquires at the end of her story, the environmental protesters of the 1990s were still able to shift the debate to the extent that topics once confined to the radical environmental fringes (such as climate change, air travel, veganism, etc) are now part of the mainstream debate. So, perhaps Swampy's powers lay in enabling more people to talk about such issues without being written off as a weirdo.

Notes

1. https://www.devonlive.com/news/devon-news/remembering-swampy-emerged-long-tunnel-3738845
2. https://www.manchestereveningnews.co.uk/news/greater-manchester-news/swampy-second-runway-20-years-19815845
3. Giros were a colloquial term for Unemployment benefit cheques in the 1990s.
4. https://commapress.co.uk/books/resist-stories-of-uprising/
5. https://www.brightonandhoveindependent.co.uk/sport/football/last-game-goldstone-ground-remembered-20-years-858001
6. https://www.comedy.co.uk/tv/hignfy/episodes/13/1/
7. https://www.youtube.com/watch?v=3NJeqpZpHUI
8. https://cris.brighton.ac.uk/ws/portalfiles/portal/442082/Fungiculture+final+as+PDF.pdf
9. https://collections.vam.ac.uk/item/O1176552/dress-fraggle/
10. https://www.theguardian.com/uk/2003/jul/09/greenpolitics.transport
11. https://www.bbc.co.uk/news/uk-england-london-56195799
12. https://web.archive.org/web/20040105180108/http://archive.salon.com/june97/media/media970605.html
13. https://www.youtube.com/watch?v=49wKgtOo0qs
14. https://www.youtube.com/watch?v=izP3YAxeMQE
15. https://schnews.org/archive/index-101-150.htm
16. A semi-regular event held in Brighton, and sometimes on tour at festivals and/or protest camps during the mid to late 1990s, this would invite activists and local celebrities (including Mark Chadwick, the lead singer of folk-rock band, the Levellers, and Mark Little who played Jo Mangel in the Aussie soap, *Neighbours*) to take a critical look at how recent events were portrayed in the media.

Mothers Need Mothers

lisa luxx

THE DARK TUNNEL TOWARDS the loading bay was long, damp and full of possibilities. Two firefighters, with skew-whiff beards and oversized uniforms were standing on the platform above the skip, beside the loading doors. Henry marched towards it with baby Ethan strapped to his back. Baby Ethan, whose tiny face was painted with tiny dots of black and white like a static TV screen. The first firefighter gave him a wink, they smiled like two neighbours sharing gossip across the fence. He adjusted his Sainsbury's uniform, straightened his magnetic 'Manager' badge, and walked into the stockroom.

Upstairs, the store deputy, who had taken a brief course on health and safety duties, was holding the staff's attention. 'A necessary systems test is being conducted across all the shops in the Piazza, we need to remain upstairs until we get the all-clear.' Henry was also there, stood watching the time on the till, this buggery had cost him two big shoppers already. What a bloody nightmare being part of this Piazza! Not half as straightforward as when he worked down at the big Sainsbury's on the ring road.

Downstairs, Henry could also be seen clearing out the stockroom – a second Henry, a Henry double, or original – nappies in all sizes, baby formula, fromage frais, and heaps of tins.

Loading the last of them into the white van, parked beside the skip, he went back in and put his coarse hands around the necks of two rosé wines. 'Why not,' bolstered the tall, slender firefighter at the door, adjusting his goatee and continuing, 'G'warn lad! If we're gonna be wrong let's be right about it.'

They pushed the stock further back into the van, to make room, shuffling two large plastic boxes full of costumes to one side just as the fire alarm sounded. Henry's chest tightened, Ethan woke up and began babbling half-words, his face censored by paint. Henry slammed the loading bay door shut, while the two firefighters started the engine. Henry pulled a stamp out of the plastic costume box, and thumped it against the loading bay door: a thin outline of a fairy dancing above a crown, encircled by the words *Not Your Servants*.

The Henry upstairs was instructed by the deputy manager to switch off the fire alarm. By the time Henry got downstairs the amount of expletives coming out of his mouth would have bought his daughter's school uniforms for the next three years in swear jar payments. If he ever paid his child support, that is.

In the front seat of the van, the two firefighters looked out across the moors above Marsden. Somewhere on the climb from Slaithwaite a sudden wave of ripples ran along the van sides and sent the nappies flying, as if the vehicle had just hit a cattle grid. 'You could have waited 'til we parked,' one of them shouted into the back.

One of the firefighters peered through the small opening into the rear. Ethan was laughing giddily, as he always did at this point. Henry was no longer Henry, but Lexi – a young woman of muscular stature. She leant forward, her suddenly baggy Sainsbury's uniform slow to re-thread itself into her usual khakis and rollneck vest, as she wiped the black and white paint off her son's face. Steadying, with her other hand, the boxes of baby supplies they'd be dropping off at food banks after a short debrief on the hills.

As the autumn wind urged beyond itself, they opened the van doors onto a heather-fringed lay-by, and the two firefighters undressed. The one who had been driving passed his uniform to the other, shouting over his shoulder: 'Got a decent stash there, didn't we, Lexi? Shall we take it down to the church on Manchester Road? We haven't topped up their bank in a while.' He proceeded to carefully unpeel his beard, massage his jaw line, and shed gender. 'Sal, pass us that vest,' said the other, who was simultaneously packing away the garments, and using a wet wipe to take the drag make-up off.

The two women took inventory on their boxes of goods, while Lexi looked on, rocking Ethan back into his afternoon nap. Dee was drawing up a tally on her old clipboard, while Sal's homemade crystal necklace swung over the nappy packs as she arranged them in size order. There was enough here for two food bank drops. The wind over the moors picked up and rocked the van gently. They'd need to pull another stunt before the week was out, no one was donating to the drop-off points since the pandemic had made everyone afraid of crowded spaces and nothing said crowded like poverty. Yes, the food banks were getting crowded. Benefit caps will do that.

They made their way back down to town so Sal could get to the school gate in time to pick up her seven-year-old, Aya, who was still attending since Sal was technically a key worker, a carer. Not that any of that mattered any more, since those she was caring for had passed away at the point in the pandemic when everybody thought it was over. Those she was caring for being her two aunts. After they passed, she started inviting Lexi round for 'Aunty René's Caribbean Curry' once a week. 'Our ancestors live in our kitchen if we cook right,' Sal would say, stirring the pot, while closely inspecting the wire twist in the latest crystal wearable she was designing – a small business she'd started and named 'Aunties' Energy' in their memory. Once Aya was sufficiently engrossed by the iPad upstairs, Lexi would shape-shift into Sal and stand beside her new self, twisting wire around crystals or deseeding scotch bonnet peppers in the way only a body that held Aunties' recipe knew how.

★

A drizzle floated down from the grey above, where light was tucked in at the hems of the sky's crumpled bedsheet. Lexi's feet moved automatically around the public gardens, known locally as Pigeon Park, as a middle-aged white man with dreadlocks sang into the neck of his Bacardi Breezer. Ethan babbled and flung himself from left to right in the pram she'd bought off Sumnah, while Lexi kept her eyes somewhere between the haphazard paving slabs and the two figures in parka coats heading towards the Barcardi breezer guy; familiar, locals to the bottom corner, rulers of the park; those treated as pigeons among people. There was more of them loitering around these days. People who wore their masks around their foreheads instead of their mouths, or had them pulled down beneath their chins. It didn't seem like it would be long before there would be more folks to stare at – more pigeons, that is – than there would be folks to stare at them and call them pigeons. Folks who gawp while spending money in the cafés and hairdressers surrounding the square, who gaze into the park during brief interludes of normality between eternal lockdowns.

As she signed in to the WomenCentre for the biweekly 'Mothers Need Mothers' support group, she listened as other single parents and their children came and went; some would spend half the day there looking after theirs and others' kids, while others would go out, one by one, to run errands that would have been impossible with the havoc of babies in tow.

'I reckon it's that Father's 4 Justice group, me. They do stunts like that, don't they?'

'I don't. I reckon it was him. That Henry's a scummy bastard, he's our Jenny's ex. Not a thing right with him, I swear.'

'But wasn't it firemen who did it?'

'Nah, they've got footage of Henry! Mind you, he had a baby strapped to his back, and that doesn't sound like Henry, does it?'

Sumnah was keeping quiet while Tina and Fifi debated yesterday's local news. She gave Lexi a sideways glance and nodded towards the kettle that had just finished boiling as a way of asking.

'No love, I've got to dash, but I'll not be long. Watch Ethan won't you?'

It was a seven-minute bus ride, at this time of day, from the centre of town to Bradley Road. As Lexi strode into the foyer of the *Examiner* building, she caught the eye of the security guard and, in the lift, became him, lanyard and all, using it to pass through the turnstile on Floor 4. Through the break-out area she caught the eye of the assistant editor, Christopher. She headed into the genderless bathrooms and came out as Christopher. Walked, walked, walked in the direction that Christopher knew so well; a body is where memories pulse, waiting to prove themselves. Walked towards Susan McGee, the journalist reporting on the rise in thefts and other stunts being pulled by a guerrilla group they were calling the 'Servants of the Fairy Queen'. He told her, in no uncertain terms, that from now on they were to ascribe all these stunts to Fathers 4 Justice following a tip-off he'd just received by phone. Susan's chest swelled with importance. 'Aye, aye,' she said, saluting him like a captain, then refreshed her inbox, and opened her InDesign document to make the edits. From scumbags to heroes, everyone loves a father fighting for his rights. Christopher, or rather Lexi, chain-linked her way back out of the building swinging like some shape-shifting Tarzan on the vines of eye contact.

Back at the centre, Sumnah was in full flow. 'My blasted tax credits got removed after I gave birth to Sameena. It's not as if I don't work either, I work every waking hour of every blasted day but because I've had my third child –'

'You're scamming off the system, that's what they call it. Three children and you must be a baghead.'

'Well, exactly. I'm an underpaid youth worker, baking cakes all night for the teahouse to try and make ends meet. But absolutely, according to *The Mail* I'm...' Sumnah fiddled with the cold tea bag in her cup, 'an unfit woman.'

Lexi put a loose bobble around her curls and sat down. Dee passed the pack of digestives followed by Ethan, before Lexi cut in: 'It isn't because of your third kid that you're an unfit mother, it's because you're not middle class.'

The middle class was, however, falling. Thanks to the glorious recession that was submerging everyone under the now seemingly endless Tory rule, and they couldn't even protest it, since their rights to protest had been scuppered last spring. Anger, instead, gathered at the threshold of churches, on the narrow pavement in front of the Fartown Mosque, in the waiting room of the Grange Group doctor's office, between cars down on the retail park, in front of the sprawling graffiti around where the Lawrence Batley Theatre used to be, and in the overflowing cemetery whose rosemary bushes could no longer be pruned back; memories invading empty space, ghosts everywhere, a swarm of grief following every lone body who had read too much. Silence was impossible, if you pushed the noise underground it would only rise up again deformed and barely recognisable. But rise it would.

Lexi combed through Ethan's hair, using her fingers to detangle his curls, massaging his scalp as she did so. Sumnah, Sal, Fifi and the group of mothers were divvying up tasks between them; which days each of them was available to cook double so they could relieve others of the daily task of survival, the daily labour of unpaid care work. They tried to partner up according to neighbourhood, so they could drop off Tupperware boxes of evening meals to each other. Rosie, one of the new young mums who had joined, said she didn't have a pan big enough to be cooking doubles. Resistance begins with agency, Lexi welcomed it, even if eyes were rolled – she welcomed that too. As they began to discuss shared entertainment days, and who had access to cars, Lexi heard a commotion in the office beside their activities room. She had a keen ear, and over the sound of the others squabbling about how best to support each other, over the raucous cacophony of children playing in the pen with plastic bricks, plastic animals, plastic microwaves, plastic dolls with plastic 'mummmmmmmyyyyy' screams, she could hear something. There was a woman in the next room sobbing.

As they were signing out for the day, Lexi poked her head round the door to the office. None of the staff were facing their screens. Instead they were huddled in the centre of the room, voices flattened by the thickness of the air. She could guess what had happened. It was only a matter of time. Her teeth clenched and her stomach tensed. She ducked back behind the door, so as not be seen, or caught – but most importantly so as not to have her assumption confirmed.

*

Ethan jolted into action after bath time. Smelling of bubble gum flavoured bubble bath, and waving his bum around, he ran from room to room throwing a sticky alien at every wall until it lost its stickiness and he burst into his usual dramatics. Typical, he had been placid all day in the presence of others but as soon as she had him alone he went haywire. It was through the 'Mothers Need Mothers' group that she had learnt it was normal to lose your cool and scream and beg 'Why do you hate me!?' at your child, and then become flushed with shame, a shame that for months sends a chill through you like rigor mortis. It was through the group that Lexi had found a way out of that pattern, had stopped taking it personally.

He slept around 2.30am. His tan, resting face and wet mouth looked so soft, as Lexi whispered half sentences, delirious from exhaustion. The sum of each sentence's parts seemed to be: 'I will never leave you.'

She pushed the safety net more tightly against the side of the bed, and quietly, as her eyes adjusted to the dark, rummaged through the draw under their bed for two flimsy photo albums. The fairy lights draped around the dresser dimly illuminated the photographs but it was enough. She found who she was looking for. Who she was always looking for. Not her mother, never her mother. No. She barely dared think about the mother-who-couldn't. This was the woman who had raised Lexi from the age of two until eleven. The first woman she ever morphed into.

The same day Jamie Harris, with his blonde highlights and straightened emo hair, said 'No wonder your parents didn't want you, you look like a mangled bird!', she had skipped maths and sat in the top fields willing herself to run away. By the time she returned to school her foster mother was looking exhausted in the principal's office. She would have been summoned in as 'legal guardian'. *Why can't you just pretend to be my mum!* she thought, staring through the glass, it was when her never-mother looked back that she felt for the first time the black hole opening up in the centre of her body. An intense suction, followed by a tingling rush of release as every cell in turn switched over. Lexi was, in less than a second, not Lexi any more.

She ran through the corridor towards the art department's always-empty toilet stalls, and stopped in front of the mirror. Panting, and hovering a shaking hand over the beads around her new old neck. This is how she disappeared twice in one day, once to hide herself, a second time to hide who she had accidentally become. This was the straw that broke the camel's back.

She was sentenced to a Pupil Referral Unit for falling below mainstream school standards, because 'mainstream school standards' were only invented for children in secure homes. As a wayward teenager, she would more and more often look strangers in the eye and wonder if they were family, if she could will them into being family. That was how the gift grew: shape-shifting into strangers, mirroring folk to convince herself she was exactly like them, that she belonged to someone, to something other than the emptiness.

Her foster mother couldn't accept housing a child in a PRU. Nobody knew her secret gift, all they saw was her obvious failing as a student. It was a Thursday, her final day in that house, in that family, before the social services lady with her stupid mint green car turned up in the driveway. She was rushed out and passed on to foster home after foster home after foster home through her next seven years until she had to find her own feet at eighteen. Each home only strengthened her gift. Each home was a current carrying her further away from her source, from any hope of ever knowing her real mother. All she was ever told was, 'Your mother couldn't cope so she gave you up.' Her birth mother was poor; her birth mother had lived with her in a mother-and-baby shelter; her birth mother was struggling with postpartum depression; her birth mother lost her baby because the system does not support poor single mothers. In truth, she was Lexi's greatest fear, standing at her elbow every time she breastfed Ethan, an absence so vast and wide it threatened to seep into any crack that formed between Lexi and her son, to seep in, to surge and rush and thunder as a river becomes an ocean, tearing them apart.

She slept a shallow sleep, with Ethan on one side of her and the photo album on the other, the fairy lights changing patterns throughout the hours of the night.

*

It had been ten months since Lexi had first trooped towards WomenCentre, down under Pigeon Park and next to the gun shop, where Sal had been taking Ethan and her own girl, Aya, while she attended meetings with a solicitor in the futile attempt to get child support from Ethan's father. Passing Maccie D's, Lexi couldn't think of a single thing heavier than the weight of nothing, the weight of her hands hanging empty as she walked towards her baby boy. Again. Again. Again.

A lot had changed since then, since she found this community. Mostly since she let the closest girls of her clique in on her gift some months after joining the group. That's how a week after hearing the commotion in the WomenCentre office, she was standing by the gun shop, watching all the children enter the side door, their small soft hands ready to hold anything. She knew now, more than she'd been ready to admit before, that the more women she let in – at this critical stage – the more women the gift could serve. It was time to amp up, to match the government's pace of destruction. She looked to the big sash window of the activities room, eyes roaming over the glass. 'Okay kid, are you ready? This is about to be brutal,' she said to Ethan, smiling at the top of his head, grateful to have him absorbing her running commentary all day.

'You are a child who we tried to love, Alexita! But you are not my child. I wish I could give you more but, little girl, I am giving you enough! Aren't you grateful?' Her foster mother's words rang in her ears. She shook her head, pulled Ethan's sleeves down around his chubby wrists, and buzzed the bell.

First the yelling was indistinguishable, the rising waves of women in outrage, mimicked by the storms brewing in their children's mouths. She signed her name on the clipboard at the entrance and let herself into the furnace. Fifi was microwaving a bottle of milk. She waited for the ping before turning to Lexi, 'They're closing the centre. For good.'

Every five years the centre had to bid for funding, and since the spending cuts after the pandemic, this year, for the first time in 28 years, the bid had been rejected in favour of XB17, a private firm, run by Tory entrepreneur Ron O'Neill, offering a cheaper alternative – in other words, paying obscenely lower wages for staff and fewer resources. Though she knew this was happening – she had felt it pooling in the heaviness of last week's air – a cold chill slipped and tripped across her arm hairs. Less well-versed women's mental health services meant higher numbers of women struggling, which meant more women driven into poverty, which meant more single mothers losing their babies to rich women. Which is essentially what the foster system was set up to support. The holes in the net beneath her feet widened. She closed her eyes and felt the suction, the black hole, and then the release. A chorus of gasps.

*

In the corridor outside the Town Hall green room, Sal, Dee, Sumnah and the rest of the sisterhood stood waiting, dressed in suits, and dragged up as corporate boys with sharp, contoured jaw lines and smatterings of facial hair. Each a bandit mask, like some knock-off Fathers 4 Justice. Heroes. On the other side of the door, Christopher, the assistant editor, was calmly adjusting his tie clip, assuring the man in front of him they had invited all the press, 'and yes, the council is in attendance too.' His knobbly fingers smoothed across his comb-over. The sisterhood burst in.

'Alarm!' bellowed Ron O'Neill, as if his own voice were a red button, as he dashed towards the square of breakable glass in the corner, but Sumnah rugby-tackled him to the ground. Dee wrapped cloth around his mouth. Sal, her goatee this time impeccable, was tying a sling around Christopher, into which a still-sleeping baby Ethan was lifted, from a pram in the corridor. His face painted like TV static, black and white.

Dee struggled to hold Ron's writhing head steady in her palms, lifting it towards Christopher who gazed deep into his eyes. The business man whimpered as the body in front of him started to transform into his mirror image.

'"Mental health services are a common land,"' the baby-carrying Ron began, '"and should be treated as such. That is why I have chosen to donate this generous sum towards women's mental health services in the local area. May they prosper in this time of need, and may our organisation XB17 forever be your allies" – what do you think? Doesn't sound like you does it? But it is. Look. Look at yourself.' The old Ron writhed, eyes wide and unblinking before his whimpering began, mouth gnawing at the cloth like a deer chewing cud. 'Look at me, Ron. You wanted to make your mark on Huddersfield, didn't you? Stepped into the wrong town, we don't buckle that like here, Ron.'

Ron, with baby Ethan strapped to his back, stood up straight. Ethan giggled and shouted incomprehensible words.

The sum of their parts seemed to say: we are not leaving. Sumnah thumped a stamp against the back of the door: a fairy over a crown, encircled by the words *Not your servants.* Then she opened the door for Ron, who, with Ethan on his back, stepped into the XB17 press conference to make his speech.

SERVANTS OF THE QUEEN OF THE FAIRIES, 1450

Origin Story: A Rebuke at Penshurst

Carl Griffin

University of Sussex

In October 1450, a group of some 130 men from the Weald of Kent and Sussex raided Redleaf deer park at Penshurst, Kent. Little about this now obscure event suggested an ordinary act of poaching. Beyond the sheer size of the gathering and the fact that this was evidently a highly-organised inter-county collaboration, several other facts are germane. Those assembled broke into the park and 'chased, killed and took away' ten bucks, twelve sores (a four-year-old fallow buck) and 60 does, making this an extraordinary act of sportsmanship and slaughter.[1] In the context of the mid-fifteenth century, stealing a solitary deer from a deer park or a Royal Forest was to risk execution, indeed it was not until 1823 that to engage in deer-stealing was no longer a capital offence.[2] Stealing so large a number of deer was so bold that it was self-evidently an act of rural rebellion, a deeply political act. While all deer parks belonged to the nobility, bishops, or the Crown – such parks at their medieval peak covering some 2 per cent of the landmass of England and Wales[3] – this extraordinary raid targeted the property of one of the most powerful and popularly despised individuals of the time, Humphrey, the Duke of Buckingham.

Some context. Over one hundred years of near perpetual war with France had culminated in the recent loss of Normandy, this followed by repeated naval attacks by the French and the men of Normandy on settlements along the coasts of Kent and Sussex. English soldiers drafted to the area to repel these attacks were poorly paid and equipped and took to raiding local towns to support and provision themselves. This – coupled with high levels of taxation, corruption in local and national government, the belief that King Henry VI was surrounded by treasonable advisers, and that the King was going to seek retribution against Kent by turning it into a Royal Forest believing the Kentish Commoners were responsible for the death of the King's widely-loathed, sometime close confidant, the Duke of Suffolk whose body had washed up on the shore at Dover – provided the spur for action. When the king did not offer them redress, from early May under the leadership of Jack Cade, men started to gather together at Calehill Heath between Ashford and Lenham, Kent, and began moving towards London, with Cade also sending emissaries to the nearby counties calling on their support. By early June an estimated 5,000 men – mainly peasants but joined by shopkeepers, artisans, several returning soldiers and sailors, and even some landowners – had assembled at Blackheath on the Kentish edge of London. A detachment sent out by the King to persuade the rebels to relent was drawn into a losing skirmish at Sevenoaks, thereafter Cade and his men marched into Southwark and then, on 3 July, into the City. Their stay was short-lived. Cade set up a tribunal to 'prosecute' those believed to be engaged in corruption, several of whom were hanged by the rebels, but the population of London tired of the rebels' debauchery and looting and on 8 July engaged Cade's men in a battle on London Bridge. Routed, Cade was persuaded by the Lord Chancellor to call off his rebellion with the promise of pardons for himself and his rebels. Despite Henry granting the pardons, these were soon revoked, and Cade was hunted down in Sussex and died from wounds sustained in a skirmish. Further, the Duke of Buckingham was charged by Henry with seeking out Cade's men and bringing them to trial, thus the Duke not only acted as the King's defacto bodyguard

– having also been present at the failed Blackheath assembly – but was also the central figure in the repression of the rebellion.[4]

The raid on Buckingham's deer, then, took on a far deeper symbolism and politics. First, given the belief that the King intended to turn Kent into a royal hunting forest, the attack on a deer park and the wholesale slaughter of the deer therein was laced with a potent irony. Second, as the deer-stealers indictment put it, they were 'arrayed for war'. Beyond the normal deer-hunting weapons of bows and arrows, they were supposedly armed with jacks and lances and dressed in saledes [salets], brygandes [brigandines], breastplates, hauberks, cuirasses'.[5] Notwithstanding the manifold dangers of the act of deer-stealing – with keepers ready to wound and maim to protect their cervid charges – to be so dressed and equipped was little to do with bodily-protection and everything to do with giving the impression of armed revolt, of a force undiminished, of a popular self-belief and fervour that was impossible to extinguish. As Roger Manning put it, poaching was a 'symbolic substitute for war', many of the rites of hunters derived from traditional land warfare.[6] The Penshurst raid had followed a second Kent-centric revolt, this led by Cade rebel and Faversham blacksmith, William Parmynter. While short-lived, his rising starting on 31 August extended to the Penshurst area.[7] Third, to attack Buckingham's estate was to strike as close as possible to the King's rule, it not only being an act of retribution for Buckingham's role in suppressing Cade's Rebellion but an evident critique of Henry's governance. It is perhaps also germane that, as Martyn Ellis put it, Penshurst 'was significant for Cade's Rebellion' not just because of Buckingham's involvement in the parish (including as Lord of the Manor) but also because a large number (23) of Penshurst parishioners came forward to seek pardons after the Lord Chancellor's promise. Further, the environs of Penshurst were also central to subsequent localised risings in the early 1450s.[8] We also know that mass acts of highly-organised deer-stealing were occasionally resorted to during periods of rebellion and were a notable feature of Kett's Rebellion one hundred years later.[9]

The Penshurst raid was no open act of revolt though; it was a war-like act rather than an act of war, something confined, discrete whatever the broader contexts. Indeed, the raid drew not just on the rites of warfare but also on established customary rituals that informed many acts and practices of resistance. The men, so it was reported, not only had long beards but had their faces painted with charcoal, being both a deliberate disguise tactic but also a mark of the carnivalesque, of the world being turned upside-down. It was also a way in which the individual could be subsumed into the collective, an allusion of being-as-one, of community unity. If these were traditions that carried on into the early decades of the nineteenth century, more unusual was the fact that the men claimed on being confronted that they were 'servants of the queen of the fairies'. What does this mean? At once, there is a simple point at play here: by deferring to someone else ('servants') they were denying that they were the instigators. But in the context of the time why not say that they were servants of the Captain of Kent, or even of Cade himself? Kaitlyn Culliton has recently argued that consorting with fairies was not something explicitly forbidden in English statute law, although harmful enchantments to people or livestock was.[10] The allusion to the Queen of the Fairies might be read therefore as assertion of their being enchanted, an attempt to deny their agency: we cannot be guilty for we were under a spell. Yet given the sheer bravado of every other aspect of the raid this seems unlikely to be the sole reason for their claim. We know that many aspects of late medieval and early modern English culture were obsessed with fairies, and certainly many individuals professed to believe in them. The works of Chaucer and Shakespeare drew on a rich vein of folkloric belief and not only contain many references to fairies and fairy-enchantment but also key fairy characters, most famously the fairy Puck and Titania the Queen of the Fairies in Shakespeare's *Midsummer Night's Dream*. To allude to fairies was also to explain mischief and misrule given that fairies were thought to be harmless but mischievous.[11]

It is also possible that the men *were* referring to Cade. Notwithstanding that on his death his severed head was placed on a pike on the Tower of London and the rest of his quartered body dispatched to parts of Kent most strongly associated with the rebellion, rumours abounded that he was still alive. Cade was also rumoured to dabble in the dark arts.[12] It is quite possible, then, that the Fairy Queen was also a reference to Cade, whether still alive, bodily scattered, or as a spirit at large. Whatever the complex symbolism at play, we do well to remember that protesters – for this is what the men at Penshurst were engaged in – drew on the cultural codes and forms that were familiar to them in informing the modes of their protests. Indeed, as scholars of popular protest, from the medieval to the modern, have shown, customary and folkloric rituals provided a ready toolbox of signs, symbols, and, critically, rules as to how to engage in misrule. And given that such rituals not only had a serious side in challenging authority and in asserting plebeian community but were also playful and fun, it is important to recognise the playfulness and dark humour of those gathered at Penshurst.

What of the deer? The number of deer slaughtered at Buckingham's park is staggering by the standards of any age. This was an act of systematic and bloodied slaughter. But this was no act of animal maiming in which the body of the maimed animal is left behind to bloodily attest the protest.[13] The deer were hunted as protest and consumed as protest. Indeed, it is highly unlikely, as Jean Birrell has noted of medieval deer-stealing, that the slaughtered deer were sold for profit, besides the sheer number of carcasses that would need to be disposed of would not only illicit suspicion but also likely draw attention. Instead, the men would in all probability have butchered and consumed the venison themselves, the feast a further war-like ritual common to many medieval and early modern poaching affrays.[14] Thus whatever the wider complexity of the case, the men, as their indictment at the King's Bench attests, were arraigned against 'the statute of parks and fish-ponds lately issued' not for treasonous rebellion.[15]

The Penshurst raid is a world away from the romanticised image of the loveable poacher that took root in the popular mind through ruralist writings in the early twentieth century. As Stephen Ridgwell has recently shown, in the final decades of the nineteenth century and into the early decades of the twentieth century there was a representational shift from the poacher being a marginal figure – someone engaged in trespass and criminal acts, potentially violent and certainly shady – to someone firmly embedded in the popular imagination as a quintessential rural figure, not written as a criminal but as roguish, as someone who did no harm but got by on their wits and with a snare, a plucky and romantic figure.[16] Such representations, typified by H. E. Bates 1935 classic *The Poacher*, acted not only to depoliticise poaching (the 'one for the pot' nature of the trope denying the element of class conflict that poaching always entailed) and denuded poaching of all complexity. Thus, if by the later decades of the nineteenth century, poaching no longer assumed *precisely* the same frames as the Penshurst affray – with deer-stealing now something rare as English rural landscapes were tended to support fox – rather than deer-hunting – the actions of highly-organised and well-armed urban gangs systematically pillaging the game reserves of nearby estates were not so very different in terms of scope.[17] We even see the practices of ritual disguise adopted in 1450 central to the *modus operandi* of the so-called 'Blacks', a group resident in and around the forests of the Hampshire-Surrey-Berkshire borders who challenged Whig attempts in the early 1720s to both revive forest law and exploit forest resources to secure political favour. The name 'Blacks' being a reference to their blacking their faces in disguise on their raids on the Crown forests and deer parks of the area. 'Their protests – and nickname – even gave rise to one of the most notorious pieces of criminal legislation ever passed in England: the 'Black Act' of 1723 making more practices punishable by death – including going about in disguise – than the rest of the statute combined and earning the sobriquet of the 'Bloody Code'.[18]

Notes

1. R Virgoe, 'Some Ancient Indictments in King's Bench Referring to Kent, 1450–52,' *Kent Archaeological Society Record Publications*, vol. 18 (1964), pp.254–5.
2. Manning, Roger. *Hunters and Poachers: A Social and Cultural History of Unlawful Hunting in England, 1485–1640* (Clarendon Press, 1993).
3. Rackham, Oliver. *The Illustrated History of the Countryside* (Weidenfeld and Nicolson, 2003), p.63.
4. Harvey, Ian (1991). *Jack Cade's Rebellion of 1450* (Clarendon Press, 1991); Ingram, Mike. 'The dark side of Blackheath.' Medieval Warfare 3, 1 (2013): 41-6; Vallance, Edward. *A Radical History of Britain: Visionaries, Rebels and Revolutionaries: The Men and Women Who Fought For Our Freedoms* (Hachette, 2013), ch.3.
5. Virgoe, 'Some Ancient Indictments', p.255.
6. Manning, *Hunters and Poachers*, ch.2.
7. Vallence, *A Radical History*, ch.3
8. Martyn Ellis, 'Was Sir Thomas Wyatt able to draw on a culture of rebellion in Kent in 1554?', *Archaeologia Cantiana*, 129 (2009): 90.
9. Wood, Andy. *Riot, Rebellion and Popular Politics in Early Modern England* (Palgrave, 2001), p.62.
10. Culliton, Kaitlyn. 'Fairies in Early Modern English Drama: Fictionality and Theatrical Landscapes, 1575–1615' (unpublished PhD thesis, Trinity College Dublin, 2019), p.6.
11. Lamb, Mary Ellen. 'Taken by the Fairies: Fairy Practices and the Production of Popular Culture in *A Midsummer Night's Dream*,' *Shakespeare Quarterly* 51, 3 (2000): 277–311. Shakespeare also dramatised Cade's Rebellion in *Henry VI* pt. II.
12. Harvey, *Jack Cade's Rebellion*, for example see pp. 143, 164, 170.
13. Griffin, Carl. '"Some inhuman wretch": Animal Maiming and the Ambivalent Relationship between Rural Workers and Animals,' *Rural History* 25, 2 (2014): 133–60.
14. Birrell, Jean. 'Peasant deer poachers in the medieval forest,' in Richard Britnell and John Hatcher (eds), *Progress and Problems in*

Medieval England: Essays in Honour of Edward Miller (Cambridge University Press, 1996), pp.68–88.

15. Virgoe, 'Some Ancient Indictments', p.255.

16. Ridgwell, Stephen. 'Poaching and its representation in Edwardian England, c. 1901–14,' *Rural History* 31, 1 (2020): 35–51.

17. Archer, John. 'Poaching gangs and violence: the urban-rural divide in nineteenth-century Lancashire,' *British Journal of Criminology* 39, 1 (1999): 25–38

18. Thompson, Edward Palmer. *Whigs and Hunters: The Origin of the Black Act* (Allen Lane, 1975); King, Peter, and Richard Ward. 'Rethinking the bloody code in eighteenth-century Britain: capital punishment at the centre and on the periphery,' *Past and Present* 228, 1 (2015): 159–205.

For the Ache of It

Avaes Mohammad

Rushed by an ebullient throng through a waste water passage, pushed and pulled to make it over a high wall only to fall onto brambles the other side, he stands wet, grazed and exhausted looking out at a wasteland nirvana. 'Welcome to Revolution HQ! Your home now. Come on!'

Sprawling over the roof of this disused factory, a defiant overgrowth of wild verdure: a dense entanglement of brambles, bushes, weeds. This is what he'd heard about through secret whispers and anxious utterances, the promised land occupied on the edge of the city. As the returning throng of generals rush past on all sides, a wave of blue and black, he stands for a moment and just breathes, his innermost thoughts giving way to lost scents of moss, mud, bark. From this height, the distant neon of the city seemed just a flicker, dimmed by the slice of sun breaking over the horizon.

'Nearly lost you there!' His hand clamped firmly by the General of Realisation, whose eyes are once again as wide as they were a few hours ago when he and his bike were brought down by this general's club. Now leading him through the moving crowd, he guides him to a patch of wet mud on the side.

'Prostrate yourself on the damp soil and press in to smear your face. This will show everyone intention. Intention, The General always says, is everything.'

Before he's fully upright again with marked forehead, his arm is gripped once more by the wide-eyed one, and he's pulled in between other bushes, emerging at an ash pit where others dressed in the same blue and black frock kneel to re-blacken their eyes.

'Move aside, move aside my generals, this one's new. Christopher! Fresh from the night!'

The General of Connection lifts his head from the pit, grey-black ash smeared all over it as he looks up at the newest recruit. 'We're all new! Constantly renewed!'

Other generals embrace him, taking his hand, smiling, reflecting his exuberance right back at him.

The General of Nurture, wild red hair with crystal blue eyes like jewels stretching the skin they're set into, pushes between them all. 'Stick this on, young man, quick! You'll have been tracked already, watched all the way out of the city!'

An oversized floral dress, blue with black print, hand-stitched, hand-pressed, cut from the same loom as everyone else's is thrust at him towards his proud chest. The young man raises his arms to the sky as the dress pours over him.

'Now kneel for your eyes!'

It was only a few hours ago this entire legion of generals had descended upon the city as a plague-like punishment. Storming down upon every symbol of the machine with their individually fashioned clubs, they unleashed elemental rage upon vending machines, street cameras, driverless taxis, automated food dispensers, and that latest step towards complete dehumanisation: police autobots. Zealously smashing a click-and-collect point, relishing each dent, each hard-won breakage, each bead of sweat, the General of Realisation with mud-dried forehead broke suddenly into uncontrolled laughter. Recoiling whilst forced to hold onto his sides, his hysterics brought him to the ground, to lay on his back. Staring through the electric hue reflected in the sky, he howled. Eventually staggering back to his feet, he stumbled out into the road, intoxicated by his own sense of invincibility, swinging his club like a madman in the face of an oncoming delivery rider. Slowing to attempt a u-turn, the rider was brought off the bike with a well-aimed throw of the club into its wheels. The rider lay on the floor with fear widening his eyes as the young general standing over him bent in closer, swinging his arm forward in a way that made the rider flinch.

'Relax, man. I just want to free you from subjugation to the system, bro!' he said with unsettling ease. 'What's your name, man?'

'Christopher.'

'I'm the General of Realisation and I'm here to free you!'

Snatching the driver's monitoring device from his arm, he threw it to the side of the road. Teeth beaming whilst walking towards it, he raised his club high, before smashing it, savagely.

'Oi! Stop! What you doing, man? I said stop!' Christopher grabbed him by the arm, forcing him to look him in his eyes, 'Are you mad? That's my work, man!'

'Relax, bro. You're more than a machine. You're the wind! You just don't know it yet.'

'I can't work without it! Do you know how much that's gonna cost me? Have you got any idea what you've done?'

'Yeah. I've liberated you!'

The mission succeeded. They broke into the outskirts of the city and made their presence known. Some generals fell, true, but for the cause. They fell at the behest of The General and how fortunate they were to do so. Just as suddenly as they'd stormed the city, they also vanished out of it, under the cover of darkness, across the stretch of wasteland, back to their overgrown nirvana. Though they'd lost comrades to police and police autobots, they'd also gained one. Gaunt young Christopher, reluctantly following a group whose collective exuberance, to him, teetered on the crazed.

'Quick, Chris, quicker! If we get to the front we might see *him*... The General.'

'I thought *you* were the general.'

'Nah mate! I'm just a general. He's *The* General. Run, man!'

'Can you at least tell me where you're taking me?'

'You said yourself you won't be able to work for the delivery company any more? So we're giving you an alternative.'

Now Christopher stands up from the ashen pit with kohl-laced eyes, The General of Nurture stepping back to admire her work.

'Beautiful,' she declares. 'It's like you've never been anyone else.'

'Come on,' interjects the General of Realisation. 'The sun's rising!'

The crowd seems mobilised again, moving as one towards the centre of the roof that opens onto ground below, from which grows a great tree rising above and beyond the roof itself. The sun's crisp light cascades like sheets over this mottled earth and as day begins to begin, The General's generals emerge from between bushes, brambles and trees to gather around this opening, excitedly awaiting word from their leader, a blue and black mosaic of moving tiles gliding around each other before settling into a final formation before their General. As The General emerges to take his place, so too does the sun, the silhouette of his hulking form cradled between branches. Reflecting the sea of blue and black beneath him, his own dress swells tightly over muscular limbs. A red headwrap tied around his ample neck and, protruding from his wild black hair, a blue strip of fabric. Ashen eyes set against black hair that swarmed across his face. He stands club in hand, fashioned from the same tree that holds his weight. The crowd below still in their paused inhalation cheer simultaneously with the raising of his club, before settling again upon its lowering.

'Congratulations, my generals!' And the crowd exhales with an almighty roar. 'Congratulations to you who strove this past evening, to you who worked. Who defied your suppression by exercising your will through your own limbs, in order to fashion this world to your own design. You are the change. You are the lever by which the balance will be restored. You are the generals and tonight you have declared war! From here do we reclaim, take back all that was ever ours. No longer are we a standing reserve! We – our land, our trees and animals, our rivers, lakes and seas – we are not resources merely to be exploited, a means to an end! We are not the machine nor slaves to it. We are more. We are life! The wind and all its force. The rain and all its vigour. The sun and all its affection. We are the earth and all its generosity! We are human and tonight we have proven it! The machines, robots, technology have slowly been eeking out our essence from us, bleeding us by a thousand installs, a million updates, until there's nothing left. But we continue to resist this servitude to the machine with all that we have. So raise your clubs, my generals! Raise these creations – fashioned by your own arms – to the sky! This is just the beginning and we won't stop till we have regained life from idleness. When night falls again, before the rage subsides in our veins and the fear wanes over the city, we will fight the darkness of night once more with the purity of all our strength and the sanctity of all our lives! So rest, my generals, for tonight will we be called upon to break through darkness once again.'

A single roar fills the night sky as a sea of clubs points up towards him. Every general collectively pulsating as one single, terrifying wave. By now the General has descended and where he walks a corridor forms as the crowd parts, making way for their leader. Reaching the edge of this sea of followers, each a self-same drop in his ocean, he leaves the crowd behind him screaming in unison, 'Resist! Desist! Destroy!' The cry saturates all space around it and, amidst arms, chests and necks bulging on the verge of outbreak, Christopher stands quite still, his eyes darting between the frenzied expressions on faces around him.

The sun has only just become fully whole and exhaustion finally caught up with the generals as they disperse to find places of rest for the day, readying themselves for the night to come. The General of Realisation ushers Christopher to a secluded spot where they lie under frayed blankets and stained sleeping bags. By the time the noon sun is beating down, most of the generals are lying splayed and spent amongst the undergrowth. But the General of Realisation is up already, scrabbling over to the newest recruit to wake him.

'What now? I'm trying to sleep!'

'Christopher, you won't believe what's just happened! My god, he knows. He knows everything! He took my hand just now, can you believe it, he held it. I felt this warmth flush all over me. He saw everything, man. My mum and dad's fights when I was little. How at eighteen I worked in factories and saved to get my own car, did taxis. How the apps that were supposed to make us the boss, became the boss. Docking points off my ratings if I was late or took a minute-longer route. Cameras to monitor how much I was smiling, talking, fuel intake, time between jobs, emissions per mile, everything... everything monitored! They wanted robots for employees, I complained, and then they got them. Electric cars! But I see now. I see that I'm much, much more. Hunched for hours over a wheel, never knowing fresh air, but I was made to fill my chest, man! I am the wind!'

Christopher leans back as far as he can, as the General of Realisation bellows his account at him.

'It's your turn now. While there's a chance. Come, now. I've arranged it!'

'Come where?'

'To The General!'

Crusted remnants of dried earth still marking his head, ash smeared over his eyes, Christopher is led between the tall brambles around the base of the old factory chimney to a den hollowed beneath the thicket. A gentle fire can be heard crackling nearby, underscoring the sound of birds and the crunch of twigs under shoes.

'I told him I'd bring you. Just go in.'

Christopher shakes his head at the General of Realisation before taking a deep breath and walking towards the entrance of the den from where he can see The General pulling back rogue branches, flattening brambles and clearing space. Christopher coughs and The General turns to face him. Up close he looks much bigger than he did when addressing the crowd, his frame blocking the light from behind him so just a silver glow outlines his contours like a halo. Thick unruly hair kept in place by a band of cloth tied in a knot; beard accentuating his chiselled profile – he has all it took to be quite the fearsome thug. Except for his ash-lined eyes. Though arresting, they reveal a warmth.

'Christopher? Have a seat.' Nervously Christopher sits among the twigs. 'Relax, you're safe here. The general who just brought you has all the zeal of a new convert. No bad thing, the cause needs that energy. And obviously the first thing he did was get you all dressed up.' Christopher is taken aback by the force of laughter that follows. 'You must feel a right wally!'

'I've felt worse, I suppose.'

'Poor you!' he chuckles. 'Look, I'm really sorry your device was smashed, Christopher. He went a little off-piste there. No members of the public are ever supposed to be hurt or directly affected by our actions. But, as you've made it here, I may as well tell you a few things.'

'What things?'

The General closes his eyes for a few moments before suddenly opening them again, his gaze full of red fire. Though Christopher desperately wants to look away, he can't.

'Gosh. It's not been easy, hey? In Albania, your parents wanted you to inherit their farm but you, you were always fiddling with little things, tying sticks together, crafting toy bridges in the garden, while they just wanted you to operate the tractor. They had the pressure of competing with bigger farms after all, needing to become more mechanised, using GM seeds. Faster, bigger yields. They needed all hands on deck. You understood. But even as your toy bridges sat unfinished on the sidelines, the bigger farms still won out all the same and ended up buying yours for half what it was worth. Nobody else was gonna buy it, they told your dad. You watched him cry that night. You were only sixteen and you'd never seen your dad cry before. They both work for the farm that bought them now, as labourers. And you figured none of it was worth anything anyway so you came to Bradford. Your dad said it'd be no better but you didn't trust his opinions any more. It's been three years since you left and you can't go back now, or at least that's how it feels, right? Admit it: you got yourself in a worse situation than the one you just left behind. Employee tracking through monitoring devices was everywhere, but at least employers gave you scheduled breaks. Now, you're gigging on your own, you're an even harsher boss on yourself. You've become the monitoring device! All you think about now is every minute you're not working is a minute you could have made money in. Add to this, the box you're forced to make a home in and you can't help but look at where you came from, and realise it's a choice between the rotten and the rottener.'

'How do you know all this?'

'And you're completely correct. It isn't a choice. Not one that befits any living creature. That's what this so-called technological progress does to us. Reduces our being to abandonment, leaving us only schedules to live by, a life only online, reliant entirely on satellites, fibre-optic signals, screen interfaces and Wi-Fi. Now our buildings compete with each other to blot out our sky, replacing what would naturally have given us a sense of awe, of celestial awareness, with what merely gives us a sense of being logged on, of a digital existence. You are something great, Christopher, some*one* great. There is an ocean coursing through your veins right now, an untameable mighty tide. Your presence can caress and comfort, or bring terror and destruction. You're all of this and much more, Christopher. You were right to act upon that voice inside you when you left your family home and country. You just didn't know what you were leaving for. Finally. You've made it.'

The General stands up and leads him out of the den, to a gathering of his closest generals, the General of Nurture and the General of Connection amongst them.

'Everyone! Our newest, general. The General of Discovery!'

Christopher is whisked around them all, and introduced to his newly kin: the General of the Watch, an older lady whose job it is to keep lookout for on-comers from on high, the General of Vision, an older man who hardly speaks but stares through everyone and everything around him, the General of Discernment, who selects the best branches from which to make clubs. After a full tour of the rooftops, he returns to the group of ordinary generals he slept with the night before. There, the General of Realisation sits down next to him and begins to show him how to fashion his own club from a piece of branch, as others repair old ones around them.

'We've joined just at the right time, you know. For years The General has convened gatherings and developed strategies and training but now, this is the phase of action. And we've just caught the start of it! He's going to speak again tonight before the next attack. At sunset.'

'My generals, I addressed you with the coming of the sun today and speak to you again before its departure because the light is ours. I commend your work through the nightly hours, your courage and commitment. But while we collectively bask in this joyous work-induced ache, it would be remiss of us to ignore the real danger we have now awakened. At this moment, photographs of us are no doubt being circulated and studied, our identities and very soon this lair, our home, will become known to them. This is not the time to rest but instead to take further action. The destruction we wreak is not an act of unfettered barbarism but a symbol, my generals, we leave in our wake, verses that make clear our message. Yesterday, we struck at the products of their enslavement – bots, autocars, devices. But now we must take our message to the core of this menace. And so, my brave generals, our next strike will include their pylons, 5G masts, communication networks and the Virgo Laboratory of Computing and Artificial Intelligence that my elite groups and myself will personally lead. So as the city awakes, they will clearly read the writing on their walls that this fight against subjugation will no longer be a peripheral activity but one that's knocking at their very door. We will resist, we will desist and we will destroy!'

★

'Mum! Mum! Don't sleep, wake up! Mum!'

Late afternoon and amber sunlight spills into the front room through smeared windows, golden, his mum's skin like an Egyptian queen's, haloed.

'What? I'm okay! I'm not sleepin'. Just restin'. God knows I deserve some rest, Son. Finally, at least I can get some rest.'

'I've got you some water, Mum. Here.'

She raises herself from being sprawled across the settee, just enough for a few sips to trickle down her throat. A bottle rolls from under her, falling onto the floor.

'Get up, Mum. Look at what I've got today. Look, you like this don't you? It's monkey! "Hello, Mrs Ludd! How are you today? Isn't everything just swinging?"'

Her eyes close again as the boy works his puppet.

'Mum, come on, wake up. Don't sleep!' He shakes her gently. 'Mum!'

'Huh? What is it? What's wrong, Son?'

'Get up, Mum, come on. I'm making beans on toast, we can share it.'

'I was too good for that factory anyway! I always said what they really wanted were machines! I wasn't born to be a machine, was I, love?'

'No, Mum. You're too pretty.'

★

As the cries rise once again, charging ahead of them all is The General, first to scale down the walls to the city below. His army follows, hitting the ground running as they reach street level, storming across the wasteland and towards the lights in the near distance, glimmering like a flagrant beacon of excess. Reaching the city's perimeters, they are once again met by police-bots racing towards them on caterpillar treads, shining blinding lights into their eyes and, having learnt from just the previous night, immediately discharging a cloud of tear gas onto the oncoming horde. The generals, lead by The General, who are also prepared with neckerchiefs over their faces, some sucking on onions to resist the gas, clubs raised like battle swords, all pour forward, out-screaming the sirens like howling banshees. Just as the two sides – being and bot – near one another, the police-bots fire pellet rounds tearing holes through the coming onslaught. Though some at the front fall impaled, those who carry on, from behind them, descend on the bots with their clubs, staving in their lenses and gun turrets. Amongst them charge the General of Realisation, with Christopher always a few yards behind, and at the helm still their General, injured and limping but far from stopped. Repeatedly they drive through with their primitive weapons, hell-bent on destruction. 'Desist! Destroy! Desist! Destroy! Desist! Destroy!' The thick, riveted metal of the bots saves them from complete destruction, but the number and force of the onslaught succeeds in incapacitating them enough to allow their charge to continue onwards into the city. Electric light illuminates The General's face, highlighting the red in his bloodshot eyes as he charges deeper and deeper with his army behind him.

As they enter the edge of the city, most generals disperse into smaller groups, over-running the streets as before, destroying any enemies they see of sweat and toil. Meanwhile, The General and his elite troops are to break away to conduct targeted strikes of a larger scale. Though still brandishing clubs, their strikes will require a wider arsenal of rope, fabric, axes, bolt cutters, circular saws, petrol and explosives. The General of Nurture is to lead the attack on an electricity pylon, the General of Connection on telecommunication network points, others on 5G masts, power stations. The General himself is to lead his own team onto the Virgo Laboratory of Computing and Artificial Intelligence. Palms clasped and embraces exchanged, the groups set off in their separate directions.

Just as the General of Nurture leaves, the General of Realisation approaches and pleads with her to let him join her twenty-strong team.

'We're under strict instruction, I'm afraid. This is for experienced generals only. You'll be able to join us soon enough, I'm sure, but the streets need you for now.'

His determined pleading shows no sign of weakening and he continues until she is forced to relent.

'…do as I say, though. Nothing else!'

The General of Realisation is so excited to have effectively been promoted into elite ranks he almost forgets about Christopher, who stands back where he has been told to wait. Running back to him, the General of Realisation explains they will meet again in the morning at their rooftop lair and instructs him to stick with another general, the General of Belief, who they've travelled with until now. Christopher gives a hint of a nod as his original recruiter runs off excitedly.

Skirting the edge of the metropolis in the darkness, the General of Nurture and her legion rush upon an electricity pylon, all of them wearing cumbersome wellington boots and thick, rubber gloves. Initially, generals of her team clamber up the mast, the General of Realisation among them, tying a long rope to the pylon before applying circular saws to it, one leg at a time: metal whirring into metal creating a fireworks display of sparks on contact. Elsewhere, 4G and 5G mobile phone masts are being wrapped in fabric by elite troops then doused in petrol before being set alight and wooden phone masts were simply chopped down with axes, wreaking havoc over roads and buildings.

Against this backdrop of focused destruction, The General leads his troops towards the laboratory. High, barbed-wired walls stand between them and the facilities which The General now scales easily using grappling hooks and a ladder, cutting an opening through the barbed-wire at the top of the wall with bolt cutters single-handedly. The troops climb up after him and scale down the other side, crouching to remain in the shadows and hiding behind other low walls. Knowing exactly where they're going, and aware it is only a matter of time before the cameras will detect them, they move fast towards a specific window. The entire platoon smash their clubs in unison through the tinted reinforced glass, setting the alarm off with it. The General is the first to rush through the opening, propelling with him any loose shards that sat in the edges of the frame. Immediately he runs to the door of the main server room. By the time the rest have reached him he has already arranged explosives at the door. The generals all take their positions, hiding behind desks and doorjambs, as The General activates the detonation. Through the cloud of dust that follows they can see the door has come off its hinges, leaving the biometrics entry system in tatters and providing the opening they require. One general shouts that security are on their way, to which The General commands everyone to leave immediately, returning the way they came. He himself remains behind though, ensuring everyone escapes first, whilst breaking through the rest of the door to access the server room. Upon entry he smashes the wall of glass panels with his club to fully expose the server racks. Having expended all his explosives, he drops his club and tears up strips of fabric from the sheets he has brought in his kit bag, before stuffing them between the racks. Reaching into his bag again for a can, he douses them all with petrol. It is at this point two security guards enter the room, brandishing batons.

'Stop exactly where you are and put the can down!'

The General turns to face them, the blue and green LED lights from the servers illuminating his face.

'I said put it down!'

Another guard comes running down the corridor, panting as he speaks: 'Archer's just radioed: the rest of 'em have set part of the grounds alight!' As soon as he delivered this news, he runs back from where he came!

Looking this hulking figure in a dress and headband, up and down, the taller of the two guards demands, 'Who are you?!' The General slowly raises the club in his left hand and steps closer to the guards, the club now pointing straight at them. Involuntarily, they both step back, lowering their own batons.

'I am Ludd!' he roars at them. 'We are generals and tonight, we have worked!'

★

'Get out of my way you pain-in-the-arse, you're always just in my way!' She throws a pan straight at the boy, who swiftly ducks. 'Who d'you think you are, telling me what I can and can't do? I'll have a drink if I bloody well want to, you runt! Move, I'm sick of the sight of you.' A plate this time. 'I look at you and I see your good-for-nothing, lying, thieving, ugly dad! Why don't you just get out of my life? I don't need you!' She attempts to lunge at him but stumbles. 'Get... Out!' Striking her hand out causes her to trip over and sprawl across the kitchen floor.

'Mum! You alright? Don't close your eyes like that? Stand up, come on. Mum! Look at this.' He grunts like a pig and scrunches up his nose. 'What's this Mum? What is it? You like this one?' He grunts again. Then he squawks. 'You remember my emu... Mum?' He mimics the walk which he's perfected, only slightly slower for affect. Chin jutting forwards and backwards, he squawks again, the young boy's anxiety for his mother causing a vein to throb across his forehead. With her cheek still pressed against the cold linoleum, and a musky-sweet smell of decaying leaves sweeping in through the cat-flap, she cracks a smile.

*

'The police are going to be here soon!'

Looking both guards directly in their eyes, a vein throbbing across his forehead, The General retrieves a box of matches from his pocket.

'I'd suggest you put that away,' the taller guard shouts.

'The police will be here now any moment!' the other guard repeats.

'Do you realise what you're doing?'

'Do you?' replies The General, maintaining eye contact. The two guards try to look away but can't. 'Why are you both here?'

'Excuse me?' the taller guard replies.

The General closes his eyelids for a few moments before reopening them in a burning gaze. 'Isn't it bad enough your wife's toilet breaks are timed and monitored by a device designed and made here! Tell me, would that enrage you any more if they hadn't affixed any plastic stars on your shoulders?'

'How do you know about my wife?'

'And you,' The General turns to the other guard, 'you wanted to be in the police, right? How long before the bots that prevent you from getting that job, take this one too? It's not like you've been very efficient tonight, is it?'

While maintaining eye contact, The General strikes the match, and holds it out flickering to the nearest scrap of fabric, which quickly roars into flames. At this moment, he closes his eyes for a second, then charges straight at them, through them, forcing them to fall to the sides as he bursts out of the room, and heads straight for the broken window. With the sound of distant sirens growing louder, the guards get to their feet, watching the wall of flames rage and consume the very nerve centre of the laboratory.

Elsewhere in the city, generals are storming through the streets, destroying everything they see. Graffiti is sprayed across the face of the city in their trademark stencil: a club with the words: 'For the Ache of It!' above it. Vending machines are not only toppled but shattered, click-and-collect points, automated food dispensers, the generals seek them out like locusts, systematically breaking them apart, their muscles relaxing with every strike, fresh air finally filling their innermost parts in complete inhalation. This is their work.

Christopher is running in formation with the General of Belief and others, across the middle of a dual carriageway. Autocars, pre-programmed to slow and stop upon encountering obstructions, pull up in ordered columns, their horns sounding in synchronised, mechanised unison. All who ride in them, able to see the cause of their obstruction, alight and run as the generals raise their clubs and pour onto the bonnets of the cars in front of them. Initially, Christopher holds back, ensuring the passengers have gotten far enough away before he joins in the destruction. Assuming a collision, each autocar, as programmed, shuts down everything except its dashboard cameras. The blue and black-frocked legion swarms over and around the vehicles and surprising himself, Christopher too finds cathartic release in this primal violence. Wing mirrors, windscreens, panels, lights, dashcams, the devastation at their feet serves only to nourish them as they stand on the bonnets and roofs of these deadened autocars, and, with every camera trained on them, raise their clubs to the sky.

'For the Ache of It!'

Suddenly all power in the city is lost. The streetlights all switch off, casting the city into sudden, eerie darkness. The lights of offices, homes, road signs all disappear into the night.

'Quick! Run back!' comes a cry from somewhere, and all the generals run back as a single swarm towards the wasteland and their rooftop lair behind it. Like ants, they hurry in their groups: a central throng forming the body of the retreat, other smaller groups joining the tail or chasing it from a distance. Among them all spread excited speculations that a key pylon must have been brought down! And far ahead, runs a much smaller group of perhaps twenty, maybe less, making its own way back to the rooftop lair.

Hundreds of generals eventually scale the factory walls back up to their hideout, the stronger climbers pushing and pulling the weaker ones until they all reach the plateau of overgrown bushes, ferns, and trees. This return is unlike that of the previous night however. Less charged, the generals walk with slower steps, speak with less exuberance and hold themselves less upright. Exhausted, the generals collapse upon entry, forming beds wherever they find space, tired bodies strewn all across the roof. Upon arriving, Christopher seeks out the General of Realisation as he'd been instructed to. But no one has seen him, nor heard anything about his platoon. Christopher searches the ash pit, the great tree and where they'd slept earlier between the bushes. Approaching The General's own den, Christopher spots the General of Connection making his bed for the night.

'Excuse me. Excuse me, have you seen the General of Realisation? He was with me yesterday at the ash pit.'

'No son,' the older general replies. 'Go and get some sleep.'

'He said he'd meet me back here though,' Christopher insists.

'He's probably knocked out somewhere exhausted. We all are.'

'Wasn't he with you?'

'No, son, he wasn't. Now go on to sleep, young man,' the general adds, growing impatient.

'What were you doing?'

'What do you mean what was I doing?'

'I just want to know. What exactly?'

'I was leading the charge against phone masts. Torched them.' He speaks without flinching.

'What else was done tonight?'

'Look, son, will you just sleep and leave us to do the same!'

'I'm sorry, I need to know. What else?'

'You heard The General's speech, didn't you? Autocars, machines, devices. Masts, telecommunications. Pylons. The AI lab. We did it all,' his eyes and chest widen as he talks.

'Will it work?' Christopher presses.

'What do you mean?' the general replies, affronted.

'Will it...? Whatever it's meant to do, will it do that?'

'What do you think?' the general pushes back.

'I don't know.' Christopher's brows furrow.

'Like The General said: when the city wakes up this morning and they see it all, how will they read it? Eh?'

'I was part of the city just two days ago.'

'So? You tell me then. The machines that enslaved you, suppressed you, now broken! How would you have read it?'

'I'm not sure,' he replies after a significant pause.

'Go to sleep, lad.'

Suddenly the older female who stands lookout at the roof's perimeter, the General of the Watch, starts running towards The General's lair. 'Police! It's a raid! A hundred of them, maybe more. They're on the North wall. Tell The General we need to go!' Immediately the man himself steps out of his den, visibly ready. Whilst some run towards points of the south wall, he, the General of the Watch and other surrounding generals, roused from their sleep, run towards the centre. Being in the vicinity, Christopher runs with them. Opening a trapdoor in the floor, they are led down a rusty spiral staircase deep into the factory below. Christopher races to keep up as they traverse the dark halls and corridors of the abandoned factory, passing through what feels like the hollowed innards of a giant metallic corpse, every step echoing like the beating of a hammer, before eventually breaking open an outer door on the far end allowing their escape into the light. As he runs, Christopher turns momentarily, attempting to see those still on the roof. All he hears are the sounds of screaming and gunshots.

After a night spent scrambling from one ditch to the next, they finally stop when they reach the cover of forest. Here they spend the remainder of the night. Anxious they've been followed, they share lookout duties till dawn, alternating slots for everyone to grab some sleep. With their backs pressed against a riverbank, they wait for the clarity that dawn always brings. When it comes, there is no great speech, no mighty address. Only the relief that the cold night has been survived. The small garrison of about twenty generals lies exhausted. The General himself rises with the sun and whispers to those awake, including Christopher, to go back to sleep, before taking himself off to become acquainted with the terrain.

'What do you think's happened to the others?' Christopher whispers to the General of Nurture. 'What's happened to the guy who recruited me? The General of Realisation? Do you remember, he went with you when we reached the city? Where is he?'

'Everyone's exhausted. You must be too,' she replies slowly.

'I'm not being fobbed off. I'm properly not! What's happened to him?' Christopher is adamant.

'Listen...young man....'

'...Don't young man me! I wanna know!'

'You sure?' After a pause in which he doesn't flinch, she continues. 'The pylon. He wouldn't let go, he just kept on pulling. I told him to let go. To run before it fell. He wanted to make sure it came down he said.'

'He was supposed to be part of your quad, your comrade? And you just left him!'

'The ground had become live. He had lost some of his protective clothing, or perhaps hadn't been wearing it in the first place. There was nothing we could do. We needed to run!'

'But you left him!' Christopher raises his voice. 'As if you've just left your comrades stranded on the roof! That could have been me! It could have been you! You're all...psychos. You could just have easily done it to me, left me like that. You're all psychos like him, the one you all follow like sheep! I'm out of here... I quit.'

★

'You still watching, Mum? Look? It's the emu, Mum, remember?' Mum don't close your eyes.' He kneels at her face. 'I know, Mum. They weren't treating you right. They were already working you to the bone, cutting your sick pay, docking your wages because you were tired all the time. I just started seeing it one day looking at you. I saw how that foreman was making you feel, constantly telling you your work wasn't right. You weren't strong enough for building drones or for operating the machinery. You were getting the riveting wrong. The company just wanted robots. Then they got them. But it's not just him is it? I see your own mum too, working herself to the bone in factories before you, coming home tired each night, defeated, screaming at you to stop dreaming about being a singer and get a proper job to help the family. So she could work less, sell herself less.'

'What you on about, lad? You never met my mum, you idiot, she died before you were born!' his mother retorted.

'But I can see it, Mum, and much more besides. I can see that you're bigger. You're greater than all this. This dirty carpet, the stained walls, these chipped plates. Mum, shall I tell you what I see. I can see the world in you: I can see trees in your hair, a forest. When you breathe, I see all the oceans of the world swelling. When you cry, whole villages are washed away in freak floods. But when you close your eyes, Mum, the sun sets. Don't close your eyes, Mum. Please.'

★

The General of Discernment reaches out to catch him as he attempts to scramble up the grassy bank and another helps to pin him down as he squirms and screams.

'Calm yourself down, lad. Stop this. You want to know what we feel? With more than half of our fellow comrades falling to the police? They were our own brothers and sisters, our kin! How do we feel? We feel how they feel. That we can't stop. Not now, not for their sakes. What you don't understand is that this is so much bigger than any one of us. Even bigger than The General! Those who have fallen and been captured, have done so for you, for us. So yeah, we wanna cry but we're damn well proud of them too, the heart in them. We pray for a heart like theirs. Standing before the police-bots, and not one of them kneeling, or begging, or asking for their old jobs back.'

'I think you'd better go after all,' says the General of Connection. 'You won't be any good to us, feeling the way you do, and we know you're not a threat. If you don't have what it takes to fight with us, you certainly won't have what it takes to fight against us.'

⋆

As the day wears on, the generals can be seen making a fire and collecting materials to make shelters under the trees. Some break off branches they think might serve well as clubs. Evening falls and the pensive company gathers around a tree as they watch their General scale it.

'My generals! All standing here as one! This will be our home, for now. From here we will reclaim all that was forever ours to begin with. We have no choice but to take it back. Just as we stand here now not fearing the night but awaiting it, so we must prepare to meet the darkness that still rages around us. But good news is upon you who have survived this far! You are the knowers. Those who have seen and those who have stood. Those still keen to feel work and the ache of it in your limbs because you recognise that ache. And know it to be life itself...'

Afterword: Ludd's Court

Dr Katrina Navickas
University of Hertfordshire

General Ludd was no one and everyone. He was a character who didn't exist in reality, but his name was everywhere in the textile districts of northern and midland England in 1811 and 1812. Artisan workers were fighting for their working conditions and their livelihoods against the imposition of labour-saving machinery. They sought a leader to unite them; they didn't have one, so they invented him.

Destroying new machinery was not a new phenomenon. The character of 'General Ludd' or 'Ned Ludd' reputedly came from an individual named Ned Ludd from Leicester in 1779, who had destroyed early machinery for knitting stockings. Working-class narratives and ballads kept the character alive until it found a potent use during the machine breaking agitation of 1811–1812. Anonymous letters and posters were a common form of protest in close communities; they were used to threaten transgressors of community norms and morals. By signing the letters with the character of General Ludd, the Luddites could be united virtually if not physically. Ludd could be everywhere and nowhere

The only known contemporary picture of General Ludd is a cartoon, 'The Leader of the Luddites', published in May 1812 by Walker and Knight, two democratic radical printers in Manchester. Apparently 'drawn from life by an Officer', it is striking and still shocking. General Ludd is depicted as a burly man with thick sideburns and neck hair, wearing a blue and pink spotted cotton dress, a contrasting pink and blue spotted scarf around his neck, and a blue ribbon in his hat. His followers are running from a burning cotton mill, and the general points them towards presumably the next target. Yet while the Luddites are jubilant, their leader is dour and maybe wearied. A missing shoe indicates his poverty.

Two men dressed in women's clothes led an attack on a cotton mill in Edgeley, Stockport, Cheshire, on 14 March 1812. The crowd referred to them as 'General Ludd's wives'. This was part of the Luddites' symbolic defence mechanism against the employers and the local magistrates. It was more than a disguise. Like many popular customary traditions drawing from carnival or charivari, wearing a costume was a deliberate subversion of authority and norms. It was a symbol that the crowd were enacting community justice against authorities whom they regarded as transgressing their moral norms. The dress itself was also an obvious manifestation of the product of workers' labour: the light printed cotton cloth that was made up into the empire-line dresses of Regency fashion were at the heart of what was at stake.

Industrialisation was regionally based, and this shaped the three waves of Luddism in England. Trade unions were effectively banned in law under the 1799–1800 Combination Acts, which weren't repealed until 1825, so there were few other options available for collective action. The stocking knitters of Leicestershire and Nottinghamshire were the first to start their machine breaking campaign against the new stocking frames. The first recorded violence against machinery occurred in the village of Arnold, Nottinghamshire, on 11 March 1811, following a peaceful gathering of framework knitters near the Exchange Hall at Nottingham. Several weeks of attacks around Nottingham ensued. Then agitation calmed down until a poor harvest and the failure of public negotiations with employers revived agitation in the autumn of 1811. But other artisans and occupations were involved too: in the close-knit textile villages in all three regions, this was a community effort. Magistrates' spies found it hard to penetrate the silence of those refusing to reveal who was the real General Ludd.

In the West Riding of Yorkshire, woollen manufacturers had introduced gig mills that lifted the cloth and shearing frames that sheared the surface of woollen cloth more quickly and cheaply. The croppers, who undertook shearing by hand in small workshops, saw these new machines as a threat to their skilled employment and the quality of their produce. The first outbreaks near Leeds occurred in January 1812. On 11 April 1812, Rawfolds' mill near Huddersfield was the site of a major attack by hundreds of participants, which the owner repelled by arming his workers with guns. Revenge was sought, and on 28 April, the manufacturer William Horsfall was shot dead in an ambush as he rode back to his home from Huddersfield. The handloom weavers of south-east Lancashire and north-east Cheshire took the hammer against the steam-powered looms introduced to the cotton mills. On 21 April 1812, Burton's cotton mill in Middleton, near Manchester, was assailed by hundreds of Luddites. Several were killed and wounded. A similar set-piece event occurred three days later at Duncough's mill in Westhoughton, near Bolton. A large crowd broke into the mill and set fire to the 200 powerlooms, though there were rumours that the attack was instigated by agent provocateurs employed by the magistrates.

The different communities of Luddites were separated geographically but united under the idea of the mythical leader. The Nottinghamshire stocking knitters corresponded with the West Riding croppers: one letter dated 1 May 1812 seized by one of Joseph Radcliffe's spies involved the correspondence of 'Peter Plush, secretary to General Ludd senior at Nottingham to General Ludd junior, Market, Huddersfield'. The local magistrates and their spies became convinced that a real General Ludd existed, and the key to suppressing the outbreaks lay in catching him. Abraham Kaye, a private in the Bolton militia, reported that he saw 'one called General Ludd, who had a pike in his hand, like a serjeant's halbert; I could not distinguish his face, which was very white, but not the natural colour'. It was a collective delusion: it was easier to believe in a mythical figure than contend with the scale of the disturbances and their root causes in economic distress and the magistrates' fellow manufacturers and merchants who caused it.

For the Luddites, military drilling on the moors under an imaginary leader was also a reaction against nearly two decades of war. The Napoleonic Wars constituted the first total war in which the whole population participated, either through military service in the regular army or navy or volunteer regiments, compulsory enlistment into the militia, or by producing food and goods for the war effort. The Luddites got creative, even sarcastic, in their anonymous letters to the authorities and employers who ruled them. The 'Soliciter [sic] to General Ludd' sent a 'summons' to Huddersfield magistrate Joseph Radcliffe, 'filed against you in Ludd Court at Nottingham'. The threat required him to desist acting as a magistrate or else 'General Ludd and his well organised army' would levy the summons against his person and property 'with all Destruction possible'.

General Ludd and his sergeants formed part of the response to years of propaganda promoting British patriotism and self-sacrificing service to the nation. General Ludd's troops subverted this patriotism by defending local communities against military compulsion and a war with seemingly no end in 1812, as well as the illegality of combining as a trade union.

Unlike the connotations of the modern uses of the term 'Luddite', the textile workers of 1811–12 were not opposed to all new machinery or economic progress. What was at stake was their skill and self-worth. They sought to defend their livelihoods and working conditions, and their communities' way of life. Since the publication of *Wealth of Nations* in 1776, Adam Smith's economic theories influenced the wealthy textile manufacturers and merchants, who pushed forward their own interpretation of industrial efficiency. For laissez-faire liberals, the removal of customary protections on wages and prices for goods heralded the success of the free market. For many workers, by contrast, the machines and large factories marked the start of a loss of control over their working lives. Factory time replaced the flexibility of domestic workshops, where male workers previously produced high-quality cloth at a pace that suited them. Dangerous child and female labour and a sharp decline in wages were the result of this change.

The Tory government was under pressure from the employers to defend their property. The Frame Breaking Act was passed in March 1812, making attacking stocking frames a capital offence. Hundreds of workers suspected of taking part in the Luddite attacks were arrested and tried at special assizes at Nottingham, York, Chester, and Lancaster. In total, 37 of those tried for various charges including riot and machine breaking were hanged and several dozen more were transported to Australia.

Agitation associated with the Luddites resurfaced after the end of the Napoleonic Wars in 1816, and anti-automation resistance continued throughout the nineteenth century to the present day. The Captain Swing movement of the early 1830s fought against new threshing machines in agriculture throughout southern England. As with the Luddites, this was not just opposition to machinery but represented wider community resistance against the degradation of agricultural workers' employment conditions and the breaking down of the old poor law system of welfare. In the 1890s, the 'new unionism' trades went on strike to protest against the introduction of new machinery in the engineering industry. In 1934, the wiredrawers of Manchester conducted a nine month strike against the introduction of a stopwatch system to force the workers to work faster. Though in many cases the protests were unsuccessful in their immediate aims, the clashes between workers and employers drew attention to growing ideas about rights, welfare, and safety at work.

In effect, the Luddites and their successors fought against what we now know as zero-hours contracts, surveillance mechanisms to track workers' every move, punitive forms of state welfare, and other manifestations of a neo-liberal economy. Environmental movements and campaigns against genetically-modified food, for example, also trace their first principles to the Luddites. Worldwide, resistance to automation in mass factory production, and campaigns against sweated labour and modern slavery similarly share some features in common with the Luddites' defence of their skill and dignity in work (though it should be noted that the Lancashire weavers as well as their employers benefited from the most lucrative produce of slavery, cotton). Current debates around 'craftism' and artisan production in some contexts have drawn from conservative and unfortunately even nativist ideas, but self-proclaimed neo-Luddites retain their connection to radicalism and anarchism in political principles and approaches to organisation.

The M & Ms

Divya Ghelani

VIRAT PACED ABOUT HIS living room, his fists clenched in anger. *Good Morning Britain* was coming live from outside Downing Street. The prime minister was talking about his party's British Values Initiative, which he was launching with a fanfare of subsidiary announcements – a new set of bank holidays, Winston Churchill Day, Empire Day and so on, to replace the old – successfully distracting coverage from another part of the same initiative, a series of immigration raids and deportation flights, including one just that morning from Heathrow.

The PM's communications team had judged the wider British Values Initiative to be 'on point' with traditional, older voters, and gimmicks like the new bank holidays as sufficiently vacuous to divide and distract the younger ones. In the weeks before this morning's launch, they had deployed new algorithms to focus-group its talking points, key words, slogans and even its logo across the whole gamut of social media platforms.

'We've sent another round of criminals packing!' replied the PM to a question about the deportations, in his usual faux-colloquial tone. 'Each one of them has committed heinous crimes, forfeiting their right to remain in our great nation. Today's flight contains 35 murderers, 59 paedophiles, as well as tax dodgers, countless drug dealers, and in all cases COVID-19 protocol violations…'

'You lot are psychos!' Virat yelled at the TV. 'Marpster was just smoking a spliff in Prestop Park. Everyone does it. So what if he doesn't have a birth certificate? He got framed to meet *your* numbers!'

Virat took a few deep breaths to stop from shaking. His best friend, Martin Marprelate, didn't even know the country he was being sent to. He was just a baby when he left Jamaica. He was from nowhere but right here – Ashby-de-la-Zouch – that's where Marps belonged. Losing him to a vote-grabbing deportation scheme had affected Virat's mental health. Since they took Martin, he'd had stomach pains, headaches, an inability to focus on anything his friends said, and when they did speak to him his anguish made him close his eyes and watch their words swirl together. He'd told his college therapist about it who suggested it might be hyper-vigilance borne of trauma. A lot of non-white kids were experiencing this thanks to the ruling party's relentless jingoistic rhetoric. He'd recommended Virat and his mother visit their GP to get a prescription for antidepressants, but since the NHS had introduced increased prescription fees Mrs. Parmar could no longer afford certain aspects of healthcare. Now, as the PM rattled off more his familiar responses, a strange new headache coursed through Virat's head. With his eyes closed, he could *feel* the prime minister's xenophobic words spiralling through the darkness.

'What is wrong with you?' Virat muttered. 'Why don't you *listen* to us? For once in your life why don't you shut up and LISTEN?'

Just then, the prime minister paused, lifted his hand to his forehead and blinked for a moment at the cameras.

'You!' he pointed to one of the reporters. 'Did you say something to me?'

The reporter shook his head. Red-faced, the PM straightened his jacket.

'Sorry folks,' the prime minister told the TV viewers, clearing his throat and jiggling his earpiece to check one of his advisers wasn't speaking in his ear.

'I could have sworn... Anyway, as I was saying... Today is a momentous day. This initiative will bring a message of confidence, positivity, and hope to millions of Britons amidst these times of apprehension.'

As the prime minister continued and his words swirled in the darkness of Virat's thoughts, the teenager became aware of a subtle and more insidious voice behind them. It was the PM's inner voice.

'You're really buying this aren't you,' it said. *'Come on then, drink the Kool-Aid you bunch of illiterate sheep! There's plenty more where this came from.'*

As the contemptuous inner voice continued to play behind the prime minister's spoken words, Virat Parmar began to see just how little any of the PM's utterances meant to him.

Not everyone's going to buy this bullshit, Virat thought.

'Not everyone's going to buy this bullshit!' the prime minister suddenly parroted to the array of cameramen and photographers.

Virat stared at the TV screen. *Did he actually just say that? Must have been a coincidence*, he told himself, and yet the words he could now see turning through the darkness also came with memories attached – ideas, recollections, fears, and fantasies. It was strange. One minute he was a seventeen-year-old Indian kid with a bad GTA6 habit, living in Ashby-de-la-Zouch, the next he's recollecting playing Pyramus in an all-Latin production of Ovid, in the New Hall in Eton.

'Prime Minister, that was an alarming statement!' a BBC journalist shouted from the press pack on the other side of the street. 'Would you care to elaborate?'

This man doesn't have any actual beliefs, Virat thought, as he passed through layer upon layer of the PM's jumbled memories. *Here's a guy who has spent his whole life winning favour, drawing attention to himself. He gets laughs out of his shamelessness, telling one person one thing, and the next the complete opposite, just to get ahead.*

'This man doesn't have any actual beliefs,' the PM replied with his arms out in his customary style. 'Here is a guy who spent his whole life winning favour, drawing attention to himself, getting laughs out of his shamelessness…'

'Whoa!' said Virat out loud, amazed at his strange new power.

'Whoa!' said the prime minister, unnerved and stammering, turning hesitantly then marching towards the door of Number 10, which didn't immediately open.

'Major goof,' he could be seen mouthing to an aide, who hurried up to the microphone on his behalf.

'Sorry folks. Press conference is over!' he said.

As the door to Number 10 was left open, viewers could see the PM stomping down the corridor shouting at thin air: 'Who was that?' 'Who are you?' It was at this point Virat realised he was no longer lip-reading the PM on the TV but being spoken to directly. 'Who is this? Are you… some spook working for the damn EU?'

No… yes. Maybe, Virat spluttered, trembling with the shock of it.

Well, get out! the prime minister hissed. *Get out this minute. I don't know who you are but I'm warning you. This is trespassing!*

But Virat Parmar couldn't stop even if he wanted to. His new power was making its presence known, unwieldy, sovereign. It continued to rifle through the PM's thoughts absorbing as much as it could in one go until, completely exhausted, Virat fell to the floor.

Hours later, he awoke to find his mother standing over him.

'What the hell happened?' he asked her.

'You tell me,' she said, furrowing her brow as she assessed her teenage son. 'Why were you sleeping on the carpet? Have you been smoking? I told you and the boys you have to stop all of that after Martin.'

'The prime minister was on the telly and I managed to get inside his head, Mum!' Virat blurted out. 'There were these words in the darkness and then, all of a sudden, I could hear his thoughts, access his memories, his dreams –'

'Too many superhero movies,' concluded Mrs. Parmar, arms folded. 'How about you do something useful for a change? Come on. Up with you. Let's make paneer wraps for lunch.'

Virat followed his mother into the kitchen, yawning and trying to shake off what he now suspected was a dream. It must have been a heavy sleep because he felt lighter, emotionally stronger somehow, as if the depression instigated by Martin's deportation had been replaced by a newfound wisdom and rootedness in himself. Virat's mum sensed it too and she kissed her son before turning on Radio 4 for the hourly news. It was while chopping onions that Virat heard the presenter go live to Number 10. The prime minister was trying to explain his earlier gaffe.

'Well, my comedy smarts clearly aren't what they were!' he was telling the presenter. '*Richly comic* was what I was going for. You see, I am a strong believer that April 1st shouldn't have a monopoly on pranks. To play Mad Tom in Lear was always my ambition at school, but I was never skinny enough. So, this morning was one of my pranks, which the journalists didn't catch onto and for this I ask your forgiveness. I wasn't explicit enough about my routine – just wanted to dazzle you all. It was a pastiche, if you will, a homage to what my enemies say about me, and who even now don't seem to get the joke. Well, the joke's on them, I say.'

As the PM rambled on, Virat found himself closing his eyes and seeing again the words of the prime minister spiralling in front of him. Through them, he began to catch glimpses of countless other memories on the other side: being drunk at a Cambridge gaudy with a tie around his head and a half-empty bottle of champers in his hand, an affair with his blonde twenty-something press secretary conducted in the Mandarin Oriental in Hyde Park, his contemptuous father scoffing at his boy self that he wasn't going to be 'world king' and that he was a 'good-for-nothing piece of shit' for not finishing all the dinner on his plate. Virat Parmar dropped his knife in wonder. It wasn't a dream. He, Virat Parmar of Ashby-de-la-Zouch, was once more inside the British prime minister's head.

'Mum,' he said. 'Can you leave the frying for a minute? Turn off the radio too, will you? I want to ask you something.'

'What is it, love?'

Virat pressed his hands to his forehead and tried to read her thoughts, but nothing happened.

'Will you buy me a hoverboard?'

'No, I bloody won't! And here's me thinking you had something important to say to me…'

'Wait. Read this,' Virat said, handing her a *'FINAL REMINDER: Unpaid council tax'* letter from the kitchen counter. 'Read it aloud.'

'Alright. I know I've got to pay it.'

'Read it. Please. All of it.'

As soon as Virat's mother started to read, the words began to dance in the darkness behind his eyelids; beyond them he was starting to hear her other voice, her secret one and then, beyond that, somehow, he found himself tunnelling through all the memories and experiences that made up the entirety of his mother, billions of them. He rummaged about at lightning speed until he found something poignant that might help him.

'Remember how much you cried when your mum didn't want to buy you that dress for your school disco?'

'Oh, love, it was awful,' said Mrs Parmar.

'It was hard coming to a new country, wasn't it? And then having nothing to wear at a big event with everyone looking at you. That's how I'll feel if you don't buy me that hoverboard. Everyone else has one.'

'Oh no. Really? I hadn't thought of it like that,' Mrs. Parmar replied, heartbroken on his behalf. 'Get me my purse. We can't have that.'

As Mrs Parmar made the online purchase for her son, Virat

realised she hadn't noticed him poking about in her head. By controlling his thoughts and not saying anything to her mind-to-mind, he realised he could get away with being neither seen nor heard.

When Virat's hoverboard arrived three days later, he felt terribly guilty for the trick he'd played. They were poor and this test of his new skill had been reckless – but it had proved his point. If he could manipulate his frugal Indian mum into being so wasteful with money, and so soon after his birthday, were there any limits to what he could do? At the very least he knew he had something like telepathy, and now it was up to him to explore it further. He skipped college the next day and sat in front of his laptop, watching live streams of politicians, sports personalities, and news reporters to see if he could project random words into the middle of what they were saying. There was a definite pattern to it. Whenever he tried to listen to interviews or discussions that clearly weren't scripted, their words didn't form in front of him when he closed his eyes. Politicians were particularly easy targets it seemed, as even their answers to live questions had a scripted feel to them. He WhatsApped his friends Penry, Job, Carleton, and Barrow.

'Something big has happened.'

'You got laid?'

The others sent laughter and aubergine emoticons.

'I'm SERIOUS. I think I can use it to bring Marpster home.'

'How?' typed Barrow.

The others were silent and Virat could feel their anguish. They all missed Martin so much.

'I don't know exactly. Let's meet at the entrance to Prestop Park. 7pm tonight. I'll tell you everything.'

It was a cool summer's night, and the stars seemed to wink at each other as the four school friends gathered on their bikes on

Burton Road, near the park entrance. Virat wheeled up on his new hoverboard, his hands in his pockets like he meant business.

'Where did you get that?' asked Penry, a skinny teen whose voice had yet to break.

'Mum. Mental isn't it?'

'I'll say,' Job replied, sporting a new rainbow drip in his box braids hairstyle. 'Thought she was skint. Wait... did you guys come into money?'

'No. I tricked her into buying it for me.'

'Sounds a bit snide,' Job replied, pulling a face. 'You should show her some respect.'

'I do. I just needed to test something. And it worked, which is why you're all here.'

'What is this about?' said Barrow, glowering. 'How is your mum buying you a hoverboard she can't afford got anything to do with bringing Martin back?'

'You trust me, right?' said Virat, as serious as the night that surrounded them. 'I got this because I managed to get inside my mum's head. I read her thoughts like they were an archive and then I found this old memory I could use against her. That's why she bought a hoverboard. Because I made her – by reading her mind.'

'Wow!' Carleton laughed. 'That's a good one.'

'I'm serious. This isn't a prank. I've got some sort of skill. It started last night. I think I can use it to bring Marpster back. Let me show you. Penry, tell me the words of a song you know off by heart.'

'Like what?'

'I don't know. You like the Sleaford Mods, right? Give us some lyrics from a song you know.'

'This is the human race,' Penry began, quizzically, *'UKIP and your disgrace/ Chopped heads on London streets/ All you zombies, tweet, tweet, tweet ...'*

Virat told him to keep going and closed his eyes, lowering his head as he felt his way towards Penry's inner voice and memories behind it, tiptoeing into the house of his mind like a svelte and elegant burglar. The broadleaf and conifer trees that surrounded them rustled as Virat Parmar rifled through the Filofax of his friend's brain. There was something magical about the steal, like he had golden fingers, like his whole being was golden. Each time Virat entered a mind it gave him such a rush, such a feeling of power that he didn't want to stop. He was in his element, but the power seemed to know when it was too much; it regulated itself when it had obtained all it needed from Penry. Exhausted, Virat collapsed on the concrete path.

'You fancy one of those identical Patel twins,' Virat said, his tired face resting against the cool ground, 'in the year above. But you're afraid to ask her out in case it's her sister.'

'Who told you that?' Penry snapped defensively.

'And your mum had an affair when she went home to China. You were nine and stayed with your grandparents.'

'Fuck me!' Penry stared at Virat. 'He's right,' he eventually told the others. 'No one knew that but me and my mum.'

'This is what I'm here to tell you all,' said Virat, scrambling up to his feet. 'I can get inside people's heads – retrieve information. By listening to them in this particular kind of way. It's easier to hear their thoughts if they're saying something rehearsed or from a script. I thought maybe I could use it to get Marpster back – but I can't do it alone. I need your help.'

The other boys were convinced that Penry and Virat were playing some kind of trick on them, so they demanded further proof. Virat gave it to them alright, listening beyond their inner voices one by one, sometimes talking to them mind-to-mind, spilling their secrets back to them. When the four of them were no longer in any doubt, they gathered around Virat to discuss how they might harness his new power. Their whispers were as hushed as the night wind rustling through trees.

Virat explained that he had already had access to a lot of personal information about the prime minister: some of it clear, other bits less so. One thing he'd been thinking about a lot was a government agency called D.I.R.T. There had been a lot of talk in the PM's brain of 'plain-clothes', operatives who seemed to be tasked with investigating aliens. But that was as far as Virat could reach. There was some kind of block. Maybe the prime minister didn't even know what was going on himself? One thing was clear: it had been plain-clothed policemen who had picked up Martin and delivered him to the cops. D.I.R.T. was somehow involved.

That next morning, the five teenagers got to work, setting up something between a slumber party and a command centre in Virat's bedroom. Virat sat cross-legged on his Star Wars duvet with his laptop on a pillow beside him, while the others stretched out across his floor, pens and notepads in hands, ready to transcribe anything and everything he told them to.

The boys tuned into a scheduled live morning interview with the PM on *The Today Programme*, during which time Virat put on the new high-tech 70s-style electric-blue headphones they'd all clubbed in to buy so Virat could better listen to what people said.

'He was bullied by his father as a kid,' Virat told them. 'His parents had no emotional connection to him; told him he was a waste of space. It's why he's prepared to be popular at any cost. It's why he race-baits, why he goes for all this bullshit ultra-nationalism. He's an opportunist who thinks power is love. He's addicted to power. He even got himself a criminal record because of it.'

'Wait! Hold up. The prime minister has a criminal record?' Job said, his eyes lighting up. 'For what?'

Virat placed his hands on his headphones to listen to the prime minister's prepared remarks in order to summon up those spiralling words once more.

'It was expunged,' he told them. 'The tabloid newspapers knew about it, along with a bunch of affairs. Gross! They tried to use it all during his first election campaign but his Eton friends in the media killed the story.'

'*You* know the names of those friends though,' Penry told him. 'Because you're in his mind, right?'

'Right.'

'And does the PM know any bad things about *them*?'

Virat listened harder.

'Illegal oil deal,' he muttered. 'A murder in Delhi. Offshore tax evasion.'

'Woah,' replied Carleton. 'That's heavy stuff.'

'Why don't we threaten the prime minister's media friends with exposure about those things *unless* they let journalists publish his criminal record?' Job asked.

'But how is the PM being exposed as a criminal going to help Marpster?' Barrow pleaded. 'We have to focus on Martin. That's the reason we're here, right?'

When the interview was over Virat opened his eyes and tore the electric-blue headphones from his head.

'I'll contact the PM directly,' Virat said. 'Next time he's on air, I can speak to him mind-to-mind and threaten him. I can say, 'I'll get your friends to reveal you're a crook if you don't return the people on those flights.'

Carleton, Penry, and Barrow all agreed on the plan, but Job resisted, saying they should think carefully about their goals. Martin's plight was symptomatic of a bigger malaise, and they should honour Martin by focusing on the bigger problem too – not just the case of deportations.

'The system has been rotting people's brains for years,' he sighed. 'We're all way too passive, too compliant. We let them get away with murder. Even if we bring Marpster back, what's to stop that party from doing it again to some other poor sod? It's the politics that needs to change and with a power like Virat's, we should think big, *really big*. We could encourage politicians to work for the people, make them accountable, make them better. Imagine it. Politicians actually behaving like human beings with beating hearts for once…'

'But what *are* the criminal records?' Carleton asked. 'What did the prime minister *actually* do?'

'I don't know exactly,' Virat said. 'I came close... but next time I'll get there.'

The following Sunday, on one of the morning politics shows, Virat read the prime minister's mind even as the politician knew he was in there.

'Get out of my head, you rascal! You rapscallion!' he spat, while continuing his answer to the TV presenter without missing a beat. 'I won't be blackmailed by a … trespasser on my intellectual property. I've got the secret police onto you,' he warned. 'I don't know what kind of mind weapon you're using on me – but D.I.R.T. will stop you, you piece of shit.'

'Wow,' Virat groaned as he collapsed to the floor having obtained the information he needed, 'You really are your father's son.'

When he came to his senses, Virat concluded that the PM wasn't making idle threats – D.I.R.T. had been assigned to come for him. The boys speculated about what sophisticated technology D.I.R.T. might use to locate Virat and perhaps themselves too.

The four were clearly shaken by Virat's findings but they said it wouldn't stop them. They focused on developing a Plan B for getting Martin back. Their college days were long behind them. (Somehow a BTEC in Retail Management didn't seem so important any more.) The summer holidays were coming up and it felt like it represented their last chance to save the country. They gathered in Prestop Park with burner phones, daisy-chaining VPNs around the world in the hope they couldn't be traced.

*

Job brought his dad's camping tent and, having erected it, installed it with an icebox filled with Magnums and energy drinks, sustenance for the boys as they watched Virat Parmar bent over his Android phone, with his 70s-style electric-blue headphones on, watching the likes of BBC Parliament, CSPAN, or Sky News. Virat with his eyes closed, clutching his head and muttering discoveries like a teen-boy fortune teller. Carleton recorded Virat's rapid mutterings on Voice Notes, while Job, Penry, and Barrow took turns jotting things down, discussing, and strategising. Carleton and Barrow, who'd been joint strongest at English in college, used aspects of Virat's information to start a blog titled *The Political Mind*. The trouble was no one wanted to read a blog by a pair of nobodies, even if the information they had seemed little short of dynamite.

'We've got barely any subscribers and the ones we've got are alt-right weirdos, conspiracy theorists, or just plain mad. Sorry boys,' Barrow told the others, after two weeks of posting online. 'We have to try something else.'

Penry and Job took the lead, attempting to podcast their findings instead, using the voice modification software Virat showed them, in case anyone in government was listening in. Their podcast, 'People Power', was advertised with a batch of press releases, and emails sent to the newsrooms of all the major outlets with headings like, 'URGENT: YOU SHOULD INVESTIGATE THIS ASAP' signed 'Anon.' This didn't work either. The boys were just amateurs, their media training non-existent. They probably sounded like the students they were. After all, their stories had no sources or witnesses that journalists could crosscheck. They had a wizard in their midst, with real-life superpowers, but no one was interested. Virat told them they had to organise better, that he'd spent enough time rooting around the minds of politicians to learn the rules of political media and its campaigns. They would have to think like advertisers.

Penry pulled a grossed-out face, but Job shrugged his shoulders in defeat.

'Telling the truth can be boring,' Job said to the others. 'This country has had lies and spin for decades. Social media has made an echo chamber of those lies. It gets people addicted to petty drama as a way of distracting them from what's outside the chamber – the bigger picture. Let's face it. We're all addicted and seeing as there's no antidote just yet. We need to deliver Virat's truths as entertainment.'

Barrow half-jokingly suggested using Virat's toy monkey, Bubu Butt, which Virat refused to throw away because it had been his only comfort when his dad had been killed on his way home from work one night. His dad had bought him the monkey for his birthday, so he still held it dear to him, even on the cusp of adulthood.

'It's a good idea,' Virat told him. 'Pass me Bubu Butt. Job, get the video camera.'

Originally Virat's idea was that Bubu Butt could be a logo or part of an ident for a YouTube channel, just to liven things up. But Barrow found ways of incorporating the toy monkey as a character in YouTube videos. He'd seen something like it before on some influencer's TikTok, and he used the toy to present the nightly news – each one breaking a new scandal. *'This just in,'* Bubu Butt would say, his head flopping forward with every syllable, Barrow's hand behind it clearly visible, *'The Home Secretary paid 21 prostitutes to celebrate his 21st birthday. Which is understandable, of course. But Zut alors! None of them were British nationals!'*

To their amazement, Bubu Butt News got the boys several thousand subscribers and over 4000 likes on TikTok. The videos always came with a link to the blog, with serious information, but their followers weren't interested in the detailed truth of the stories as much as they were the goofiness of the idea. Besides, followers were mainly teens like the boys themselves, and awareness needed to be spread across the entire electorate. How else to get rid of the present government other than at the ballot box?

Job and Penry set to work again, using Job's dad's new Apple Mac to create a series of political memes based on Virat's revelations about the prime minister's hidden criminal record. They were meticulous in their planning, bolstered by their knowledge of the PM's wrongdoings. The duo spent weeks studying memes from previous elections, from both sides of the political spectrum in the UK and the US – 'Fields of Wheat', inexplicable clips of former prime ministers laughing hysterically at the dispatch box or looking ridiculous as they mocked their own inability to dance. Job and Penry explained to the others how they'd been studying the polling data curves and how they corresponded to the spread of these memes, which is what made them convinced of the necessity for such tactics in their own campaign. After all, it was satirical and 'funny' memes that had helped Trump and every British PM since get into power – created by real fans and troll farms. The boys set about making their own, ripping into the prime minister and his party, ridiculing cabinet members, showing all of them to be the charlatan self-aggrandising crooks they were – and all in the 12-month run-up to an election. At the end of each meme, they signed off with 'M & Ms', which was what they decided to call themselves after the kid it was all about. Barrow (the digital artist of the group) drew a bunch of masked protesters as a kind of logo for their new tag, at the centre of which he added a skinny Indian boy with a gold lamé eye-mask and a pair of wireless electric-blue 70s-style headphones: Virat Parmar as Major M. This is when their project really took flight.

★

The M & Ms' very first meme depicted the PM in a launderette. He was sitting on a pile of freshly washed British Flags with a confused look and a speech bubble that said: 'Why does laundering my money make it dirty money?' It was a reference to the prime minister's expunged criminal record; the fact that he had been laundering millions via businesses in the Cayman Islands for him and his latest wife to amass huge wealth which not only had they not declared on the ministerial register, but whose origins no one knew anything about. He should have been facing questions around the transparency of his financial affairs, but his friends had killed the story in the media.

The meme didn't get much attention, but a celebrity gamer retweeted it 'just in case it's true' and this is how a helpful outsider got in touch via the comments section of Job and Penry's now abandoned blog. It was a criminal lawyer who knew everything about the prime minister's financial dealings, despite there being a super-injunction not to talk about it.

'It's important the country knows how immoral its leader is,' he said in a follow-up email. 'Attached is a letter confirming that the PM was indeed arrested and charged in 2019 for money laundering in the Cayman Islands. Did you know he also created and gave billions in Covid-19 emergency funding to old Etonian business friends? Good luck re-sensitising people to the fact that they've elected a morally hollow automaton to run the country!'

It was their first big coup and the publication of the lawyer's letter via a meme 'reveal' featuring Peter Falk as popular 80s detective Columbo saying, '*Alright it seems you won the last election fair and square. Have a good night. One more thing though…*' The signed lawyer's letter plus the cheeky meme garnered the M & Ms 50k followers across Twitter and Instagram, followed by another 10k on Reddit. As soon as a well-known journalist confirmed the lawyer's letter to be true and it was discovered the lawyer had fled to Russia fearing for his life, it got picked up by mainstream media and the M & Ms' social media follower numbers exploded.

The five young men worked all hours to nurture their dissemination channels and prepare a series of memes with enough virality to reveal their central claim: Irrefutable proof that the PM of Britain was a criminal. That he helped set up billion-pound Covid-19 deals for his friends was next on the fact-based character assassination agenda, and the boys used their new mainstream media contacts as well as Virat's skills plus new informants to uncover photos of him shaking hands with shady businessmen they were able to disgrace one by one. Each image was followed by an anonymous quote once attributed to George Orwell, that called upon people to act: 'A People That Elect Corrupt Politicians, Imposters, Thieves and Traitors are not Victims but Accomplices…' Any serious journalist who hadn't pledged allegiance to the ruling party got in touch via *The Political Mind* and the M & Ms, via the growing horde of informants and Virat's superpower, provided all the proof they needed.

Since they had started the project, the M & Ms had been frantically trying to contact Martin in Jamaica, who was now living with his uncle and helping out at his grocery store. After seven weeks of searching border agents' minds Virat finally got a new WhatsApp number for him, and video-called him out of the blue. Martin looked like he'd lost a lot of weight, and almost immediately confided in Virat that he thought his phone had been bugged.

'Can you call me back on Signal, audio only?' Virat asked.

Martin did so and Virat put on the eye-mask he'd mind-controlled his mum into sewing for him as well as his wireless electric-blue headphones – both helped him get into character and concentrate.

'What the hell?' said Martin, on seeing his best friend dressed like a masked crusader.

'Promise me you'll follow my instructions,' Virat said.

When Martin agreed Virat asked him to read the shop signs he could see around him.

'You're kidding, right?' Martin said.

'I'm deadly serious,' Major M told him. 'And when you run out, start again.'

'Galveston Flower Shop, Lenny's Hardware, Jessica's Nails, Yam Bar…'

As Martin read shop names Virat read his beloved best friend's mind, learning firsthand the distress he'd suffered, how thankful he had been that his estranged uncle had agreed to look after him – a fate much better than others he knew on the plane. His depression had been much worse than Virat's own, and the pain of being separated from his family, home, and friends had changed him. The sound of Martin's inner voice, all that he had experienced through and beyond, gave Virat a renewed sense of purpose and he vowed to himself that he would help anyone in Martin's situation.

'I've had a lot of time think over here,' Martin told Virat outright after Virat revealed to him his new identity. 'My uncle is quite political. We talk about global politics, not just what's happening in Jamaica and the UK. I want people in every country to wake up and realise they're being lied to. I mean, we're at the edge of a climate catastrophe. We've got to think bigger than stupid nationalism and isolationism. We're better than this. I know we are. You say you have a superpower and I believe you. Use it, Virat. Show the people they're being lied to. Tell them to open their eyes. This is major. It's bigger than you or me.'

Virat passed Martin's message to the boys, who responded by becoming a nocturnal meme machine. Each day's political secrets, tapped into by Virat in his electric-blue headphones, were transcribed and transformed overnight into mash-up memes, riffing of classics of the meme genre like 'Keep Calm and Carry On', Nyan cat, double rainbow guy, 'Delete Your Account', and so on. Often the M & Ms would produce eight or nine memes per night and come the morning none of them would have reached exit velocity. But it only took one meme to attain virality, every three or four days, for their momentum to build. Job and Penry weren't so much creating fake accounts by this stage as farming whole flocks of them, while Carleton had begun writing a programme that would delegate many flocks at a time to automated 'shepherds'.

One day, on Virat's advice, they stopped putting the M & Ms logo on memes, and before long other memes they'd never seen started being attributed to them by the likes of Buzzfeed and Thrillist. Their following grew and even celebrity endorsements followed: Stormzy spoke about them during a live Radio 1 interview (with a bit of mind-to-mind encouragement from Major M who was big fan), the Queen derided them (which got the anti-monarchists' attention), and, Carleton (by far the group's best hacker) cloned the login to Number 10's official Twitter account and renamed it 'FACT CHECK UK' – an old election campaign reference that got the mainstream newspapers talking about 'democracy-threatening pranksters'.

The last stunt got the government's attention and they hit back with a series of raids based on tip-offs from members of the public, suspicious of their neighbours, and young people on their street corners. Plain-clothed police stormed houses and abandoned buildings in Birmingham, East London, Brighton, and Glasgow. One night, someone guessed right and a whole fleet of black cars with tinted windows came swooping into Prestop Park with a horde of armed plain-clothed D.I.R.T. men who could do little but trash the boys' tent while they watched via camcorder from Virat's bedroom. The M & Ms made the evening news then, not just in Britain but also in the US, India, Denmark, Russia and China. The boys realised they were being hunted but also that their reach was now global, allowing them to critique far more than the fledgling British two-party system and to interrogate a whole generation of politics, moving beyond national border debates in order to focus on that arrogant, gaudy, out-of-control monster of mass delusion, which was now super-sized, gorging on fear, trashing the truth.

'Always remember what Marpster told us,' said Major M, rallying the M & Ms from the empty garage near Job's house the boys had relocated to, cadging off the free Wi-Fi from a local café. 'This is bigger than us.'

The boys had learnt to use different routers and VPNs, to cover the camera lenses on their laptops and burner phones with packing tape, to flush their SIM cards down the drain, and use code words they changed each day. Meanwhile the PM and his communications team retaliated with their own memes and what could only be described as a full-on media assault. Using DeepFake Reboot – an AI application developed by one of

Downing Street's big data friends – combined with a bunch of voice actors, they created videos of young men who bore striking resemblances to the characters in Barrow's logo and with them claimed they'd arrested 'the pranksters', further broadcasting their apology to the nation with a false strapline that read: *'Government Verified Information'*.

'Bunch of lying pricks!' Virat commented from his makeshift workstation behind a broken-down old Volvo. 'We strike tonight, and we strike together. Come boys. Let's show them how it's done.'

Job created and posted a meme featuring the Number 10 press secretary as a lady from the classic British sitcom *Allo Allo,* with the line, 'Listen very carefully. I shall say zis only once' and a subsequent line that said, 'The prime minister's Paedophile Business Partner Hired Prostitutes For His Rich Friends' Parties'. This was followed by a damning photo sent to them by their latest anonymous informant via their *Political Mind* blog, which was now very much back in action. The other boys each produced a meme based on the prime minister and his party's misdeeds, and then they made even more. To their delight they made *The Trevor Noah Show* in the US, where the host suggested that Major M and the M & Ms were like Robin Hood and his Merry Men because they were rumoured to be from the East Midlands. Cerebral articles were soon written about the 'pranksters' describing them as 'carnivalesque disrupters'. Meanwhile, art critics proclaimed them to be the performance artists of our age whose 'intertextuality transcended the left and right of orthodox politics', calling them 'The New Banksy's.' The boys didn't understand all that was being written about them but they high-fived with mugs of Virat's mum's masala chai when their work made *Newsnight*. Deep down, however, Virat was extremely anxious for his friends.

'It's only a matter of time before D.I.R.T., or one of the one other security agencies, gets hold of us,' Major M told the M & Ms from the Star Wars duvet in his bedroom, now knowing full well the deviousness of the ruling politicians' minds. 'Either we stop now, or we keep working knowing the risks – that we're on borrowed time. If you don't want to do this with me, I understand...'

The boys renewed their commitment in the name of Martin Marprelate, but also for a bigger cause – that people the world over deserved the truth, because the truth was potentially world-changing, and therefore more important than any of the boys themselves. They pushed ahead with political seriousness, creating tweets, and social media posts as weapons, turning the government's PR memes against them like missiles hacked into and reprogrammed mid-flight. Their productivity was that of a machine gun powered by anger: 'We're mad as hell' it said, 'And we're not going to take it any more.' Their following grew, reaching further than the overblown echo chambers of social media. People on the streets began learning about Major M and the M & Ms through conversations in workplaces, high schools, care homes, and community centres. The idea that an anonymous group of vigilante justice-seekers were uncovering governmental political secrets and revealing them to the world using satire, comedy, and all backed up by a growing grassroots fact-checking movement was setting the world alight: volunteers, academics, independent and retired journalists across the globe were forming their own 'M & M's of the Media' clusters, complete with Signal groups that even began to acquire a few quiet, conscientious professionals within corporate media, all taking it upon themselves to verify each piece of information issued by the M & Ms – and with electrifying results.

It must have happened when the free Wi-Fi the M & Ms were bumming off dropped out, kicking out one of the VPNs on Job's devices that then automatically switched to an ordinary traceable 5G signal. It was impossible to know *who* exactly in central government found them – be it D.I.R.T., MI5, or some other intelligence agency hired by the prime minister and his men in grey suits. But their enemies came in broad daylight, plain-clothed with dead eyes and silencer guns driven by the sole intention of stopping the M & Ms. Virat was threatened and kicked in the ribs, whereas Job, Barrow, and Carleton got broken limbs and black eyes. Penry's fate was the worst – he got his nails pulled off one by one until he couldn't take it any more and revealed Martin Marprelate's new hideout address in Jamaica. Virat was told to make a video for the government's PR team 'or your friends die', in which he asked for forgiveness, and pledged his new allegiance to the nation, the PM, and The British Values Initiative.

'We're just a bunch of kids having fun,' Virat was forced to say. 'We're not to be taken seriously. Not at all. We were just joking around.'

Plain-clothed agents travelled to Jamaica to threaten Martin Marprelate, who was now living with his uncle in a brand-new hideout, having been tipped off by Virat via Signal about how dangerous the situation was becoming. In case their line was bugged, Virat had spoken to him, mind-to-mind, while Martin read aloud the menu of the restaurant he was in.

'They told me to tell you,' Martin confided, 'or rather they told me to tell Major M to stop what he's doing or he's dead. I think it was D.I.R.T. They roughed me up and my uncle pretty bad.'

'What did you say?'

'I told them the truth matters.'

After Virat's public humiliation on international TV, Major M and the M & Ms were made to sign contracts that stated they should never gather, stand against the government, or the police. If they did, they'd be charged with terror laws. The police then charged Virat with violent disorder, assault on police, and public order matters (all lies) before throwing him in a cell for two months. When Job visited Virat's detention facility, he hugged him as tightly as he could before revealing that D.I.R.T. had killed Martin in Jamaica –a final warning to

Major M and the M & Ms that the government meant business. Heartbroken by Martin's murder and despairing at his own inability to help him despite his powers, Virat lost it with guards, leading to the institute's psychotherapist declaring him 'delusional' and 'a danger to himself and others.' Virat was placed in a padded cell. As he rotted alone in there, the PM proceeded to frame the whole controversy as an attack on national security and British values and rode the wave of jingoistic rhetoric to yet another election victory, his entire campaign built on a towering scaffold of intersecting lies. In his acceptance speech, the PM proclaimed that, 'Anyone who is a decent citizen of Britain should be vigilant that Major M and the M & Ms do not regroup or inspire copycat cells! Their anarchic and demonic teenage aim is to trash this great nation of ours.' His meme team showed the PM crushing a packet of chocolate M & Ms underfoot after which he sauntered down a street with British Jack flags fluttering on either side.

On the day a highly drugged, beaten, and depressed Virat was released from prison, the boys visited him and Mrs Parmar in Prestop Park. They agreed it was too dangerous to keep meeting because of the newly draconian terror laws granting police 'shoot to kill' protocols for public gatherings where named terrorists were present. The boys had something important to tell Virat.

'They're watching our every move from now on,' Carleton explained. 'Especially yours. Marpster's gone. You've got to think of you and your mum now. She needs you. We've got to think of our families too. This is our last meeting.'

'But what about the movement we started?' said Virat, blinking back tears. 'We said it was bigger than us.'

'It is,' Job said, holding his burner mobile phone for Virat to see. 'Look at this. Martin saw that video they made of you saying we were just a bunch of jokers. It pissed him off, so he made his own before they got him. His uncle posted it online when he found him dead.'

'They'd planned it,' Carleton added. 'Watch the video.'

It was a video of Martin wearing an eye-mask and headphones just like Virat's.

'I'm Martin Marprelate, the man behind the M & Ms,' he told the camera. 'I'm Major M, too. Major M is not just a person. He's an idea. I was unfairly deported to Jamaica as part of the British Values Initiative. The M & Ms began as a means of getting me home, back to the UK, but we realised our movement was instantly bigger than any of us. If you know you're being lied to, if you choose to stand up do something about it, you're a superhero and you have pledged allegiance to the M & Ms. By the time you'll get this message, I'll be dead, my friends might be soon… so it's over to you. If you believe in truth in politics, if you love this world that I can no longer be a part of, then join us. Our voices, united, *can* make a difference. I'm Martin Marprelate. I'm Major M. I'm truth to power. And if you want me to be, I'm you.'

'Oh love.' Mrs Parmar looked at Virat, wiping his eyes. 'It's over for Martin but it's far from finished, see? There are live protests happening all over the world.'

Virat gazed down at Barrow's screen, amazed to see hoards of protesters gathering in Trafalgar Square, all of them wearing Major M masks.

'I'm Martin Marprelate!' one of them shouted. 'I'm Martin Marprelate!' another shouted. 'We're the M & Ms. You can kill us, but we won't die,' they chanted. 'Truth matters! Facts matter! Evidence matters!'

'It's not just in Trafalgar Square,' Carleton told Virat. 'It's all over the world. Look.'

Virat gazed down at Carleton's phone in amazement – a CNN news clip showing protesters taking to the streets wearing Major M eye-masks or photocopied masks of Martin Marprelate's face in Berlin, Paris, New Delhi. 'Ich bin Martin Marprelate!' they shouted. 'Je suis Martin Marprelate!' 'Meera naam he Martin Marprelate!'

'It's not just in-person protests,' Barrow explained. 'They're producing their own content now: memes, sketches, pranks, rap songs – all in service of political truth. Some of it is proper genius. Last night the PM signed off on a big illegal arms deal and they've exposed him already, *without us.* They've made a pop song from it already, containing only facts. Imagine that! Fact-based rap songs, pop songs, toppling rotten politicians. They're singing it in schoolyards, Uni campuses, everywhere. The PM's going to be tried in court. I think he's on his way out. *They* did that without us.'

As Mrs. Parmar and the boys fell to the task of convincing Virat of all the good work people had done in Martin's name, and as Virat's face gradually lit up at some of the funnier posts on TikTok, Vlog, Snapchat, Twitch, Insta, and Reface, a fleet of black cars with tinted windows quietly slid along Burton Road, from which dozens of plain-clothes disembarked and stealthily made their way across the grass to deal with this 'congregation of terrorists.' By the time they reached the M & Ms, Virat's heart was singing, lifted by the satire, rhymes, jokes, songs, and stories that their movement seemed to have inspired, like hundreds of golden fingers reaching through darkness into light. Under 'shoot to kill' protocols, Virat received a bullet to the chest, Mrs Parmar rushing to hold him and rock him in her arms.

'My baby boy,' she cried.

'I'm Major M now,' he told her as the lights went out. 'I'm Martin Marprelate too. We're alive in them. In a truth that matters...'

MARTIN MARPRELATE, 1588-1589

Origin Story: Paper Bullets

Dr Ariel Hessayon
Goldsmiths, University of London

ON 6 APRIL 1593 the Cambridge-educated religious separatists Henry Barrow (*c.*1550–1593) and John Greenwood (*c.*1560–1593) were hanged for treason at Tyburn – a notorious site of execution outside the city of London. They had been found guilty of writing and publishing seditious literature with malicious intent. Just over a month later another Cambridge-educated religious dissident, the Welsh preacher and pamphleteer John Penry (1562/63–1593), was tried twice: firstly for inciting rebellion and insurrection, and then for attacking the Church of England through the publication of scandalous writings. Penry was found guilty and on 29 May 1593 likewise hanged, this time in Surrey. As for Penry's co-conspirator, the Warwick MP Job Throckmorton (1545–1601), he too had been put on trial in 1590. In Throckmorton's case this was a result of the government crackdown on Protestant dissenters suspected of being involved in the writing, publication and circulation of a series of texts issued under the pseudonym 'Martin Marprelate' and its subsequent variants. Throckmorton, however, pleaded innocence: 'I am not Martin, I knew not Martin,' he claimed. And because of his relatively high social status and extensive connections, not to mention legal technicalities, Throckmorton escaped the fate that would befall Barrow, Greenwood and Penry. Instead, he died in relative obscurity.

More than a century ago it was argued that Barrow was the main author of the Martin Marprelate tracts, although few scholars accept this now. Slightly more recently the case was made for John Penry as lead author. But this too failed to gain much support, with most specialists downgrading Penry's role to that of minor literary collaborator or perhaps chief orchestrator of the conspiracy. Rather, both for some contemporaries and several modern experts, the evidence points to Job Throckmorton as the principal pen responsible for these writings. Another figure too must be mentioned who, like Penry's, Throckmorton's and Barrow's namesakes, appears in Ghelani's story. This was George Carleton (1529–1590), a Northamptonshire gentleman who had served as a Justice of the Peace and an MP. In 1589 Carleton married the rich widow, Elizabeth Crane, and it was at her house in East Molesey, Surrey near Hampton Court Palace that the first Marprelate tracts were printed. But whether Carleton merely facilitated the enterprise or whether his role extended to taking a hand in the authorship of the texts is unclear.

Turning to the choice of pseudonym, Martin was a fairly common proper name derived from the Middle English Martyn, with Martinmas or the feast of St Martin celebrated on 11 November. The prefix 'mar' (now obsolete), meant a hindrance or that which impaired something. A prelate was a high-ranking cleric, for example an archbishop, bishop or superior of a religious house. Hence Martin Marprelate could be understood as a sort of everyman who obstructed the exercise of authority by the ecclesiastical hierarchy in Elizabethan England.

There are at least seven works associated with the name of that 'worthy gentleman' Martin Marprelate. Issued between October 1588 and September 1589 in print runs of between 700 and 1000 copies and priced between 6*d*. and 9*d*., these include *The Epistle*; *The Epitome*; the broadsheet *Certain Mineral, and*

Metaphysical Schoolpoints; *Hay any work for Cooper*; *Theses Martinianae* (by 'Martin Junior'), *The Just Censure and Reproof* (by 'Martin Senior'), and *The Protestation*. More than one printer was involved. Initially Robert Waldegrave (*c*.1554–1603/04), a freeman of the London Stationers' Company notorious for printing material by the 'hotter sort' of Protestants (i.e. puritans), who had suffered imprisonment as well as the seizure and destruction of his equipment as a consequence. Using a new and distinctive continental black-letter type, Waldegrave printed the first four Marprelate pieces on a secret portable press at various locations: East Molesey, Surrey (Elizabeth Crane's house); Fawsley House, Northamptonshire (home of a sympathiser named Sir Richard Knightley); and Whitefriars, Coventry (residence of Knightley's nephew John Hales). Afterwards John Hodgkins and his assistants took over. They printed the remaining works at Wolston Priory, Coventry (home of another sympathiser named Roger Wigston) and Newton near Manchester. While Waldegrave fled abroad to Scotland (where he temporarily joined Penry), Hodgkins and his assistants were not so fortunate – they were captured, sent to London and tortured.

As for the wider context, the continental Reformation had begun more than 70 years previously in Wittenberg, Saxony. Among the mainstream European leaders were another Martin – Martin Luther (1483–1546), as well as Philip Melanchthon (1497–1560), Huldrych Zwingli (1484–1531) and Jean Calvin (1509–1564), a French theologian who had established a theocracy in Geneva. In England the Reformation started somewhat later. Although scholars do not agree exactly when, the 1530s – the decade during which Henry VIII (*d*.1547) declared himself head of the Church of England and then dissolved the monasteries – is widely accepted. Under Henry's eldest surviving legitimate son Edward VI (*d*.1553) the process of Reformation accelerated, only for the national church to revert to Catholicism during the reign of Henry's eldest daughter Mary I (*d*.1558). During the persecutions of 'Bloody

Mary', as her enemies dubbed her, several hundred Protestants fled into exile – including a few who sought shelter in Calvin's Geneva. Mary was succeeded by Elizabeth I (*d.*1603), Henry's daughter by his marriage to Anne Boleyn.

At the time the first Marprelate tract was published Elizabeth had been on the throne almost exactly 30 years. For complicated political reasons she was still unmarried, which meant that the Virgin Queen's dynasty could not be secured. Elizabeth was eventually succeeded by her cousin James VI of Scotland – although only after she had executed James's Catholic mother Mary, Queen of Scots in February 1587 on the charge of treason. Mary had been accused of scheming to assassinate Elizabeth in what was known as the Babington Plot, just one of a handful of attempts on Elizabeth's life that decade. Yet a greater threat still was foreign invasion by forces loyal to Philip II of Spain, whose second marriage had been to Elizabeth's half-sister Mary I. In July 1588 the Spanish Armada set sail for the English Channel, its prime objective to depose Elizabeth and replace her with an amenable Catholic monarch; its secondary aim to prevent English Protestants providing assistance to their co-religionists in the Netherlands who had rebelled against Spanish rule twenty years previously. Nonetheless, the Armada was defeated after which in August 1588 Elizabeth delivered a famous victory speech at Tilbury, Essex.

Against this backdrop the Marprelate tracts appeared. Their objective was, in a manner of speaking, to push the Church of England further away from Rome (Popery) and closer to Geneva (Calvinism). The middle way – as they saw it – that had been navigated in the form of the Elizabethan Religious Settlement, with its reintroduced Book of Common Prayer (1559) and modified Thirty-Nine Articles (1571), did not go far enough. Rather, the tightly knit and well-organised network of 'Martinists' responsible for the tracts wanted a separation of secular from ecclesiastical power, that is distinct spheres of influence for the magistracy and ministry. Moreover, they placed great emphasis on the Bible as the word of God, a divine word which had greater authority than traditions and the pronouncements of bishops. Indeed, it was high-ranking ecclesiastical officials and academics – 'petty popes, and petty antichrists'– that the Martinists initially had in their sights. Among them was a dean of Salisbury called John Bridge, who had written an exceptionally lengthy and tedious defence of the Church of England; the Archbishop of Canterbury; the Bishops of Winchester and London; and the master of a Cambridge College. This was at a time, it must be stressed, when printed works were strictly censored by the Archbishop of Canterbury, Bishop of London and those delegated by them for that purpose. And while there was no Inquisition in the manner of Catholic Spain, there was still a Court of High Commission for investigating and punishing those found guilty of committing religious offences. Mercifully, this court could not sanction torture to extract confessions nor could it impose the death penalty. It did, however, operate in tandem with the secular Court of Star Chamber, whose officials investigated and heavily fined some of those suspected of being involved in the Marprelate affair.

Not all the Martinists' accusations were accurate, or even coherent. Nonetheless, they succeeded in breaking the mould of how religious disputes should be conducted. Indeed, a striking feature of the tracts was that they were written in English rather than Latin so that they could reach as wide an audience as possible; even those unable to read might still hear the words spoken aloud. The prose was colloquial and playful, relying on spontaneity, irony, parody and alliteration: 'proud, popish, presumptuous, profane, paltry, pestilent and pernicious prelates' gives a flavour. Most likely the author(s) were influenced by the extemporisation of actors on the Elizabethan stage as well as jest books and ballads. As for the satire, it was comparatively savage. Indeed, it did not follow accepted norms which derived from Roman models. Rather, Marprelate mixed sometimes well-informed anecdotes with sexual insults and subversive rhetoric.

The official response was outrage. Scandalised, the Bishop of Winchester declaimed in *An Admonition to the People of England* (1589) against these 'odious libels' crammed with 'untruths, slanders, reproaches, railings, revilings, scoffings and other intemperate speeches' that never before had been seen committed to print. Further propaganda intended to maintain the status quo appeared, including a royal proclamation and a sermon. Yet the most remarkable aspect of the officially sponsored counter-narrative was how the ecclesiastical authorities, with full governmental support, managed to swiftly adopt the Martinists' innovative polemical strategies and turn those weapons against the very people who had developed them. To accomplish this they hired skilled writers, most likely including the prolific Thomas Nashe (1567–*c.*1601) and the playwright John Lyly (1554–1606). Altogether more than twenty anti-Martinist works were published with titles like *Pappe with a hatchet* (1589), *An Almond for a Parrot* (1589), and *Martins Months mind* (1589). Even so, in an unanticipated irony, at least one of these anti-Martinist pamphleteers became so infected with the Martinist strain that he began writing some pieces in a Martinist vein.

In the short term, as we have seen, the Martinists were defeated. Not only that, but their more cautious and moderate puritan brethren – many of whom had been quick to distance themselves from the Martinist project – were damned by association. A further blow was struck in July 1591 with the execution of William Hacket, a self-proclaimed prophet from Northamptonshire. Hacket and his accomplices planned to abolish church government by bishops and depose Queen Elizabeth. Their widely publicised fate, however, served only to bring the puritan movement into further disrepute. But in the long term, like a phoenix rising from the ashes, Martin Marprelate re-emerged together with a fictional offspring. In 1637 his spectre was invoked by seditious parishioners in Northamptonshire refusing to pay tithes and ship money. Then, with England on the brink of Civil War between Royalists and Parliamentarians, a pamphlet entitled *Vox Borealis* (1641) printed by 'Margery Mar-Prelat' appeared. Here the printer directly addressed the reader in verse:

> Martin Mar-Prelate was a bonny Lad,
> His adventures made the Prelates mad:
> Though he be dead, yet he hath left behind
> A Generation of the MARTIN kind.

The following year, Marprelate's *Hay any work for Cooper* was reprinted by 'Martin the Metropolitan'. Thereafter a number of similar titles were issued, notably a satirical plea for religious toleration by 'Young Martin Mar-Priest, son to old Martin the Metropolitan'. Many of these works were by the future Leveller leader Richard Overton. Appropriating and refashioning the identity of a famous if pseudonymous Elizabethan antagonist of ecclesiastical authority, Overton's purpose was to fire shots with paper bullets against persecution and tyranny in the pamphlet wars of the English Revolution. Leaders die. Their followers die. But ideas can and do endure – as do the innovative ways in which they can be expressed and spread.

The Captain

Karline Smith

June 12th – Five Months Ago

LEAVING LONDON'S EAST INDIA DLR station, high-heeled and power-suited, blending with the swarm of early workers walking past Canary Wharf, Bridget felt the familiar adrenalin rush freed finally from the packed underground carriage.

The morning sun shone in a blue, cloudless sky. Work was a five-minute scurry across the elevated glass walkway and down its sister escalator towards DataSky Global. Her usual coffee spot was on Cotton Street, and already her taste buds were craving for her regular cheese and ham toastie; her tongue hankering for the smoothness of the accompanying skinny latte. On her way in, Bridget had noticed a homeless woman and a little boy, huddled in a doorway, a sign near them on the ground asking for money. Withdrawing cash from a nearby ATM, Bridget handed it to the lady, whose mouth opened wide at the sight of the ten fifty-pound notes.

There was a new system of ordering via an app, to ease the queues since the Covid-19 outbreak a couple of years ago. Bridget sat at a small, vacant table near the window, gratefully unburdening her heavy laptop bag onto the floor. All around, the wealth of London announced itself through jagged skyscrapers, glass-box wharf-side apartments, and unimaginably expensive penthouses. The money she'd given the homeless woman wouldn't have got her a decent room for a week around here. And every day brought more desperate faces begging onto the streets. Silent and invisible lives.

At the table opposite, a construction worker in a helmet and high-vis vest, paused momentarily midway through a bacon sandwich, to stare at her gloved hands with a curious wrinkled forehead. Outside it must have been 23 degrees and rising. Her sunglasses and gloves contradicted each other's purpose.

Bridget smiled softly, flicking her long blonde hair behind her, until the inquisitor lowered his gaze. Her skin condition was nobody's business. Releasing a long breath, she took out her iPhone, idling through Facebook, waiting impatiently for her order. Twenty-four likes for a tagged photo of her daughter from her husband, one new friend request and meaningless updates in her news feed.

Sensing a presence, Bridget jolted up from her phone. Seated opposite, was a young mixed-race woman, eighteen, twenty at the most, studded nose, black mascara, eyeliner circling her brown eyes, and dreadlocks trickling from under the navy-blue hoodie.

'Mind if I sit?' she asked. The question was pointless because she was already seated. The table where the construction workers had sat was now empty. Bridget fake-smiled, like a magazine advertisement for whiter-than-white toothpaste, shifting her weight in her seat. A lover of personal space, even before the pandemic, it rattled her that this person was deliberately invading it.

'I'm Zayda.' Bridget felt something familiar about the girl, vague images trying to reactivate in dormant brain cells.

'Okay. Hi.'

Bridget's head dropped down to the phone screen.

An assistant came over with Bridget's latte and cheese and

ham toastie. He bade her enjoyment of her food drearily, before departing.

'You have a superpower.'

'*Excuse me?*'

'Don't deny it. I saw you. You gave that homeless woman cash by withdrawing money with your hand, no card. The assistant came with your order, yet you didn't use the app or go to the counter to place it. You come in every morning. At the same time. You don't even interact with the staff. The order just appears… like magic… just like that money.'

Now the stranger had Bridget's attention.

'I also know why you hide your eyes behind dark glasses, the real reason you wear those gloves, and that you don't need a mobile to make or receive calls.'

Bridget's heart performed a triple-beat, as she slid her phone into her trouser suit pocket. Looking for a quick exit, she realised she had made a mistake. She was hemmed in, her back to the window, a woman and her family moved to the vacant table nearby and a couple with luggage blocking her path, were at the other table.

'It's okay. Please don't be wary. I am here to –'

Bridget stood up, chair scraping on the tiled floor, scooping up her coffee and toastie hastily and snatching her case.

A ringing mobile filled the air. Bridget felt her right gloved hand vibrating. Her mobile in her pocket wasn't vibrating.

'Receive the call… please,' Zayda said, narrowing her eyes. 'Take off the glove and receive the call.'

The youngest child, at the table next to them, a girl aged around four, stared at the two women, caught in a standoff.

The phone stopped ringing. Zayda's lips pulled upwards at the corners with admiration.

'Ahhh, you've blocked it. You're better than I thought.'

An assistant at the counter complained loudly about a system failure. The contactless payment machine wasn't working. The computerised till register had malfunctioned. Around them, people looked bewildered, as several ring tones trilled in the atmosphere in unison, signifying incoming mobile calls.

Bridget felt her pale complexion burning. She knew that behind the tinted shades, her eyes would reflect zeros and ones, the binary codes accessed by her mind and body, that her special magnetic gloves were not filtering, because of this woman's presence, indicating they were similar, clashing with each other's data fields. Abandoning her food and coffee on the table, Bridget pushed through bodies and luggage, almost falling over, exiling herself from the procession of ringing phones, flickering lights, and disrupted software. Fleeing Zayda's eyes trying to enter her core, like malware.

With trembling hands, Zayda made a phone call, watching through the coffee shop window as Bridget disappeared around the corner.

'It's her, definitely, one hundred per cent.'

She punched the air in jubilation, laughing as exhilarating tears fell.

The caller asked, 'Do you think she recognised you?'

Zayda paused, welling up.

'No, Franklin. How could she recognise the future version of the child she dropped off at nursery this morning?'

October 1st

Heavy rain slashed the pavements, leaving large puddles in dips and holes. By the time D.I. Ward reached the location, Europa Global Bank Vault, situated next to the Rochester Hotel on Park Lane, the team were already assembled, taking photographs, dusting for fingerprints, analysing CCTV footage. A media blackout was in place.

His colleague, Detective Inspector Bilal 'Billy' Khan with a computer bag over his shoulder, met him at the entrance to the basement of the Grade-II listed, 140-year-old former mansion. Like him, in his early thirties D.I. Khan was young for such a high-ranking position. Square-jawed and taciturn, though some people confused this quietness for weakness, his intelligence, not to mention fiery temper, were characteristics that often caught people by surprise. Both ex-military, they had been friends for nine years, since week one when Billy defended Aiden against a racist knobhead in their unit. From that day, the guy left the only Asian and Black officers in the unit, alone.

On the ground floor entrance, Billy did the honours, introducing the vault's owner – who had cut short his holiday in San Paulo, to fly over – to his boss, Aiden, who'd also cut short a long weekend in Margate, with his wife and child:

'Mr Di Marco, this is Detective Chief Inspector Ward – Digital Forensics division of the Metropolitan Organised Cybercrime Unit, and myself Detective Inspector Khan – also Digital Forensics, as I explained earlier.'

Oliver Di Marco's leathery skin looked like ash, as if someone had tipped him upside-down and drained out all his blood. It was understandable. Aiden remembered watching a TV profile about the facility once, where the guy had boasted his security system was unassailable, and that his clients' assets were in the safest vault in London.

'How the hell has this happened?' his voice was mangled with apprehension.

Ward had been partly briefed on his drive from headquarters. So far CCTV had revealed nothing. No images of any persons entering or exiting through the front upstairs lobby or the back entrance, both of which are heavily secured. The building had four routes leading to the single corridor downstairs going to the vault, each with hourly rotating passcodes. A sophisticated entropy-based random-generator produced the codes, restricted to a server hermetically sealed from external access. Clients could only access their high-value items if they gave a week's notice, and had their ID verified independently by the vault's biometric system, and only then if escorted by a custodian and two security personnel. Along with its titanium-reinforced blast doors, bullet-proof glass, electronic timers, and additional biometric scanners, the vault insisted every member of staff, from the cleaners to the directors, were thoroughly and continually vetted.

There was only one way in and one way out.

Nobody would be able to escape the cameras or the computer system.

Or get through the heavy, double-locked, steel-reinforced door.

Not even an insider.

As they headed downstairs, into an area flooded with bright neon light, the sound of pounding rain above began to fade. At the vault entrance, the soon-to-be ex-head of security, Toby Philips met them and began explaining the security protocols. All four had to remove their coats and suit jackets and dress in white, crime-scene overalls and white cotton shoe-covers to eliminate cross-contamination. Then, suitably attired, they walked into the chasm of the vault, Toby, the taller of all the men, leading the way.

'All mobile phone signals are blocked down here. We try not to make our clients feel as if they are on a prison visit, but if they choose not to leave their phones in the lockers upstairs,' Toby explained, 'they won't work down here.' Aiden observed the deliberately visible CCTV cameras on all sides, silently tracking the small congregation as they moved around the vault.

Five hundred and fifty security boxes were in the vault, containing valuables and documents for whoever could afford the thousand-pound-a-week fee for the smallest of boxes. Only, *one* box had been opened illegitimately. Box number 22. The fact that this box had had its contents removed with no one seeing or detecting a thing was now a threat to the company's entire business model. Wiggling his white-gloved fingers, Aiden walked towards the box, which Toby informed him, had its own randomly generated 8-digit passcode, like all the others.

'Do you know which passcode was used?' Aiden asked, licking his upper lip.

'Yes, I ran a report. The code was overridden,' Toby said.

'You mean you were hacked.'

'It's not possible.'

The flesh on Toby's forehead puckered into tiny lines, while his eyes widened to appear even more bloodshot.

'Hmm. Why are we here then? You were hacked, your routers were compromised, your firewalls breached, your network monitoring system, your CCTV – all invaded by an extremely agile hacker,' Aiden said, making no attempt to hide his haughtiness.

As he eased the security box door open, a stream of what looked like grain trickled out onto the floor.

'Is this what was in here? I don't understand,' Aiden said.

'According to the inventory, box 22 contains, or rather *contained,* a family heirloom, a green pendant, silver chain, worth a fair amount given its age, in the family for four centuries,' Toby said.

'Stolen and replaced with – what is this, wheat grain? No other boxes touched. Just *this* one,' Aiden said, spinning around on his feet.

Looking as if he was about to cry, Di Marco left, leaving the head of security with the detectives.

'I would like to know your thoughts,' Toby said.

Aiden put his hand out, indicating for him to stop, feeling a sudden excruciating pounding in his head. He took out his mobile to check the battery. It was dead. Billy checked his also, shrugging to acknowledge his was dead too. Aiden looked at the overhead cables sitting in the rack above.

'This is a complex hack. It's deep within your network infrastructure, able to manipulate petabytes to exabytes of data, and to move wirelessly outside, in.'

He looked around. All evidence pointed to what they'd already suspected: they were up against Variant Bi-Data beings who mostly used their abilities for small-scale, petty operations. But this one felt different. Stood out.

Aiden motioned for Billy to hand him the computer bag. Placing the laptop on the floor, he switched it on, logged into the government's maximum-security Quadrant application and linked it with a wireless handheld scanner which he also retrieved from the bag. Billy huddled next to him so that he could see the dashboard of graphs, blue and red flashing bars, and reports. Aiden sensed Toby watching silently, imagining the man's anxiety like something creeping under his skin. Billy lifted the scanner towards the cables above. Instantly the digital graph software began analysing frantically, black zigzags peaked and troughed erratically until it spiked high off the chart, and the dashboard of flashing bars all turned red.

A surge of disbelief and excitement filled Aiden.

Quadrant seemed to be indicating the source of the hack was in the room itself, just metres away, as if in the fibre-optic cables above them.

Observing.

None of the others were capable of that.

June 28th

Bridget walked into the meeting room where the new recruits waited for her to facilitate the training. Her thoughts were digressing to anywhere but the present; she couldn't stop thinking about Zayda, the girl who had intruded into her life two weeks ago, and forced her, among other things, to give up her beloved coffee shop. Halfway through the morning, a strange nausea forced her to visit the toilets, having to pass through their floor's reception, and hearing complaints about the systems going offline en route.

At the toilet sinks, Bridget removed her gloves. Bright sunlight poured in through the windows making the binary codes coursing through her veins more visible on her skin. A female co-worker entered the toilets wearing a friendly smile, her eyes descending towards Bridget's hands. Bridget plunged them under the tap which automatically triggered a stream of water. Smiling nervously, Bridget pretended to wash her hands thoroughly.

'Did you get one of those 3D tattoos? Looks amazing,' the woman remarked, entering a cubicle.

Drying her hands, Bridget replaced her gloves hastily, glancing at her blonde hair sticking against her perspiring forehead, tinted glasses hiding her blue eyes. Exhaustion consumed her. She leant on the sink area for support. In her teens, Bridget visited her GP over the strange, pulsing welts. A skin specialist remarked that it was an allergy. Bridget discovered the disfiguration worsened around computers, with other symptoms such as a pounding headache, and tingling fingertips. Life got worse for her when an ex-boyfriend freaked out, saying he saw his Insta account in her eyes, after making love. She discovered that magnets controlled or lessened her body's data absorption, after playing with her daughter's new fridge magnets one day. A manufacturer she found online had made the lace gloves for her, minuscule magnets sewn into the cloth. Most people, including her employer and husband, thought she wore her gloves for medical reasons. All was going well until this Zayda girl turned up causing an 'emotional' data-related surge, ultimately wreaking havoc with the systems at work.

The woman who had complimented her on her 'tattoo', washed her hands and left.

Breathing heavily, Bridget felt the first heaves of a panic attack. These episodes had not surfaced since childhood. As much as she didn't want to remember, the images insisted on replaying themselves in her mind. Her parents were poor. Always fighting and arguing about money, constantly moving from one squalid dwelling to another, owned by rich slum landlords who treated them like cattle. No banks would lend them money. Food was scarce. She remembered, on her hands and knees, picking between the crevices of dirty, scratched floorboards, looking for pieces of stale food, as her stomach felt like it was eating its own lining. Her father couldn't seem to hold down a job. Then one day, she never saw him again. Vanished. Her mother told her never to say his name again, ever. She did everything to put food on the table. Bridget knew what she did. For *her*. Men coming and going. Rich men. Her mother died before she ever saw her daughter's abilities with computers reap any rewards.

Bridget heaved air in and out of her lungs, gloved hands holding onto the edges of the sink, resisting, controlling her breathing, until it passed.

She knew who the caller was before she heard the ringtone. Checking no one else was in the toilets, even though she saw the other woman leave, Bridget picked a cubicle and dropped down onto a closed toilet lid, locking the door behind her. Removing her glove, she brought her three middle fingers down, and tilted her hand visibly teeming with blue lights under her skin, to the angle of a phone.

'For God's sake, stop calling me. Please. Leave me alone.'

'I can't. I need you. You need me,' Zayda said.

Bridget closed her eyes, rocking back and forth on the toilet, trying to swallow the lump in her throat.

'Meet me at the corner of Blackfriars Road near Southwark underground in twenty minutes.'

'I'm in work.'

'Make some shit up. Tell them you're sick. It's important. You won't regret it.'

'What choice do I have?'

'You *do* have a choice. You can pretend you never saw me the other day and keep living your life in ignorance of who you really are, or you can come with me. You can stop hiding, stop pretending.'

'I don't understand any of this.'

'Meet me at Southwark and I'll explain everything.'

Zayda logged out.

The lights faded from Bridget's palm.

October 6th – Present Day

D.C.I. Aiden Ward sat examining the report he had just typed up on the previous week's cyber-theft at the Bank of Scotland,

Westminster branch. The crime was similar to the vault, only this time it was money spread across multiple accounts. Notable accounts, too, exclusively very rich people's accounts. The money left the bank, was deposited into various clearly fake accounts, and transferred to offshore sterling accounts, probably to re-emerge sometime later on these shores as crypto currency, if previous moves like this were anything to go by. The weekend before that, two other banks had been hit with the same modus operandi. A total of five million pounds. Scotland Yard and The Met were getting edgy. There was a sense that any bank in the world could be targeted if they didn't act fast. The pressure was building, and as Senior Investigating Officer, Aiden was desperate for a breakthrough.

Aiden finished off his fourth coffee, ignoring the Superintendent's glare as he passed by his office's glass window, disappointed that his two specialist officers seemed to be costing the department time, money, and reputation. The team were still analysing hours of CCTV from the vault. No matter how sophisticated this character was, there had to be a glitch somewhere; everyone gets careless. Even the tiniest data fragments could be pieced together.

The rain, hitting the windows outside, sounded like tapping feet. Inside the office, a warm light, combined with the shimmer from the server stacks, cut through the greyish darkness. Between the light and the dark, dancing dust could be seen falling on the desks, cluttered with files and paperwork. One long night was merging into another, with no sign of progress.

Aiden didn't want to lose it. Opening his desk drawer, he looked at the small bottle of Jack Daniels, and risked a quick drink, straight from the neck. The framed photograph of his wife and child on his desk, whom he had not been spending any time with lately, made him pause mid-swill. Recently promoted, his wife was attending conferences most weekends, and their child stayed with his sister. He wondered if they were drifting apart.

Interrupting his thoughts, Billy blundered into the room energetically, waving an iPad, which he thrust under Aiden's nose.

'I was looking at possible dodgy business acquisitions and came across this from *The Guardian*,' Billy said, almost breathless.

Aiden read the headline, biting his upper lip.

UK Charities Benefit from Anonymous Benefactor.

Leaning back slightly, Aiden continued to read.

Charities and organisations across the United Kingdom have benefited from huge sums of money over the last week from an unknown sponsor, known only as Eht Niatpac. Unite to Save the Children received 1.5 million pounds. Shelter 4 Children received 1 million.

Aiden clicked on the link to a video showing the beaming face of the founder of a small Essex-based charity Food for the Needy. He looked directly at the camera, with ecstatic eyes.

'We're delighted, and of course, extremely grateful, to have received a donation of £2.5 million,' he said. 'It's the single biggest donation we've ever received. With this money we can do so much more to help impoverished children and parents struggling with basic necessities. The benefactor has indicated that some of the money should also be invested in community-owned, cooperative farms in the developing world, so that we can deliver food parcels directly from them.'

The off-camera interviewer asked: 'If you don't know who the donor is, what makes you think this?'

'The donor is clearly a lover of symbolic, some might even say theatrical, gestures. This morning we received, by mail, a bag of grain, accompanied by a note using the same alias, along with a brochure for a community-owned farm in Uganda, outlining the various benefits of this type of ethical investment. Beyond that, I can't say any more.'

Aiden paused the video on the director's smiling face. Tilting his head sideways, he looked at Billy.

'Exactly five million in total for all three charities. The

same amount of diverted funds. ... and the bag of grain? Did anyone speak to the family of box 22 at the vault?'

'Yes, Jeremy did,' Billy said, video-calling D.C. Jeremy Parker on his PC, sitting eagerly waiting for him to join them. They didn't have to wait long. Jeremy's face appeared on the screen. He got straight to the point.

'The pendant has belonged to the Cocker-Merritt family since... 1629. More of a sentimental asset than a monetary one. The family is quite distressed by its theft.' Jeremy shared his screen with an image of the pendant.

'Any disputes about ownership within the family?' Aiden asked, sending the image to print.

'You mean like it could have been an inside job? No. They were all in agreement to keep it somewhere safe,' Jeremy said, blinking.

'So, it's been with them since 1629?' Billy asked. 'That's a long time.'

'Yes,' Jeremy said, 'passed down via a John William Cocker. John Cocker was an Executioner in Essex, Maldon. The family said he took it from the neck of a woman who was hung that year.' His voice was full of sarcasm. 'What a great entertainment piece at dinner parties.' With that he ended the call.

Aiden Googled, 'Executions', 'Maldon', '1629', clicking the first link by Professor John Walter from The University of Essex.

In May 1629, a Maldon housewife was tried and hanged for rioting. In March of the same year, over a hundred Maldon women and children, from Witham and the squatters' colonies, boarded a ship taking grain at the Hythe, and forced the crew to fill their aprons and caps with rye. They had been protesting about severe food shortages caused by poor harvests, exacerbated by profiteers transferring scarce grain to areas paying even higher prices.

On May 22nd, two months after the first demonstration, Maldon experienced one of the country's largest and most serious grain riots when a crowd of 300 from surrounding areas, descended on the town's port, Ann Carter took a leading part in this second riot, in May 1629, attacking boats taking on grain, in apparent defiance of a recently renewed ban on the export of grain. They boarded a ship, assaulted the crew, and stole some of the grain from the ship, taking more grain, later, after breaking into a house. Carter coordinated this action, apparently touring clothing townships to drum up support via letters styling herself 'Captain', in cahoots with a local baker, John Gardner, acting as her secretary.

The scale of the rising was exceptional, causing great alarm, and a swift government response. Within days, arrangements were made for a trial of eight of the ringleaders. A week later, four of them were executed, among them was Ann Carter.

'This woman was an actual legend. Incredible,' Billy remarked, clapping his hands, brown eyes widening. 'Wow. They hung her just for trying to feed her family and others when the government was ripping off the grain. Bloody Tories!'

'Never took you for a liberal, Bilal Khan.'

'It's not about that. She had to make a stand, didn't she? This was a bold play for a time when women were ranked so much lower than men in society.'

'Would you say that of whoever is moving inside London banks and vaults right now, un-encrypting data, digitally removing vast sums of money to give to the less fortunate? Is that a bold play?' Aiden asked, hands under his jaw, contemplatively. 'Hmm. Still a criminal in my eyes. We need to put an Account Freezing Order on those charities' accounts. So the money doesn't go anywhere.'

'Freeze all of their assets? On what charge?'

'Money laundering,' Aiden answered. His voice had a sharp edge to it.

'But freezing their accounts would cripple them, Aiden. Staff won't be paid. The people who rely on them won't get their food parcels. Besides, we can't prove anything, you know that. We have to show a direct link from those robberies to the charities. It would take months to try and work out how they got into the system.'

'Billy, why do you think we are here, hmm? We're supposed to be the best team in London. We're supposed to get results. We're supposed to shut hackers down. They're running around wirelessly walking in and out of vaults and laughing at us. I don't care if it's for the poor or for God-fucking-zilla. I don't care if this is 1629 or 2029, they're taking us for absolute fools!'

'But it's money the account holders don't even need, they're so rich. Surplus money sloshing about. Money is just a construct, invented by the rich while others starve. I don't see why –'

'I'm going to shut her down, Billy. I'll find a way.'

'So, you think it's a woman?'

Aiden paused and let loose a deep breath before he answered. 'Eht Niatpac is obviously The Captain backwards. She reclaimed the pendant. She likes grain. And she's also not acting alone. But I am going to get her, I swear. My career depends on it.'

Something else was troubling Aiden, scratching away at his senses.

He glanced at the image of the stolen pendant for a moment then looked up at Billy.

'This pendant story… it doesn't make sense… like how she could afford such a classy piece of jewellery if she was so poor and had to riot for food?'

'Maybe she nicked it from the ship and was about to sell it?'

'Nope, this would have been removed from her before she hit the jail chambers. Ask Jeremy to look into it… like maybe speak to that Professor Walter. At the moment it doesn't add up; and why was it so precious to the Cocker-Merritt family that they had to hide it in such an elaborate vault?'

Billy got up and left. Aiden didn't notice him pause in the open doorway to look back at him.

When he was sure Billy was gone, he took another swig from the whisky bottle, before sliding it back, under a pile of files.

It was nearly eleven o'clock. He still had work to do.

June 28th – Five Months Ago

After waiting for over fifteen minutes, and about to lose her nerve, Bridget finally received a text message from Zayda, instructing her to turn left onto the next street, walk 100 yards and go into the Turkish restaurant directly facing her. Entering the place, Bridget was glad to get out of the hot summer sun, as she was still dressed in her work suit. Why had Zayda told her to come to this grubby takeaway? Bridget couldn't help but wonder about the place's food hygiene rating. An old man sat in the corner reading a newspaper. A woman sat at a table with a toddler, cursing the child's father on the phone right in front of it. The takeaway assistant glanced up at her, serving kebab to a customer.

'Are you the inspector?'

Bridget nodded.

With a flick of his head, he indicated she should go through to the back. Bridget lifted the hatch and passed through.

Zayda texted. *Head down to the basement.* Bridget walked straight into a locked door, with a digital keypad next to it.

Zayda texted. *Use your power.*

Clearly Zayda was observing her, wherever she was. Bridget took off her glove and placed her hand over the unit. The door opened. There was another text. *When you get down to the bottom, do the same at the door there.*

At the foot of a steep, dingy stairwell Bridget found the second door, opened it, and then stopped, startled for a moment. Expecting to find a dark, smelly cellar she was instead dazzled by the lights and sounds of a computer room filled with an array of monitors and cables; some screens showing code, others offering multi-screen live feeds from CCTV cameras overlooking the takeaway, its entrance, and the street outside. Zayda sat at a computer with triple monitors, alongside a young, dark-haired man, busy with code. The computers were hooked up to two large glass vials, big enough to take a shower in. The vials were attached to wires and electrodes, leading to cables hooked to a main computer.

Zayda's words broke her gaze from the glass cylinders.

'Bridget, this is Franklin. He's our junior technician. You heard about the neo-Nazi site that Twitter claimed it shut down accidentally last week – that was Franklin.'

'What is this place?'

Bridget walked around examining the computers, impressed by some of the hardware in the room.

'It's the hub. It's our backup. It's where we watch everything and everyone. It's where we offload our data, wipe it or reuse. But we won't need to do that now because you possess the power to store a shit load more than this place, just like the data company you work for.'

'Don't be silly. No one has power like that.'

'*You* do. You just don't know it. Data and energy live within you.'

'I am just an ordinary woman. A mother. A wife. I happen to be good with computers…'

Bridget felt Zayda's eyes piercing into her.

'Don't you know me?' she asked softly, after a moment.

'No. I don't think so?'

'Your daughter has a butterfly style birthmark on her back, right?'

Zayda pulled her top up, turning around to reveal her back. Bridget backed away the moment she saw it, almost falling into the chair behind her, which she gladly sat down in, hand over her open mouth.

'It's me. I'm twenty years old now. From the future.'

Bridget looked and, in the woman's features, suddenly the face of her daughter appeared: the eyes, the silky light-brown complexion, the long eyelashes. This *was* her daughter, the same feisty girl but all grown up. Bridget closed her eyes, shaking her head from side to side. Her heart felt like it was climbing up in her throat, her mouth dry.

'I'm hallucinating. This is a dream. I know there's something different about me, but this is too much. It's not real. This isn't happening.'

'For my third birthday, you bought me a pair of silver roller skates and a doll that spoke many languages because you realised I had the ability to absorb data too. One day before Christmas you discovered that I could take money from ATM machines using my hand. You told me off. I took that money out to help you because you were sick, because of the virus. You have never told a soul that I had the same ability as you. You told me never to do it again. We are who we are many times over, we just don't know it.'

Franklin stopped coding and smiled at Bridget.

'I want to help you finish your mission. Your purpose. Let me help you regain it. Trust me, Mum, you *have to* trust me, Mum.' Zayda walked over to one of the vials and opened its door. 'This one is yours. Please, step inside.' Hesitation held Bridget to the spot. 'I want you to travel down the wire and find yourself. If you don't like it, you can go back to your dreary big tech job, and you'll never know the power you have to change things.'

Zayda was right. Her life was dreary. And all the poverty and injustice she saw in that life only made her feel helpless.

Bridget stepped inside the vial, watching wearily as Zayda closed the door. She had no choice but to trust her. This was her daughter. Bridget realised she could hear nothing inside apart from her beating heart, pounding in her ears. Zayda indicated for her to place a halo type instrument on her head. The vial tilted backwards slightly, and Bridget felt her back pressing against the glass gently as it continued to tilt until she was horizontal. The sounds in her ears were like high pitch screeches. Carefully, Bridget closed her eyes. The colours behind her eyes were like the clashing of atoms, and she longed to join them. To be within and without. To hear shooting stars and see two moons spin around the earth. The feeling was like the highest point of a roller coaster ride before it angled down into a hundred electric colours. She thought she couldn't control it. Thought it weird she couldn't see her body. Felt trapped between the centre of night and the first light of day and felt herself drifting outward, towards a satellite. Had to learn to coast and float, back down the cables. How was this possible? This liberation. She was cables. She was wireless. She was Bluetooth. But all the time she was down the wire, she could feel an ominous presence, travelling close behind. Bridget struggled, fought until her eyes popped open and she was bolt upright, the door to the glass vial already open, and staring at her future daughter, mouth wide gasping for breath, exhausted.

'Those are viruses. We will teach you how to mutate and outnumber them. What did you think? Did you like it?' Zayda pressed her hands to her mouth, suppressing her excitement.

'It was amazing,' Bridget said, laughter bubbling up and out, stepping out of the vial, Zayda taking her hand.

'By the way, you didn't have to avoid the Satellite. As long as there is data, inside earth or in space, you can utilise it. You can go anywhere.'

'What happens to my physical body?'

'Franklin uses an application he created to monitor breathing and bloods... the vials are oxygenated well, are you in?'

Bridget nodded, head bobbing like a ball bouncing on gentle waves, happy, feeling as if she had finally found the place she knew was always deep in her heart and soul.

August, September, October

As the months passed, Bridget started to notice that this future-daughter was quite different to the girl she was raising. Zayda was entertaining a lavish lifestyle. Restaurants, clubs, cars, concerts, plastic surgery, yachts. Enjoying the attention from social media platforms with huge followers. Zayda was materialistic. She loved money. And Bridget wasn't that way. That's not the way she wanted the persona of The Captain to be. Bridget hadn't yet been able to convert the funds to other currencies – currency markets had better security; it was too risky, Bridget thought. So it had yet to reach many of the places it was most needed, like the developing world. But they were just starting.

Bridget drained her glass of house red and put it down, waiting for Zayda to join her at the corner table at The Seven Stars in Alwych. Blue-skied summer days had turned into grey, rainy autumn ones, and the pub was deprived of its busy lunch time rush, thankfully. Only a few stragglers remained, probably entrepreneurs owning their own time, not clock watching like other people. Feeling hungry, Bridget studied the menu. Twenty minutes past the agreed time, her daughter eventually turned up, wearing new boots, struggling with a cacophony of rustling paper bags emblazoned with designer names. Large Bvlgari frames covered her eyes, hair combed out of their dreadlocks and styled in extension tresses. Bridget barely recognised her at first, until she saw her dark painted lips parted in a smile, exposing her newly whitened teeth. Piling her bags up on a spare chair beside her, Zayda sat down and immediately took out a mirror to re-apply lipstick to already heavily-worked lips. The glint of the girl's diamond earrings caught Bridget's already-widening eyes.

Bridget poured herself another glass, took a swig, and poured one for her daughter.

'Why d'you meet me here? There are far better places to eat.'

'This place has history, Zayda. It's been here over 400 years. I like it.' Bridget cleared her throat, leaning forward, putting her hands under her chin. 'Anyway, I need to talk to you.'

'You could have called. Or sent a text.'

'No, you've been too busy. We need to talk face-to-face.' Zayda put the mirror and lipstick away in what Bridget noticed was another new handbag.

'Damn, why so serious?' Zayda sipped the wine, looking at Bridget, a playful smile teasing the corners of her lips. Bridget didn't return it.

'We have to stick to the plan, Zayda. Not divert funds for expensive clothes and luxuries.'

Zayda gave Bridget a look of fake aghast, laughing.

'Live a little, really, you're such a workaholic.'

'It's getting a little messy. I notice you're not staying with me when we plug in, you're doing your own thing. And now this shopping habit. I thought we were in this together. Last week, when you followed me in, you disappeared and didn't come out for hours. It's dangerous for you. You're not like me. And we risk losing everything here. Then we wouldn't be able to help anyone rise out of poverty.'

'What's the point of working this hard to help people if we don't reap some of the benefits ourselves?'

Bridget could feel a stubborn fury in the girl. A trait she recognised from the younger version of her daughter, a dislike of being told what to do.

'Are you listening to me, Zayda?'

Zayda let loose an aggrieved breath before answering without meeting Bridget's eyes directly. Her tone sounded petulant.

'All right then. Have it your way. We'll cool off until *you* say so.'

November 2nd

The briefing room was full: men and women from the analytics team, as well as others he didn't know from some internal task force who hadn't introduced themselves; all waiting for Aiden to update them with the latest regarding Operation 1629. Four floors up, the rain outside could still be heard, pounding down on the pavements below. Drawing in his breath and licking his upper lip, Aiden began to speak.

'Not everything is as it seems, and not all weapons look the same. In this department, we investigate some of the most complex, high-profile cases anywhere. Over the past two months we have been collecting, exploiting, assessing, and interpreting a range of overt and covert information sources to deliver valuable, influential analysis to tackle this latest so-called "digital vigilante",

The Captain, who we believe is a single, British individual, rather than a collective, a foreign adversary, or a piece of self-perpetuating AI, possibly assisted by one or two other persons as yet unknown.'

Aiden flicked on the overhead projector. A blurred image of a woman appeared on the screen.

'After several weeks of analysis, Billy has been able to enhance a glitch in the CCTV images at the Bank Vault somewhere between 18.30 and 07.30 on 29/30th September.'

'Well done Billy!' someone shouted. Billy's smile was modest, his face turning crimson, as if he wanted to play down his role.

'This clip is just two frames long, lasting one twenty-fifth of a second; the hacker left a gap in the CCTV footage that she overwrote,' Aiden continued in a level, unemotional tone.

'Everyone makes mistakes,' Billy muttered.

'We believe this to be one of the perpetrators, most likely The Captain herself,' Aiden went on. 'Facial recognition software came up with an online match.' Silence descended on the room, people stopped rustling their papers, everyone's full attention was on the image. The image was of a young, mixed-race female, studded nose, late teens or early 20s. 'We have several pseudonyms for this woman: Amelia McAllister, Alexandria Jones and Zayda Canning. Amelia was arrested for unlawfully withdrawing funds from an ATM around four years ago. Since then, she has been untraceable. The internet however provided a number of face matches: in particular Twitter and Insta profiles under a second name, Marisha Blake. Blake is a minor celebrity on social media with over six million followers. She appears to have money, lots of it, and is well-travelled. A request for information revealed IP addresses in New York, Toronto, Rio, and Sydney, Australia, all VPNs. We have no physical address so far, no National Insurance number. No bills. No bank accounts. No digital footprint, outside of social media.'

'Over the last week, we've fed the image into our CCTV facial recognition cameras out in the community in conjunction with other UK police authorities, and the result came up that she is right here, in London, as we suspected. We tracked her a couple of times on the underground. The cameras tracking her have detected multiple appearances in or near a takeaway at 29 Isabella Street. This is where the raid will take place tomorrow morning, backed by an Armed Response Unit – no terrorist links have been established, but it's best to err on the side of caution, just in case. Let's get her, guys. Let's get The Captain.'

From the corner of his eye, Aiden saw DC Parker trying to get his attention as the team disbanded, wafting a piece of paper. With a discreet side-nod, Aiden motioned Billy to follow him into the office. Both sat opposite Jeremy, who fixed them with his eyes.

'I have an update about the pendant. Walter confirmed he'd never heard of anything like it and said, like you, it was highly unlikely. He directed us to The Bodleian, in Oxford, and it took us a while, hence the delay, but I came across an odd text from a clergyman and medical practitioner called Richard Napier who treated poor people in Buckinghamshire for "sickness or anything caused by devils or astronomical events". On a visit to Malden, he came across a man in the marketplace "consumed with lunacy" who used to be a jailor. The man was purported to have turned into a "tosspot" after no one believed him that he witnessed a woman appear inside the chambers of the jail he was guarding. The woman did not enter through normal, earthly means but walked through the wall, he claimed, and spoke to a prisoner, a female prisoner, who was due to hang the following morning: Ann Carter. The former jailor described the woman as "a Moorish wench with hair like snakes, a jewel in her nose and appareled in strange breeches, white shoes with a peculiar mark on them". She did not look like a "spirit", and the jailer had thought he must have been dreaming. All the same, he hid from sight so he could eavesdrop without being seen. The woman seemed as solid as the clergyman in front of him. He saw her remove something from around her neck, which looked like a necklace with a light glowing from a stone hanging from it.

Then he listened as the woman instructed Carter to give the jailor (him) the necklace in exchange for her freedom. On seeing this, the jailor stayed away from Carter's cell for the rest of the night, petrified she was in league with witches and demons, until it was time for her execution. Nothing in the world would make him sell his soul to the devil for an *accursed necklace*.'

Aiden moved his eyes from side to side, digesting the information.

'Folklore.' Billy said, folding his arms, blowing out a pent-up breath. Jeremy's eyes passed from one man to the other.

Aiden looked lost in thought. 'A Moorish wench with hair like snakes,' he repeated slowly, 'a jewel in her nose and appareled in strange breeches, white shoes with a peculiar mark on them.' He saw Billy draw in long, troubled breaths, unfolding his arms, leaning forward, 'What description did we get of the younger suspect from the CCTV footage: dreadlocks, nose piercing, jeans and designer trainers? Feels like we're being pranked here.'

'We'll get all the definite answers tomorrow.' Billy said, 'when we nick them.'

The next morning, armed with a rifle, Billy sat in the front of the van waiting for the command. When it came, he leapt from the vehicle and dashed through pouring rain towards the takeaway, surrounded by the rest of the team. The assistant's jaw dropped as they burst in, demanding he stay where he was and not move, waving their guns at him. They marched past him through to the back where they met the first door entry system.

'What's the code?' Aiden shouted. The assistant said he didn't know. He only worked there to pay for his student loan. Several uniformed officers wearing bullet-proof vests tore the door down with battering rams. After two attempts, the door gave way. They went downstairs cautiously, backs to the wall, guns trained at the second locked door. The door was given the same treatment, bursting wide open. The team bust in, guns poised.

The room was empty.

No computers. No life. Nothing.

He saw a piece of paper poking out from under his right boot.

Picking it up, he read it: *Better luck next time. Eht Niatpac (and crew).*

November 23rd

Sometime after 3am, Aiden tossed so hard he fell out of bed. It had been like this every night since the raid. The same dream: opening the door to the basement in the Turkish takeaway, to nothing. Four weeks leave was forced on him, and he spent most of those playing PlayStation games in his custom-made chair in front of a gigantic widescreen monitor. Nothing like a shoot 'em up to de-stress, rapid gunfire and booms tearing through the 3-D surround speakers. He never discussed confidential cases with his wife, but he could tell she felt locked out from him. Besides, she had a life of her own, busy with her job, working late, at weekends. His wife left early for work each morning, leaving him to take their daughter to school.

Aiden looked at his bearded face in the bathroom mirror: his hair growing into inch round curls, circles under his dark eyes, his brown complexion looking distinctly greyer. Over the last few weeks, he had found new hiding places for his whisky bottles, and it was showing. Billy kept him updated, of course. No new robberies with the same M.O. No sightings on street CCTV cameras. No sudden financial gifts to charities or individuals. The Captain and her crew had gone to ground. Temporarily, of course. The clue was in the note. There was definitely going to be a 'next time'.

As he entered the department, later that morning, it was clear from the looks on everyone's faces that no one was expecting his return so soon. He'd cut his hair, shaved, splashed aftershave over himself, even manicured his nails. He looked, and smelt, good.

'Don't you have another week's holiday to go?' Billy asked,

following him into their office, and closing the door. The compact space looked neat and tidy.

'No. I told them I was coming back in. I have a plan.'

Billy squinted his eyes, waiting.

'We should lure them out,' Aiden said, biting his lip, eyes moving around as if fearing The Captain was somehow in the room, listening.

'What do you mean?'

'Do our own version of a Trojan horse and hit the infrastructure with a super-virus. We create a fake new bank in the City, providing for the super-rich only. One million pounds minimum opening deposit. Then we can get third-party comms to run a hoax story to all news agencies, bragging about state-of-the-art security, and so on. In short: we challenge them.'

'I'm inclined not to bother, to be honest,' Billy mumbled. 'Banks have insurance, and this is going to cost the force a pretty penny in real money, not fake money; and they may not even take the bait. For all we know, their little Robin Hood episode might be finished.'

'I think the commissioner will agree. We have to try, though. It's the only way we are going to stop The Captain making a mockery of London's financial systems.'

'I don't know, chief. It's not the most heinous crime to cross our desk.'

'What if, ten years from now, this e-vigilante has wiped the world of all of its currency? What if she achieves the opposite of what she's supposed to be about: everyone, you, me, our families, children, end up bankrupt and starving, on the streets, with the world in chaos. What then, Billy?'

Billy blinked. 'What virus would we use?'

'It would have to be bespoke, specially made. She'd have vaccines for all the existing viruses.'

'How long would that take?'

'Two weeks max. It will give us time to put everything else into place. I've got dibs on what we call it.' A smile spread across Aiden's face. 'Check this. I'm going to call it "The Executioner"!'

December 7th

Zayda applied black gloss evenly to her lips, smiling at her big-eyed reflection in the large mirror. Bridget was becoming distant. Zayda sensed it. Their comradery had become frayed, bringing a heaviness to their work. When they first met, they'd had fun together. Bridget had confided in her about how her special skills had alienated her to the point of having no friends. She'd never spoken about them to anyone until Zayda appeared. Now she missed Bridget. She needed them both to be back to where they'd been before.

The sky was clear, and a bright sun lit up her nine-million-pound condo overlooking the River Thames. Flicking through the news channels on her wall-high flat screen, Zayda was about to move on to painting her toenails in much the same colour, when a business news report caught her attention.

'Dubai Commercial Bank has just opened in London's financial district, boasting the eighth-highest sigma rating of any bank in the world, leapfrogging giants like Barclays and HBOS, from day one. The new bank offers a broad range of financial services to international markets, specialising in day-trading, derivative and currency services.' The reporter went on to say that it had an e-commerce security system like no other, unbreakable. 'On the high seas international finance, this ship claims to be unsinkable,' the reporter signed off.

Zayda called Bridget.

Bridget was travelling through London Euston underground, on her way to a business meeting, sailing through gates using only her hand to open each barrier, with no one noticing. Once out in the open again, she found a side alley, donned her glasses, removed a glove, looked around cautiously and took Zayda's call.

'We have our Titanic,' Zayda's voice declared.

'The original ships were Flemish,' Bridget corrected her. 'Although popular rumour at the time claimed they were from Dunkirk. A little smaller than the Titanic, either way.'

'I mean, a bank that says it's unsinkable, right from the start. All dirty money. Dubai – an economy built on slavery you always said.'

Bridget paused.

'I thought we agreed we were easing off after the raid. It was too close.'

'I thought your mission was to help people. You've barely scratched the surface. Don't you want to help more poor people, Mum, worldwide?' Bridget sighed audibly down the line. 'This is a big one. Just opened. Filthy rich clients. You'd really, *really* make a massive difference.'

A low feeling clung to Bridget.

'I don't know. It's too soon. You know it exhausts me each time I do it.'

'Don't you enjoy it, Mum? The whole bag of grain thing? And you know it's for the greater good. People are depending on you.'

Bridget released the words cooped up in her mind for days since their meeting in the pub.

'And what, exactly, are *you* doing this for, Zayda? Your followers? Your crib? Your lifestyle? I really want to believe that you're in it, like me, to help people.'

'You know what? I don't need you,' Zayda spat back. 'I don't need your help especially if that's what you think of me. I'll do this by myself, and I am not wasting another minute with you and your high-horse bullshit.'

Zayda disconnected the call before Bridget could respond, leaving Bridget staring at her hand in disbelief.

Bridget tried to call back, but Zayda's number rang out, unanswered.

Within an hour Zayda was at the new place, a disused barn in the Essex countryside, kitted out with the shower-sized vials and the rest of the command centre. Franklin was waiting for her. Zayda plonked herself down on the couch with an iPad to study the architectural plans of the building as well as network charts and security tests. There was no doubt in her mind that she could travel through the optic fibres just as transparently as her mum had, absorb data, unencrypt data, infiltrate accounts, shift money, in short become the system.

10.00pm

Franklin attached Zayda to the leads and cables in the glass vial, giving her one long look before he closed the door.

'Are you sure you want to do this without Bridget?'

'She's out. Her choice. I can do this.'

'I don't think you should…'

'Just hook me up, Franklin.'

As she wirelessly downloaded the bank's network to the computer, terabyte by terabyte, the whites of her eyes showed tracks of running noughts and ones. The same numbers pushed through the surface of her skin on her palms and hands. Unused to the intensity of light normally absorbed by Bridget, Zayda felt her body shaking.

10.01pm

The large computer room at the cybercrime unit looked like Houston mission control, anxious technicians and scientists awaiting lift-off, as everyone sat at their computers, headphones on, watching the beta network monitoring software devised in collaboration with several university departments. Everything in the room linked them to the bogus bank, a previously vacant office on the fourteenth floor of an otherwise typical City tower block. Billy and Aiden stood in front of the largest monitor in the room, watching. A red light flashed in the top right-hand corner of the screen, indicating an anomaly.

'She's in,' Billy said.

10.02pm

Zayda felt a shock wave passing through her energy field. Then saw a blinding light coming towards her. Something almost undetectable snagged and tugged her to where she wasn't supposed to be going.

Franklin hammered at his keyboard frantically, commanding the software to increase the oxygen levels to the maximum. Through the vial, he saw Zayda's body convulsing. Her oximeter numbers were plummeting dangerously. He saw the whites of her eyes as the pupils rolled upwards no longer showing binary codes. Sweat formed on his brow. He was losing her. A movement behind him made him spring around to see Bridget, unexpected, marching across the wide expanse of the barn.

'She's in trouble,' Franklin heaved the words out in gasps.

Bridget already knew. She plunged into the vial next to the writhing body of her future daughter, and pulled the halo down to her temples, attaching the electrodes with shaking hands.

10.03pm

A second red light flashed in the top right-hand corner of the screen, indicating another anomaly.

'Christ,' Billy screeched. 'There's another one. There's two.' There was a surge of movement in the room, as everyone leant forward, eyes wide, staring at their computer screens. 'We didn't anticipate this. How's this going to work with two? The virus is only designed to infect one host at a time.'

Taking off his headphones, and turning towards his partner, Aiden answered confidently: 'It will seek out the strongest. Whichever one is The Captain; the virus will destroy.'

10.04pm

Zayda saw the thing snaking towards her. It looked like a cross between a green worm and a rope, sliding and squirming towards her, coiling itself round her midriff, tightening. Bridget had seen it too as she rushed directly towards her daughter. Sensing the intruder, it stopped crushing Zayda, and shifted its energy, releasing its first prey in the process. Whatever it was, it whipped itself around Bridget, coiling round and round her neck. Bridget couldn't move. There was a crowd of people inside the cables, confusing her.

The rope around her neck tightened until she heard the words: 'Let her drop.'

December 8th

Aiden stirred in a tangle of bedsheets. From the angle of the sunlight coming in from the garden, he could tell it was late afternoon. He had propped up the bar at The Crown Tavern on Old Street, well past midnight. The boys had celebrated the success of Operation 1629 and he had been the toast of the pub. The Executioner had done its job. He barely remembered how he got home. Turning over he called his wife's phone, then remembered she was in work early, after working late last night. He threw the phone back under his pillow. That's how they were now, passing ships in the night, with their daughter often being dropped off to school by a friend or relative where she'd stayed overnight. But all that would change now. Promotion was a certainty. His head started to vibrate. Stretching and yawning, he reached back under the pillow top, retrieved the phone, and accepted the call.

'Is this Mr Ward?'

'It is.'

'It's Robin Docherty, the head of year at St Andrew's. Your wife hasn't collected Ella. We've been calling her since 3.15pm.'

Aiden looked at the time. It was 3.45pm. He scratched his head, wondering where she was, bolting upright, naked in the bed, his lean, muscular body desperate for a shower and shave.

'Oh. Ok. I'll... that's really strange... can you bob her in a taxi home for me?'

'It's against our child-safeguarding policy, especially if this is not a pre-arrangement. You need to come and pick her up. Besides, there's something I was going to discuss with your wife. Seeing as you will be coming, I can discuss it with you.'

Driving to his daughter's school, Aiden called his wife with his Bluetooth in. No answer. He called her office. After asking to be put through to her boss, her manager came on the line.

'Mr Ward. Bridget resigned months ago.'

It hit Aiden like the wallop of a spade. Why was she going to weekend conferences and working late? When did she quit her job? He called her phone again. Still no answer.

Agitated and awkward, Aiden waited in the school reception until Mr Docherty met him holding his daughter's hand, with a strange look on his face.

'Mr Ward we have some concerns.' Aiden was barely listening. None of this was making any sense to him. Where was Bridget? 'Ella came into school with a thousand pounds cash this morning. It was in her rucksack.'

'What? Where the hell did you get that from?' he barked, turning to the girl.

Aiden glared at the Peppa Pig rucksack on his daughter's back, before bending down to her level.

'I got it from the cash machine,' Ella said, smiling coyly.

'Sweetheart, baby, you don't have a card.'

'I used my hand. Mummy told me not to.' Aiden's heartbeat thundered. 'Mummy is sick daddy. She needs help.'

The teacher's next words hit him like slow-motion bullets.

'She kept saying that all day too Mr Ward. She keeps saying that her mummy is sick because you put a virus in her and she keeps telling the staff she has another name. Zelda or Zayna or something like that. While we encourage imagination in our...'

'It's Zayda,' the child corrected sternly, before releasing Aiden's loosening hand and skipping towards the car parked near the main entrance. Then she stopped, turned and looked at Aiden. From that distance, Aiden couldn't see her brown eyes, let alone the flecks and imperfections in each iris, which if looked at through the right kind of microscope would have showed nothing but ones and zeros.

'And I can see Mummy in the future.'

CAPTAIN ANN, 1629

Origin Story: Crowd Actions in the Politics of Subsistence[1]

John Walter

FOOD RIOTS – MORE PROPERLY crowd actions since, then as now, 'riot' was a linguistic label employed by authority to deny any legitimacy or reasoning to acts of protest – had occurred since the Middle Ages. But they began to increase in number towards the end of the sixteenth century. In March 1629 in the small Essex port of Maldon, a crowd of over 100 women with their children in tow boarded a Flemish ship and forced its crew to fill their caps and aprons with grain from the ship's hold. In the aftermath of the women's protest, Maldon's rulers were forced to put their hands in their own pockets to purchase the grain and to write, unsuccessfully, to the king's government for a ban on such exports. Quite exceptionally, Maldon experienced a second 'riot' in the same year. In May a much larger crowd several hundred strong, this time dominated by unemployed male clothworkers, again attacked boats taking on grain at Maldon.

Scarcity and fear of famine provoked the protests in Essex in 1629. Poor weather at the start of the year had signalled a bad harvest. Harvest failure was a recurring threat in early modern England. It drove up prices and, in an economy where demand for non-foodstuffs was determined by the price of the staple food of grain, it drove down employment. A trade slump in

European markets had already had a disastrous impact on the cloth industry that dominated much of the north Essex economy. An over-expanded domestic industry whose workforce formed a large, near-landless rural proletariat spinning and weaving in their own homes, was scarcely in a position to weather the storm. With little or no land, few savings and no hopes of alternative employment, it was the clothworkers who bore the brunt of the crisis.

In Essex in 1629, an already fragile situation had been further exacerbated by the extensive taking up of grain within the county by English and foreign merchants for export to European markets. The merchants competed on unequal terms with the urban poor for what grain was available, sweeping local markets of their stocks and pushing up prices in the process. A popularly held moral economy, which privileged local subsistence in the marketing of foodstuffs, was echoed in government policy in policing the market and grain trade against hoarding and excessive profit. The activities of foreign merchants at Maldon's port was therefore ill-received by the crowds since they were popularly held to be flouting laws designed to cope with a situation of impending dearth which banned the export of grain when prices rose beyond prices set by the royal government.

In the first crowd, the women may well have felt that their crucial role in the provisioning of their families gave them special licence to notify authority of its failings in this crucial area of their lives. They were probably more aware of the licence afforded them by their ambivalent legal status at the margins of the law's competence. In the 'riots' of the period, women consciously exploited the ambiguities of their position within the political culture and explored the freedom of action this brought them. In rioting, they were able to turn their marginal relationship to the structure of power within the community (of which their legal dependence on their husbands was only one aspect) to their temporary advantage, since their intervention, if short-lived, was less likely than male violence to threaten the underlying relationship between the poor and their governors. The actions of the women and children at Maldon therefore parallel the deliberate use elsewhere of their ambiguous socio-legal status to articulate the community's sense of grievance. If they did not openly voice the common claim made by their defiant sisters in early modern agrarian protests, 'that women were lawless, and not subject to the laws of the realm as men are but might ... offend without dread or punishment of law,' doubtless some such reasoning helps to explain their exclusively feminine gathering at Maldon and elsewhere in crowd actions over food. Interrogated by the town's rulers, the crisp retort of one of the Maldon women to the question of who [*sc* which male] had incited her to 'riot' was: 'the Crie of the Country and hir owne want'.[2]

The actions of the second crowd had similar motivation. Taking away some of the grain stored awaiting export in a warehouse, the crowd had assaulted the leading merchant, a Mr Gamble, and forced him to purchase his freedom by the payment of a twenty-pound 'fine'. Their fining of the merchant responsible for exporting the grain was a deliberate appropriation of the penalties imposed under government policy for illegal exports. But the repetition of crowd action was a direct challenge to the unwritten protocols of early modern 'riot' in which, after the event, crowds were expected to express contrition in exchange for conciliation by authority. While the March rioters had escaped scot-free, the second 'riot' ended in the execution of several of the rioters, including the crowd's leader, Ann Carter, a participant also in the first action.

Ann Carter had been active in the first 'riot'; she played a leading role in the making of the May protest. According to a report of her subsequent trial, she had made a tour of the clothing townships to drum up support and had had letters sent out in which she styled herself 'captain'. Unable to write herself, she had employed a local baker to act as her secretary. Captain Ann may well have carried her leadership into the actual 'riot'. In an attempt to mobilise the town's inhabitants, she was reported to have cried, 'Come, my brave lads of Maldon, I will be your leader for we will not starve'.[3]

Remarkably, unlike so many of those in the past whose only appearance into the historical record is a note in the criminal records of their punishment, research has uncovered evidence of Ann Carter's past. This may help to explain her willingness to lead the protests, and certainly also cast her for the role she was chosen to play in the judicial aftermath as a sacrificial victim of seventeenth-century 'justice'. Her previous history as well as her behaviour afterwards – her surviving judicial examination suggests a confidence to challenge any description of her action as violent or illegal – certainly qualified her for that role.

Married to a local butcher, what little that can be recovered of her personal life suggests that the couple had unsuccessfully struggled to maintain a living. After her death, a jury found she had nothing to her name. Something of her personality, but also her poverty, is reflected in a series of confrontations she had with the town's rulers. Questioned, for example, by one of the town's rulers over her absence from church, she had flung back at her examiner, 'If he would provide one to do her work she would go,' telling him that, 'she served God as well as he'. That Ann, driven by her struggle to feed her family, had been prosecuted for a minor infringement of market regulations, while the town's rulers failed to prevent the more damaging activities of foreign merchants, had doubtless increased her own sense of outrage.

Tried and found guilty before a swiftly-convened special commission packed with the leading aristocratic families of the county, Ann Carter was hanged the very next day, on 30 May 1629. Apparently the only woman in protests over food to suffer such a fate in this period, there is a strong case for seeing her punishment as a sordid piece of street theatre, as a show of judicial vengeance intended to demonstrate, at a time of political as well as economic crisis, Charles I's government's ability to restore order. Now remembered in Karline Smith's story, following her recovery from the historical record Captain

Ann has belatedly become something of a local heroine – as well as a continuing source of controversy – in her home town.

By the late seventeenth century, the food 'riot' had become the most common form of collective protest within the politics of subsistence, The lazy stereotype of the food 'riot' as a collective form of violent theft rarely captured the reality of such disorder. As the continuing record of twentieth-century famines has shown, 'riot' was seldom, if ever, an automatic and unpremeditated response to hunger and starvation. It needed a sense of injustice, moral outrage and legitimacy for crowds to take action. Nor in early modern England was the food 'riot' simply a form of immediate self-help on the part of the poor and harvest-sensitive (whose numbers in years of harvest failure might stretch well beyond the everyday poor). The crowd's appearance was not designed to end its grievance unilaterally, but to do so by securing (or coercing) the necessary exercise of authority. By publicly confronting authority with its failings, crowds attempted (more often than not successfully before the late seventeenth century and even thereafter) to recall their governors to their self-proclaimed duty of protecting the poor. As the ultimate political weapon of the poor, the food 'riot' was often the culmination of a preceding exchange between the poor and their governors in which the threat of popular violence had been used (unsuccessfully) to coerce authority into action on their behalf. At the heart of government policy, encoded in printed books of orders, re-issued after the Maldon crowd actions, was a belief that it was manipulation of the markets by farmers hoarding, merchants exporting, and middlemen inflating prices that caused dearth and suffering. Government policy therefore called for policing the grain trade and market, privileging, in theory but by no means always in practice, in years of dearth the access of vulnerable consumers to grain at under-prices and for the very poor in years of harvest failure cheap or free distribution of grain or flour within towns and villages.

Protesters then had other tactics available to them that stopped short of the need to 'riot'. Petitioning authority to implement its own policies and to prevent malpractices in the market might then be the first step taken by those facing the threat of starvation, as it was before the second Maldon 'riot'. But petitioners might also introduce an element of threat into their pleas by delivering their petitions *en masse* and by referring therein to the threat of violence; as the contemporary proverb ran, 'Hunger will break through stone walls'. Public grumblings in the marketplace or increasingly in anonymous bills with threats to stick the heads of middlemen in the grain trade on poles before their doors served a similar role. Wise magistrates took the hint.

That crowds sometimes did not take the grain they seized reflected their concern to distinguish their actions from simple theft. While those transporting the grain might be physically threatened and on occasion assaulted, the aim of the protesters was to avoid the label of 'riot' and to secure the intervention of central and local government on their behalf. Since the most frequent protesters were either clothworkers or the urban poor of generally smaller towns and ports, their actions in defence of the moral economy nevertheless reflected their understanding of their increasing dependence for food on a market economy and its agents. Frightening away the dealers in grain upon whom they depended would prove self-defeating. There was therefore a politics to the food 'riot'. Riots were necessarily triangulated: crowd actions had as their immediate target those manipulating the grain trade, but as in the first 'riot' at Maldon, they were intended to prompt action by the magistrates. The legacy of the food 'riot' was, then, double-edged. It brought not just a restoration of order by authority, but also an increased responsiveness to the demands of the poor.

Into the eighteenth century, accelerating urbanisation, regional industrialisation and growing landlessness increased the numbers of those dependent on the market for both food and employment. The increasing penetration of a national market saw local markets increasingly becoming bulking points for the onward movement of grain for export or to the capital and larger cities, while an increase in buying crops in the field or 'at pitch' (from samples of grain) began to undermine the public space of the market as the primary site for dealing in grain and other foodstuffs. Against a background of increased agricultural productivity, royal government actively encouraged the export of grain and increasingly abandoned its policy of policing the market and grain trade. But in reality, both central and local government remained inconsistent; at moments of crisis triggered by harvest failure, the authorities might reintroduce aspects of an earlier regulative policy, thus keeping alive popular knowledge and expectations of how authority should behave in the face of threatened famine. All of these changes help to explain why, even as the reality of famine receded, crowd actions over food increased and disciplined protest began to break down. A set of attitudes that had previously been the shared possession of both Crown and crowd was well on the way to becoming 'the moral economy of the eighteenth century crowd', with protesters now proclaiming that 'they were resolved to put the law in execution since the magistrates neglected it.'[4]

Notes

1. John Walter, 'Grain riots and popular attitudes to the law: Maldon and the crisis of 1629', in John Brewer & John Styles, eds., *An Ungovernable People: The English and their law in the seventeenth and eighteenth centuries* (London, 1980).
2. Essex Record Office, D/B3/3/208, no. 14 (exam. Dorothy Berry).
3. T. Birch, *The Court and Times of Charles the First*, ed. R. F. Williams (2 vols.,1848), i, 17.
4. There is a large and growing literature on eighteenth-century grain 'riots', but the classic study, now much debated, remains E. P. Thompson, 'The moral economy of the English crowd in the eighteenth century', *Past & Present*, 50 (1971), 76-136, reprinted in his Customs in Common (London, 1991), 185-258.

The Seed

Irfan Master

A TINKER WALKS THROUGH a field, skirting the hedgerows, navigating a well-trodden path. He sees a figure traversing the same field diagonally, towards him. The figure is him, changed, in different garb, but the same nonetheless. From a third corner emerges another figure, masked, caped with high boots, the gait the same as the other two. This field, verdant, lush, speckled with wildflowers, is a perfect square. On the thick hedgerows are perched thirty birds. Among them a duck, a falcon, a kestrel, a hawk, eyes unblinking, witness. The melodic sound of another bird, the hoopoe, rings out then stops. A call to history.

The three meet in the middle. Each figure is engaged in an act that will alter the path of the other. Hanging from each figure's hip, the same small pouch. They stand at three separate points, creating a downward pointing triangle. The pouches begin to throb at their sides, an itch that becomes a sudden burst of heat; waves ripple through the field, cresting and falling, until time is stilled.

The tinker, the first of his kind in this land, looks across into the dark hazel eyes of his future self.

'So, here we are again.'

'This was not planned, this meet,' says the masked figure, impatient.

'But we know what this means,' says the second figure, dressed in a simple shirt, tie and trousers.

The tinker smiles, at seeing the two again. It has been a thousand years since they last met in this field. There were six of them then.

'It means the stories are merging.'

'We cannot maintain this, *us*, if...'

'One more of us dies?'

The tinker holds out both hands, palms up in supplication. The other two do the same.

'When the time comes, when our stories merge, we will know what to do. Perhaps we have held onto them too long?'

The tinker's words, heavy with what is to come, weigh on the other two figures, their heads bowed.

All three loosen the drawstrings of their pouches and clasp the object within. The three who were one, open their palms, and for the first time in a thousand years, all stories merge once again.

The Tinker

A tinker, John is his name, stands in a perfectly square field on bended knee. It is hard to know if he has just emerged or whether he has always been there. In his hand, a grain of wheat. A single, small, hard seed. He carefully places the seed into his pouch and stands up. All around him looking on, a sea of faces, birdlike. A bell rings out, three times, a sound that resonates in this time, and another. They call him 'Captain' as he walks by, but he is no military leader. He is a tinker, was only ever a tinker, before this day, someone who repairs what he can, salvaging an object or remaking it to serve another purpose. The eyes are on his pouch, nestled on his hip, as he raises his hand and all across the three counties of Warwickshire, Leicestershire and Northamptonshire, it begins. This pulling up of fence posts and routing of hedgerows, the freeing of land from enclosures.

It is quiet work. The work of men, women and children. A labour of deep love for the common. With hands calloused and cut by the thistles and bushes, John joins the effort, quietly urging, a gentle voice amidst the assembled crowd. Although he knows how this will end, the pride and defiance he sees in the people fills him with urgency, as the ramparts of ever-encroaching ownership are removed and the people stand, united, on once-more common ground. When labour is complete, there is silence. A moment given over to words to recognise the deed. People reconvene on that first, square field, sitting in three concentric circles around their Captain.

'I am not a leader. I am only a tinker. I travel where my feet take me, wandering these paths, navigating these hedgerows and gorse bushes for what feels like millennia. From a time long before enclosures existed. I have never tried to own the land, or claim it inch by inch as I have witnessed encroach upon it. This common belongs to all of us, yet here we are turned criminals just for recognising it. They will not let this rebellion stand. They will send their lieutenants and soldiers to stop us. And they will. But understand one thing, this victory today will always be ours.'

Opening the pouch at his side, John produces a small seed. Kneeling on the dark earth, he cups his thick hands and digs a shallow hole then places the seed in the clotted soil. The hushed crowd stands up as John fills the hole and pats it flat. Still kneeling, he can feel the tremor of the hooves in the distance, and all around the boots of soldiers on common earth.

*

A man walks through heavy double doors into a perfectly square courtroom. Well ordered, symmetrical, the empty room fills with a bottled silence. He is dressed in a suit, tie, white shirt, yet his shoes are dirty, encrusted with mud. The courtroom begins to acquire occupants, tense bodies, intent minds. A multitude of thoughts swirl around the act of uprooting a simple piece of bronze. The man notices his dirty shoes then takes out a single sheet of paper from his briefcase. What sky he can see through the tall arched window is opaque: a large tree, tangled branches reaching towards the pane, and perched on a thick stem, a hoopoe bird, silent.

In the lobby, a seething mass of people pour in from the street. Men, women, children. Staring at the court guards posted in front of the double doors, and every other entry point. They have come to pay witness. Back inside, three defendants rise to hear their names. They are not young, not yet aged; black and white. The judge and jury enter; a shuffling of boots on the ground, kicking up dust. The case, such as it is, has now to conclude. The jury, weathered under the public scrutiny of the case, and having witnessed so many retrials and appeals, finally anticipate an end. The judge senses a shift of something that is beyond him but proceeds.

'Can the Crown please commence with its closing statement.'

'On Sunday 7th June 2020, a public demonstration degenerated into a public disturbance resulting in the defacing and destruction of public property. The property was then dragged and dropped into the river very much led by the three defendants. The case of the Crown is, whatever the present-day feelings associated with what was, at the time, a legitimate trade, to allow this act to go unpunished would be an irreversible precedent. How many statutes, plaques, nameplates, on how many schools, libraries, hospitals, parks and other properties, public or private, would need to be torn down for the accused and those who follow their lead to be satiated? How far back in history must we go before we come to a stop? What then will be left? Our responsibility should not be to rewrite history but to engage in civilised and intellectual discussion about it. Can we not speak of these matters, now, in public discourse? Can our identity as a nation not also encompass historical wrongs? Or are we not a nation of laws; or may we suspend these so-called 'laws' on any passing whim? If the accused are innocent, what next? The uprooting of borders, jurisdictions, county lines? The pulling up of ownership itself? What else will be dug up and tossed aside in this war of historical correction? Where does it stop?

'What does it teach our future generations about public debate and civil behaviour? That if something offends you, why, simply tear it down and drag it to the nearest ditch? Your task, as the jury, is to return a guilty verdict and stem the flood of emotion that such wanton destruction and flagrant civil disobedience can cause. We must tackle the sins of our past, but with a careful and considered approach. One worthy of a civil society.'

There is silence and the judge, distracted and tense, is staring out the window at the hoopoe. Pouch clears his throat and brings the judge back to proceedings.

'There has been a request by the defence for each defendant to issue a short statement, before mine. If the prosecution has no quibble with this, we will proceed.'

Pouch grips the hand of each defendant and urges them on.

A young black man, Jermaine, grips the railing in front of him, his knuckles pointed, close to the surface.

As a child holding my mother's hand, I often walked past it, though my mother would hurry me along not wanting to linger in its shade. Even my mother knew, this statue was a blight on our ancestors. As a young boy, I would cycle through 'the square' (it isn't a square but we'd call it that), and rest my bike against the plinth and meet my friends there. I still remembered my mum squeezing my hand as we walked past, but he was just another dead white guy to me. I don't remember everything about the day in question. It was just another day, until I saw a text saying people were gathering there. I'd been to a few BLM rallies but I had never seen anything like this. You could almost taste the anger. And it wasn't just the anger of that day, but of all the days before that off into the past. I remember joining the wave of people, some with masks on, some smiling, some tense. I saw young people, kids, families and elders, and then I knew, this protest was part of a movement. I found myself standing at the foot of the statue overcome with emotion. I wasn't there just for me, but for my mother too. For all those times we walked home and I'd look over my shoulder at the long shadow that statue cast over us. I don't remember climbing onto the statue but I do remember the noise when I got up there. The crowd was euphoric, cheering me on, but I didn't know what I was supposed to do. A lot of people had camera phones out and were recording which made me feel a bit nervous because I knew that would bring trouble, but I wasn't scared. I knew the young people I mentored would be proud. That's when I saw a hand passing up a rope to me and instinctively I took it and looped it around the statue's neck. Another rope tapped at my feet so I reached down for it and looped that round it too. The noise was incredible, a rising wave. I was lifted off my toes, the energy in the crowd was palpable. After I jumped down, I felt a hundred hands on me, patting me on my back, my head, I felt completely out of my body. After that, it was largely a blur; I remember pulling on the rope with others – dozens, maybe hundreds of others – and bringing it down but by that point I was exhausted and stood back. I couldn't process what had happened and after a while, I walked home and went to sleep. I didn't even see the statue being thrown in the river. It was only the next morning when I heard knocking on the door that I'd realised what that moment was. It was my mother and she stood there with a newspaper and right there on the front page was a picture of me. My mother didn't say anything. She stepped in to give me a hug and left the paper with me and walked home. I don't want to go to jail, I want to stay in the world and talk about why I did what I did. The papers will make out it was wrong and all that and paint us as the villains, but we're not the ones that made our fortunes from slave trading are we? How are we the villains?

A tall white man, Eric, stands up and nods at Pouch.

I've been part of a group that have been petitioning to remove that statue for years. We pursued every legal avenue we could. We organised, we protested, we wrote and distributed information. No one listened.

When we warned people that eventually it would come to this, we were still ignored. For me, it was a day of celebration. I cycled and got there early. I'd already arranged to meet my friends and some family there. This had been building up for some time. A pressure valve if you like, and you could just see that it was going to explode. Saying that, I still didn't expect that many people to turn up. But then this is the movement of our times. We can reach so many people now, and that one act was in the news in a thousand places instantly. I let the years of frustration wash over me, that day, and was strangely calm. We'd tried everything else, so I wasn't scared. I'd bought some rope and when Jermaine jumped up on the statue, I knew what I had to do. The moment the statue came down is hard to describe. I mean, it's just a piece of metal, right? But for so many, it was a symbol of oppression. And when it fell, it felt like a correction. I've had too many conversations that tried to justify letting the statue stand, but I was ashamed to let it stand. That statue falling on that hard concrete is a message to all those who would soothe their conscience by saying, let the past be. It was a peaceful enough process. Nobody was hurt on the day. I – we are not criminals, just normal people who happened to be there when history was being made.

A young black woman, Nicole, stands, composing herself. She looks at each jury member and nods.

I am a member of BLM. I joined as soon as it started here, and I'm proud of my work organising events in the city. I helped get as many people there as possible on the day. I was one of the first to arrive at the traffic island, where Colston Avenue tangles the A38, under the shadow of Colston Tower. It was quiet to begin with, and I remember standing there rereading how the statue had been 'erected by citizens of Bristol as a memorial of one of the most virtuous and wise sons of their city.' There were people sitting on the benches having their lunch, walking under the trees on their way to work. Just another day. And for a moment, I wondered if anybody would turn up. I sat at the foot of the statue and waited until a trickle of people turned into a flood. There were people everywhere, standing, shouting, waving placards. People of different races, not just supporters of BLM. The statue, and the way the city memorialises him, is hard to live with. Like someone spitting in your face every time you walk down a certain street. That's how it felt. But on that day, it was different, we were part of something bigger.

It was my idea to throw the statue into the river. The same river that had shipped those slaves back and forth flowing into the same seas that had taken so many of their lives. And that's where I met Eric and Jermaine and our lawyer. He was there after all the cheering had died down, and he gave me his card. Just as he gave it to Eric and Jermaine too.

The judge makes a note. 'Mr Pouch, you may begin your closing statement.'

'There have been a lot of questions asked on behalf of my defendants. I have a few of my own: Like what's the difference between uprooting hedgerows and bronze statues? Both are reminders of division, difference, and indenture. As for my learned friend's question: where does it stop? This war of historical correction? The question is rather: where does it *start*? And to that my answer is 'Today'. It *starts* today. There is a stillness in this current moment. Can you feel it? As we speak, all around this country, groups of people stand ready to remove other physical mementos of a subjugated past. At a hundred different locations, they wait upon this precedent, ready to tear down these reminders of our shameful history. Are we to rationalise this reminder of dehumanisation by espousing civilised discussion? The Crown contends that the destruction of public property is an illegal act. Yet what is or was legal, or illegal, changes, and in the case of slavery it took more than just discussion to bring about that change; in the United States, it took a civil war to change it. The time for discourse is over. It was over the moment this statute hit the water. What is that smell that lingers? What are we still trying to protect? What is on trial here? It is certainly not three individuals who sought to do what was long overdue. To tear down the symbols of oppression that exist singularly to uphold an idea of the past is precedent, the past defines us.'

Pouch looks up at the window, the hoopoe again. Slipping his fingers into the small leather bag attached to his belt, he produces a single, almost invisible seed. Placing the grain between thumb and forefinger, he crushes it into powder and blows the grey dust into the air. The hoopoe, silent until now, sings out, and there begins a great shuffling. Outside the courtroom, an urgent chatter. People look at their phones to see an extraordinary sight. Word filters through to the courtroom and finally a court attendant asks to step up to the bench to speak with the judge who looks at Pouch and points.

'What is happening?'

In countless locations around the country, groups of people are pulling up bronzes and other metal objects – statues, plaques, nameplates, from universities, parks, and public buildings. It is quiet work. The work of men, women and children. A labour of deep love for the common. Hands calloused and cut by stone and spikes. Live news feeds relay footage of the disturbances to people's phones. Once this labour is over, there is silence. Cameras scan the gatherings, looking for more. But all is silent: a moment given over to words to recognise the deed. People reconvene in small groups, around their devices, to look back at the spectacle of the trial, to bear witness.

Pouch, sitting down, points up to the window, the hoopoe now gone.

'We will no longer be prisoners to history.'

The Pirate Pouch

A pirate walks on the deck of her ship. A ship that flies, *The Hoopoe*, crested with gold. She wants to say something. Something poignant and fitting for the occasion, but she has never been a woman of words, this Pouch, only action. Through the eyeholes of her mask she looks over the last remaining members of her skeleton crew, all similarly masked and looking to her for guidance. The moment has come.

'It's time,' is the best she can muster.

The crew disperse and set to work at their terminals, fingers tapping on screens, eyes scanning lines of code.

What does it mean to lose your sense of self? It is a question Pouch asks herself all the time. When she stood on that field, she felt not only the land through her heavy boots, but a dissonance of her other selves. Back then, a patch of land could carry your labour, and give you back what you earned. It was the vessel of your freedom. Now, in the eyes of another self, she has seen the pain of having that land stripped from you, and the torment of being rendered an object, much like the land itself, of being renamed, owned. A millennia has passed since a minor bronze statue was pulled down in a leafy traffic island. It had been the beginning of something monumental, for a while. But in the meantime a new era has arisen, one in which people can no longer truly possess even themselves. Their own identities have been encroached upon, enclosed, and fenced off into packets of metadata, a grid of personal information penned up in corporate repositories, to trade for currency or other data. When people's lives are given internal boundaries, chequered with fences – their work, their likes, their dislikes, where they've been, where they'd like to go – their personalities become like private land, to be farmed privately. No one can now exist outside this system. Algorithms follow them everywhere. No one can obscure themselves. Everyone exists as a file number that unlocks their entire personal history. A single grain of information.

Pouch knows the cost of what they have set out to do. There has been half a century of resistance. Of collectives organising to regain individual freedoms, but all has failed. Collective thought has been dimmed by the algorithms. People can organise, voice their discontent, even revolt, but this is soon commodified and traded. Even their anger can be monetised, even ideologies can be bartered back and forth. Original or revolutionary thoughts are all anticipated by the algorithms and when they're sanitised, recuperated and sold back to us, we buy it!

As her ship gains altitude, picking up speed, Pouch reassures herself this is the only way. She and her crew have managed to evade all the security bots and drones they sent. The owners of the algorithms have cast them as pirates. That is the narrative. They are thieves and they embrace the moniker. They do steal. Valuable information, knowledge, forgotten histories long since removed and rewritten. They conserve it, building huge archives in archipelagos both digital and physical, ready to be read and understood again one day.

They have spent years planning this moment. From the first time Pouch arrived among them, targeting small online communities where dissent occasionally raised its head, before the algorithm could disperse such seeds of frustration. She would organise gatherings in remote, wide-open spaces, fields, deserts, islands, where the signal was weak enough to be jammed and the algorithms blocked. She returned to the same spots each year, and awareness bloomed. New pockets of resistance sprung up everywhere. In exchange for people's action, Pouch promised freedom. But for all their sophistication in the art of disruption, the only path they were left with, in the end, was brutally simple. To be the hand that wielded the hammer.

Turning to her crew, the pirate produces a single, small grain from her pouch and sets it down in the centre of a small square disc. Inserting it into the terminal in front of her, she nods to her crew as the ship lurches sideways. The contents of the disc, for a moment, scramble millions of servers, sending whole tranches of the tech corporations' global networks into a momentary lapse. Pouch steps back. She can feel the inertia of the atmosphere outside. It is the same inertia that exists in the world. A deep lassitude that drags the spirit to a halt. There had to be a correction. A moment in which people could see themselves reflected in a prism that hadn't been constructed for the purpose of turning the viewer into a sellable commodity. It wouldn't free everyone. In fact, it would only allow a scattered few to exist beyond the algorithms' reach. Unplugged, unseen, adrift in the void, they would be free to commune again, to organise, to live under clear skies. Disrupting the servers would only give Pouch and her crew a moment. They needed more time. For that, there has to be a physical breach, and Pouch's crew have spent years searching for a weak spot, finally finding it hidden in the blackness of space. An armoured satellite. If destroyed, it would flatten the algorithms just long enough for a ripple to start, perhaps twenty-four hours, before bigtech took control again. Pouch's ship will be the nail. A diversion, and a warning. Under that cloud, both cover and daylight. The darkness envelopes them as they hurtle further and further upwards. The satellite will fire, but Pouch and the ship named after the wisest of birds, knows its blind spot, and it will be too late. Bracing herself for impact, Pouch thinks back to when she stood before her other incarnations and admonishes herself for being so impatient. She wishes she had smiled and embraced her other selves and waited for the light to change.

The Old Pouch

No matter how sharp the bite of the north-westerly this evening, the old man remembers past storms better. He sits in a small boat. By his side nestles a small leather satchel. It has been many years since he last loosened its strings and held what was inside. The past is within him now, his many selves butting up against him at this, the farthest shore. Known as Captain to some, Pouch to others, and to those who first launched his tale into the centuries, simply the tinker. But for all the lives (and deaths) he, or rather they, have lived, this is the last. He is the last. The world, such as it is, has no need for him. Untying the satchel that has hung from his belt for over a thousand years, he removes the one remaining grain and places it on his palm. A small seed, almost translucent, nothing extraordinary. Bringing it to this tongue, Pouch remembers the wild, rough days and the sudden, clear moments of calm. The past is what he has lost and the people have found. Closing his eyes, the last seed dissipates within him, as all the many lives merge, floating against the currents of history, cutting a way perpetually into the present.

Afterword: Captains of the Field

Professor Briony McDonagh
University of Hull

In the early summer of 1607, a large group of perhaps as many as a thousand men, women and children assembled at Newton (Northamptonshire) and began digging up hedges. The hedges surrounded enclosures recently put in place by the local landowner, Thomas Tresham of Newton, a cousin of the much more famous Sir Thomas Tresham of Rushton. Arriving at Newton on the 8th June, the deputy-lieutenant of Northamptonshire, Sir Edward Montagu, twice read out a royal proclamation demanding the rioters disperse. When they did not, their forces charged the crowd. After initially putting up fierce resistance, the crowd fled as the mounted horsemen charged for the second time. Forty to fifty of the rioters were killed in the field and many more captured, some of whom were later executed and their mutilated bodies displayed at Northampton, Oundle and other local towns. The events at Newton were the culmination of more than a month of unrest in parts of Northamptonshire, Leicestershire and Warwickshire, much of it focused on the issue of agrarian change – specifically the enclosure of common-field arable land and its conversion to sheep pasture – and recorded either in government papers and letters or in subsequent court cases.

The reputed leader of the Midlands Rising was a man called John Reynolds, who was said to be a tinker or pedlar from

Desborough in Northamptonshire. He was known as Captain Pouch for the leather satchel that he wore and which he claimed contained magical material which would protect him and his followers from harm. Relatively little is known about Reynolds, his role in coordinating the unrest or his precise movements during it. He may have contributed to an anonymous broadside that was sold in alehouses in the early summer of 1607 and helped to forge connections between communities in the weeks before the events at Newton, and his followers said that Pouch claimed the authority to 'cut downe all enclosures betweene … Northampton and the cytie of Yorke'. Reynolds was not at Newton however, having been arrested at Withybrook (Warwickshire) a week earlier. He was identified by the authorities as 'the chiefest leader' of the rebellion and – predictably enough – swiftly convicted and executed.

But there were many Pouches: not only did someone else command the field at Newton, but there were numerous men and women who came both before and after Pouch whose actions contributed to ongoing negotiations by which modern concepts of property – as private, absolute and spatially exclusive – came into being. The Midlands Rising was preceded by more than a century of small-scale, local unrest over enclosure and associated agricultural change, which on occasion erupted into significant episodes of popular opposition to the activities of enclosing landlords. The Westminster equity court records reveal an extended history of anti-enclosure rioting and other forms of direct action in Northamptonshire and the neighbouring counties, with evidence of widespread tensions over enclosure which stretched back decades before 1607.

In the late 1580s, for example, another local landowner complained that a group of around 80 inhabitants had interfered with his attempts to plough land in the manor of Badby and Newnham to the west of Northampton. He said they had sent secret messengers about the town 'in manner of a rebellion to raise the people'. They assembled together under the leadership of a mounted captain who commanded the crowd with watchwords and signals. The crowd refused to disperse even after a local justice of the peace arrived, saying they would lease – in other words, lose or let go of – their lives before they leased their lands. This was genuinely radical stuff – or so the landowner wanted the court to believe.

The captain at Badby was a man named Anthony Palmer, but the landowner later pursued a related case against a similarly-sized group of women who had driven his cattle through his planted fields, thereby destroying the crop. Importantly, once we start to look for women – something previous historians sometimes forgot to do! – we find them. At Kingsthorpe (Northamptonshire) in 1599, married, single and widowed women were said to have dug up hedges amounting to 80 perches (equivalent to perhaps 400m), while at Adstone in the same year, more than a hundred people – mostly women – assembled in order to drive cattle into recently enclosed land as a means of resisting the landowner's attempts to depopulate and enclose the township. At Chilvers Coton (Warwickshire) in 1604, a large group of women cast down the hedges and banks around twelve acres of woodland in order to open it up to common grazing. Further afield at Hoddesden (Hertfordshire), a married couple were said to have conspired to raise 'a great multitude of women' who worked together to drive the plaintiff's cattle out of a close. Here we see (typically) working-class women acting collectively to defend common rights and resist the agricultural, social and economic changes brought about by enclosure.

Negotiating enclosure – in the sense of both promoting and resisting it – was dependent on assemblages of people, animals and things and their convergence within particular spaces and temporalities. Hedges acted as both symbols of ownership and a physical means of excluding unwanted people and animals, defining the grid against which animal and human occupations operated. Hedge-breaking, grazing animals and mass trespasses inserted human and animal bodies into enclosed property, physically occupying disputed space, reestablishing access and reasserting common rights over the land. Mass ploughings physically – and very visibly – resisted the remaking of space brought about by enclosure, turning over new pasture closes so as to sow them with wheat or other crops and thus return them to common-field arable. Even walking paths and trackways blocked by an enclosing landowner could be a bodily assertion of rights of access, and thus an important strategy for resisting enclosure. In this sense, we can point to a range of very mundane and everyday objects – cattle, sheep, spades, billhooks, ploughs, and human bodies – that were all implicated in resisting enclosure, just as hedges, maps and court cases enacted the enclosures, rolling private property out across the common-field landscape of the English Midlands.

The physical contents of the mythical satchel are important too. A near-contemporary chronicler records that on examination, the satchel was found to contain nothing but mouldy cheese – seemingly a deliberate attempt by the chronicler to dent Reynolds/Pouch's posthumous power. In Irfan's story, Captain Pouch's satchel contains a grain of wheat which he plants in Newton field in the moments before the approaching militia arrive. Fifty rioters were killed in the field at Newton and the supposed ringleaders hanged in nearby market towns soon afterwards. But Pouch resists, even whilst feeling the tremor of hooves and boots 'on common earth' and knowing the inevitable, bloody outcome. Here the story has echoes both of the early modern men and women whose actions we see imperfectly refracted in the equity court records and of the final scene in Jim Crace's *Harvest*, in which as a last act of resistance the hero ploughs and plants a single furrow in the field set to be enclosed and converted to pasture. Like the mass ploughings we find in the archives, this was a physical marking – and remaking – of the land as a form of resistance to enclosure.

Irfan's story signals beautifully the complex entanglements of place, people and things through which protest is enacted. I love the sense in which particular places – specifically, the square field – are the sites at which past, present and future are folded together; or as Irfan puts it, 'time is stilled'. Those involved in enclosure riots were typically well aware of the importance of history. They mobilised earlier disputes to give meaning and legitimacy to their actions, narrating long histories of exploitation by grasping landowners as well as many years or even decades of opposition to enclosure and agricultural change in their locality. Occasionally, defendants and witnesses in enclosure cases also referenced the depopulation and enclosure of nearby parishes in their efforts to protect common rights in their own village, drawing on other commoners' experiences as both a geographical parallel to and historical warning of what might be to come.

The Midlands Rising was also *remembered* long after the rioters were dispersed from Newton and the ringleaders put to death. The events of summer 1607 were referenced in litigation from the region in the years immediately following the Rising, typically by landowners who referenced the spectre of rebellion as a means to up the ante in pursuing cases against commoners who resisted enclosure. Moreover, as others have noted, the term 'diggers' was first coined in reference to the rioters of 1607 only to reappear in the late 1640s to describe Winstanley's experiment at St George's Hill and Cobham (Surrey). That name has echoed through the centuries since, the seed that grows and bears (countercultural) fruit. From the Hyde Park Diggers and the Digger Action Movement of the 1960s and 1970s to the eco-camp established a decade ago close to Runnymede by a group calling themselves the Diggers 2012, the idea of physically occupying land as a means to counter dispossession and/or argue for land reform is a powerful one.

As in the early seventeenth-century English Midlands, the physical occupation of space continues to be a key tactic today, part of the range of strategies available to protesters in resisting hegemonic versions of property relations – and hegemonic (read: white, male, straight, able-bodied) versions of history set in stone. Or bronze. Hedges thrown down or sent up in flames;

statues of slavers pulled up and dumped into rivers; the enclosure of the digital commons and a world in which – as Irfan puts it – people can no longer truly possess even themselves. But some things continue to matter – men, women and children bodily occupying space, standing against dispossession and oppression, writing histories from which we can only hope others will learn. Long live Captains Pouch!

Note

This afterword reproduces material from B. McDonagh and J. Rodda (2018) 'Landscape, memory and protest in the Midlands Rising of 1607' in C. J. Griffin and B. McDonagh (eds), *Remembering Protest in Britain since 1500: Memory, Materiality and the Landscape* (Palgrave Macmillan), pp. 53–79, reproduced with permission of Palgrave Macmillan. The author and publishers are grateful to Joshua Rodda for his work on the original chapter.

Post-Credit

Lillian Weezer

'IT DOESN'T LOOK GOOD, does it?'

Scattered across the desk, torn-out pages curled at the edges as if wilting under the office strip light: dark pencilled cross-hatch fought with concentric pentagons to give the paper an almost sickly sheen. 'Blueprints' Gauch had called them in his Creative Therapy class; though blue would have given them some life.

'Do you mean the artwork or your chances of an appeal?' Migram intoned.

'I mean me being here with you; our little art appreciation sessions. It's not like the other creatives in here get weekly psych appraisals. Being called out every Tuesday...' Gauch sipped from his polystyrene cup, 'makes the others look at me queer.'

Not to be baited, Milgram took one of the drawings and pretended to examine it; a circle of spidery clusters orbited what looked like a contour map; the topography of a small hill or earthwork detailed with outcrops and depressions. Not a blueprint for anything new, he thought. 'But what you pulled off was a little exceptional,' he tried again. 'You can't blame the agency for allocating a bit of extra shrink time, to draw up a profile, you know, in case there are others like you out there. Quiet ones.'

Gauch finished his drink. Setting the drawing down, Milgram flicked through others, pulling out one piece that appeared to depict, in intricate detail, an aerial view of a bombsite: with rubble strewn in all directions, toppled signposts at the fringes of the picture, and in the middle of it all, dragged from God knows where, a single mattress with a man idly resting on it.

'Some people argue that self-deception is a process very close to the surface of consciousness, even in schizoaffective disorders. Subjects choose to be confused, almost deliberately. Like when they arrive here, and they're suddenly mystified as to the actual nature of the place.'

'Why am *I* in here? *I'm* the sane one... that sort of thing?' Gauch punched the tip of his index finger through the base of the polystyrene cup. 'Sorry, Doc, no dice.' Retrieving his finger, he set about picking away at the hole in the bottom making it wider and wider. 'But if you want, I can tell you why *you're* in here.'

'Pray tell.'

'Your job is to find out – for the rest of your department – why Subject Twelve has been sent to a T Category facility though he has no discernible special talents. The Faraday Wall is wasted on a dweeb like me, your colleagues think. Four square walls and a couple of bars in the window would've been sufficient. No need for your grunts outside the door to be packing piezoelectrics, a cudgel to the nape would've done the job, right? So the boys in the staffroom can't figure it out. It's bugging you too. What are the higher-ups not telling you about me?'

'*A cudgel to the nape,*' Milgram repeated, pretending to be taking a note.

'Your job is to find out what my particular "special talent" is.' Gauch flicked a chip of polystyrene onto the desk: 'It's clearly not drawing.'

'*Subject believes he has a su-per-po-wer?*' Milgram continued in his fake note-taking.

'No,' Gauch snapped. '*You* think I have a superpower.'

A blend of grease fumes and ammonia hung in the air that lunchtime as subjects processed into the T-Block canteen. Given the effects of the medication they were all on, it was difficult to tell sometimes if they were queuing patiently or just walking as fast as their stiffened joints could take them. For Milgram, the lunch queue was too obvious a metaphor for what D.I.R.T. had done to them, too simplistic, but it stuck in his head as an image: stripped of their 'assets', denuded of any personality beyond base biological needs, they shuffled forwards, lifeless spectres of what they had once been. Only the little green lights twinkling at their wrists all along the length of the queue showed any evidence of life, monitoring their vitals, reassuring the grunts upstairs that as well as breathing and functioning, they were still at least manageable.

Milgram had permission to be there; he'd secured clearance from his superior, Travers, to pose as an inmate at lunchtimes and even occasionally wander the exercise yard, complete with grey jumpsuit and his own Subject number, 23, so as to quietly further his observations. Unlike most facilities he'd worked in, where canteens and exercise yards were testosterone-drenched amphitheatres, and every interaction a clichéd power play, here, in T-Block, lunchtimes passed without incident. Meals were finished or they weren't. Drinks occasionally got spilt or plates clattered to the ground, but only out of clumsiness caused by the neuroleptics, and never as a warning, or a false pretext to a new debt. It was all thoroughly anticlimactic. If it hadn't been for the time that Milgram had spent memorising Subject 23's back-story, he would've given up on these observations by now and returned to his carefully prepared quinoa salads in the staffroom.

In front of him, Subject Six had reached the dessert section and was grappling with a bowl of crumble and congealed custard, the surface of which quivered with the same seismicity as his own drug-induced tremor. Rhubarb stalks didn't writhe new-sprouted foliage out of the crumble and around the tray; the limp cabbage on his plate made no attempt to effloresce around his utensils or twine its way up his wiry forearms. Likewise, ahead of him, the emaciated figure of Subject Five stared into the middle distance; dank hair clinging to the side of her face; no trace in her eyes of the woman who would've thought nothing of setting fire to the tray stand, the cup trolley, or any of the other dismal sights that seemed to mock her with their inertia.

Taking a seat across from his usual dining buddy, Milgram caught sight of Gauch already seated in the far corner. One arm spooned rice mechanically into the side of his mouth, while the rest of his body folded around a dog-eared paperback. From the lack of design on the cover, Milgram assumed it was another academic text. 'Your move.' Subject Nine was itching to start their lunchtime ritual: perched in the centre of a cross-shaped grid of dots that he'd scored into the tabletop many weeks ago, a small red shirt button sat ready to take on the fifteen variously lined-up white buttons. Nine loved it when it was his turn to be the fox. Milgram obliged, moving one of his 'geese' into what he suspected would prove another trap. Naturally, Gauch had clocked Milgram on day one of his canteen observations but his embarrassment over the Tuesday call-outs was enough, Milgram hoped, to keep him from ratting on him. To everyone else in there, he was just like them: a wandering shadow whose back-story was of no more interest to himself than it was to others.

'Your move.'

The game progressed and before long, Milgram was surprised to find himself mounting an apparently coherent attack on the red button. His strategy of never letting his vanguard pieces stand undefended for more than one go proved, for once, almost sustainable and, by the time they were onto the custard, he had only lost four buttons to his opponent. The nine-dotted square to his left seemed ready to fence in his quarry.

'You're learning, geese, I think you might now be worthy of my next trick.'

Officially Milgram wasn't there to watch any one subject, but all of them, or rather how they interacted as a group. The Boorde Serum had worked, in terms of stripping them of their talents, and while the facility as a whole was surrounded by an army of grunts and a Faraday Wall that no EM wave could penetrate, inside it felt more like a day care centre than a maximum-security wing. Today, though, Milgram couldn't take his eyes off the solitary Gauch, his 'Tuesday morning' as he called himself. Perhaps he was looking at him too much for at some point the slow back and forth shuttle of the spoon stalled mid-air and Milgram could tell he had stopped reading.

'Can I help you with something?' Gauch's tray clunked onto the table beside Nine's.

'Pay attention, geese,' Nine interrupted, 'blink and you'll miss it...'

'If you're going to take a photograph,' Gauch continued, 'we may as well make it a close-up.'

'My bad, my bad,' Milgram muttered, standing up, suddenly flustered, and hurriedly clearing his plates back onto his tray. 'You reminded me of someone else.'

'Pay attention, little geese; though your poulterer has abandoned you,' Nine continued to the white buttons ranged around his red one.

'We'll have a do-over tomorrow, I'll let you be fox again,' Milgram muttered, before offering another 'my bad' to Gauch as he turned with his tray and walked straight into the wall of abdomen that was Subject Eight. Coffee seeped into the grey fabric around the giant's crotch, and craning upwards Milgram could see the creases around Eight's eyes tightening, his chest rising. Before he could find a new set of words to apologise with, the green light on Eight's wrist-monitor blinked red, and a squad of masked grunts charged into the room with piezosticks, prodding the now twitching Eight into a kneeling position. Tranquiliser vapour engulfed the canteen, it's hiss deafening Milgram even more than the klaxon.

As three green-uniformed guards dragged Gauch, kicking and thrashing towards the wing, he bellowed back: 'Nobody cares that you're a screw, Milgram! Nobody cares that you...' His kicking eased to a limp drag. It was true, the revelation barely stirred a second glance from the other subjects now being strong-armed back to their cells. Unaccompanied, Milgram calmly picked his way through the clumps of mashed potato and spilt pudding around him, only noticing as he glanced back at the table, that where the red shirt button had previously stood, so cleverly hemmed in by all his white ones, a dull, rusty peg now stood in its place, balanced on its tapered end for a moment, before toppling over.

'Quite a scene you created last week.' On the wall of Milgram's office, a kitsch pendulum clock ticked ostentatiously, its dumb weights stretching halfway to the floor. Most of the screws' offices here had one, Milgram had noticed. On the table in front of him, the Voice Memo app of his phone showed digits racing forwards, counting the seconds and centiseconds so far recorded.

'It worked, though, didn't it? Got my lunchtime privacy back, and your fake ID revoked.'

'Your drawings are often about nests,' Milgram began.

'Ha. This again.'

'Do you see the facility you're in as a kind of nest? One you've been inserted into, where you don't rightfully belong?'

'As I explained repeatedly to your predecessor, that was a name the press gave me. And I'm not sure they came up with it alone. It's not one I respond to.'

'Ironic though, isn't it? That a Cuckoo should end up in a loony bin?'

'But you said it *wasn't* a loony bin. It's a research facility for the previously talented. And with all the false mirrors around the place, the idea of you going native *inside* the cage seems a little indulgent, don't you think. But that wasn't the point, was it?'

'Let's talk about Endcliffe Wood, again.' Before he took up the post, Milgram had sat through hours of shaky bodycam footage, presented at the trial, and read all the statements given by security contractors and bailiffs on the day. 'A performance piece,' Gauch had called it in his own testimony. Dozens of HS2 protesters, known to have been living in treehouses along the planned route, could be seen in grainy video, screaming like banshees, chasing after what turned out to be paid actors dressed as JCB operators. The real operators could be forgiven for turning and running as timidly as they had. The terrain was unfamiliar to them and littered with old mine workings, recently uncapped and loosely re-covered with bracken by the protesters. The sight of mud-faced hippies with what looked like blood around their mouths, chasing heavy-set, uniformed contractors till they plummeted from view, and then jumping down into the holes after them, was enough to turn the burliest bailiff's stomach. What had unnerved Milgram about the footage was the strange poses the activists seemed to strike for the bodycams after each catch. As protesters at the front of each pack piled into the hole after their victim, those at the back would turn to face the bodycam wearer, stick out a hip, pout, and throw up a V-sign, like some cannibalistic version of sixties peaceniks.

When the dust eventually settled, none of the actual eviction crew were found to be missing and only very minor injuries had been sustained. But the bailiffs and JCB operators refused to go back. There was something about the stunt that unnerved them, a seriousness to it. Word spread among other employees, and a whole new contractor had to be brought in to finish the clearance. It was a clever stunt, as were the other actions Gauch had been linked to, though never charged with: a hoax Ebola outbreak in a residential tower block in Radford to thwart an immigration removal; a mass sleep-in supposedly caused by a gas leak outside an Ilbet drone factory in Tamworth. Any one of these would have warranted a 24-month stretch, for sure. But in none of them had any 'special talent' been displayed of the kind D.I.R.T. would find interesting. Gouch's being here didn't make any sense. There had to be a fourth incident Milgram wasn't being told about.

'There's nothing new to say. I admitted my part in it. I fessed to the tres. We both know that's not why I'm here.'

The unlikely clock chimed the quarter-hour mark. Above its face, a wooden bonnet held aloft a peculiar finial – a small metal globe that reminded Milgram of the transmitter on the perimeter fence turret from which the Faraday Wall was projected. Gauch had resumed his routine of slowly removing the base of a polystyrene cup.

'OK. Let's try something you *do* want to talk about then. In a previous session, you made a number of references to Galileo, and a story about a bell and a boat. I didn't quite follow you at the time. Would you care to go back to either of those?'

Gauch waggled his index and middle fingers through the bottom of his cup. 'The people of the village became convinced that enemies were about to invade the country,' Gouch began, 'and resolved to hide their most precious asset – the church bell – at the bottom of the village pond. With the bell brought down and heaved into a boat, they rowed to the centre of the great pond, and hoisted it overboard, only to then worry that they had been too hasty and wouldn't be able to find it again. Then, the wisest of the villagers realised all they needed to do was cut a mark in the side of the boat exactly where they had thrown the bell overboard. "It was right here that we heaved the bell out," the wise man said, so they rowed back to shore confident they could find it again.'

Placing a white chip on the palm of his hand, Gauch flicked it into the air, in the direction of the clock.

'OK, and where does Galileo come in?'

'Galileo wrote a Corollary that made a similar point; inside the cabin of a boat, with the curtains drawn, there is no experiment in the world you can perform that will tell you whether the boat is moving smoothly across flat water at a constant speed or stationary. The idea that you can ever tell the difference is as dumb as the wise man of the village cutting a mark in the boat to remember where the bell is.'

'Meaning?'

'Meaning, Doc, you never really know who you're working for. You can't tell what kind of reference frame you're in – a stationary one or a moving one. The analogue in ethics is you never know how biased the system you're born into is; the biases are hidden; there's no window you can just stick your head out of to see if you're moving. You're trapped in the curtained cabin of your own head.'

'It would be like marking the side of your boat...'

'So, you have to make a guess, Doc. The Earth is turning; you're never likely to be stationary. But how do you redress it? Unless you're happy to go with the flow, all you can ever do is pick a direction, one that feels unfollowed, and run that way. Chances are it'll reduce your overall speed, your overall bias.' Gauch took a pen from Milgram's desk and scored a hole near the lip of the cup. 'Galileo wrote the original Corollary, but Newton plagiarised it, called it his Corollary Five.' He raised his right hand, and with his index and middle finger made a five in Roman numerals.

Gauch flicked another chip of polystyrene into the air, this time reaching the clock, and landing on the hood, right beside the finial.

'The cabin we each find ourselves in,' Gauch continued, 'has more than just curtains blocking out the light, it has a thick Ilbet tech.'

'Zero escapees or your money back,' Milgram beamed.

The following Tuesday, snow fringed the tops of half the vehicles in the staff car park. Those who had driven over from Derbyshire had seen the worst of the night's fall, and now it perched in thin ridges along wipers and wing mirrors like prizes awarded to those who commuted the furthest. Even against that sky, it was depressing how the hazy blue dome over T-Block had something summery about it.

For Milgram, arriving at the perimeter gates each morning felt like a judgement on his own personality. Three card scans in, his blood would start to boil and a feeling that the system had it in for him personally couldn't be dismissed from his thoughts. An inanimate, neutral system of checks and balances was somehow wronging him.

'I *am* holding it against the glass,' he snapped, his thumb pressed white against the third gate's vertical fingerprint-scan, the klaxon horn that followed, indicating he was clear to pass, being as predictable as his look of contrition as he mouthed 'sorry' at the screen-lit guards inside.

At the fourth gate he was snapped out of his mood by the realisation there was no one behind the security screens this time to get impatient with. The lights on the barrier were off and there wasn't any point holding the card up to it. At the same instant his phone pinged. From the lock-screen notification, he got the gist of it. 'Disturbance on T-Block, all staff report to Briefing Room on B, immediately.' At last, Milgram thought to himself, something to observe!

By the time he reached the Briefing Room, a phalanx of grunts, already kitted out in full Kevlar, stood ahead of him, visors down, facelessly listening to the operational briefing. Milgram was filing into another part of the room, partitioned for auxiliary staff, when his name was called out, and he was beckoned to leave his queue for a side office.

'It's Cuckoo,' Travers, Director of Rehabilitation spoke first. Milgram had never particularly taken to his Nottingham line-manager; he had a neatness to him, and an energy that seemed suspicious. 'He's breached the fence between T-Block's exercise yard and the general yard, and now he's holding court with most of the inmates in C- and D-Block. It's like he's holding a rally.'

'How? Did he use a talent?'

'It's not clear yet. All the others have come back online though. We have hawthorn bushes climbing up the perimeter fence; the library's on fire, and the CEO of H5T seems to have lost his marbles, tweeting denials of things that haven't even happened. Travers handed Milgram his phone: 'There's no truth in the rumour that all @HMPNotts inmates have now broken free,' the CEO's tweet read, closing with a smileyface. 'Looks like the work of the little M&M dude.'

'But what about the Faraday Wall? I thought it was strong enough to contain the T-Categories, even if they came back online.'

'Cyber attack we suspect,' Barton, Travers' deputy, chimed in. 'But it switched to its default, surrounding the entire prison.'

'Is it Lent? Making a late appearance?'

'That wouldn't make much sense. She'd just portal them all out?'

'From what we can piece together, after the glitch in the Shield, Ludd came online first and reduced the guards to blubbering snowflakes; Swampy then brought the goddamn rhododendrons in from the front lawns, breaching the perimeter and four internal fences. Then the default kicked in. So long as we keep the transmitter safe, there's no need to call the cavalry.'

'And now he's asking for you,' Barton added.

Milgram's heart pounded. He'd covered hostage negotiation in basic training, but never seen anything like it in the field. Taking the headset Travers held out to him, he plonked himself down on the one empty swivel chair in front of the monitors.

'Good of you to join us, Doc.' Milgram's ears filled with the sound of inmates bellowing an indecipherable, prison-wide chant. In front of Milgram, a bank of CCTV screens showed the general and T-Block exercise yards from multiple perspectives. In most, Gauch could be seen perched halfway up the perforated dividing fence, on what appeared to be an office chair, beside an ordinary office desk, the whole ensemble woven like a shelf into the high fence by brambles thick as suspension cables. In the middle of the bank of screens, Milgram blinked into a single monitor showing a Zoom session, with Gauch's face gurning into it. On his head he had attached two upturned polystyrene cups, like horns, tied together with string. 'We had an appointment for 10.30, Doc,' Gauch quipped, 'I didn't want to stand you up just because of a little team-up.'

'Team-up,' Milgram repeated, adjusting his headset nervously.

'You know, now we have an audience,' Gauch gestured to the hundreds of C- and D-Block inmates assembled beneath him, 'it might be opportune to answer that burning question of yours.'

'You hardly need to tell me any more, Gauch; it'll all be on tape. Unless you've got The Captain to mess with the CCTV, that is.' He looked around at the surrounding screens, 'But all seems good up here.'

'No, no, no. You'll want to hear this. But I have to show you something else first.' Gauch swung his desktop monitor 90 degrees, past the far wall, the exterior of C-Block, and down to the exercise yard beneath him. Among the two hundred or so men simply standing looking up at Gauch, there were gaps in the crowd where inmates appeared to have fallen into activities of their own. Gauch held the screen still and, as the autofocus resolved, Milgram could make out half a dozen men lifting aloft a gate, ripped from a barrier somewhere, which now bore a solitary prisoner standing on it, dancing and waving his arms erratically as if shooing away an unseen pest. In another pocket of the crowd, a group of prisoners were sitting on the concrete floor in a peculiarly tight ring, so close together in fact that their legs entwined with each other's. Above them, a fellow inmate stood taking turns to hit the feet of each of those entangled with a screw's truncheon, this being their cue to untangle and get up. Further off, one of the playing-ground's sit-on lawnmowers was being awkwardly winched up by its steering wheel towards the gymnasium roof, and on all sides the relentless, indecipherable chanting continued.

'Mass hysteria,' Milgram muttered. 'That's his power. The protesters at Endcliffe weren't faking it; it was all real to them.'

For the first time, Milgram caught sight of the other T-Block subjects over Gauch's shoulder; first Ludd, scaling the side of the turret like it was a climbing frame, to beat at the dome of the transmitter with a post, then Skimmington being lifted upwards to join him on the tip of a what looked like a blooming thicket of wisteria.

'Milgram, Milgram, Milgram... it's quite the opposite,' Gauch laughed centre-screen. 'My special talent, my superpower, as you insist on calling it, is the ability to make people realise they're *not* mad. The hedge doesn't go that high. They can just fly... fly fly fly!'

For a moment, the ridiculous clock on the wall seemed to stop ticking. To Milgram it came as a blessed relief. But then next thing he knew, a ripple was fanning out through the air around the transmitter, and just like that, the hexagonal mesh of thin, blue lasers that had for so long been the subjects' only sky, blinked out.

As the prisoners charged towards the fence, Milgram finally managed to make out the words they had been chanting all along: *'The wise men are risen again! The wise men are risen again!'* It seemed to be coming not from his headphones but from the world around him, down the corridors, through the library, across the rectory, into the very room he sat in.

Afterword: The Wise Fool

Frank E. Earp

As a young schoolboy in the early 1960's, I would often hear the playground taunt 'You're going Cuckoo!' called out, usually accompanied by a sing-song chorus of 'Cuckoo! Cuckoo!' from all around, as well as a hand gesture: the index finger revolving in small circles by the side of the temple. It wasn't until I was in my mid-teens when I began my journey into local folklore that I discovered the fantastic origin of this jibe. The answer to the question 'Why should an enigmatic bird be associated with foolishness?', lies in one of the strange events that supposedly took place in a small Nottinghamshire village in the thirteenth century.

Gotham – (pronounced 'goat-ham') – is an unremarkable village some six miles south-west of Nottingham. According to folklore and local tradition, for one day during the reign of King John (1199-1216), the entire population of the village engaged themselves in acts of 'madness'. The first indication that something strange happened in Gotham comes from the fifteenth century. An act of foolishness by two men from Gotham appears in *The Wickirk Play*, written by an unknown hand sometime between 1425 and 1450. Here the title of 'Fools of Gotham' is firmly bestowed on the villagers. In the reign of Henry VIII around the year 1540, a collection of twenty stories that describe foolish events taking place in Gotham was published anonymously, under the title of *The Merry Tales of the Mad Men of Gotham*. With subsequent editions, the word 'mad' was changed for 'wise' and the myth of the Wise Men of Gotham was born.

The twenty tales in the 1540 chapbook contain examples of over 100 foolish acts attributed to Gothamites. One example from the chapbook tells how a man chained a wheelbarrow to a barn door. He said that it had been gnawed by a rabid dog and he was afraid less the barrow turn mad and bite someone. A second example tells of a how a man and wife worked out a way of ridding their thatched cottage of grass growing over it. They decided that their only cow might enjoy eating it. Tying a rope about her neck and throwing its end over the roof the couple began to haul her up. As the rope began to tighten and choke the life out of the animal, she let out a desperate bellow. The woman was alarmed at this and stopped pulling. 'Pull harder wife!' the man shouted. 'The cow is near the top and is excited at the prospect of her new pasture.'

Not all the acts of madness take place in Gotham. A man taking his ripe round cheeses to market in Nottingham noticed that one had slipped out of his saddlebag and had rapidly disappeared down the hill. 'Ah!' said he, 'you know your own way to town'. Immediately he untied his bag and emptied out the remaining contents. 'There, follow your brother along the road, but be sure to wait for me in the market. I will be along shortly'. However, on arrival at the market, his cheeses were nowhere to be seen. Intent on finding them, he began to enquire as to their whereabouts. When one of the stallholders asked the man who had brought his cheeses to market, he replied, 'No one!' 'They knew their own way here, so I sent them on ahead by themselves. I fear now that they were in such haste that they have overshot Nottingham and have gone to York'. Straight away, he hired a fresh horse and set out in pursuit of his wayward dairy products. Another man from Gotham was returning from Nottingham when he spied a fat round cheese lying in the road (presumably one of those released from the first man's bag). Drawing his sword from its scabbard, he reached down to try to pick up the tasty treat. However, no matter how hard he tried he just didn't have the reach. 'Curses! My sword is not long enough!' Turning his horse about, he set off back to the market to buy a longer blade. When finally he returned to the spot, the cheese had gone. 'Someone has taken my prize. If I had but this long blade one hour ago, I would have had a fine cheese for supper!'

One cannot fail to notice that these tales have a kind of perverse logic to them. And when we dig a little deeper, we find that they are not unique to Gotham. In fact, they are found all over the world. However, there is one very special tale which stands out as having very ancient origins: Briefly, the tale tells how the men of Gotham heard a cuckoo calling from a bush. In an effort to preserve springtime eternally, they set about to build a hedge or fence around the bush to keep the bird in place. Their efforts were thwarted when the cuckoo suddenly flew away over the top of the hedge. Lamenting their loss, one of the men concluded: 'If only we had made the hedge higher, she would not have escaped'.

The chapbook of twenty tales remained in print for over three centuries. Throughout that time the Cuckoo Bush tale always had its place as the third tale in the book. There has only ever been one illustration accompanying the tales – the front cover – offering different versions of the same image: the cuckoo in the Cuckoo Bush. On a hill high above the village, to the south, are the remains of an ancient mound at the centre of which was once a thorn bush said to be the actual tree from which the cuckoo escaped captivity. For hundreds of years the 'Cuckoo Bush' – possibly the sole physical origin of the phrase 'a bird in the bush' – attracted visitors until sometime in the late the nineteenth century when the landowner, tired of trespassers, had the bush cut down and the land around planted with trees. The trees have grown and there is now no official access to the mound, although it is still marked on modern O.S. maps. Like other elements of the tales, the story of the penned cuckoo isn't unique to this Nottinghamshire village. There are around 45 other villages in England and one in Wales that have a 'cuckoo penning' legend. Ancient earthworks and mounds labelled 'Cuckoo Pen' exist in Berkshire and Wiltshire, and the story varies considerably. Sometimes the pen isn't a bush or a hedge, but a high wall. In the village of Heathfield in Sussex, a local witch, called Dame Heffle, is said to have once caught any early-arriving cuckoo and locked it in a cage, only releasing it (and marking the start of spring) when she was good and ready. But Gotham is the only village that preserves both the tales of 'madness' and physical evidence – the mound and originally the bush.

The cuckoo has always been considered a mysterious and magical bird. Before the concept of migration was understood, it was a mystery as to where the bird went in winter. One idea suggested that the cuckoo transformed into a hawk – the male bird, when in flight, very much resembles a raptor. Most importantly, there was a belief that the bird slept in a 'fairy mound'. Could it be that the Cuckoo Bush Mound and the other Cuckoo Pens were originally constructed as places where the cuckoo might spend the winter?

A story from Celtic mythology tells how at the beginning of time, the door between this world and that of the gods was always open. Humans and animals passed freely between the worlds at will. After a time, however, the gods became tired of humans requesting favours. They decided that the door would be closed to all but those they deemed worthy. Before they did so they asked every creature including humans which world they wanted to live in. The only animal which could not decide was the cuckoo. The gods agreed that the cuckoo could spend half a year in both worlds. However, there was a caveat; Its young, born in this world would be raised by other birds whilst their mother was in the world of the gods. In return for this, the bird was to become a messenger of the gods. At the 'Callanish Stones' in the Outer Hebrides, at dawn on midsummer morn, an entity called the 'Shining One' is said to walk down the central avenue of standing stones heralded by the call of the cuckoo. In this story, the 'Shining One' is an ancient 'Celtic sun god' and the cuckoo his messenger herald.

When the *Merry Tales of the Mad Men of Gotham* first appeared in print, only around eleven per cent of the population would have been able to read it. Those that could, the king (Henry VIII) and the rich and powerful, would have seen the work as an amusing book of jokes told at the expense of a village full of mad men. However, if Henry and his court had known the supposed reason behind the feigned madness of the Gothamites, the book would have been considered an act of sedition against the Crown. Before they were ever written down 'The Twenty Tales' were a part of a storytelling, oral tradition which originally contained a story explaining exactly why the Gothamites behaved the way they did. This involves that tyrant, King John. There are two versions of this story, in one John is making his way towards Gotham – in the other, he intends to build a hunting lodge or castle in Gotham. In either case, the Gothamites would lose out. In the first instance, if the king travelled through or by Gotham his route would become a King's Highway and the Gothamites would be responsible for its upkeep along their stretch of road (which would have meant imposing tolls). In the second instance, the building of any royal residence would mean at worst, the total destruction of the village, or at best the loss of valuable farmland. Both stories have the same end. The Gothamites, being aware of the king's plan, organised so that when John's herald arrived in the village, he would find them all performing their mad capers. The servant reported what he witnessed and, madness being considered contagious at that time, John quickly changed his plans, not wishing to risk becoming infected, never ultimately visiting Gotham.

There is a third version of the story which was preserved in Gotham itself and was told to the historian Alfred Stapleton in 1899. The story begins as previously with King John making his way from Nottingham towards Gotham in a chariot. When he reaches a spot on Gotham Moor to the east of the village, he is ambushed by three young farmers from Gotham. (We must note here that those who passed on this story insisted that the king was in his *chariot* – not the vehicle of a twelfth-century monarch). One of the young men seizes hold of the lead horses and the other two chain the chariot's wheels to a post which they had previously fixed into the ground. Recognising the men as Gothamites, John swears revenge on them and their village. However, fearing that this act was the start of a rebellion, John turns for home as quickly as possible, thinking to return with an army and destroy Gotham and its inhabitants. This delay gave the Gothamites time to come up with the plan of feigned madness. When the king's spies arrive in the village, they discover a village of madness. Fearing he might catch it and relieved to have found he wasn't facing a full-scale war, John pardons the people of Gotham. To commemorate their victory the Gothamites raised a mound over the post to which the king's chariot had been chained.

To support this story, Stapleton was taken by his informant to Gotham Moor to the east of the village and shown the remains of the 'actual mound'. He describes this as looking like the ploughed-out remains of a tumulus. Stapleton reports seeing a second, less well-preserved mound a few yards away. There is a disputed reference in the Nottinghamshire volume of *The Victoria History of the English Counties*[1] to the opening of a tumulus at Gotham and the finding of a bronze spearhead. Like the cuckoo story, the presence of prehistoric mounds and the mention of an ancient vehicle indicates the story is far older than the reign of King John (the links with sun worship and references to a chariot even put one in mind of the Greek legend of Phaeton, also known as 'the shining one'). At this point, it is worth disclosing that the writer has discovered a long-distance prehistoric trackway which crosses Gotham Moor and runs close by the Cuckoo Bush Mound as a bridle path. With the sun-worship elements of the story in mind, one could be forgiven for conjecturing that the lost mound(s) on the moor to the east may have been part of an alignment marking the spot from where, at the winter solstice, the sun (or the sun king in his chariot) appears to stop, over the Bush Mound, and stand still, just before it sets.

It is interesting to remember that although the elite readers of the 1540 chapbook may have enjoyed its apparent mockery of the 'cuckoos' of rural Nottinghamshire, what they were overlooking was a much older tradition, according to which the figure of the fool, generally, was highly revered. In almost every culture a notion of a paradoxically 'wise fool' can be found; the bringer of chaos, the provider of reason through irrationality, the challenger of authority. According to Jung, the trickster figure (a variant of the 'divine fool') is deeply rooted within the human mind, an archetype who, through his apparent foolishness, possesses wisdom and a state of near-divinity. There is something shamanistic about him; he can enter the otherworld for the benefit of the community. It is also interesting that, in Court, the fool or jester is the only person present allowed to gainsay the monarch. It could be argued that it was the collective enactment of this role – the fool defying the king – that the people of Gotham were participating in.

But communal attitudes towards 'foolishness' and so-called 'madness' were changing, turning from reverence and respect to fear, and the Gothamites' trick of avoiding authority (not just defying it) exploiting this new fear. There is another tale of Gotham that repeats the trick (within the trick): it talks of a man riding home late one night, spotting the reflection of the full moon in a pond, and believing it to be a cheese. Dismounting he tries to pull the 'cheese' from the water with a broken fence-rail. At that moment the horse bends down to drink from the pond and simultaneously a dark cloud covers the moon making the reflection disappear. Thinking his horse has swallowed the cheese, the man takes his sword and slays it, cutting open its belly to retrieve it. As with cuckoo-penning, the origin of this 'moon-raking' tale is much older and not unique to Gotham: it is said that smugglers along the Dorset coast once hid barrels of brandy and other contraband at the bottom of village ponds, only to retrieve them on a full moon. If a customs officer should come by, they would simply tell them that they were trying to rake a cheese from the pond, at which the officer would leave them to it, thinking them all mad. Indeed, folk of Dorset are often called 'moon-rakers' by Wiltshire folk, who in turn are called 'cuckoo penners' by Dorset folk.

In Lillian's story the protagonist is called Gauch. This is a version of the Scots name for the cuckoo, 'gowk' (from the Old Norse 'gaukr') which was eventually replaced with the French loan word 'coucou' after the Norman Conquest. Interestingly, Scotland boasts a number of solitary standing stones known collectively as 'gowk stones' and there is a theory that the term 'gowk', also meaning fool, originated in the Dark Ages as a name the Saxons used for Britons, their arch enemies, as it compared them to the devil himself (the devil is often likened to a fool in *Proverbs*).[2] So it seems, our seemingly innocent book of amusing tales about a small village in Nottinghamshire might have inadvertently uncovered an emblem by which the whole of Britain was once known: a people defined by their defiant, impish, anti-authoritarian nature.

Notes

1. *The Victoria History of the County of Nottingham*, Volume 1. ed. edited William Page (Constable, 1906).
2. There is also a theory that the word 'gowky', which in Nottinghamshire at least means 'clumsy' has the same origin as the French word 'gauche', for left, making the cuckoo a potential symbol, also for the left. Anatoly Liberman, 'Cuckoo Birds in Gawky Park, or, Our Etymological Ailing Tooth', OUP blog, 10 May, 2006 https://blog.oup.com/2006/05/cuckoo_birds_in/

About the Authors

Yunis (M.Y.) Alam works at the University of Bradford, specialising in and writing about ethnography, ethnic relations and popular culture; his latest book explores the sociology of the car, particularly in relation to ethnicity, social class and 'taste' (*Race, Taste, Class and Cars*). Whilst his academic interests are broadly around the sociological, he has previously enjoyed teaching creative writing as well as English and Postcolonial literatures. He has also produced various works of fiction, including novels *Annie Potts is Dead, Kilo* and *Red Laal*, several essays and short stories. 'Absence' is the second short story published by Comma Press.

Bidisha is a broadcaster, journalist and film-maker. She specialises in human rights, social justice and the arts and offers political analysis, arts critique and cultural diplomacy tying these interests together. She writes for the main UK broadsheets and broadcasts for BBC TV and radio, ITN, CNN, ViacomCBS and Sky News. Her fifth book, *Asylum and Exile: Hidden Voices of London*, is based on her outreach work in UK prisons, refugee charities and detention centres. Her first short film, *An Impossible Poison*, received its London premiere in March 2018 and has been selected for numerous international film festivals. Her latest publication is called *The Future of Serious Art* and her latest film series is called *Aurora*.

Divya Ghelani is a writer who holds an MA in Creative Writing from the University of East Anglia and an MPhil in Literary Studies from the University of Hong Kong. Her short stories have been published by *BareLit*, *Litro*, Comma Press, BBC Radio 4 and more. Her novel in progress has been longlisted and shortlisted for four literary awards. Divya lives in Berlin where she leads a BIPOC Reading Series for The Reader Berlin and co-hosts a short story club for the UK's leading literary salon, the Word Factory. Divya is represented by The Good Literary Agency.

Luan Goldie is a Glasgow-born author and primary school teacher who grew up in East London. Her debut novel, *Nightingale Point*, was longlisted for the 2020 Women's Prize for Fiction and the Royal Society of Literature Ondaatje Prize. It was also a BBC Radio 2 Jo Whiley Book Club Pick. In 2018, she won the Costa Short Story Award and her short stories have since appeared in *HELLO!*, *Sunday Express* and *The Good Journal*. Her second novel, *Homecoming*, was released by HarperCollins in 2020.

Gaia Holmes lives in Halifax. She is a cat/dog/house sitter, freelance writer and creative writing tutor who works with schools, universities, libraries and other community groups throughout the West Yorkshire region. She runs 'Igniting The Spark', a weekly writing workshop at Dean Clough, Halifax. She has published three collections of poetry, *Dr James Graham's Celestial Bed*, *Lifting the Piano with One Hand*, and *Where the Road Runs Out* (all with Comma).

Peter Kalu is a poet, fiction writer and playwright. He cut his teeth as a member of Manchester's Moss Side Write black writers workshop and has had nine novels, two film scripts and three theatre plays produced to date. He gained his PhD in Creative Writing at Lancaster University in 2019. He has a first degree in Law from Leeds University, studied software engineering at Salford University and Languages at Heriot Watt University. In 2018, he was writer in residence at the University of West Indies (Trinidad campus). For many years he ran a carnival band called Moko Jumbi (Ghosts of the Gods) which took to the streets at Manchester Caribbean Carnival on three feet high stilts.

lisa luxx is an activist and poet of British and Syrian heritage. Her poems are published in *The Telegraph*, *The London Magazine* and by publishers including Hatchette and Saqi Books. Her work is broadcast on Channel 4, BBC Radio 4 and TEDx. In 2021, she toured UK theatres with the show for her 60-minute poem, *Eating the Copper Apple*, produced by a team of all Arab women artists. She is founder of The Sisterhood Salon in Beirut, and works within an economy of sisterhood. Her debut book, *Fetch Your Mother's Heart*, is out now through Out-Spoken Press.

Irfan Master is the author of *A Beautiful Lie*, which was published by Bloomsbury and shortlisted for the Waterstone's Children's Book Prize and Branford Boase Award for debut authors. His short fiction has appeared in *Lost and Found* (Dhalia Publishing), *This Side, That Side* (Yoda Press), and a short story, 'Once Upon a Time', was adapted into a touring show, aimed at Bangladeshi, Pakistani and Somali families. His most recent novel, *Out of Heart*, was published by Hot Key Books in 2017.

Avaes Mohammad is a writer working across forms. His scripts chronicle post 9/11 multicultural Britain. As a performance poet his influences range from the Sufi Saints of South Asia to the Dub Poets of Jamaica. His essays and opinion pieces engage with topics that include integration, identity and the arts. Avaes is enjoying long form fiction.

Courttia Newland is the author of eight books including his much-lauded debut, *The Scholar*. His most recent novel, *A River Called Time*, was longlisted for the Gordon Burn Prize. He co-edited *The Penguin Book of New Black Writing in Britain*, and his short stories have featured in various anthologies and been broadcast on BBC Radio 4. As a screenwriter, he has co-written episodes of Steve McQueen's 2020 BBC series *Small Axe*.

Born to Jamaican parents who arrived in Britain in the 1960s, **Karline Smith** was one of the first black female crime writers to deal with the subject of drug gangs in inner-city Britain. She is the author of three novels, *Moss Side Massive*, which was dramatised by Liverpool's Unity Theatre, *Full Crew*, and *Goosebumps and Butterflies are Fairy Tales* (published by Black Sapphire Press). Smith won the Vera Bell Short story award in 1988 and her short fiction has been published in *The City Life Book of Manchester Short Stories* (Penguin), *M.O.: Crimes of Practice*, and *Resist* (Comma).She is currently a trustee of Manchester City of Literature.

Lillian Weezer has an MA in English from the University of Manchester, and has previously published poetry in *Rialto, Smiths Knoll, PN Review*, and *The North*, among other places.

About the Consultants

Dr Chris Cocking is a Principal Lecturer in the School of Humanities and Applied Social Sciences at the University of Brighton, with a research interest in the psychology of crowd behaviour (particularly during mass emergencies). This interest stems from his early experiences of being involved in the anti-roads' movement of the 1990s and his PhD study of the protests against the Newbury bypass. His current research has looked at mutual aid during the COVID-19 pandemic and he regularly appears in the media to talk about emergency behaviour and effective public messaging.

Frank E. Earp is one of Nottinghamshire's leading folklorists and historians, having written on the county's folklore, mythology and history for over 40 years. For many years he wrote a weekly column in *The Post Lite*, and is author of numerous local history texts, including *The A-Z of Curious Nottinghamshire* (The History Press), *May Day in Nottinghamshire* (Heart of Albion Press), *Secret Nottingham* and *Secret Beeston* (both with Amberley Press).

Niklas Frykman is an Associate Professor of Atlantic history at the University of Pittsburgh, where he researches and teaches the history of capitalism, revolution, and the sea. He is the author of *The Bloody Flag: Mutinies in the Age of Atlantic Revolution* (UC Press, 2020), and co-editor of *Mutiny and Maritime Radicalism in the Age of Revolution: A Global Survey* (Cambridge, 2014) *and Free and Unfree Labor in Indian and Atlantic Ocean Port Cities, 17th-19th centuries* (Cambridge, 2019).

Carl Griffin is Professor of Historical Geography at the University of Sussex and Visiting Professor at the Centre for

History at the University of Highlands and Islands. Carl's research focuses on histories of popular protest and resistance in the English countryside, and environmental and more-than-human histories. His latest books are *Moral Ecologies: Histories of Histories of Conservation, Dispossession and Resistance* (with Roy Jones and Iain Robertson, 2019) and *The Politics of Hunger: Protest, Poverty and Policy in England, c. 1750–c. 1850* (2020). He also co-edits the journal *Rural History*.

Dr Ariel Hessayon is a Reader in the Department of History at Goldsmiths, University of London. He has written extensively on a variety of early modern topics: antiscripturism, antitrinitarianism, ball games, book burning, communism, environmentalism, esotericism, extra-canonical texts, heresy, crypto-Jews, Judaizing, millenarianism, mysticism, prophecy, and religious radicalism.

Richard Hingley is Professor of Roman Archaeology at Durham University. He is interested in Roman imperialism and Iron Age reactions and has written a number of books on Roman topics, including *Conquering the Ocean: The Roman Invasion of Britain* (Oxford University Press, New York).

Rhian E. Jones is a writer, critic and broadcaster on history, politics and popular culture. She is co-editor of *Red Pepper* and writes for *Tribune* magazine. Her books include *Clampdown: Pop-Cultural Wars on Class and Gender* (zer0, 2013); *Petticoat Heroes: Gender, Culture and Popular Protest* (University of Wales Press, 2015); *Triptych: Three Studies of Manic Street Preachers'* The Holy Bible (Repeater, 2017), the anthology of women's music writing *Under My Thumb: Songs That Hate Women and the Women Who Love Them* (Repeater, 2017) and *Paint Your Town Red: How Preston Took Back Control and Your Town Can Too* (Repeater, 2021).

Briony McDonagh is Professor of Environmental Humanities at the University of Hull, where she is also Director of the

Leverhulme Doctoral Scholarships Centre for Water Cultures. She is a historical geographer and environmental historian, with research interests in the green-blue humanities, women's histories and the historical geographies of protest and the commons. Her book, *Elite Women and the Agricultural Landscape, 1700–1830* (Routledge, 2017), won the Joan Thirsk Memorial Prize and Women's History Network Book Prize. She is co-editor of *Women and the Land, 1500-1900* (Boydell & Brewer, 2019), *Remembering Protest in Britain since 1500* (Palgrave Macmillan, 2018) and *Hull: Culture, History, Place* (Liverpool University Press, 2017).

Dr Katrina Navickas is Reader in History at the University of Hertfordshire. Her latest book, *Protest and the Politics of Space and Place, 1789-1848*, was published in paperback by Manchester University Press in 2017. She has written widely about Luddites, Captain Swing, and other machine breakers of the nineteenth century.

Dr Richard Sheldon is senior lecturer in social and economic history at the University of Bristol. He is working on a book *The Politics of Bread in Eighteenth Century Britain* and is also currently working on global histories of protest movements.

Rose Wallis is a senior lecturer in British Social History and Associate Director of the Regional History Centre at the University of the West of England. Rose's published research considers the dynamic relationship between the law and society, with a particular focus on the regional judiciary, criminal justice and social protest. She is also consultant historian at Shire Hall historic courthouse museum in Dorset, and works with a number of heritage partners on public engagement with criminal justice histories and their relevance in the present.

John Walter, Emeritus Professor of History at the University of Essex, researches and publishes on the politics of early modern crowds in the period leading up to and during the English Revolution. His publications include *Understanding Popular Violence in the English Revolution: The Colchester Plunderers* (1999 Whitfield Prize, Royal Historical Society) and *Covenanting Citizens: The Protestation Oath and Popular Political Culture in the English Revolution* (2017 Pepys Award), and a large number of essays, a selection of which were published as *Crowds and Popular Politics in Early Modern England* (2006). His articles have inspired both an award-winning beer and the film *Robinson in Ruins* (Patrick Keiller, 2010).

Special Thanks

As well as all the contributors, the editor would like to thank Lewis Brennen, Becky Taylor, Graeme Hayes, Brian Doherty, Anthony Taylor, Richard C. Allen, Gordon Pentland, Jane Whittle, Trudi Shaw, and especially Dr Katrina Navickas for their help in the development of the project. Huge thanks are also due to Inez Hickman for her help in the visual development of the characters.

ALSO AVAILABLE FROM COMMA PRESS

The American Way

Stories of Invasion

Ra Page & Orsola Casagrande (eds.)

Following the US's bungled withdrawal from Afghanistan, and the scenes of chaos at Kabul Airport, we could be forgiven for thinking we're experiencing an 'end of empire' moment, that the US is entering a new, less belligerent era in its foreign policy, and that its tenure as self-appointed 'global policeman' is coming to an end.

This anthology explores the human cost of these many interventions onto foreign soil, with stories by writers from that soil – covering everything from torture in Abu Ghraib, to coups and counterrevolutionary wars in Latin America, to all-out invasions in the Middle and Far East. Alongside testimonies from expert historians and ground-breaking journalists, these stories present a history that too many of us in the West simply pretend never happened.

'Challenging, engaging, and at times deeply unsettling'
– *The Irish Times*

Featuring: Talal Abu Shawish, Gabriel Ángel, Gioconda Belli, Gianfranco Bettin, Najwa Bin Shatwan, Hassan Blasim, Paige Cooper, Ahmel Echevarría Peré, Ahmet Haluk Ünal, Hüseyin Karabey, Wilfredo Mármol Amaya, Lina Meruane, Lidudumalingani Mqombothi, Fiston Mwanza Mujila, Payam Nasser, Fariba Nawa, Jacob Ross, Bina Shah, Kim Thúy & Carol Zardetto

ISBN: 978-1-91269-739-7
£14.99

ALSO AVAILABLE FROM COMMA PRESS

Resist

Stories of Uprising

Edited by Ra Page

In the wake of the social and political turmoil of Brexit and a climate crisis that continues to be ignored, it's easy to think these are uncharted waters for us, as a democracy.

But Britain has seen political crises and far-right extremism before. In this timely collection of fiction and essays celebrating key moments of British protest, writers fight back with well-researched, historically accurate fiction. From Boudica to Blair Peach, from the Battle of Cable Street to the tragedy of Grenfell Tower, these stories demonstrate when people have stood up and resisted in the face of injustice.

In our age of fake news and post-truth politics, these stories celebrate the occasions when people have stood up and resisted.

'Resist is about how important it is to question the status quo as governments and right-wing movements attempt to set our agenda.'
– *Stylist*

Featuring: Bidisha, Julia Bell, SJ Bradley, Jude Brown, Lucy Caldwell, Steve Chambers, Martin Edwards, Uschi Gatward, Luan Goldie, Gaia Holmes, Nikita Lalwani, Zoe Lambert, Anna Lewis, Irfan Master, Donny O'Rourke, Kamila Shamsie, Karline Smith, Kim Squirrell, Lucas Stewart & Eley Williams

ISBN: 978-1-91269-731-1
£12.99